The Heartbreak Hotel

The Heartbreak Hotel

Ellen O'Clover

Berkley Romance
New York

BERKLEY ROMANCE
Published by Berkley
An imprint of Penguin Random House LLC
1745 Broadway, New York, NY 10019
penguinrandomhouse.com

Copyright © 2025 by Ellen O'Clover
Readers Guide copyright © 2025 by Ellen O'Clover
Penguin Random House values and supports copyright. Copyright fuels creativity, encourages diverse voices, promotes free speech, and creates a vibrant culture. Thank you for buying an authorized edition of this book and for complying with copyright laws by not reproducing, scanning, or distributing any part of it in any form without permission. You are supporting writers and allowing Penguin Random House to continue to publish books for every reader. Please note that no part of this book may be used or reproduced in any manner for the purpose of training artificial intelligence technologies or systems.

BERKLEY and the BERKLEY & B colophon are registered trademarks of
Penguin Random House LLC.

Book design by Daniel Brount
Interior art: Mountain landscape © Invato Design/Shutterstock.com

Library of Congress Cataloging-in-Publication Data

Names: O'Clover, Ellen author
Title: The heartbreak hotel / Ellen O'Clover.
Description: First edition. | New York: Berkley Romance, 2025.
Identifiers: LCCN 2024057341 (print) | LCCN 2024057342 (ebook) |
ISBN 9780593952542 trade paperback | ISBN 9780593952559 ebook
Subjects: LCGFT: Romance fiction | Novels
Classification: LCC PS3615.C5825 H43 2025 (print) |
LCC PS3615.C5825 (ebook) | DDC 813/.6—dc23/eng/20250303
LC record available at https://lccn.loc.gov/2024057341
LC ebook record available at https://lccn.loc.gov/2024057342

First Edition: September 2025

Printed in the United States of America
1st Printing

The authorized representative in the EU for product safety and compliance is
Penguin Random House Ireland, Morrison Chambers, 32 Nassau Street,
Dublin D02 YH68, Ireland, https://eu-contact.penguin.ie.

To Mom and Dad—my first love story

One

It happens past midnight, in a fluorescent-lit room. I'm shaky with adrenaline and not a little bit sweaty. I'm having trouble hearing.

"Louisa," Nate says, an edge to his voice like he's repeating himself. "What did you honestly expect?"

Not this, *honestly*. Not Nate, who's only ever called me Lou, pulling out *Louisa* like a weapon. Certainly not the mottled bruise along the sweat-ringed neckline of his T-shirt, evidence of someone else's mouth.

"We've been so scared to call this what it is, but it's actually obvious, right?" He keeps talking, the end of every phrase turned up like a question he expects me to agree with.

I let his voice haze out, become wordless as I watch his lips move: the freckle just off-center of his Cupid's bow, the thin white scar from his near-feral childhood cat. He raises a hand to scrape his fingers through his hair, fidgety, then tugs at the leather bracelet slung around his left wrist. I made it when I was twenty-three and briefly consumed by handicraft.

Bad timing, I think he says. *Less than ideal.* He starts fiddling with things on his dressing room desk: a haphazard stack of picks, a tin of cinnamon breath mints. The set list is taped to the mirror, *Purple Girl (Acoustic)* highlighted yellow. He opened with it tonight, not making eye contact with me where I sat in the VIP section, and for once I didn't sing along.

"Say something," I finally make out. A demand, halfway petulant, as Nate turns to face me. He's always been this way: defensive when he's wrong, made accusatory by his embarrassment. "You owe me a response, here, at least."

"I *owe* you?" My voice surprises me, like this is a scene I've been watching from a distance and I'm disoriented to hear myself in it. Someone whoops from the hallway—Kenji, maybe. Nate's drummer. Everyone else is packing up to go home, or go out. But I have the paralyzing feeling that I'll never exist outside this moment again. "I don't think so."

"No?" Nate tips closer to me, and I bite the insides of my cheeks so hard I taste iron. "After six years, you don't have a single thing to say?"

Six years. *Six* years. Six *years*.

I do have one thing to say. When I tilt my chin upward, Nate tracks the movement like a sniper.

"Don't think for even half a second that you're keeping the house."

He blinks, surprised. It's a victory, however small, to shock him.

And it's what I'm thinking of, as Nate Payne—my first love, my first everything—dumps me backstage at his own concert. Not the humiliation of being cheated on right under my nose.

Not the fallout when the press learns that Louisa Walsh—Nate's *purple girl*—is out of the picture. Not even the anticipatory shame of telling my mother, my sister.

It's this, simple and salient:

I cannot lose that goddamn house.

Two

Three hours earlier

I never get floor seats anymore. It used to be a physical thing, watching Nate play: the press of bodies against mine, the bass vibrating up through my sneakers, the guardrail crowded into my spleen as I tipped over it to get closer to him. Now his tour manager, Roger, always books me into the VIP section. Tonight it's stage left, separated from the pit by a railing and a smattering of security guards in yellow polo shirts. Roger says it's to keep me safe, but I've always had the distinct suspicion it's to keep me out of the way.

Kenji's waifish girlfriend sits next to me, white sneakers propped on the rail, phone glowing in her hands. She doesn't look up, even when they take the stage. I think her name is Florence—though it could be Frances, or Frieda. Kenji's girlfriends are hard to keep track of; they come and go, each one more beautiful than the last, sort of incomprehensible to me. When I met Kenji he was a greasy-haired nineteen-year-old with a "hard-line moral stance" against deodorant and a grade point average so precarious it could only be salvaged by a string of expensive tutors. The only thing he cared about was drums, and—sometimes—Nate.

Onstage, Nate waits for the screaming crowd to quiet. "*Hellooo*, Denver!" he shouts. A woman in the very front row, once my place, shrieks so loudly in response I see a vein throb in her neck. Beside me, Florence/Frances/Frieda is shopping for face serum.

"We're Say It Now," Nate says, his lips brushing the mic. "And it's a dream to be in our hometown, singing our songs." Kenji hammers out a drum riff that sounds like the train jingle at the Denver airport, and a laugh ripples through the stadium. "If you know the words to this one, sing along for us, all right?"

He plucks out the opening chords of "Purple Girl" and suddenly I'm twenty again, writing an essay in my Boulder dorm room, Nate cross-legged on my bed with his guitar. I close my eyes and think of us like that: children. I loved him like a fever, with an intensity that left me sleepless. Before Abe and Mateo joined the band, before "Purple Girl" took off, before the record deal or the tours or any of it at all—just Nate Payne, the first and only boy I ever loved, writing me a song.

"*But I'd give it all up,*" Nate sings, "*these purple mountains, the alpenglow . . .*" He steps back from the mic and smiles into the stadium, waving his hand to give them the stage. And they step up, twenty thousand voices, to finish the verse: "*. . . for my purple girl.*"

For years Nate sang those words right to me, no matter how big the crowd. His eyes on mine and the time collapsing between us, making us college kids again. He doesn't look for me, now, and the truth is the song isn't mine anymore. We haven't been those kids in a long, long time. Nate called me purple because he said I was like a bruise: hurt beneath the surface, carrying the remnant of something painful. *You try to hide it*, he said. *But it's right there under your thick skin.* Nate could be poetic like that—around his huge laugh and his scrappiness. There was something tender inside of him.

Last fall Nate posted an acoustic version of "Purple Girl" that went viral overnight, eleven million views by morning. He recorded the video in the attic office at the house, sitting in my desk chair with afternoon light coming in from the garden behind him. The song was five years old, by then. It had always been one of their most popular—but not like this.

It's the version he sings tonight, the one that catapulted Say It Now to the level of fame that's had them on tour since winter. I haven't seen Nate in months. When the song hit the Billboard charts and everything changed, his story did, too: *Lou's a kaleidoscope*, he told the press. *Full of every surprising color—purple most of all.* It was happier that way, if less true. And I couldn't quite blame him: we haven't been those people in years. It's been a long time since I've been the girl he wrote the song about.

My phone buzzes, and I pull it out of my pocket. My sister, Goldie. The reply to a text I sent hours ago. What are you waiting for, though? Can't you just get a date on the books for your licensing exam?

My throat gives an involuntary grumble, a strangled noise that makes Frieda(?) glance over at me. I stuff my phone back into my pocket and feel it vibrate again. I try to focus on the music, but I can imagine what else Goldie's saying: *You're wasting time.... You can't put off your career forever.... Twenty-six is too old not to have a 401(k)*. Goldie was nine when I was born, and when we were kids I called her Vice Mom, like a vice principal but worse. She's been on my case since I was an infant.

When Nate and I were students in that dorm room, imagining our life together, I had the future mapped out exactly as Goldie wanted it. I was going to be a therapist. I was going to have the steady job, the reliable income, the health insurance. Nate was going to play guitar. But before we even graduated that all changed—Nate was touring and then I was in grad school and now we're here: in a packed stadium, together in the same room for the first time in months with a sea of people separating us. Nate's given me the exact thing Goldie hates most: a safety net. An excuse not to stand on my own two feet.

With Nate paying for our lives, I can keep putting off the inevitable for a little longer, and then a little longer after that.

I don't need Goldie's approval, I remind myself. The band transitions into "Louder," and everyone in the pit starts jumping. I watch Nate's face on the big screen—his full lips, the dimple in his right cheek, the jut of his nose where he broke it rock climbing at sixteen. *I have my own life*, I remind myself. And then, even though it grates—even though it hasn't felt true in a long while—I think, *I have Nate*.

Frieda follows me backstage when the set's done, finally dropping her phone into her shoulder bag and giving me a thin-lipped smile that doesn't touch her eyes. I've had two hard seltzers—those giant-barreled cans they only sell at stadiums—and I'm feeling a little fizzy. I tell myself I didn't think of Goldie when I ordered the second one. Didn't think about how she'd never drink on a school night, because she always has work in the morning. Certainly didn't think about the fact that I have no plans tomorrow—or any other day, really.

"Flooooooo!" Kenji bounds down the hallway toward us, his voice bouncing from the concrete walls. It's Florence, then. When he scoops her into his arms and spins her around, she looks genuinely repulsed. In her defense, Kenji's pretty sweaty. "What'd you think, baby?"

"It was great," Florence says, adjusting her hair as he puts her back down. "You ready to go?"

"Where's Nate?" I ask, and Kenji notices me for what seems like the first time. A weird look storms over his eyes, there and then gone. "Uh, he's . . ."

"Dressing room?" I prompt.

"Yeah," Kenji says slowly. His hand's wrapped around Florence's waist, rucking up her shirt. "But look, Lou, he's not—" Kenji breaks off, swallows. Kenji's a lot of things, but *taciturn* is not one of them. I hike my eyebrows.

"I don't know if you want to go back there," Kenji says. There's a flush spreading over his cheeks. I feel it start to mirror in my own.

"Why not?"

Kenji's eyes flicker down the hall, back to me, down the hall. *"Kenji."*

"Ah, Lou, it's really not my place—" He breaks off again, grimacing. And I know, fully and all at once, like a shoe dropping. A door slamming shut.

I start to walk, autopiloting my body down the concrete hallway even as he calls after me. Kenji's been my friend for years—but he's Nate's friend first. It's not me he's trying to protect.

". . . Abe always gets so pitchy on 'In Flux,' but he's insistent on that solo." I hear Nate before I see him, his voice carrying through the cracked door of a room with his name on it.

When I push it open and step inside, he's standing next to a girl. *A woman*, Goldie would chide me. She's tall and curvy, with tumbling red hair and a shirt that dips low enough for me to see that her breasts have significantly more *presence* than mine. His hand is on her ass, all four fingers tucked into the back pocket of her jeans, and in the same moment it registers that I recognize her, she reaches to unwrap Nate's earplugs from around his neck.

The photo, I think. That damn photo, from the spring.

She's nobody, Nate had said. *Nobody*.

But here she is.

Three

I get home past two o'clock and don't turn any lights on. Nate stayed downtown—whether with his bandmates or that woman, I don't know—and I went home to the house we've shared for the last four years. A historic wood-and-stone cabin in the mountains (if you can call something a *cabin* at five thousand square feet and six bedrooms). With its wraparound porch and stained-glass windows and vaulted, gnarled-beam ceilings, it's my happiest place. A home that Nate's almost never in, that feels like it's mine as much as my own face, my own fingernails.

It was nearly ninety degrees in Denver, where August's always sticky and sweltering. But up in Estes Park the evenings are cool all summer long, and when I step out of my car in our smooth driveway it's clear and breezy. It smells like pine trees. The stars are otherworldly bright.

I kick off my sandals inside the front door and walk through every room of the house: moonlight coming in through the tall windows, whispers of wallpaper and doorframes under my fingertips. Trying to memorize every piece of it. Trying to imagine my life anywhere else.

Seriously? Nate had said, when I told him I wanted the house. *That's really all you have to say?* Not an answer to whether I could keep it, and it *was* all I'd had to say, at least right then. His words from the stadium are still swirling through me: *What did you honestly expect? We've been so scared to call this what it is.*

I would never have admitted it to him, that he was right. That it's been at least a year—longer, probably—since Nate and me have been *Nate and me.* We settled so invisibly into our shared but separate lives that I can't see the seam, looking back. The line where things changed. I only know that they did: that Nate had become my long-term plan by default, not choice, and that there was a part of me—not insignificant—that stayed with him only to prove something to myself. That I'm capable of an everlasting relationship. That I'm settled and grown-up and taken care of. That I'm, maybe most of all, not like my mother.

It was unfair to him, to hold on for reasons like that. But now we're here, more than even in our unfairness. I'm insulted and humiliated and relieved.

The house had been Nate's idea, out of college. The front door alone looked like it cost more than my entire Boulder apartment—all burled wood and brass hardware. There was one of those copper, wall-mount thermometers on the porch, and a cluster of aspens in the front yard, and a storybook gate that led around back to the flower garden. It was gorgeous: stone paths winding between rows of mountain lupine and purple columbines. You could see clear to Longs Peak from anywhere you stood. The house belonged in *Architectural Digest*, not in my life.

Nate grew up in a low-slung suburb of Denver, in a small brick bungalow with two brothers. Every summer his family drove up to Estes Park and camped for a full week: the only vacation they could afford. The house was down the street from the ice cream shop he'd go to with his brothers, the three of them tumbling over each other on the weed-cracked sidewalk. It was lodged in Nate like an old splinter—the way only things from our childhood get stuck in us. It was more than a house, to him; it was an idea. One that, after a record deal and a national tour, he could afford to rent for himself.

It didn't make much difference to me, where we landed. The splinters of my own childhood had only ever pushed me in one direction: away. I'd never go back to Ohio, but pretty much anywhere else seemed fine. I was two days past graduation and starting an online master's program in the fall. I had an empty summer spread before me, a plan for the future, a twenty-two-year-old boy holding my hand. When he tugged me through the front door of his dream house, I went willingly.

Nate gave me creative control over the house (within reason—we were renters). The landlord, a man named Henry I never met, lived in town but didn't come by. So long as we didn't do anything obnoxious, Nate said, we could pretty much do what we wanted. With Nate gone so often—on tour, or out of town for press, or staying in Denver for weeklong stints to record with the band—his dream house ultimately became mine. I painted the kitchen a woodsy green and installed vintage light fixtures; I themed each bedroom after a Colorado plant—pine, spruce, lupine, juniper, aspen, fir; I applied peel-and-stick wallpaper in the attic office, where a bay window looked out over the back garden.

There was already help for the garden by the time we moved in, a woman named Joss who came by most summer afternoons to manage our small wilderness. It was just as well; I've always been an indoor cat. I wouldn't have known what to do with the yard, and Joss worked magic out there. On nice days we'd drink lemonade on the porch together when she was through; she was only in her midthirties, and a great storyteller. With Nate gone and all my college friends over an hour away in Denver, it was nice to have Joss around. For the garden, and for me.

There weren't close neighbors. Each house sat on a wooded lot that elk roamed through at will, grazing on pine needles and bunches of lichen. The house across the street was nearest, a stately cabin where a retired couple from Kansas—Martina and Bill—lived with their old St. Bernard, Custard. He was enormous, bearlike, all droopy jowls and soulful eyes.

When Nate was home we cooked the kinds of simple foods twenty-three-year-olds tend to: pasta with cherry tomatoes from the yard, burgers that Nate grilled on the gas range on the back porch. We went barefoot everywhere and christened every room of the house the way twenty-three-year-olds also do. Nate was gone so often that having him home always felt like Christmas morning: a fleeting, frantic gift. I felt like I could've sustained myself on Nate alone, never mind the pasta and the burgers. His mouth and the inner curves of his elbows and the warm skin of his belly pressed to mine. The weight of him. He was always a meal enough for me.

And then he'd be gone again, kissing me on the front steps while Kenji honked at us from the road. When school or clinical hours prevented me from traveling with him, he'd send me a video of "Purple Girl" after every single show. "This one's for Lou," he'd always say. And, eventually, "You all know who this one's for." And, after that, only, "Sing along if you know the words."

I missed Nate when he left. Especially at the start. But the longer I lived in the house, the more I missed it, too, when I was away. If something prevented me from touring with him, it was always tinged with a bit of relief. I wouldn't have to leave my home, my beautiful refuge in the mountains. I wouldn't have to wake up without the stained glass above the kitchen sink casting my morning flickering rainbow; I wouldn't have to fall asleep without the hush of aspen boughs caressing my bedroom window. Goldie and I never stayed in one place for long—growing up was a blur of rentals and motels and living rooms of my mother's friends. But this house felt like it was mine, more than any place had ever been.

When I whispered this to Nate, my lips at his ear in our quiet, mountain-ringed bedroom, he smiled sleepily in the dark. *It's all for you, Lou*, he said. I believed him implicitly. Because I wanted to, because he'd never given me a reason to doubt him, because I'd loved him long before the rest of the world.

Eventually, the house stopped meaning, to Nate, what it had always meant. Eventually, he had all the trappings of a life that anyone could want: rentals in Miami and Los Angeles and a transparent sapphire watch that cost more than my car. It was a mark of the change in us, that the things that had always meant something *more*—the house, Estes Park, me—were just things again.

I'd intended to start working in the spring, after passing my

National Counselor Examination and officially earning my license. But then there'd been the photo. That woman. And the fallout from all of it, leading like a trail of breadcrumbs to this night.

Instead I spent early summer *languishing*, as Goldie put it. Reading books in my attic office and sitting in the garden with Joss and having weekend-long sleepovers with Mei, my best friend, when she could get away from Denver. I'd let Nate sweep me under the wave of his life. I'd done what Goldie always feared I'd do, what we grew up watching our mother do and be destroyed by: I let a man take care of me.

I'm not sure I even recognized it as it was happening—not really. The sands shifting beneath me, putting me flat on my back in the surf. And even as it all changed around me, I never thought I'd lose it.

I let myself believe—naively, foolishly—that this life was mine for the keeping.

Four

"We'll find a way for you to keep it." Mei's sitting in my kitchen, slicing a peach. I haven't eaten since before the concert last night. "You have money saved, yes?"

It's Friday morning, a workday, but Mei showed up a little past nine. *I'll keep an eye on my email*, she said, dismissive, when I balked at her skipping work for so depressing an occasion as my breakup.

Now, she passes the cutting board over the table. She's arranged the peach slices in a perfect fan, their spiky red centers radiating like small suns. It's so pretty, my eyes fill with tears. Mei has her life so entirely together she even cuts fruit the right way.

"Lou," she says, and I look up at her. "It's just a peach. You need to eat."

"I can't," I say, but I pick up a slice anyway. Nate texted me at seven to say I could keep the house. I know him well enough to know that those dark morning hours after the show were long enough for his guilt to fester—that by daybreak, he'd have been sufficiently ashamed about what he'd done to throw me a bone. But it wasn't until I read his text—You're right, you should keep the house. I'll move out—that I remembered Nate was hardly the start of my problem. There's no way I can afford to stay here on my own. "I'd rather drown in my stomach acid than face this."

"Stop that." I've been peeling the fuzzy skin off my peach slice and Mei plucks the whole thing out of my hand, setting it back on the cutting board. "No one's drowning in their stomach acid. Nate is a monster—we can't do anything about that. But we can figure out this house thing."

Mei's known Nate and me since sophomore year at CU; all three of us lived on the same hall and she was there when I met Nate, when he wrote "Purple Girl," when we moved to Estes Park and started this life. She's not only my favorite person, but Goldie's, too. The person Goldie wishes I was: Mei's had a full-time job since the day after we graduated, coordinating marketing campaigns at an agency downtown. Her LinkedIn has the word *manager* on it. She *has* a LinkedIn.

I haven't told Goldie about the breakup yet because I can imagine exactly what she'll say: *If you'd figured out a job by now, you'd be able to support yourself. Now what, Lou?* Now what, Lou, indeed.

"The rent is ridiculous," I tell Mei, licking peach juice off my fingertips and feeling my stomach turn. I look around my beautiful, familiar kitchen: its farmhouse sink below the stained-glass window overlooking the garden; its wide, antique floorboards; the cream-colored Smeg fridge that looks like something out of a vintage fever dream. The smell of it, like a library: aged wood and filtered sunlight. "We only live here because Nate has stupid money. You know this, Mei. I'm not even *employed*."

"That can change," she says. She chopped all her hair off at the start of the summer and it's this lovely, blunt bob—exactly to her jawbone and shiny as sun on water. My hair's an unbrushed mess. "Right?"

"Not soon enough." I look at Mei and cough up the lie. "I haven't even booked my licensing exam."

"Okay," she says evenly. "How long will that take?"

What she doesn't know—what no one knows but Nate—is that I failed the exam the first time around, back in April. That it's only offered at certain times of year, and that I have to wait until the fall to retake it. My fear of failing all over again has stopped me cold every time I've gone to schedule a date, but I'll have to. Soon, I'll have to.

I bite my lip. Through the screen door, I see Joss cross the backyard. "A couple months, minimum?"

Mei follows my gaze, tracking Joss's movement through the garden. She ducks below the sight line of the back porch, and Mei looks back at me. "And how long can you float the rent here on your own?"

My eyes glaze with tears, turning Mei to watercolor. I can't believe the mess I've allowed myself to make of my life. "A month, if I spend most of my savings. And rent is due Monday."

If Goldie was here, she'd tell me to move. It's the logical choice: I can't afford to stay in this house. But Mei, my angel on earth, my very best friend in the entire world, just reaches for my hand across the table. "I know what this place means to you," she says. "If you need to stay, pay the rent Monday and then we have a whole month to figure out the next move."

The truth is, this house is the first place that's ever been *mine*. It took me years to realize that the nomadic lifestyle I grew up with wasn't typical—that my friends from school didn't have their pack-it-up routine down to a science; that they couldn't fit their entire lives into a single, broken-zippered suitcase. Aside from an eighteen-month stint with one of my mother's longer-lasting boyfriends, we never stayed anywhere for more than a few months.

It wasn't until I left for college that I called one address home for longer than it took for me to memorize it. And even then, I had a different dorm—a different apartment—every school year. This house is the only place where I've ever let myself exhale, let my guard down enough to actually think of somewhere as a place *I* belong. To get rid of the suitcase.

The thought of losing the house—its rooms shimmering with light cut by dancing aspen leaves, its familiar sounds, every inch of it curated to be my own idea of home—feels like vertigo. Like the world won't be right side up if I don't live here anymore.

"Mei," I say now. "I love you, but the only move that could keep me here is winning the lottery."

"What if I move in? And we split it?"

"Stop." I sniff inelegantly and shove a peach slice into my mouth. "You're too pure for this world."

"I'm serious." She waves one arm around the kitchen. So much of my life, of my friendship with her, has happened in this room—leaned toward each other over opposite ends of the granite island, sipping wine as we wait for water to boil; Scotch-taping string lights to the tops of the green cabinets at Christmastime; slicing peaches as my world falls out from beneath me. "This place is amazing. Obviously I would love to live here."

I shake my head. "We're over an hour from your office *and* Andy."

"Andy loves the mountains," Mei says. She points through the screen door, where Longs Peak is emerging from behind a cloud. "They'll visit all the time."

"No." Mei met Andy at a bar last spring, and they've been inseparable ever since. The healthiest relationship I've ever seen her in, and not one I'm going to let her sabotage just because mine has shredded itself like food scraps through a garbage disposal. Besides . . . "I can't even afford half the rent here, so it's moot."

"Morning." The screen door thwacks open, mewling on its hinges, and Joss pokes her head into the kitchen. Joss looks like an Icelandic milk maiden: white-blond, blue-eyed, with sinewy arms from lifting heavy planters and bundles of tree roots all year long. She frowns at the door. "God, it's still making that noise? Can't you get Henry to fix it?"

Henry—a name I barely recognize; the landlord I've never met. Asking Henry to silence the screen door would've fallen firmly into *Nate* territory.

"I like it," I tell her, my voice thick. The sound of the door and all of the house's sounds are strung together like a soundtrack to my life. It's reassuring to open the door, and step onto the porch, and hear the same squeaked greeting every time.

I swipe roughly at my cheeks, and Joss realizes that something's wrong. I clear my throat and sit up straighter, but it's too late.

"I'm sorry," she says quickly. "I'm interrupting."

"No, no." I flap my hands uselessly. "We're just, um—we're just—"

"Lou and Nate broke up."

I look at Mei. It's not that I *wouldn't* have told Joss—we're friends, in all the ways that matter. But hearing her say it out loud makes it feel real all over again, not to mention makes it seem like Nate's the reason I'm crying over stone fruit, when in reality it's the thought of my entire life crumbling apart.

"Oh, Lou," Joss says. Her eyebrows draw together, mouth turning down at the corners. "I'm so sorry to hear that."

"We hate him now," Mei says, turning to Joss. She has a peach slice in one hand. "Just to be clear."

Joss puts a hand over her heart. "I've always been Team Lou." She nods her head at the empty seat across the table from Mei and me. "Can I sit?"

"Of course," I say, kicking out the chair with my foot. She steps inside and the door whines shut behind her. "Have some peach."

"Don't pawn it off on Joss," Mei says. She glances at Joss as she sits down. "Lou's not eating."

"I'm *eating*." I pick up another slice for emphasis. "But the thought of losing this house does not whet my appetite."

"Don't tell me you're moving out," Joss says, pulling off her gardening gloves. "Is Nate staying? He's never even here."

"No," Mei says emphatically. "Nate's moving out, and Lou's staying, and we're going to figure it out."

"Maybe," I groan, slumping into the chair until my socked foot collides with Joss's under the table. "Sorry. I just don't see how I *can* stay."

"Because rent?" Joss asks. She takes a bite of peach and swipes juice from her lips with the back of one wrist.

"Because rent," I confirm. "The landlord makes a killing on this place, and I do not have one single killing to my name."

"I offered to move in," Mei tells Joss. "But she won't—"

"Splitting it isn't enough," I say. "Joss, you'd have to move in, too."

She gives a breathless grunt of a laugh and wipes her fingers on the thighs of her work pants. "I can't do that."

"Well, Mei can't, either," I say. When she opens her mouth to protest, I lift a hand. "You have a whole life in Denver, Mei. A partner waiting for you."

"You're my partner," Mei says, dropping her head onto my shoulder and nuzzling into me.

"You have a *nonplatonic* partner waiting for you."

"What if you sell a kidney?" Mei suggests, reaching for another peach slice. "Is that a thing you can do for money, or only as a Good Samaritan kind of gesture?"

"I know you can sell plasma," Joss offers. "There's a place off Highway 7—you wouldn't even have to go very far."

"*Great*," I say, but the smallest gurgle of a laugh rumbles through the word. "I'll just vampire myself into affording rent."

"Good." Joss smiles at me, a little sad, over the table. "I can't really imagine this house without you anymore."

"Was the previous tenant horrible?" Mei asks, sitting back up. "Some old-money snob with disgusting taste in landscaping?"

Joss laughs. "Something like that."

This place was pristine when Nate and I moved in—if a little lifeless. The house was more than seventy years old but immaculately renovated: a surprise to Nate, who remembered it as colossal but disheveled. The kitchen had been gutted and remodeled with brass fixtures and soft-close drawers; each bathroom had a new shower, sleek tile, a wide vanity mirror with warm lighting. The wood floors refracted the high Colorado sun, freshly lacquered.

There were no traces of them, whoever had lived here before us. Just a gorgeous canvas of a home, whispering for me to fill it with color.

"Well," I say on a sigh. "Hopefully the next tenant's even cooler than me."

"The next tenant's going to *be* you," Mei says, reaching over to smack my hand. "Without No-Spine Nate to hold you down."

My throat tightens, and I nod. Reach for another peach slice so I don't have to meet anyone's eyes as my own fill back up with tears.

"If you need help getting rid of Nate's things," Joss says gently, "I'm around, okay?"

"Oh, god." My head drops directly onto the table. "I hadn't even thought about his things. *Six* bedrooms' worth of things."

We'd filled this house like mice, nesting. Every side table was cluttered with my thrift store treasures, every picture rail hung with paintings and photographs and cross-stitched landscapes, still in their hoops. Nearly all of it was mine—but Nate was everywhere, too. Stacks of his records in the front bedroom; his clothes in the closets, smelling of smoke and sage and his skin. A tube of Carmex lip balm dropped into a drawer in every single room of the house.

Mei makes a soothing sound, and I feel her hand land on my shoulder. I breathe, my eyes pressed shut. And as my words hang between us—*six bedrooms' worth of things*—I feel them start to blur. Going fuzzy at the edges, blooming, shifting into something else entirely. *Six bedrooms.*

Four upstairs bathrooms.

A circular driveway with plenty of parking.

A massive kitchen with seating for ten.

A way, maybe, for me to stay—without having to sell my kidney.

Mei can't live here, but other people could. The kind of people with money to spend and calligraphy art on their walls—the kind that says, *The mountains are calling and I must go.*

I sit up and look between Mei and Joss through blurry eyes. "I think I have an idea."

Nate always dealt with the rent; it's humiliating to admit that I don't even know our landlord's last name. I don't know if Nate paid online or by check. When I text him late Saturday morning, I need the landlord's contact info, he just replies with a name—*Henry Rhodes*—followed by an address and phone number.

When I call the number, I'm expecting the grumbly voice of an old, harried man. No one young is named Henry, for starters. And what young person could afford to own this house? But it's a woman's voice, clipped and professional.

"Good afternoon, this is Rita speaking. How can I help you?"

"Rita, hi." I turn on my heel in the living room, plastering a smile on my face as if she could see me. "I'm looking for Henry."

"Yes, you've reached his office. How can I help you?"

"Um." I squint out the window, where sun cuts through the boughs of a juniper tree in the side yard. "I'm his tenant out on Cedarcliff? The stone house with the porch? I was hoping to discuss something with him in, um, in person?"

There's a brief pause. "Dr. Rhodes had a cancellation for four o'clock today. Otherwise, we're closed Sundays and Mondays and I'm booking appointments two weeks out. The earliest I have available is September thirteenth."

Dr. Rhodes? I glance at the coffee table, where all my frenetic research is scribbled out on scrap paper. Mei slept over in spite of my protests—*Andy's at dinner with college friends! I don't want to listen to them reminisce about Habitat for Humanity anyway! Shut up right now!*—and we spent most of the night researching vacation rentals. What the other options are in Estes Park, what kinds of rules I'd need to follow, what I could charge for a place like this. She left a couple hours ago but it's only noon; I can get this jumble of information presentable in four hours.

"I'm . . . not sure I need an appointment," I say to Rita. "I just need to discuss a matter about the house? But I can do today at four, too."

"Great," Rita says. I hear her tapping at a keyboard. "What was your name?"

"Louisa Walsh," I say. "But he might only recognize my boyfriend's name, Nate Payne. He usually deals with the rent."

The word *boyfriend* seeps through me like vinegar, burning all the way down. Rita is unfazed.

"Thanks, Louisa. We'll see you at four."

The phone clicks off. I catch my reflection in the mirror

above the fireplace: pale cheeks, rat's nest hair, enormous *NSYNC T-shirt with a hole in one shoulder that I haven't peeled off my miserable body in forty-eight hours.

I point one finger at my face. Meet my own, red-rimmed eyes in the glass. "Get your shit together."

Five

When I park at the address from Nate's text—a business park on the other side of the lake—there's a Bernese mountain dog blocking the front door. It's got to be at least a hundred and twenty pounds, with more hair than an entire sorority pledge class. There's a felted pink lily tied to its collar—giant, floppy petals and spindly orange stamen.

The dog's owner shuffles out after it, shouting a thank-you through the door behind her. She promptly loses her rein on the dog, who bounds toward me with all the limb control of a puppy. I shriek when it gets to me—not because I don't like dogs, but because I'm wearing my *one* good blazer—and it barks heartily in response, like we're playing.

"Stop it!" I say, hopping backward in my heels. The sun is high and hot; I can feel myself starting to sweat as the dog hops right after me, salivating profusely.

"I'm so sorry!" The woman scrambles after the leash, finally pulling her dog away from me. There's a glistening ribbon of slobber on my pencil skirt. "Mabel is so friendly, but *so* enthusiastic."

"It's okay," I say. Mabel looks up at me balefully. "I love dogs, I just—" I gesture at my outfit. "I'm not dressed to play."

"Of course," she says. She's in running shorts and sneakers, a faded *Estes Park Turkey Trot* T-shirt. They did it at Lake Estes last year—a fogged-breath, early winter morning that Nate and I spent with coffee in bed while half the town pounded the cracked pavement around the lake. "I'm sorry. She gets so excited when she sees Dr. Rhodes."

I stare at her for a second, then at the door. HENRY RHODES, DVM is right there on the glass in crisp vinyl letters. He's a *vet*? I'm in a matching skirt and blazer, carrying a briefcase. I brought *printouts*. Shit.

"Bye, Mabel." I pat her wide head and hustle into the building, where a woman in braids—Rita, I presume—sits behind a desk in the small waiting room. There are heartworm prevention posters on the walls.

"Hi," I say, approaching the desk with a confidence I don't feel. "I'm—"

"Louisa." Rita taps at something on her computer and gives me a perfunctory smile. "I'll take you back."

I swallow. I feel like she's walking me to detention as she motions me into an exam room. There's a vet school diploma framed on the wall, along with a pastel portrait of an incredibly disgruntled-looking cat. It smells like Clorox wipes.

"He'll be right in," Rita says before shutting the door. I sit in the plastic chair with my briefcase in my lap, unsure what to do with myself. Should I get the printouts? I open the clasp on my bag and pull out the stack of papers inside: local comps, recipes, even a mock listing I wrote at one in the morning. When I spread them on the exam table and step back they look absolutely ridiculous, and I'm in the middle of shoving them back into my bag when the door creaks open.

"Louisa," Henry says. His voice is soft and husky: the exact voice you'd want soothing your dog when they're afraid. "How can I help you?"

I feel my lips part. Henry fills the room like overhead light: nowhere, then everywhere at once. He can't be older than thirty-five, dark hair just silvering at his temples. A white coat hangs crisply from the cut of his broad shoulders, his name stitched over the heart. There's the ghost of a beard along his jaw and faint circles under his blue eyes.

"You—" I don't know where my sentence is going, and it comes out as, "—know who I am?"

He blinks at me. "You live in my house—of course I know who you are."

I think what I meant was, *You recognize me?* Because there's no way this man and I have ever laid eyes on each other. I'd remember.

"Is there a problem with the house?"

"No," I say. "I just wanted to—" I root around in my briefcase and pull out a check, the bulk of my savings, and thrust it at him over the exam table.

He takes it, glancing at my scribbled handwriting before looking back up at me. "You didn't need to come in for this. Nate usually just mails it."

I take a deep breath. "It's not only that. I have a—proposal for you."

One dark eyebrow lifts. "A proposal."

I nod, and Henry stares at me for another beat before setting the check on the exam table. He adjusts his slacks and sits on the stool waiting behind him. Laces his fingers together between his thighs. "All right."

I clear my throat and slide one piece of paper across the table at him: a photo of the house with *Majestic Mountain Getaway* splashed over it in the most elegant word art I could find on short notice. A couple strands of dog hair have floated across it, and I wipe them hastily away.

"Imagine," I say, and Henry's eyes flick up from the photo to meet mine. "Your beautiful home, *the* short-term rental destination of Estes Park, Colorado."

Henry doesn't look keen on imagining. When he tips back on the stool, his lips press into a line.

I slide another paper toward him. "Five individual guest bedrooms, beautifully appointed." And another. "Homemade breakfast. Curated recommendations from a local. Meticulous maid service."

"Who's the meticulous maid?"

"Me," I say, and now both of Henry's eyebrows rise. They're good eyebrows: dark and severe. "And I'd cook breakfast, too. And manage everything, every detail, and pass all of the profit along to you. With five rooms, we could easily bring in double what you're currently asking in rent."

He studies me. At some point while I was speaking, he crossed his arms over his chest. "And Nate?"

I raise my chin. "Nate's not in the picture anymore."

Henry's face doesn't change. His eyes only cut back and forth across mine, like he's weighing this—or deciding what it means.

I think he'll probably do the polite thing and tell me he's sorry to hear it, but instead he says, "Is he transferring the lease to you, then? We'll need to sort it out in writing."

I can feel it start to unfurl in me: fear. It seeps up from the floor of my belly, and I press one hand to my blouse, as if I could trap it there. Henry tracks the movement before looking back up at me.

"That's the thing," I say. "I want to run the house as a bed-and-breakfast instead of taking over the lease."

"What's in that for you?"

I swallow. It does nothing to push down the rising tide—the feeling that I'm drowning in myself. He's going to say no; I can already tell. And I'll be out of a home, out of a relationship, out of a future. "You'd let me live there for free."

There's a long silence. Henry's arms are still crossed. He says finally, "Ah."

"I know it's a lot to ask," I say, and a muscle tics in his jaw. "But I do think it makes sense, financially. For you."

"And you." Something about his gaze feels punitive, like he's caught me in a lie. My eyes start to burn, and I will myself to keep it together. I think of Goldie, who's always been irritated by my propensity for tears, the way it *makes people take you less seriously*. There's no space for my heartbreak in this room.

But then Henry says, "I'm sorry, but no," and immediately goes blurry in front of me. "You can't run a vacation rental without the right permits, and I'm not interested in strangers cycling through my home, and—" He breaks off, and I wipe quickly at my face. "Are you all right?"

"Yeah," I say thickly. "Sorry, I must be allergic to—cats, or something." When I gesture at the portrait on his wall, he doesn't look away from me.

"I can easily transfer the lease from Nate to you," Henry says. His voice is even, but when I look back at him his face has gone the slightest bit pink—right along the ridges of his cheekbones. "There's no need to go to all this trouble."

I think of Mei, when I called her before driving over here, the pep talk she gave me as I stood in front of the mirror. *You go in there like the badass, empathetic, beautiful businesswoman that you are and make him see the genius of your plan.* I draw a long, slow breath and blink my eyes clear.

"I can't afford it," I tell Henry. He holds my gaze. "Without Nate. I'm looking for work as a therapist, and even then, I won't be able to afford it." Henry rolls his stool sideways to open a cupboard above the sink. I'm humiliated when he pulls out a spool of paper towels and extends it toward me. "I love your house," I tell him, taking the towels. I rip one off and dab it under my eyes, hoping my mascara hasn't turned me into a rabid raccoon. "It's my home. And I really, really don't want to leave it."

Henry watches me as I carefully fold the towel and drop it into a small metal trash can. When he still hasn't said anything, I find myself carrying on just to fill the silence. "It's the first place that's ever felt like home to me. The attic office, and the garden, and the window in the upstairs bedroom that overlooks the street—where sometimes I can see Custard the St. Bernard in Bill and Martina's yard." Henry's face is all sharp lines: the cut of his mouth, the rigid set of his eyebrows. But I see the quickest flicker of something—sympathy, or surprise. Something soft in his eyes, there and then gone. I cling to it like a buoy. "It's my favorite place in the world. And if I could share it with other people, instead of having to leave it, I mean—" I hesitate, drawing a steadying breath. "I'll take such good care of it. I promise."

Henry's quiet for a long, slow minute. His eyes are shocking, white-ringed blue, like lake ice in the sun.

"I have a friend in city hall," he says finally. He seems surprised at the sound of his own voice, and when he shifts on the stool he looks distinctly off-kilter, like he's baffled by himself. "Who might be able to help with the permits."

I grin, such an intense slice of a smile that it makes my cheeks ache straightaway. "*Thank* you," I say, a rush of words that propels me toward him across the exam table. When my hand lands on his forearm, squeezing, I feel the muscle jump under his sleeve. "I can't tell you how much this means to me." His eyes flick up to mine, startled, and I let go. "Seriously. Thank you."

"Let's try it for six months," Henry says, something stilted about his speech—like he can't quite believe he's agreeing to this. He clears his throat and sits up straighter on the stool. "Until March? And if it's not working, that's it."

"That's it," I echo, nearly breathless. "Thank you."

Henry slides my rent check back across the exam table toward me, angling it through the maze of my printouts. "We'll let September be month one."

It's a gift I don't deserve. When I meet Henry's eyes his jaw is tensed, his eyebrows knit together, his face still flushed. He looks like I've confused him so entirely, like maybe he needs to lie down. I have the indecent urge to tip forward and smooth my thumb between his eyebrows, erase the worry from his face. *It's okay*. Instead, I lift the check and press it to my chest like something precious.

"Thank you," I say quietly. "You can trust me."

Henry swallows. His voice comes as quietly as my own. "I hope so."

Six

My sister's favorite time to video chat is while she's making dinner, phone propped against her backsplash to give me a straight shot of her tiled kitchen ceiling and the upper third of her face.

"It's like they have no concept of a career woman," she says now. "It's a *runny nose*, for god's sake, not Ebola. I can't keep him home for producing snot. What am I even paying them for, you know? It's day care, not maybe-some-days care. I'm not sitting around my house in a caftan, here, waiting for my child to come home at the end of the day. I'm *working*. In an *office*. Where I cannot *take him*."

"I know," I say, half an eye on Goldie's forehead and half on my browser, where I'm building out the house's rental page. I'm in the attic office, an A-frame hobbit hole of a room with floral wallpaper and a bay window that overlooks the garden. The house is old and thin-walled; something about the architecture makes the sound travel straight up to this room from the first floor—anytime Nate needed me from the kitchen, all he had to do was lean against the wall and shout. "How's he feeling now?"

"Oh, he's fine." Goldie picks up her phone, giving me a clear view up her nose as she leans in, and changes the angle so that I can see Quinn in the living room. They live in a loft in the West Village, a tiny box with tall ceilings and windows over the Hudson. "Say hi to Lou-Lou, Quinn." He waves at me, and I wave back.

Quinn is five years old and perfect. It's criminal that he lives across the country from me, but I'll get to see him this fall when Goldie comes to Denver for a conference. I told her weeks ago that he could stay with me while she's downtown at the hotel, and it only occurs to me in this exact moment that I nearly didn't have a home for him to stay in.

"Anyway." She sets her phone back on the counter and leans over the stove. Steam rises from a pan to obscure what little I can see of her face. "How are you? You've been ignoring my texts."

I take a long, slow breath. "I'm going to need you to look at me for this."

She cranes toward the phone like an ostrich. "What is it? Oh my god, are you sick? Is Mom sick?"

"Why would I know that Mom's sick before you? No, no one is sick."

"What, then?" I stare at the pixels of her face, and she leans closer. "Hello? Lou, what did you do?"

"Why do you assume *I* did something? Nate broke up with me."

Her intake of breath is theatrically sharp. She reaches for her phone, whipping it up into the air and storming out of the kitchen so fast I could get motion sick. She waits until she's shut in her microscopic bathroom—out of Quinn's earshot—to say, "He broke *up* with you?"

"Yes."

"Oh my god, Lou, I told you men are vipers. What a snake. When did this happen? Why did he do it? What will you do? Where are you living?"

"*Goldie.*" She stares at me, wide-eyed, her familiar face washed out in the bathroom light. "You're raising my blood pressure."

"You're raising *mine*, Lou. This guy has sustained your entire lifestyle!"

I rub at the spot between my eyebrows. "Can you be supportive for, like, one minute before laying into me about getting a job?"

"It's not about a *job*, Lou, it's about *independence*." I've heard this diatribe two-point-seven billion times. "It's about setting yourself up so you don't wind up in this *precise* scenario where your older sister is terrified for your well-being from the other side of the country because you have no means of caring for yourself even though you have *two* entire degrees from accredited universities that cost you enough money to float the entire economy of a small island nation and you haven't even *scheduled* your licensing exam—"

I glance back at the rental listing on my computer. She'll run out of steam eventually.

"Lou? Are you hearing me right now?"

"I don't need you to lecture me." I pick up the phone and turn in my desk chair so I can look out over the garden. The house has a first-floor office, too, but I've always preferred it up here, where I can see the stone paths through the garden like trails on a map. Nate bought me a desk that fits just right in the trapezoidal nook. "I'm going through a breakup, remember?"

My sister blinks. She never liked Nate, but I was always unsure if it was because of Nate himself or just the idea of him. He grated on all of Goldie's sensibilities: he was a dreamer, running on blind faith and cheap beer, who'd built his success without any of the things she believed in. Advanced degrees, savings accounts, budget spreadsheets. He came from a *gentle parenting* family. He moved through the world like water: taking every dip and turn with grace, barreling ahead even if his direction changed unexpectedly. Goldie was the tree growing from the riverbed. Battered but unmoved, her roots white-knuckled.

Mom made her this way. Just like Mom made me a therapist. Goldie was the head; I was the heart. And still, all these years after leaving home, we're always trying to tug each other in our own direction.

"I know," Goldie says. "And I'm sorry, Lou. But there are logistical concerns."

"And I'll deal with them. Eventually."

She pulls the phone closer to her face. "Really? What does that even mean? I barely have room for Quinn and me in the apartment and you're obviously not moving back in with Mom."

Obviously. I haven't lived with Mom since I was a preteen; when Goldie moved out for college, I went with her. I had friends whose parents worried about this: Was it a good idea for such a young girl to be living at Ohio State? Exposed to all that chaos, all that drinking? What I didn't tell them, of course, was that my mother was the source of chaos in my life—and my exposure to drinking.

During those years, we mostly saw Mom at the holidays. We'd go wherever she was staying, a short-term lease or friend's apartment, and do our best to make merry. It wasn't that we didn't love our mother. Mostly, she tried to be on her best behavior with us. She was loving, and loud, and when you told her a story, she really listened to you. But she was unpredictable, naturally, and only more so when she was drinking.

Her moods were a game of roulette. One that always felt, to me, worth playing. Because sometimes I'd get her rasping laugh, her hand clutching mine, an entire evening where all she wanted was to cuddle me on the couch while we watched old movies. But just as often—more often, if I'm honest with myself—I got her anger. Her fury at Goldie for *taking me* from her, though we all knew she didn't want to manage my care, or my education. Her rage at the injustice of the world, at how men treated her, at how her bosses didn't value her. In her worst moments, the thinly veiled threat that we'd all be better off without her.

There was nothing that bothered our mother that she wouldn't share with us—even when I was nine. Even when I was younger.

Goldie loved me and resented Mom in equal measure. Her college years were consumed by parenting me—a sacrifice that she never complained about, but one that I knew wore on her. How could it not? When I left for college, hightailing it to Colorado, she moved to New York and didn't look back. We didn't communicate with Mom much after that; without us close by, she rarely reached out. Goldie and I spent holidays together, or with friends. I missed my mom, and I felt stupid for it—the shock of her disinterest in my life still hasn't worn away, not even seventeen years after I first moved in with Goldie.

Goldie stayed in Ohio all that time for me. It's clear, in retrospect, that it wasn't what she wanted, but what she felt she needed to do. And while my feelings toward our mother are an inextricable knot of longing and fear and loss and love, Goldie's are simpler. She's angry.

Now, down in the garden, Joss swings open the gate. I tell my sister, "I'm staying in the house."

"With what money?"

I take a breath and test out the words. "I'm turning it into a bed-and-breakfast. The landlord's letting me stay for free in exchange for managing it."

Goldie's lips part. "You don't even know how to scramble an egg."

I look at my sister. Remind myself that this is how she loves me. "I'll learn, Goldie."

"Okay, no." Mei pulls the plate out of my hand and dumps the eggs back into the pan. "These are too soupy. No one likes a wet egg."

I shudder. "Don't say 'wet egg.'"

"Don't *make* a wet egg." Mei jabs at my mess of scrambled eggs with a spatula. Morning light dances in through the stained glass over the sink, sending small rainbows over her cheeks. "The only runny part of a scrambled egg should be the melted cheese. Wet eggs give people the ick."

It's Sunday morning, a week later, and Mei slept over to give me a crash course on breakfast prep. There are six bedrooms upstairs, but Mei passed out in the king bed with me—her breathing soft and even, steadying me as I struggled to fall asleep. When I showed her the recipes I'd printed out for Henry—eggs Benedict, ricotta-stuffed French toast, ginger-lemon muffins—she'd looked me square in the face and said, "I admire your beautiful, ambitious soul, but this is not going to happen."

So far I've mastered dry, crumbly blueberry muffins and oven-baked granola. The eggs are a work in progress.

"Lou?" Joss's voice sails through the front door. She usually comes through the back, but it's unseasonably cool for early September and I've left the door open for a cross-breeze. It carries down the front hall, smelling like pine and soil and sun. "You've got a package—want me to bring it in?"

"Yes!" I crane away from the eggs, and Mei catches my wrist before I yank the pan off the stovetop. "Thank you!"

Joss comes into the kitchen, blond hair hidden under a wide-brimmed sun hat. "Investing in some new security?"

The box she slides onto the dining table is peppered with DefenseLock logos.

"Oh, good. No, those are my—"

"Okay," Mei says, guiding my hands to slide the pan off the heat, "they're probably done."

"—new bedroom locks. To convert the rooms for the vacation rentals."

Joss's eyebrows shoot up. "So he said yes?"

"Yep." I shoot her a smile between shoveling eggs back onto the plate. "At least for a six-month trial."

Joss had been worried Henry would veto the rentals—*grouchy* was the single word she'd used to describe him. Now, she grins. "You must've made a good pitch."

I think of my printouts on the exam table. Of the paper

towels Henry handed to me when I teared up. Of the bemused look on his face when he agreed to this, like even as he said the words, he couldn't quite believe them. With the rent check he passed back to me, I have enough money to manage things here for the next six months—updated décor, new locks, food—if I'm scrappy.

"I guess?"

"Well, I'm glad." Joss cuts around the kitchen and gives me a warm, one-armed hug. "Let me know if you need help with anything, yeah? I'll be outside continuing my futile quest to get rid of the dandelions."

"We'll be on our own futile quest," Mei mutters, and I gasp.

Joss barks a laugh and makes for the back door. "Smells good, at least."

"*Thank* you," I say indignantly, raising my eyebrows at Mei. She watches me pepper the eggs and accidentally dust the entire counter with a shower of black specks, then raises her eyebrows right back.

My phone trills from the table. My heart does this hot, painful clenching thing, like it's trying to squeeze out from between my ribs. I'm always ready for it to be Nate, admitting that he made a mistake. Not because I want him back—because I want to be someone with enough gravity for him to regret losing me.

But it's only Henry, a few simple words.

Have an update on permits. Can I come by 2pm?

Seven

By the time Henry shows up, Mei's gone back downtown to meet Andy and I've set the entire kitchen island with the spoils of our morning together: a platter of my crumbly muffins, little glass jars of yogurt with granola on top, buttered toast piled with scrambled eggs, plain pancakes burned only on one side (stacked burned-side-down), a giant bowl of glistening berries, and two fresh mugs of coffee.

I'm expecting Henry in his vet clothes: dark slacks, a checkered button-down, the white coat with his name stitched over his heart. But it's a Sunday, and when I open the front door he's on my porch in worn-looking Levi's and a CSU Rams T-shirt. He's holding a thin stack of papers. When I offer him one of the coffee cups, he extends the papers toward me.

At the exact same moment, we both say, "What's this?"

"Coffee," I tell him, as he says, "The Estes Park Vacation Home Regulations."

I riffle through the pages, clocking the edge-to-edge fine print. "Ah."

Henry lifts the mug at me. "Thanks."

Behind him, across the street, I see Martina step outside with Custard the St. Bernard. She waves at me, and when I return it, Henry glances over one shoulder and lifts his own hand. Martina looks startled to see him, her smile wide and surprised, and when he points to his watch she nods.

I wait for Henry to explain, but he only turns his eyes back on me and stands, frozen, with the coffee cup.

Well. I step backward into the entryway. "Do you want to come in?"

Henry tips his head, eyes casting over mine. His gaze flicks to the hall behind me and he swallows, like he's bracing himself, before he finally says, "Okay."

Inside he stands perfectly still and keeps his gaze trained to his coffee, like he needs to be invited to take up space here.

"We can get the permit by the end of the month," he tells me. The stubble traced along his jaw is dark and rough. When I dip past him to shut the door, he smells like soap—bright, unexpected citrus. "But there's a lot in there you'll need to take note of. Occupancy restrictions, and quiet hours, and rules about vehicles."

"Absolutely," I say. I meant what I told him in that exam room: he can trust me. "I'll give it a read. Is that—" I hesitate, and he finally looks up from his coffee to meet my eyes. In the afternoon light the hallway is bright and warm. "All you needed? Because I was hoping to show you what I've been working on."

I want Henry to be excited about this. I want him to understand how seriously I'm taking it. I also, admittedly, want to see if I can get him to crack a smile.

"Oh." He glances back at the coffee, which he still hasn't taken one sip of, and then down the hallway into the kitchen. When he swallows again, I watch it move through the long column of his throat. "No, I didn't have anything else."

"Great." I smile, and he doesn't return it. Instead, his eyes cast over the house: taking in the photos I've framed on the walls, the turtle-shaped lamp on the side table, the maple-scented candle crackling from the dining room. I hardly use it and it's more of a library, these days: a long table framed on all sides in bookshelves, stacked high with my favorite poetry collections and mythology retellings. With Nate on the road, I always had time to read.

"Well," I say. "I've been working on the breakfast menu." When I start down the hall, Henry follows me quietly. "Muffins and eggs and granola and fruit. If we're still going next summer, we can do Palisade peaches. And coffee." I turn back to raise my mug at him, but he's staring across the living room at my gallery wall. It frames the fireplace, extending like scattered seedlings on either side: a photo of Goldie and me when I was in high school, bundled like mummies in a snowstorm; a pencil sketch of the Flatirons Mei drew for an art credit during our senior year of college; every little painting and memory and talisman I've added to my collection since moving in here at twenty-two.

I sniff a little and wave a hand over the spread on the counter. Henry's eyes flick across it in silence.

"Any input on the menu?"

He swallows, and it looks effortful—like he's choking. His voice, when it finally comes, is quiet. "No."

I paste on a smile. "Well, I'm open to feedback. Or I can

show you the guest rooms—I'm working on installing individual locks, and I've got little nameplates for each one, like, 'The Aspen Room' and 'The Juniper Room,' that sort of thing."

Henry steps past me, his bare forearm brushing my own as he sets his mug next to my platter of secretly burned pancakes. He clears his throat, a tic I recognize from his office. "Look, Louisa." He backs away from me, toward the front door, his eyes finally coming to mine. "I think it's best if you run with this. If I'm not involved."

I think of my conversation with Joss last week—*grouchy*. But Henry doesn't strike me as grouchy; he strikes me as a trapped animal. I can see the tense line of his shoulders through his shirt.

"Okay," I say, pulling my lip between my teeth. Henry's eyes flick to my mouth. "I just want you to feel good about it."

I've always craved validation but been horrified to ask for it. Growing up in Goldie's shadow was a study in second place: she was good at everything, entirely self-sufficient. And then came Nate, who packed stadiums with roiling oceans of fans screaming his name. I'm so used to the background, the passenger seat, supporting actress. I don't want to need the praise—but swallowing the need feels like drowning.

"I do," Henry says, though it comes out a bit like a question. "It seems that you have everything perfectly under control."

I think of Mei, fixing my wet eggs, and manage a frozen smile. "Thanks."

Henry glances toward the dining room and adjusts his watch, a thick leather strap with a gold face. Ropy veins race up from his wrist to his elbow.

"You should keep some of the money that comes in." He casts a hand over the kitchen island without looking at it. "Whatever you need to pay for this. And compensation for your time, of course. Just—" His eyes flick to me, then toward the front door. "Just give me the numbers when you have them."

It's generous—and surprising, considering his tone. But Henry doesn't even give me time to respond before saying, "I'll let you know when the permit comes through."

He turns, then, heading for the front door.

"Thank you," I say quietly. He's the first man in the house since Nate, and as he's framed by the hallway I'm struck by the differences between them: Nate's jangliness, the looseness of his limbs as he careened through the house with pent-up energy and an echoing laugh. Henry is stoic, zipped into himself. He moves so carefully, like he's afraid to touch anything.

When he reaches the door he turns back to me, sun from outside lighting his blue eyes so they look snow-bleached and frigid. "Don't forget to look over the regulations."

"I won't," I say, and his eyes flicker to something behind me. When I turn to look, there's nothing there.

"Henry!"

We both whip around at the sound of Martina's voice, reedy and high from across the street. She's still in the yard with Custard—she's sitting in a folding chair now, with his heavy snout in her lap. She waves, beckoning.

"I need to be going," Henry says, ducking his head like an apology.

I glance from Martina to Henry one more time. "To Bill and Martina's house?"

"Yes." He clears his throat again, twisting his body toward the driveway, his car, away from me. A flush, pink and warm, rises from the neckline of his T-shirt. "Once a month, I—"

"Bring Lou with you!" Martina shouts, cutting him off.

Henry swallows as he turns back to me. He's tall—taller than Nate and Mei and my sister. In the afternoon sun, he casts a shadow over my face.

"Um," I say. *I think it's best if I'm not involved.* "I don't want to—"

"You don't have to—"

Our mouths snap shut in unison. Henry takes a step backward; he moves like there's a magnet pulling him from the house. "I guess we should—"

Custard starts barking, watching us now from the fence. His tail whirs like a wind sock.

"Okay." I yank the door shut behind me. Flap my hands at Henry, who can't seem to get rid of me. "Let's just go."

It's not my fault Martina invited me over, but as I wait for Henry to pull a zippered leather bag from the back seat of his SUV I feel distinctly burdensome—like I'm a burr he's spent the last ten minutes frantically trying to shake off and I'm still clinging, stubbornly, to his pant leg.

"Hello!" Martina calls, standing from her chair as we cross the street. My flip-flops thwack the asphalt, my shoulders burning around the straps of my tank top. Late afternoon is the hottest time of day in the mountains—at two thirty, early September, the sun feels like it's cast through a magnifying glass.

Henry opens Martina's gate like he's done it a hundred times. Her yard is a postage stamp of verdant grass on the flat, brown envelope of our street; lawns are rare in Estes Park, but Bill's outside watering theirs every morning. Custard promptly shoves his nose into Henry's hand, and all five of Henry's fingers disappear into his fur.

"Hello, my friend," Henry says. His voice is soft, none of the uneasy edge he had at the house. "How are you feeling today?"

"He's so good," Martina says, reaching us and dropping her own palm onto Custard's head.

"Well," Henry says, more to the dog than Martina, "we knew that." He lowers into a squat, dropping his bag to take Custard's face in both hands. Custard drags his tongue over Henry's cheek and he laughs. "Any more vomiting?"

"Not so much since the last time," Martina says. "Maybe we do the injections out here, in the shade? He just loves to be outside in the grass."

"Sure." Henry stands, reaching for his bag, and motions to the shady spot where Martina's chair is set up. "How's he tolerating the new oral medication?"

"Seems okay," Martina says, and as Custard lumbers after Henry she puts a hand on my elbow. "Hi, honey."

"Hi." I smile at her, completely disoriented by this moment—the news that Custard's sick, but even more the way Henry has changed around him. It's *me*, apparently, that sets Henry on edge. My plans, my house, my mess.

"What were you two chatting about over there?" Martina asks. She's never been especially nosy, but we're really each other's only neighbors—we keep tabs. "I haven't seen Henry at the house in years. You're not moving out, are you?"

"Oh, no," I say. I feel very warm—from the sun, or from Henry, or from this question. "Nate is, though."

From the grass, legs crossed in front of him and Custard sprawled across his lap, Henry glances up.

"We broke up," I tell Martina. "And I'm going to be running the house as a bed-and-breakfast."

"Oh, *no*," Martina echoes, her fingers clenching around my arm. "I'm so sorry. Nate was always . . ." She hesitates, and Henry digs around in his bag. His neck is still very, very pink. "Well, I know you were together a long time."

I swallow, pasting on a smile. "We were. But it's all right, thank you."

"Bed-and-breakfast?" She glances at Henry. "It's not going to be loud, honey, is it?"

"No," Henry says, before I can reply. He doesn't look at us; he's snapping on a pair of blue nitrile gloves. It's jarring: his old jeans, his T-shirt, the dog gazing up at him as he uncaps a needle and sinks it into a vial of clear liquid. "I was just here dropping off the regulations, and there are strict rules about noise. Don't worry, Martina."

His eyes flick to mine, like he's checking this with me. I nod, and he turns away to part the fur between Custard's shoulder blades.

"What's going on with Custard?" I ask, desperate for a change of subject. Henry's ducked over him, and I look away when I realize he's giving him the injection *right now*. I've never been good with shots.

"He's got lymphoma," Martina says, looking down at him. I follow her gaze without even thinking, but the injection's over with—Henry's rubbing Custard's ears, murmuring to him in a low voice. *Easy, now. Good boy.* Custard's tongue lolls out of his mouth as he blinks up at Henry like he's hanging on his every word. "He's nine, now, you know. But we aren't ready to say goodbye."

"And you don't have to," Henry says. He doesn't look at us;

he's taken the gloves off and his long fingers are running through Custard's fur—a steady rhythm along his rib cage. Henry smiles up at Martina. "Not so long as we're keeping him feeling good."

"I know," Martina says, swatting at him. Henry looks back down at the dog and I know—I *know*—that I'm staring at him, but I can't make myself stop. Who *is* this person? The tense set of his shoulders, that worried line between his brows—all of it's gone. It's like a magic trick: this isn't the same Henry who stood, trapped and stiff, in my kitchen a few minutes ago. The wind moves through his hair and he smiles down at Custard, the muscles shifting in his forearm as he rubs his belly. When he murmurs, "Good boy," it feels like a secret between the two of them.

"Henry comes by to give him treatments because it's so hard for us to lift him into the car these days." Martina waves a hand at me. "Don't get old, honey, it's terrible."

I force a laugh, though nothing about this feels funny. Custard can't be sick. I can't lose the house. Henry can't stand me. I don't want this many things to change—not all at once.

"I've got to go," I say too abruptly. I'm already stepping backward when Henry looks up, the ghost of a smile falling from his face. The sun's in his eyes, and he squints at me—like he can't quite see me; like there's something blurred and unspoken between us. "I hope Custard feels better."

"Thanks, honey." Martina brushes her hand over my arm one more time as I turn away.

"Bye," I say. My voice is loud; too loud, to my own ears. "Bye, Henry."

I don't look back as he responds. I don't let myself think

twice about it when a sudden breeze carries his reply, "I'll be seeing you," after me through the summer air.

I've spent twenty minutes trying to get the nameplate straight. I have one stub of a pencil in this entire house and a pocket-size level that I got for free in a Lowe's-sponsored swag bag at a summer food festival in college. Plus, I'm crying. The really self-indulgent kind, snot running onto my lips and periodic wails bouncing down the upstairs hallway.

I let out a hiccup and collapse onto my ass on the antique wood floor. Henry's lack of enthusiasm this afternoon—coupled with Custard's diagnosis—shook something loose inside of me. Whatever resolve I've built since the breakup has been knocked directly out of place. It's not that I expected warmth from Henry, exactly. But I'm still so raw from Nate's betrayal that any semblance of rejection—anything even *breathing* on the same plane as rejection—feels like a barbed knife directly through my rib cage. And the tense, strained way Henry moved through my house felt personal. Especially after seeing him with Custard and Martina—that gentle, smiling stranger he turned into once he got away from me.

You're alone, the whole exchange reminded me. *The world is all strangers who owe you nothing. You failed your exam and you'll fail at this, too.*

I stare at the level in my palm through blurry eyes. *Let's get one thing straight!* is emblazoned across it. The nameplate I've been trying to install, beautiful brass with a little tree and the words THE PINE ROOM, hangs sideways from one screw. It'll be a miracle if I get one thing straight today, or maybe ever. I wish

I had someone here to help me. I wish I didn't have to do any of this at all. I wish—

My phone starts to ring from the floor beside me, a jaunty jingle that feels offensive given the circumstances. Mei takes up the entire screen, a photo of her at seven years old making a heinous little face while poised over a soccer ball. It's framed in the entryway at her parents' house in Pasadena; I took a picture of it when I spent Thanksgiving with them during our junior year of college.

"Hey," I say wetly, lifting the phone to my ear. Sobs echo through the line, and it takes a few full heartbeats for me to realize they aren't my own.

"*Lou*," Mei wails. I sit up straighter immediately, swiping at my cheeks. "Andy's breaking *up* with me."

"What?" The hallway seizes around me, closing in. *No*. Andy's obsessed with Mei. Andy's one of the good ones. Andy's not supposed to go anywhere, especially this swiftly after Nate. "No, they're not."

"They are!" Mei yells. I have to hold my phone away from my face so she doesn't burst my eardrum. "They're moving to fucking *Costa Rica* and they don't want me to come with them!"

"Costa Rica?" I repeat, and Mei bellows, "Costa! *Rica!* To build houses with their Habitat for Humanity friends! Because apparently, after more than a year spent dating me and not mentioning it even half of one single time, they've realized this is their passion!"

"Oh my god." A wave of calm rises through me, starting at my feet and moving all the way up. I feel myself shifting out of my own misery and directly into Mei's. "Okay, it's okay. You're going to be okay."

"I'm going to be *okay*? Lou, Andy was the best thing I—I mean, we had all these plans and—and I just—"

"I know," I say. My voice has smoothed out, my own tears dried up. "Can you drive back up here? Can you come stay with me for a bit?"

"Yeah," Mei mumbles. "I think so."

"Good," I say. "Here's what we're going to do."

And then I lay it all out for Mei: The email she'll send to her boss, asking to work remote for a while. The bag she'll pack with only her favorite, comfiest clothes. The Thai food we'll order. The walks we'll go on. The sunshine we'll get.

By the time I'm done talking, her sobs have quieted to muted sniffles.

"Thanks, Lou," she whispers. While we've been on the phone I've stood up. Pinned the nameplate in place. Screwed it in, perfectly level. "I'll be there in a couple hours."

"Drive safe." I pull in a deep breath, settling into the role that I'm best at. Being needed. "I'll see you soon."

Eight

Mei is significantly taller than me, but she's pretzeled herself into the smallest possible surface area on my couch—head propped on a pillow in my lap, wad of tissues pressed to her nose that she whimpers into like a wounded animal at regular intervals. I lit every candle I could find in the house. Put *Treasure Planet*—Mei's comfort movie—on the TV with the volume nearly muted. Set out a bowl of Sour Patch Kids, which have so far gone untouched. I run my fingers over Mei's hair.

"It's just such a *shame*," she says for the thirteenth time. She's in shock, still, repeating herself to get used to the ideas. A fire crackles in the fireplace; no matter the heat of the day, nighttime's always cool. "Like, you love someone but then they *physically* need to move their *human body* away from you and that's why you break up? In this day and age? Technology has failed us, right? Why can't we teleport?"

"I know," I say quietly. "When you're feeling better, we'll figure out teleportation."

She lets out a wet laugh that turns into a sob halfway through. "Fuck, and their *family*? I love Andy's family. Andy's *mom*?"

"Andy does have a great mom," I say. "And you do, too. And so many other people who love you and will make sure your life still feels full."

"But who will I text when I see a meme about Mexican hairless dogs?"

I hesitate. "Um, me. I would love to laugh with you about Mexican hairless dogs."

"But they were Andy's *favorite*," Mei says weakly, her voice dissolving into the tissues. I know what she's doing: remembering. Even with the distance Nate and I had let grow between us, there's a version of me—younger, buried—that feels it like a fresh cut every time. Nate's voice when he was halfway to sleep. The Jack Skellington suit he wore every Halloween. The way he'd text me a photo anytime he saw someone walking a dog that looked like them.

"What's your favorite?" I ask, and Mei whines, "Who *cares*, Lou?"

"I care," I say. When I lean forward to pick up a Sour Patch Kid, she groans at the movement. I hold it to her mouth and she opens up like a baby bird. We sit in silence, candles flickering around us, as she chews.

"I guess those fluffy black ones," she says finally. "With the white-and-brown faces? That save people from avalanches?"

I think of Henry, the rigid set of his jaw in my kitchen. "Bernese mountain dogs?"

"Yeah," she says miserably. "Bernese mountain dogs."

I pat her head. "Good choice. Much cuter than Mexican hairless, if you ask me."

"Yeah," she says again. For a while, she just breathes—steady, in and out. On-screen, the crew of 2D pirates crash-lands on an unfamiliar planet. The movie's a stark contrast to the room around it, which is all wood paneling and carved finials and antiques I've spent the last four years collecting.

When Mei speaks again, she sounds clearer. More serious. Like after getting her jokes out of the way, we've finally arrived at the tender core of her hurt. "But it's like, did I waste all that?"

I look down at her, and she turns onto her back to look up at me. "Waste all what?"

"All that time." Her lower lip trembles. "I spent a year with them, you know? I thought we were building toward something. But now I'm just back to square one and I—god, sorry, I sound like such an ass right now. You were with Nate way longer." She smashes a hand over her face. "*Fuck*, sorry, Lou."

I swallow. I was with Nate long enough to have trouble remembering how things felt before him. Long enough that a year felt like a blink. But Nate was also gone so often—more than half the time—that I'm used to being without him. That I don't miss him, if I'm being honest with myself. I just miss knowing that I had someone out there, planning to come home to me.

"It's okay," I tell her. I pry her hand off her face, and we meet each other's eyes in the firelit living room. This is how it's always been, with Mei and me—with everyone and me. I'm more comfortable taking care than being taken care of. "You didn't waste it, Mei. Think about everything you've learned about yourself over the last year. What you want in a partner, and maybe some things you don't. And how big of a love you're capable of giving to someone else." I try to hear the words as I say them. "You get to keep all of those things. How much better you know yourself now. That's yours forever, and it's so valuable."

For the first time, Mei offers me a weak smile. "You're really good at this, Lou. It's like you could be a therapist or something."

I roll my eyes, and she sits up. Pulls the bowl of Sour Patch Kids into her lap. "I'm serious."

"Thank you."

She picks an orange gummy out of the bowl—my favorite—and hands it to me. "Can I stay here forever?"

"Of course you can."

"Even when you start renting out the rooms? Can I get a friends and family discount?"

"I'll charge everyone else more so you can stay here forever for free."

She smiles again. Smashes two red gummies together and eats them. "Or at least until my heart's not broken."

"At least until then," I agree. "We the brokenhearted have to stick together."

"So true," Mei says, leaning her head onto my shoulder. She melts back into the couch. "We the brokenhearted."

As we watch the movie, the words ring between us: *We the brokenhearted.* We the vulnerable. The left-behind.

I picture my house full of people like us, leaning on each other. Eating candy and watching kids' movies and doing the soft, quiet things that make us feel a little less raw. Talking about all the small, awful memories of the people we won't know anymore. Saying them out loud so they don't have to live, trapped, inside of us.

"Mei," I say quietly. She looks up at me. "What if I did that, with the rentals?"

"Did what with the rentals?"

I swallow against the swell of it, rising in me. "Offered them to brokenhearted people. Like a retreat, to recover."

She sits up again. "Like heartbreak rehab."

I nod. "Like—get away to the mountains and recover from your heartbreak with hiking and a therapist to talk to and good food." I correct myself. "Almost therapist."

"Decent food," Mei amends.

"Right." The truth is I've felt more like myself this evening than I have since the breakup. Having someone to care for—putting my energy into someone else's pain—lessens my own. I've always been like that. *Bleeding heart*, Goldie calls me.

Maybe this is exactly what I need. Not only the thing I'm best at, but the thing that makes me feel best. Being useful, creating peace, giving people someone to sit beside in their hurt. It would be like therapy *lite*: channeling all the reasons I wanted to be a counselor in the first place, but doing it in a way that'll fill my time—and patch my heart—until I can retake my licensing exam and start my career in earnest. Using this house I love so much to help people heal, the way it's healed me over all these years.

I look at Mei. "Do you think—I mean. Is it a good idea?"

"Lou." Mei takes my hands. Her wad of tissues is stuffed between our palms. "It's a *great* idea."

The first heart I ever watched break was my mother's. My father was never in the picture—Goldie's, neither—but I grew up marking time by Mom's heartbreak. In kindergarten it was Ross, a contractor whose big boots sit by the front door in all my earliest memories. In second grade, Matthias with his blue pickup truck, the sticker shaped like a German shepherd on its mud-splattered back window. In third grade, Darren—not around long enough to be buried with a talisman in my memory. It wasn't the men who stuck with us, making a pattern of our family. It was their going: the sudden absence of them, and the fallout we repeated like clockwork.

It was worst when we were staying with them—when it wasn't just a breakup but an eviction, too. We didn't always live with Mom's boyfriends, but it certainly made things easier for her. Rent was our boogeyman, creeping out from the baseboards with cold fingers. We moved more than any of my friends—usually living in someone's spare room, the three of us snuggled like sardines in a queen bed, or on a month-to-month lease Mom could break when she needed to. Her boyfriends' places tended to be small and spare, but we didn't pay rent there.

If we weren't living with him, the break was cleaner and less complex. I tracked her phases through a breakup like checking days off a calendar; she always followed the same process. The sharp-toothed, uncontrollable anger—the cursing, the redness of her face. Then the sorrow—the way she became small, folding into a meek and miserable version of herself. This was the part Goldie hated most, but the easiest for me. She'd start sleeping on the couch, away from us—so her crying wouldn't wake us, maybe, or so that she could play something on TV all night and knock out the loop of her own thoughts. I'd wake up, finding her gone, and shuffle out to join her on the couch. It's almost sweet, in my memory: the picture of my mother lifting the throw blanket in the glow of the television, making space for my body against the curved shell of her own.

Then came her defiance. She'd get preachy, two weeks into a breakup—teaching my sister and me that men couldn't be trusted, shouldn't be sought after, didn't deserve love. Then she'd meet someone new, and she'd forget it all until the next time.

I was seven, Goldie sixteen, when one of Mom's boyfriends got her into therapy. It was Matthias—his muddy blue pickup a stark contrast to the softness hidden beneath. It was unclear to me, a child, exactly what was going on; I only knew that our mother was suddenly at the doctor with novel regularity. It scared me. It was only after I'd woken Goldie up in the middle of the night for the third time in a week, panicked that our mother was sick and dying, that she told me Mom had been diagnosed with borderline personality disorder. *Finally*, Goldie had said, but I didn't understand what a personality disorder was—or how someone like my own mother, who I'd learned everything from, could have one.

To me, Mom's temper was part of being human. Her impulsivity was what made her fun. The messes she got us into—forgetting to pay rent, or spending all of it on things we wanted but didn't need—seemed like honest mistakes. It wasn't until Matthias—until counseling—that I came to understand some of the things that I thought made my mother who she was weren't personality traits but symptoms.

When Matthias left, less than a year later, so did the incrementally more even-keeled version of our mom. I understood, later, that he was paying for her psychotherapy and that, without him, we couldn't afford it. Mom wasn't in treatment long enough to experience lasting healing or change. She went back a few times—the first after an unexpected holiday bonus at work when I was in sixth grade; again after an aunt died sophomore year and left her some money. She wanted help. I believed that, more than Goldie did. But she could never get it for long enough to stick, and when her sporadic attempts "didn't work," she eventually stopped trying.

Mom's boyfriends—coming, going, leaving her brokenhearted—remained inextricable, for me. The way she dove in heart-first every time horrified Goldie. *She's sick*, she'd tell me, after we listened to Mom rave about someone she'd only just met. But it didn't feel that way to me. Maybe because I was younger; maybe because I didn't want to believe that our mother's unyielding desire to find love—after all the times she'd been burned—could be anything but a virtue.

Maybe because it was me, every time, picking up the bloodied pieces. Me, who she needed; me, who was useful. Me, sliding in beside her on the couch in the most vulnerable hours of the morning, our breaths syncing up in the darkness.

Nine

"No, more charming." Mei nudges my hands off the keyboard and starts typing. I'd written *Run by an innkeeper with a counseling degree,* and she edits it to *Run by an empathetic, caring innkeeper with a therapy degree and years of experience counseling clients through heartbreak.*

"I don't want to overpromise," I say. We're back on my couch in our pajamas, morning light coming through the stained-glass windows. It's sunny again today—the drippy butter yellow of September. "Or give the idea that I'm doing free therapy or something illegal like—"

"Show me the lie," Mei says, gesturing at what she's written. We have the vacation rentals website up on my laptop, which is propped on our knees between us. Her computer sits open on the coffee table behind it, where she can keep an eye on her work email. "This is all true."

"I mean, technically—"

"Okay, then." Mei keeps scrolling, reviewing my work. "What we really need to figure out is what we're calling it."

"Calling it," I repeat, looking at her.

"A name," Mei says. She tucks hair behind one ear and meets my eyes. "Every trendy spot needs a trendy name. Like, Pewter and Rye. Brimstone Sage. Exhale on the Water."

I squint. "Those all sound like candles."

"I think that first one might actually be a restaurant in Denver. My point is: we need a name for the B&B."

I tap a fingernail against my laptop. "It's not meant to be *trendy*, though. It's meant to be a real experience. Like, with some staying power."

"Of course," Mei says, reaching for her coffee mug on the table. "But we've still got to market it."

I draw a long breath, thinking. I'm not good at this kind of thing, and when I say, "Haven House?" Mei rolls her eyes.

"That's definitely the name of some overpriced rehab in Malibu. What about the Getaway?"

"Too vacationy," I tell her. "If it needs a name, it should convey that this is, you know, a place to come feel your feelings."

Mei eyes me. "The Feeling Spot."

We burst out laughing in unison, and I offer, "The Lightheart Lodge? Like, you could leave more lighthearted than you came?"

Mei rubs her chin. "It's got potential. A little cute, though."

I reach for my own coffee, taking a sip. "It's about working through grief," I say, thinking out loud. "About a safe place to come and sit in the experience you're having. Nothing else to focus on, no distractions, just taking care of yourself, and processing, and finding yourself again." I look at Mei, who's nodding. "Coming back to yourself."

"Everyone likes a comeback story," she says.

"The Comeback? Comeback Cottage?" I raise my eyebrows at Mei, and she tilts her head back and forth, squinting like I haven't quite hit it yet. "The Comeback Inn?"

Mei gasps. "*Yes*."

"It's not too punny?"

"People *love* puns." Mei leans closer as she talks, the way she always does when she's excited. "Plus all the important stuff you said: Come back to yourself. Come back in, because it's safe here. Yadda yadda."

"Yadda yadda," I agree, and Mei starts typing again. It's good to see her like this—creative; sure of herself; laughing, even—after last night.

We have less than a month before the permit goes into effect: three weeks to get the word out about the rentals and inspire enough bookings to make this worth Henry's while. As Mei continues to bejewel my descriptions—adding words like *cozy* and *endearing* and *picturesque*—my phone buzzes on the side table. I put down my coffee mug and pick it up.

It's Goldie: Be strong today and DO NOT let him weasel back in.

It takes a full beat for me to remember what she's talking about, but when I do, I gasp so sharply Mei stops typing.

"What?" she says.

"Nate's coming today." I worm out from under the throw blanket we're sharing and swivel around the living room, taking in the disaster of it. There's food everywhere—the Sour Patch Kids from last night, an open box of cinnamon rolls that Mei and I decided we needed this morning, empty glasses ringed in dry red wine. "To get his stuff." I look down at myself—wrinkled pajama shorts, legs prickly with stubble, hideous Peter Pan sweatshirt I got at Disneyland when I was nineteen. "Oh my god."

"When?" Mei slides the laptop off her legs. "Like, soon?"

"Ten, he said." I scramble for my phone again, and it glares up at me: 9:18. "Oh my *god*."

"Okay, go shower." Mei flaps her hands at me. "I'll clean up down here. Don't wash your hair, just do that low bun thing, and maybe mascara and, like—" She hesitates. "Concealer? You look tired." I groan, already making for the stairs, and she shouts from behind me, "But beautiful! *So* beautiful."

In the swirl of Mei's breakup and the new angle for the rentals, I've somehow managed to forget about Nate. We set this date last week, after I'd asked for Henry's contact information. The band leaves for Australia soon, and Nate wants to clean house before he goes. After talking about it with Goldie I decided not to pack all his things for him—they're everywhere in the house, still. Our winter sweaters mixed together in the Juniper Room's closet, his small collection of paperbacks stacked on the dresser in our bedroom. *Make him do it all*, Goldie said. *Make it hard for him*.

But I know it won't just be hard for Nate. It'll be hard for me—to have him back here, moving through my space. The indisputable fact of his body. The heat between us cooled a long time ago, but it doesn't change the fact that for so many years, Nate was the most familiar thing in my life. My nose starts to burn just thinking about it as I strip my pajamas off in the bathroom, and by the time I step into the shower my eyes are glazed over with tears. *Fuck*. Fuck, fuck, *fuck* this.

By the time I'm dressed and downstairs it's 9:57. I've sucked my tears back inside, taken enough deep breaths to power a hot-air balloon, put on Nate's favorite perfume. Just to be petty. Just to feel like someone he desired, once.

"Okay, so Henry is stopping by," Mei says. She's at the kitchen sink, sudsing up a wineglass.

"What?" I shove the mail on the front table into a pile, as if seeing how organized I am will make Nate regret his choice.

"Henry, your landlord? He texted." Mei juts her chin toward my phone, which is sitting on the kitchen island. "He said he has this espresso machine he doesn't use and asked if you wanted it for the B&B, so I said yes."

I blink at her. What's Henry *it's-best-if-I'm-not-involved* Rhodes doing offering me an espresso machine?

"Um," I say, shaking my head a little. Yesterday made it clear that this house—that *near me*—is the last place Henry wants to be. "Okay? He's coming right now?"

"I guess?" Mei says. "He didn't really specify—"

The doorbell rings, and we both freeze. My heart seizes, hot and violent. When I turn, I can see the top of Nate's head through the narrow window in the door: his light hair, just the right shade of disheveled, and a thin strip of his tan forehead. The place I used to press kisses, right at his hairline, when he was sad.

Suddenly behind me, Mei whispers, "I love you. You've got this."

"Okay," I tell her, and then I open the door.

"Hi," Nate says immediately, a little too loud. I know he's as anxious as I am when he pinches the skin behind one elbow, a nervous tic he's had for as long as I've known him.

"Hi." My voice is quieter. "Come on in."

Nate waits for me to pull the door wide and steps over the threshold, toeing off his sneakers. It was a debate, in the beginning—he came from a shoes-on household; I was staunchly shoes-off. I look at his socked feet on the hardwood floor and will myself not to cry.

It's not Nate himself, not really. It's the weight of an entire life we built up around each other, suddenly just *gone*. It feels like a death.

"Hey, Mei," Nate says.

"Nathan," she replies coolly. She's perched on the bottom landing of the carved wooden staircase: a strategic choice, maybe, because it makes her taller than Nate. It occurs to me that he might think she's here because I wanted backup for this, which makes me feel like a fool. "I'd say it's nice to see you, but."

"Yeah," Nate says. When our eyes meet, he looks sorry. I wanted him to be an asshole today. I didn't want him to be nervous. I didn't want him to hold my gaze the way he does now; the way he's done so many times before. I wanted to hate him, and I know—as his hand lifts, as his fingers brush my wrist, as I watch him stop himself from comforting me—that I don't. That even after all of this, Nate and I meant something to each other once, and nothing can undo it. "Lou."

It's almost like he doesn't realize he's said it. I can tell he has no idea where to take the sentence, and as my name hangs between us in the sunlit entryway I nearly forget that Mei's here. Nearly forget that Nate came to empty the rest of himself from my life. His lips part, and I force myself to speak first.

"Your things are where you left them."

Nate shuts his mouth.

"Did you bring a box or something?" Mei says. Nate glances at her, like he forgot she was here, too.

"Uh, yeah." He jerks one thumb at the door, then lets his hand fall to rub the back of his hair. "I have a suitcase in the car. Um, Lou, can we—" He looks at me, hesitates. "Talk upstairs?"

"I'll go," Mei says. She catches my eye. "So you can talk down here. If that's okay, Lou?"

I swallow. Hear myself say, "Sure."

When Mei disappears up the stairs, Nate and I walk into the kitchen. He sits at the island and I stand across it, my hands flat on the cold granite. The expanse of stone is a wall between us, and I lean on it for support. I fight myself from sinking into the familiarity of this: Nate in our kitchen with the sun in his eyes. Nate spooning cereal while he reads the news. Nate mixing cocktails the night he gets home from tour. Nate telling me he loves me, so quiet, as he pulls the strap of my dress over one shoulder and presses me against the cream-colored fridge.

It's not my heart pulling me toward him, it's my muscle memory. But in the frenetic rush of my blood, the tumble of my pulse, it's hard to discern the difference.

"You look good," Nate says, softly.

"Thank you."

He wets his bottom lip, and I have to look away. "I owe you an apology, Lou. I handled this all wrong."

Ice clunks into the freezer bucket. I meet Nate's eyes.

"I should have talked to you when I met Estelle." *Estelle.* Of course it's Estelle. If "Lou" and "Estelle" were cars, Lou would be a Prius and Estelle would be a Maserati.

"I should have been honest when you sent me that photo," he

continues. "Back in the spring." This is how Nate's always been: after his defensiveness, his thoughtfulness. Given time, the angry, obtuse person who broke up with me in Denver has always turned into the self-reflective one sitting, now, at our island. But I wish he wouldn't; I wish he was awful. "I should have been honest even earlier than that, and ended it then."

"When?" I say quietly. I don't want to know, but I'm desperate to know. To rifle back through all my memories for the breadcrumbs of this betrayal.

"In the winter," he tells me. My fingertips press into the counter. The first time I saw Estelle, a nameless woman kissing Nate in a photograph, it was April. *April.* "I met her in February, at this—"

"I don't—" We both stop, watching each other unblinkingly. "I don't want the details."

"Okay," he says, nodding. "That's fair. I'm sorry. I just want you to know that you don't—" He breaks off, looking across the kitchen. He takes in our living room, the couch we picked out together, the fake fiddle-leaf fig he teased me for buying until he saw how nice it looked. Especially at Christmas, string-lit and glowing. He draws a rickety breath and looks back at me. "You don't deserve to be lied to. This isn't an excuse, but things had been so distant between us for so long and I just—" He draws a breath. I watch him force it back down, whatever he was about to accuse me of. "I was a coward, and I'm sorry."

I don't thank him for apologizing. I don't ask what it is about her. I don't say, *I hope you think of me every time you play "Purple Girl," and I hope it hurts you.*

I stand in silence, not wanting to give him anything at all. And then the doorbell rings.

"I'll get it!" Mei shouts, muffled, from upstairs. When she thunders down the staircase, Nate turns on his stool to watch her open the door. Morning light floods in, cut by the outline of Henry holding an enormous espresso machine.

"Morning!" Mei chirps. Henry looks at her, then at Nate, then at me. He holds my eyes over the length of the hallway, sun reflecting from the metal surface of the espresso machine and making him squint.

"Nate," Henry says. "Hi." Nate lifts a hand in greeting, and then Henry's eyes flicker back to mine. He sounds uncertain when he says, "Louisa?"

"Hi," I say, and my voice betrays me. It's reedy and wavering, right on the edge of tears. It makes Nate turn back toward me, and the pity in his eyes is enough to take me out. He doesn't need to feel *sorry* for me. We got here together—he's just the one who sealed the coffin.

I cut around the island and head for the front door, clearing my throat. "This is my friend Mei," I say, gesturing to her. Henry's eyes stay on me, and I fight to swallow my tears before they become indisputable, before I become the woman who's always weeping in front of him. "She's helping me get things set up for the rentals."

"Rentals?" Nate says, close enough that I realize he's followed me.

"Yes," I say curtly, as Henry's eyes shift from me to Nate and back again. I reach for the espresso machine. "Thank you for this."

I try to lift it out of Henry's arms and immediately lose my balance from the weight of it. I gasp, stumbling backward, and both Henry and Nate jerk toward me to help, which results in all three of us with our hands on the machine and my fingers crushed under Henry's. I yelp, and he lets go, and the machine smacks him in the kneecap before he catches it again. He curses, a guttural rumble of "Fuck" that I feel squarely in my stomach.

"I'm so sorry," I squeak. Over the top of the machine, Mei looks at me with her eyes wide in horror.

Henry's eyes are pressed shut. He exhales through his nose and they break open—unreasonable, biting blue. I think of Quinn, babbling to me over video chat a month ago, telling me how poison dart frogs are so brightly colored to warn everyone else they're dangerous. When Henry's eyes lock on mine, I feel it like a threat—like I'll find myself deep, deep in trouble if I keep looking. Absurdly, I remember his fingers in Custard's fur. His low, soothing voice: *Good boy*.

I swallow, and Henry makes a noise in his throat that eventually turns into the words, "Where do you want this?"

"Kitchen," I whisper. Nate's and Henry's faces are inches apart, each of them supporting one end of the machine. They don't make eye contact as they shuffle down the hall.

After sliding the machine onto the counter, Henry looks at me. My gaze swivels down to my feet as I say, "I'm so sorry, I didn't realize how heavy it is."

"It's fine." Henry looks at Nate. "I was under the impression that you don't live here anymore."

Nate reddens. He looks like he might deny it, like he's reaching for the right words even though there's really only one thing to say.

Henry's eyes flick back to mine. A small line forms between his dark brows—the one I wanted to swipe away with my thumb, back in his office. The one that lingered there while I tried to tell him about the breakfast menu just yesterday. "Louisa?"

"He doesn't," I say softly. "He's here to get his things."

"Are you renting our house out?" Nate asks me. *Our* snags on my ribs, chafing against my heart. Even before the breakup, this house felt like mine alone.

"It's Henry's house," I tell him. "But yes."

"To who?"

The brokenhearted, I think. But I'm still massaging the details of this plan, so I say simply, "Vacationers."

"Lou." Nate steps closer to me. His voice drops an octave. "You don't have to do that. I mean, if it's about money, I can—"

I close my eyes. "Nate, stop." The air stills around us. No one moves, or speaks. I can feel Henry watching me from across the kitchen. "Please."

"Hey." His hand lands on my elbow, warm. "Lou, I care about you. I can help with—"

"She told you to stop," Mei says. Nate's hand drops, and I open my eyes. When I glance at Henry, those blue eyes hold mine—but this time, I don't make myself look away.

"I think you should get your things and go," I say quietly, barely sparing him a glance. I look, instead, at Henry: the quickly reddening skin on his knee, the stretch of his shirt over his shoulders, that line between his eyebrows—like he's trying to figure this out. *Why are you here?* I want to ask. *How is it that you're here, again, witnessing my humiliation?*

Nate searches me, looking for the person he knows. The Louisa I used to be, in a different life, needing him.

"I'll help you," Mei says. She extends her arm toward the stairs. "Let's start in the Pine Room, there's a shitload of your coats in there."

Nate glances at me, then Mei, then Henry. He clears his throat. "Yeah, okay. Let me get the suitcase from my car."

"I'll get it." Henry steps forward, extending his hand for Nate's keys. From behind me, I hear Mei's surprised intake of breath. "So you can get started."

Nate stares at him. Henry doesn't blink. I wonder about the times they've met before, without me—when Nate first toured the house, when he put down the deposit. What those conversations sounded like. If Henry's always been this cold toward him, or if it's only for my benefit.

Nate glances at me, then lets out a small scoff before digging into his shorts pocket and dropping the keys to his hatchback into Henry's palm. He turns, wordlessly, to follow Mei up the stairs.

When Henry comes back inside, depositing Nate's huge black suitcase in the front hall, I twist my hands together. I can't imagine a scene that could have convinced him any *less* that I have things under control here.

"Hey, I'm sorry," I say. "This wasn't, um . . ." Henry meets my eyes and holds them. "Professional."

"This is your home," he says. He doesn't look around this time—not like yesterday. He doesn't look away from me at all. "And I interrupted. You didn't need to be professional."

I manage a small smile. "Thanks for the espresso machine."

He nods. I get the sense he wants to say something—the way his eyes flit past me down the hall, glancing over the staircase where Nate has disappeared. But he only looks back at me, steady and stoic as ever. "If you have any questions about how to use it," he says, "you have my phone number."

Henry takes a step backward onto the front porch. The sun hits his face, his eyelashes, sending shadows over his stubble-flecked cheeks.

I lean one hand against the door. "I do."

Ten

"Stop worrying." I say this to my sister knowing full well it's not something she's humanly capable of. "I've already got a booking."

"From *who*?" She's video calling me as she walks, Manhattan a gray blur behind her. "They could be a serial killer. They could be a squatter. What kind of person books a *heartbreak retreat*, Lou?"

"The kind who wants help, Goldie." We stare at each other through the pixels. "The kind who doesn't want to bury their feelings."

"Okay." She rolls her enormous eyes. Goldie has cartoon eyes, baby deer eyes, fringed in impossibly long lashes I wasn't lucky enough to inherit. "So this is about me now?"

I raise an eyebrow at her. "You said it, not me. And the hosting platform does some kind of background check. No one's going to be a serial killer."

"No one ever thinks anyone's going to be a serial killer."

"Goldie, I need you to trust me on this. I'm going to make it work."

"And I'm helping!" Mei shouts from across the living room. She's in pajama pants and a silk blouse, laptop balanced on her knees. Her company agreed to let her work remote until November, and she's been fielding video calls all morning.

"And Mei's helping," I echo. We screamed, standing together in the kitchen, when the first booking came in a week ago. This was actually going to *happen*. "She even got one of her media contacts at *The Denver Post* to run a story about it."

They sent a photographer up yesterday, a guy in his forties who took pictures of me standing on the front porch and leaning over the kitchen sink and fluffing a pillow in the Juniper Room. I was proud of the photos, when he sent them to me. Each of the guest rooms that I've spent the last couple weeks so carefully curating: the Aspen Room's iron bedframe and antique framed postcards; the Pine Room's double beds and thrifted coatrack; the Lupine Room—small but mighty—with its Turkish rug and wicker bookshelf.

The story runs tomorrow, a week before my permit goes into effect. No turning back now.

"Okay, but who's the renter?" Goldie presses. A car horn wails behind her. "Do they seem normal?"

"Very," I assure her. "Mom of two who's recently divorced. She's staying four nights."

"When does she arrive?"

"My permit starts October first, and she shows up the following weekend."

Goldie hesitates, and suddenly she's inside—out of the

sidewalk chaos and into the marble-walled lobby of her law firm. She brings the phone a little closer to her face. "Did you tell Mom?"

In my peripheral vision, Mei turns to look at me. "No," I say. "I haven't heard from Mom since July. Have you?"

"No," Goldie says. She steps closer to the wall, out of the flow of people returning from lunch. "I just didn't know if you'd given her an update on Nate or the house or any of it."

As a general rule, I don't give my mother updates. Mom tends to claim space in our lives when she needs something and hardly ever else, so I learned to stop sharing myself with her years ago. When enough time has passed I'll start to feel guilty about it—I always do—but I'm not there yet. I was nine when Goldie graduated from high school and started at Ohio State; her scholarship covered housing, her meal plan, all of it. It's been a long, long time since Mom's had a vested interest in either of our lives.

And besides—she loved Nate. I don't want to hear her lament the loss of him.

"I haven't," I tell Goldie. "And I'd rather you didn't, either, if you talk to her."

"You know I won't," she says. Goldie doesn't carry the same guilt I do about avoiding our mother.

"Well, her home and auto insurance draws next month," I say. "So we may be hearing from her if that becomes a problem."

Goldie sighs. "And if we do, we can send her to voicemail."

This is the game we play: Goldie reminding me that I can ignore Mom the way she does. I won't do it, but she likes to pretend that I could.

"I know," I say.

Goldie glances at something across the lobby, then back at me. "I've got to get back up there. I love you. Don't get killed by the divorcée."

"I'll try not to," I tell her, but she's already gone.

I wake up on Tuesday to voices—angry ones, floating up from the garden. I can't make out what they're saying, just the rumble of someone unhappy, then the gentler lilt of someone trying to soothe them. When I pull back the curtain just far enough to peek down, all I can see is Joss. She's in a sun hat and long sleeves, spade in one hand. The garden is in full, frantic bloom: frothy zinnias and towering Russian sage, nearly shoulder height and arcing toward Joss where she stands on the stone path. Next month, when October sets in and the nights get frosty, the flowers will start to pale. But for now, they're as arresting as the voices rising up to my bedroom.

Another hand waves into my field of vision—a male one. A familiar one. One that may have recently crushed my own hand beneath it on an espresso machine.

It's clutching something. Joss takes it, and when I squint, pressing my nose to the glass, I clock it as a copy of *The Denver Post*, open to the article that ran yesterday. Henry's voice rises again, his pointer finger appearing to tap the photo on the page. Me, on the front porch, beneath the headline NEW ESTES PARK BED & BREAKFAST OFFERS A SOFT LANDING FOR THE BROKEN-HEARTED.

When Joss glances up at the bedroom window, I suck in a breath and retreat behind the curtain. I scramble to get down there, yanking on a pair of ancient sweatpants and raking a hand through my hair. If Henry's mad about the article, he shouldn't be taking it out on Joss. The last thing I want to do is cause an issue for her with her boss, and why would he even bring her into it? Why would he even be mad in the first place?

I hit the first floor in my bare feet, hardwood warm from the sunlight spilling across it. The back door to the garden is open, screen letting in the morning breeze. Mei must've left it like that before heading into town—she told me she was getting up early to go on a walk. The microwave clock says it's 8:22.

". . . not here, Joss." Henry's voice is clipped. "Of all places, in this house—"

I push open the screen door, its hinges whining conspicuously, and his mouth snaps shut. Both of them freeze, faces turned toward me. Henry is in running clothes—a gray shirt ringed in sweat, blue sneakers, shorts that hit midthigh and give me a clear view of the faint, yellowing bruise on his knee. He pushes sweat-damp hair off his forehead and says, "You're awake."

"Yes." It occurs to me that I'm not wearing a bra, and I cross my arms over my chest. "What's going on?"

Henry snatches the article out of Joss's hands and points behind me. "We need to talk inside." He casts half a glance back at Joss, who says, "I don't see the big deal."

"Joss." Henry's voice is nearly a snarl, and I tense as she lifts her chin and holds his eyes. "Please."

"You're overreacting," she tells him, wiping a bead of sweat from her forehead. She looks at me before turning toward the garden shed. "Lou, don't worry about him."

Joss has been tending to this house forever—long before I came into the picture. Maybe one day I'll have the same resolve when it comes to our shared boss, but right now, when Henry turns his gaze back on me, I feel like I'm in big trouble. I think of the poison dart frogs, the blue of his eyes, the way meeting them feels like having the wind knocked out of me.

Henry says nothing, just jabs his finger toward the kitchen again. His cheeks are pink, stubble scraped along his jaw, shoulders tensed under the thin fabric of his shirt. Inside, the door wheezes shut and he slides the newspaper toward me across the island.

"We didn't discuss this."

"Press?" I say. When I meet his gaze, he doesn't blink. "I'm just trying to drum up bookings."

I edge toward the living room as casually as I can, reaching for the throw blanket on the back of the couch. When I wrap it around myself to hide my barely covered breasts, Henry's eyes track the movement like a cat—quick and unblinking.

"Not press," he says as I lower myself onto one of the island stools. He stays standing, rigid. "'The Comeback Inn'? 'A haven for the heartbroken'? You told me this was going to be vacation rentals, not some kind of rehab."

"It's not *rehab*," I say on half a laugh. Henry does not crack a smile. If anything, his lips press into an even more sinister line. "It's just a—" I hesitate, and Henry's eyebrows hike upward. "A soft place to land."

"A soft place to land," he repeats. His voice is different—not the gentle rumble he used with Custard, not the carefully restrained tone that so offended Nate. This is something new, something scraped and unchecked. "Meaning what?"

I force myself to hold his gaze. "A safe place to come and heal." His eyes flick back and forth between my own, like he's searching for something he understands. A muscle jumps at the corner of his jaw, sharp and angry. "I'm good with heartbreak."

Henry blinks. "You're good with heartbreak." His eyelashes are long and dark, almost pretty against the austere set of his face. "Because you're a therapist?"

I hesitate for half a breath. It's not true, quite yet—not until I pass the NCE. But I can tell it's what he needs me to say. I think of that moment, back in his office, the worried line between his eyebrows. *Trust me.* "Yes."

"And there was no other angle you could have chosen?"

I bite my lip. Henry doesn't look away. Outside, a squirrel trills in the garden. "I know this one best."

His hands are pressed flat on the counter, half covering the article, one thumb on my printed face. His voice softens, hardly enough to notice. "Because of Nate."

Because of my mother, I think. But it's too much to admit—and given what Henry saw between Nate and me the last time he was here, this makes its own kind of sense. "Yes," I say, and Henry's eyes drop from mine, down to the article framed between his hands. They're big, his hands, his fingertips pressed white against the granite. "And because my friend just went through a breakup, too, and I feel like I have the experience—"

"With breakups," Henry says stiffly. The muscles in his forearms flare, like he's barely holding himself here. He looks back up at me. "That's what this is about? Come stay here to get over your ex-boyfriend?"

I flinch. He makes it sound silly and small. But nothing about the way I grew up—nothing about Mei sobbing on my couch—has been little. It's been enormous. It's been big enough to knock both of us out entirely.

"I'm picking up on your tone," I say coolly, "and I don't appreciate it. Recovering from a broken heart isn't trivial, whether you believe it or not."

Henry clenches his teeth, the corners of his jaw sharpening. "No," he says, and there's wavering heat in his voice that betrays something hidden. Something he hasn't shown me. "It's not trivial."

I straighten my spine, force myself not to look away from him—from those dangerous, inescapable eyes. "Then what's the problem, Henry?"

"The problem, Louisa, is this isn't what we discussed. I don't want my house full of—of—" He breaks off, and his chest rises. He draws breath like he's drowning.

"Sad people?" I say. The line forms between his eyebrows. "Whether I host other people here or not, it's going to be. I'm going to be."

Silence hangs between us. On the counter, Henry's hands have uncovered my face. I stare down at myself—that smiling, self-sure person who was gripped by this idea and *knew* it was the right one. Who felt so much more confident than I do now, faced with this man who can't seem to stand me.

"And I'd rather use that energy to help other people through *their* pain," I say finally, "than sit here boiling in my own. If I need your permission to do that, then I guess this is me asking for it." When Henry doesn't immediately respond, I keep going. "You told me to run with this. You said that you *didn't* want to be involved. What else do I need to check with you?" My voice is rising. It feels good to be angry, so much better than being sad. "Do you want to approve the guest list? The check-in procedure? Should we go back to the breakfast menu? Should I call you every time I—"

"No," Henry says softly. He stands up, nudging the article across the counter toward me like he doesn't want it anymore. In the quiet that falls, I realize I've been yelling at the person who holds my entire life in the balance. He could cut it all out from under me anytime he wants.

"I'm sorry," I say. Henry's shoulders are up around his ears. He rolls them out, blinking slowly, like he's unwinding something inside himself. "That wasn't—I got carried away." He opens his eyes and looks at me through dark lashes. Something's softened—just barely—in his gaze. "That wasn't professional."

One corner of Henry's mouth twitches upward. On anyone else, I'd call it a smile. "You never are, are you?"

I bite my lip, face warming. "I'm sorry."

"Me, too," he says. When he draws a deep breath, it sounds like he's bracing for something. "You don't need my permission. I got carried away, too."

Oh. I shift on the stool, unsure what to do with his apology. I think of his voice, just moments ago, threaded with an unfamiliar anguish: *It's not trivial.* And the way he moves in front of me now, like he's a little embarrassed. His cheeks are still pink— not from his run anymore, maybe. From this conversation.

"I'll get out of your way," Henry says, starting around the counter. "I need to get to work. Proceed with your heartbreak hotel."

"It's not—" I start, but the way he glances back at me over one shoulder makes me realize he's kidding. Henry Rhodes, making a joke.

I lift a hand in farewell. He opens my front door.

I think, *Who broke your heart, Henry?*

Eleven

"What about group sessions?" I reach for my wineglass and take a sip, angling on the kitchen island stool to look at Mei. "Where we can all vent about stuff together?"

"Oh, definitely," she says. There's a bowl of cheddar popcorn in front of her, and she plucks out a disconcertingly orange piece and pops it in her mouth. "There's nothing more powerful than a group of women talking about their feelings."

"Well, there might be men, too."

Mei grimaces, and I swat at her arm.

"I'm kidding," she says, reaching for her own wineglass. But then she slants her eyes at me while she takes a sip. "Maybe."

We've been at this all evening: plugging program ideas for the heartbreak retreat into a Word document, open on my laptop between us. We're a few days into October and, like clockwork, the evenings have turned chilly. A fire crackles from the living room and the warm lights below the kitchen cabinets are turned on. The rest of the house is dark—it feels close and cozy, like the whole space is lit by fireflies.

Mei reaches across me and types: *Guided hikes*.

"Who's guiding them?" I say. "Me?"

"I mean, obviously." In an oversized CU sweatshirt and leggings, Mei could be twenty again, studying beside me in the library. She tucks hair behind one ear. "I know you aren't an award-winning outdoorswoman, but you're aware of enough trails up here to take some tourists out for a couple hours."

When you live in Colorado, everyone assumes you've become one with the woods—but this *house* is my happy place. The nature's always been a bonus.

"I know, like, two hikes."

"Two's fine," Mei says. She reaches for more popcorn and leans back on her stool to eat it. "People are going to be coming and going—you can just repeat the same two."

"Okay, I can probably handle that." As I add the names of the few trailheads I know to the document, my phone buzzes on the counter.

It's Goldie, a linked article with two words above it: *Fuck him*. My ribs curl in, bracing my lungs for what my body already knows is coming—something about Nate. I shouldn't click it. I should stay in this moment with Mei, building my new life, moving forward. I *should*, but I don't.

The article is from *People*, a publication Nate couldn't have dreamed of seeing his name in before the "Purple Girl" re-release. But there he is: walking down an L.A. sidewalk with a lanky arm thrown over Estelle's shoulders, his chin tipped down as he listens to her speak, his eyes hidden behind the sunglasses we picked out together after he lost his favorite Ray-Bans on the Fourth of July. My finger hovers over my phone screen, afraid to touch it. The headline is offensive in its simplicity: NATE PAYNE STEPS OUT WITH NEW GIRLFRIEND IN LOS ANGELES.

"Lou?" Mei's voice brings me back to myself, a rope thrown down a well. "What is it?"

I blink up at her, then thrust the phone over the counter so she can see it for herself. This was coming, of course. Nate's life will keep being visible to me, even when I'm not looking. It feels like a stomachache—the unsettled roil of your insides completely disagreeing with you, like my body's working to reject this.

I don't want to be that girl anymore, tucked under Nate's arm. But I don't want this to have a place in my new life—in my kitchen, as I plan a project I'm so excited about—either.

"Oh, *hell* no," Mei says. She turns my phone face-down on the counter. "Why would Goldie send that to you?"

I shake my head. "I think she thinks she's helping—or, like, commiserating, or something."

"Well, she's not." Mei reaches for the wine bottle at the edge of the counter and splits its remaining contents between our glasses. Then she thrusts my glass toward me, meeting my eyes. "Let's get drunk."

It's only nine when the power goes out. Between the two of us, we're a bottle of wine and two margaritas deep. Mei has a revenge playlist blasting from the living room TV, and we're dancing like wet noodles in the kitchen—flailing, sweatshirt sleeves flopping, heads tipped back as we sing along. Mei wriggles over to the blender with a cup full of ice. Halfway through its whir—tequila churning at warp speed—the lights go out. The music stops; the microwave clock blinks off; we're left in sudden, total stillness. I can barely see Mei when she turns around to gasp at me.

"It's probably a breaker," I say, reaching for my phone flashlight. My cheeks are very, very warm. "They're in the basement."

"The creepy murder basement?" Mei stumbles forward to grab my arm. She giggles out a hiccup. "Are we going down there?"

"Yes," I say, dragging her across the kitchen toward the basement door. "We're strong women. We're full of tequila. We're powerful."

"I only wish I had another margarita in my hand to power me through this visit to the murder basement." Mei freezes, jerking me to a stop. "Should we do a shot?"

Standing there, clutching each other in my pitch-black kitchen, it sounds inspired. It sounds like the smartest thing she's ever said to me.

And the tequila does, somehow, make the murder basement feel less murdery. We trip over each other down the wooden stairs, our phone flashlights bouncing like lasers at a rave. The basement is damp and ancient, like a root cellar or an apocalypse bunker. There's nothing down here but the breakers and a few storage boxes.

"Hurry up!" Mei says, nudging me forward when we hit the bottom of the stairs. "I'm going to need another shot if we spend more than ninety seconds down here."

"Calm thineself," I say, cutting across the cement floor toward the breaker box.

Mei cackles, her voice filling the room. "Okay, Shakespeare."

"It felt right coming out."

"That's what she said." Mei careens into me as I open the breaker panel. We train our flashlights to the rows of switches, scanning. They're all labeled in neat block print that goes a little blurry the harder I try to bring it into focus. FIRST FL. BATH, KITCHEN APPL., DISPOSAL.

"What's kitchen apple?" Mei says, and a laugh bubbles from me like carbonation.

"Appliances, genius."

"This is the *apple power supply*, madame, and you shall not disrespect its gravitas."

I find the switch labeled MAIN, but when I throw it, nothing happens. Mei and I look up at the ceiling, like the universe herself might intervene. I try every other breaker in rapid succession. Clicks fill the basement. But nothing happens—no light coming through the open basement door from upstairs, no music coming from the TV, nothing at all.

"Well, shit," I say. "Now what?"

Mei sighs. "I'm not too big to admit that I usually call my dad in these situations."

"I guess I could call Nate," I say, unlocking my phone and scrolling through my recent texts. He's a ways down—we haven't spoken since he picked up his things.

"Did you sustain a brain injury I don't know about?" Mei plucks the phone out of my hand and keeps scrolling. "Absolutely not."

When she starts tapping out a text, I wriggle around to read over her shoulder—and when I see who she's texting, I let out a strangled noise and try to swipe my phone back. But she's too quick, spinning away from me. "We need his help!"

"But he's mad at me! He's super mad at me for that article in the—"

"Here." Mei hands the phone back to me, the smug look on her face barely visible in the dark. When I look down at the text to Henry, my eyes struggle to focus—but even I can tell half the words are misspelled.

"*Mei*," I wail, and she throws her arms up.

"What else are we going to do, Lou? Get murdered in the basement? Let's go upstairs while we wait for him to respond."

She tugs me back up to the kitchen, and she's reaching for the bottle of tequila on the counter when my phone buzzes. Henry's text says only, What?

"Mei!" I cry again, thrusting it at her. "He's going to think I'm a sloppy mess."

"Tell him it was a typo!" she counters, pouring us two more shots. "Calm thineself."

Sory! I send, closing one eye to focus and still managing to misspell it. Power out an can fix with braker

Three dots appear, then disappear. It happens twice more in the time it takes for Mei to pass me a shot that I knock back without thinking. Then my phone starts buzzing in earnest—Henry's calling me.

"Shit!" I say, dropping the phone like it burned me. "He's calling."

"So answer." Mei rolls her eyes. "And he can tell us what to do."

"Okay," I say, picturing the flush of his cheeks in my kitchen last week. The shredded quality to his voice as he thrust the article at me across the counter. "Okay. Okay, okay."

"Henry!" I cry when I pick up, both too loud and too enthusiastic. I wince, and he pauses on the other end of the line.

"Louisa," he says finally. His voice is soft and close, and I press the phone to my ear until it hurts my cartilage. "What's going on?"

"The power's out. And we tried to flip the breakers but none of them did anything and it's so dark in here and I'm not sure if—"

"We?" Henry says. I hesitate, my brain lagging three steps behind me. *Nate*, I remember. He thinks I mean Nate.

"My friend Mei," I say, and she lifts another shot glass in the air as if cheersing me. "You met Mei, she was here that day when Nate—with the espresso—I mean—" I bite my lip, squeezing my eyes shut. Why did I drink all that tequila?

"I remember," Henry says. "You tried all of the breakers?"

"All of them," I confirm. A laugh chortles out of me, obscene. "Even the kitchen apples."

Mei cackles, and Henry says, "The what?"

"The appliances for the kitchen—the breaker is labeled, like, A-P-P-L, and Mei thought it was apples—" My voice dissolves into a gasping laugh. Across the kitchen, Mei's clutching her abs, tears in her eyes. Kitchen apples.

"I'm going to come over there," Henry says, and it shuts me right up.

"Oh, you don't have to—"

"Hold still." Then he hangs up, the call clicking off in my ear.

I look up at Mei, then back down to my phone. "He's coming here."

"Party!" Mei cries. She shimmies her hips in the dark. "Think he'll want a shot?"

By the time Henry arrives, I've been slapping my own cheeks for five minutes. I was trying to sober myself up, but all I've managed to do is make my face even redder than it was before. When I open the front door Henry's eyes sweep from my hairline to my toes, and I feel every centimeter of his gaze as it moves over me. I lean against the door, trying to appear casual.

"Thank you for coming," I say. He's holding two giant flashlights and his car keys, black SUV parked behind him in the driveway. It registers somewhere in the very back of my brain that Bill and Martina's lights are on across the street. I hear Henry's voice from that day in their yard, his fingers moving rhythmically through Custard's fur. *Easy, now.*

"It's no problem," Henry says, and I blink the memory away. He's wearing a utility jacket and jeans, his face clean-shaven. It's the first time I've seen him without the ghost of a beard—it softens him in a way that I feel right at the center of my pelvis. "You sounded . . ."

I bubble up a laugh. "Like a mess?"

His eyebrows tic. "Like you could use a hand. Can I come in?"

I make a grand gesture of sweeping my arm into the house and it sends me off-balance so that I stumble backward into the door and smack the edge of the handle with my funny bone.

"Ow," I yelp, clenching it in my other hand. "Damn."

"*She is beauty,*" Mei sings from the kitchen, where her phone flashlight is face-up on the counter. "*She is grace . . .*"

"Come in," I manage, motioning Henry around me so I can close the front door. Immediately, we're swallowed by darkness. Henry clicks on his flashlights and hands one to me.

"Are you okay?"

"Stellar," I squeak, taking the flashlight. "Thanks."

Henry toes off his boots and waits for me to lead him into the kitchen, where Mei stands with three shots lined up in front of her. "Henry," she says grandly, taking a deep bow, "welcome to the Power's-Out Party. May I offer you a beverage?"

In the dark, I can just see one corner of Henry's mouth start to hitch up. I jerk my flashlight around to get a better look at it—a smile!—and he winces, reaching out to angle the light away from his face. His hand covers mine on the flashlight. I choke a little on my own spit.

"I'm good," Henry says, his fingertips sliding off the backs of my knuckles. "But thank you."

"Should I show you the breakers?" I say, tipping into his space. "They're in the murder basement."

"I know where they are," Henry says, and just as I feel my center of gravity start to slip, his hand comes to my waist. It's light, his grip—open palmed, gentle through the thick fabric of my sweatshirt. Once I'm righted, he lets go. "Let me take a look"—his eyes connect briefly with mine—"in the *murder* basement."

Henry makes for the basement door, and I look at Mei. She's swiping the back of her hand over her forehead, and when she whispers, "He is *hot*," I'm not fully convinced it's quiet enough for Henry to miss it. I shush her so violently it makes my head pound, and she erupts into a loose guffaw of laughter as I spin in my socked feet to follow Henry down the stairs. I feel fizzy and light, like Nate's a world away, like all I need is in this house with me—Mei, laughing in my kitchen. Henry with his flashlights. The foreign feeling that ached through my belly when his hand landed on my hip.

"See anything?" I ask, lumbering down the stairs with all the grace of a newborn elephant. Henry's bent over the panel, flashlight trained on the breakers. He swings the light over to me and, just as I hit the last step, says, "Be careful."

I make a noise like *Pffft* and swat my hand at him. When I come to peer around his arm at the panel, hooking one hand on his shoulder, he looks straight at me. Our faces are very, very close. "Well?" I say, and his eyes track back and forth over mine.

Henry blinks, and when he stands up my hand slides off of him. "There's nothing flipped here. Were you running power to anything upstairs that you don't normally use?"

I shake my head, rocking back and forth on my heels. "TV, lights, fridge. Were *you* running power to anything *you* don't normally use?"

Henry's mouth twitches, and I lean in close, pointing to his lips. "Ha!" I cry. "Smile."

Now he smiles in earnest—but it's bewildered, unsure. "Smile?" he repeats.

"You never do." When I tap his mouth with my outstretched fingertip, his pupils blow wide in the dark. "But you just did."

"I smile," Henry says quietly, and my hand drops.

"Not around me," I say. "You hate me."

The line forms, severe, between Henry's eyebrows. "Why would you say that? I don't hate you."

I frown right back at him, yanking my own eyebrows together. "You tell me."

"I don't hate you," he says again, firmly.

"But you hate being here." I wave my arms around the basement. "With me."

Henry's eyes flicker over my face. He doesn't answer me, not really. "Are you okay, Louisa?"

I spin like a ballerina, arms arched above my head. "Of course!" When I stumble out of the pose his arms jerk out to steady me, flashlight beam arcing across the room. My ribs are framed between his hands. "Why?"

He shakes his head, drops his hands. "You just seem . . ."

"Drunk?"

He tips his head back and forth, lips twitching like he's embarrassed. Like he doesn't want to call this what it is. "Is there a reason?"

"That I'm drunk?"

His lips pull between his teeth when he nods. I watch him press them together, watch his tongue scrape over his bottom lip as he waits for me to respond. His mouth is full and soft; with his cheeks shaved clean he looks young and gentle—like that angry person from my kitchen isn't here at all; like he's someone I know.

"Just this dumb article," I say directly to Henry's mouth. His hand lifts, his fingers angling my chin so I'm looking up at him. He drops his hand as soon as our eyes meet.

"The *Denver Post* article?" he asks. I see him across the kitchen island: sweaty T-shirt, angry eyes. Hot flush breaking over his cheekbones.

"*People*," I say. I'm suddenly having trouble getting his face in focus. I blink once, hard. "About Nate and his new girlfriend."

Henry's quiet for what feels like a lifetime. When he says, "Ah," it sounds clipped. Like he's that stranger again, walking through my house with a mug of coffee he's too scared to drink. I remember, hazy, what he said the last time we spoke—*Come stay here to get over your ex-boyfriend?* How he made it sound so petty. And I have the desperate urge, consuming, to make him understand.

"I'm not hung *up* on him," I say, reaching out both hands to plant them on Henry's shoulders. He's tall enough that it makes my own shoulder joints twinge. "Did you know he cheated on me with her?"

Henry goes very still under my hands.

"After six years together," I say. "He couldn't just *tell* me, like a courtesy. It would've been decent. But no." My fingertips dig into the ridge of muscle that races from Henry's shoulders up his neck, and I realize that I'm using him for balance. "It's so annoying not to be rid of him, that he's always going to *be there* in the press. Because honestly, it's been done. We should've broken up years ago."

"Why?" Henry asks quietly. At some point while I was talking his free hand rose to my waist to keep me steady. With the other one, he's got his flashlight pointed up at the ceiling so it illuminates the basement.

"We didn't even know each other anymore," I say. I rub my thumbs into Henry's collarbone, studying the way it peeks from beneath his shirt, dips at the base of his throat. "We didn't even try to. We didn't *care* to try to. Which should have been enough of a sign, but I was stupid."

"You aren't stupid," he says softly.

"No," I agree. Our bodies are very close. I've had more tequila than I can remember and I want to make him smile again; I want *that* Henry, the soft one, the one that opened up for Custard like a flower after rain. "I just didn't want to lose the house."

Henry laughs, then. It's breathy, a great gust, moving through his entire body so spectacularly that I step back from him to watch it happen. My hands drop from his shoulders; his hand drops from my waist. All the tension he carries, every bit of him he zips away—all if it changes when he laughs.

"What?" I ask, grinning. Henry shakes his head, smiling like he's trying to swallow it.

"You stayed with someone for six years just to keep living in this house?"

"Maybe not all six," I say. There was a time, once, when I loved Nate in every real way. "But definitely the last few."

"Why?" Henry watches me like I'm a science experiment, like a model volcano, like he's trying to figure out how I work. "That's a high price to pay."

I shrug, and catch myself before stumbling backward. "I'd pay any price for this place."

Henry pulls his lip into his mouth again, tongue running over it like he's thinking, like he's not even aware of it. "Louisa—"

"Why do you *call* me that?" I tip my chin up to the ceiling. His formality, his stoicism, I don't want it—I want him laughing, loose, like he was just a minute ago. "*Louisa*. Always Louisa."

"Is that not your name?"

"It *is*," I say, driving one fingertip into his chest. Right over his heart, warm and firm. I'm fascinated by how he feels; I spread my entire palm over his T-shirt, tucking my fingers under the lapel of his coat, and Henry watches me do it. "But so formal. Everyone else calls me Lou."

When he's quiet, I pull my eyes up to his. Blue, blue, blue. Unbelievable.

Henry's voice comes softly. "Maybe I don't want to call you what everyone else calls you."

"Any luck?" Mei shouts down the stairs. I yank my hand out from under Henry's coat like I've been caught shoplifting. "I'd love to get this blender going again before I hit old age."

"Blender," Henry says, looking at me. "You were using a blender when the power went out?"

"Frozen margs," I confirm, with a little shimmy that pulls Henry's gaze from my eyes to my hips. "Want one?"

"No," he says, and then he takes my elbow in one hand to guide me up the stairs. "But the kitchen outlets are all GFCI—if you tripped it, it would've taken the power out."

"What's GFCI?" I ask, and from the top of the stairs, Mei calls, "Is that related to the kitchen apples?"

Henry ignores us both as we collide into breathless laughter at the top of the staircase, arms coming around one another. Across the kitchen, he fiddles with an outlet and all the lights come back on. The music starts up immediately, blasting through the house. I wince at Henry, blinking as my eyes readjust to the light.

"Ta-da!" Mei shrieks, and then she whirls across the room, hip-checking Henry out of the way so she can get back to the blender. "Our hero."

"You should stay," I say, still holding Henry's eyes from across the room. It feels very important, suddenly, that this moment doesn't slip through my fingers. That this new version of Henry—the one who laughs, the one whose warm hand holds me steady—doesn't disappear.

"Should I," he says, his voice low. Not quite a question. *I don't want to call you what everyone else calls you.*

"I think so." I come closer as the blender starts up, closing the distance so we can hear each other over the ice and the music. "I think you should have a margarita."

Henry reaches out, unsticking a piece of hair from my cheek. "I think you should have some water."

I cross my arms. I feel feisty. I feel free. I feel like I'm on fire. "I think you should stay and make me."

Henry's eyebrows rise. At the corner of his jaw, a muscle twitches.

He says, "Okay, Louisa."

Twelve

There is no shame like a hangover. This one lasts nearly all of the next day, as Mei and I moan through our headaches on the couch. I'm sick with nerves. My first guest, Grace—the divorcée—is checking in tomorrow, but it's not her sending me into a tailspin. It's Henry. Henry, who wasn't here when I woke up. Who left at some point last night, though neither Mei nor I can remember when. Who I'm pretty sure I said things to that no professional adult should ever, ever say to another.

"You were on him like a monkey up a tree," Mei says unhelpfully. She's nursing a coconut water and wearing gold eye masks. "I don't know that I've ever watched a rebound unfold in real time like that."

I groan, thunking my head back against the couch. "Henry's not a rebound."

"No?" Mei looks over at me. "Sure seemed like you wanted him to be."

"*Mei.*" I press the heels of my hands into my eyes. I don't say what I'm thinking, which is that even through all the tequila, the way I felt last night wasn't fleeting. I didn't wake up horrified that I'd come on to Henry because I don't feel the same way sober; I woke up horrified to find myself feeling the exact same way. "What am I going to do? He's my landlord. He must think I'm a disaster—what if he backs out of the rentals?"

"He won't," Mei says, gripping my forearm and shaking it. "You were cute. From what I remember. Just text him and say sorry."

But the thought of texting Henry paralyzes me. A texted apology isn't enough, not for the broken moments I remember from last night: touching his mouth with my fingertips, bracing myself on his shoulders, challenging him to stay over. I need to either apologize in person or never, ever see him again. And I'm too ashamed to apologize in person.

Mei intercepts me at the top of the staircase, gesturing wildly down the hall at the Spruce Room's bathroom. She's got headphones in, and when I say, "What?" she points at them before darting another pointed look at the bathroom. Then she lifts her shirt so I can see her stomach and grins.

"Yes, Ma," she says, skirting past me to get down the stairs. "I'm drinking enough water. Heaps and heaps, I promise."

I glance down the hall to the bathroom, where Henry's been for the last twenty minutes. Grace arrived last night, and her shower isn't working. So when I finally texted Henry after the unforgivable show I put on the other night, it was just a cowardly request for his plumber's contact information. He'd responded: Kitchen apple clogging the drain? I'll come take a look this afternoon.

I'm so embarrassed that I made Mei answer the door when he arrived. Then I hid in my room like a hermit until I knew he was safely tucked away in the bathroom.

Now I stare at the door I know I'll find him behind. Wonder if whatever Mei's on about is worth the risk of seeing Henry's face. Or worse, him seeing mine. Something clunks from inside Grace's room, startling me.

In her first day at the Comeback Inn, Grace has kept to herself. She showed up in a Subaru just as the sun was starting to set, looking weary and overheated. I put together a check-in guest survey to gauge how interactive people want to be: *Would you like company at breakfast, or to eat in your room? Would you like to join me (Louisa) and other guests for a group discussion in the afternoons? Please check which of these programs appeal to you: Movie nights. Group hikes. Crafts. Gardening.*

Grace had elected to eat in her room, and apparently none of the programs appeal to her. I'm not hurt, *exactly*. It was one of the first things I learned about counseling, about supporting other people at all: you can't make people want to be supported in the way that *you* want to support them. The inn is for everyone—even the people who want nothing to do with me. Who come here for silence and mountains. Never mind all the thought I put into supporting everyone in the softest, warmest ways. It's fine. *I'm* fine.

The most Grace has said to me was when I picked up her breakfast tray from the hall floor this morning. She opened her door at the sound of my footsteps, tired-eyed in one of the matching waffle robes I ordered. Over her shoulder, I could see a framed photo of her children that she'd added to the nightstand.

"Um," she said. I'd thought, *This is it. She wants to talk about her heartbreak.* "There's a problem with my shower?"

And now, Henry in the bathroom.

I edge down the hallway as quietly as I can, craning around the bathroom's doorframe to catch a peek at whatever Mei was flailing about. Immediately, I jerk back around the corner. Henry's flat on his back on the bathroom floor, half in the shower stall and half out of it, a wide strip of his stomach exposed as he reaches upward to fiddle with the shower handle. This bathroom is the smallest in the house, but my favorite: Its original copper faucets are mixed with new, moss-green subway tile and LED-outfitted light fixtures. And, now, Henry.

I swallow, looking down at my hands. One of them is clenched around my grocery list—I came up here to find a pen—and the other is holding a glass of water that I've managed to dribble all over my arm.

The hot flare of longing that licks along my pelvis is like an old friend, home from a long trip. Nate was always gone—and when he was home, there was no more of this. Of the way it feels to see the muscles move on Henry's stomach—or the dark hair that curls there, disappearing into the blue cut of his jeans. *You're confused*, I tell myself. *You drank too many margaritas and touched his mouth like some kind of horny goblin and now your body's all mixed up.*

"Louisa?"

I jump. "Yes?"

"Can I get a hand?"

I press my lips together and turn back into the doorframe, wondering what of that he saw—me glimpsing his torso and promptly spilling all over myself? When our eyes meet, it comes back to me in a sickening flash: my finger on his lips, his hands bracketing my rib cage, the way I ran my palm along the line of his jaw sometime after the lights came back on and said, *I like your baby face.*

"Will you pass me that screwdriver, please?" Henry looks up at me from the floor. There's a towel spread beneath him on the shower tile, a small pile of tools next to his head. "On the sink?"

I swallow and reach for it, catching my own reflection in the beveled mirror. My cheeks are smoldering pink.

"How's it going?" I ask, handing Henry the screwdriver. I keep my eyes trained very purposefully to his face, which is clean-shaven again.

"All right," he says, his gaze flicking to mine. He reaches above his head to twist a screw into place, and his biceps move in a way that I have to look away from. "The valve was broken, but I'm almost finished."

I can tell he's going to make me bring it up. And I *should*. I have to. So I sit down on the closed lid of the toilet across from him and force out, "I'm so sorry about the other night."

Henry adjusts the shower handle. "Which night?"

"Henry."

He glances at me, smiling, and I can't believe I touched his mouth like that. "How are you feeling?"

"Mortified," I say. "Like I should live out the rest of my days under a large, flat rock."

"I wasn't sure if you remembered any of it." He tightens another screw and this time I watch the muscles in his forearms tense. "I didn't hear from you."

I drop my head into my hands. I need to stop looking at him. I need to *stop*. "I didn't know what to say. I'm so sorry."

"Do you?" Henry asks. I risk a look at him and he's pulled himself up to sitting against the tiled wall of the shower. He props one elbow on his bent knee. "Remember any of it?"

"Enough." His eyebrows lift, and I add, "Like the part where I basically assaulted you."

Henry's lips twitch. "I don't remember that."

"Oh, great," I say, "maybe I made it up." Then I realize how this sounds, and start scrambling. "Not that I thought about—or, I didn't mean I've been—"

"Louisa." Henry's smiling again. All it ever took, apparently, was me making a fool of myself. "It's all right."

"It's not," I say, raking a hand through my hair. "It was so unprofessional, and I'm really embarrassed, and I'm really sorry."

Henry shakes his head, making to stand. "I'm just glad you're okay. And that we got the power back on."

I bite my lip, and Henry's gaze drops to my mouth. A great rush of heat whooshes up from my belly, and I wave an arm toward the shower to change the subject. "Were you a plumber in a past life?"

"No." He starts packing his tools into a black case sitting on the vanity. "But I did a lot of the remodel on this house myself, a long time ago."

I've always known the house had been meticulously updated—its stained glass, its claw-foot tubs, its beautiful transom windows. But I never imagined Henry as the one who carved it apart to make it what it is now.

"When was that?"

"Ten-ish years," he says, glancing at me. It's tight in here; from where I'm sitting on the toilet, my knees are nearly brushing his legs. "I took it over from my parents, who took it over from their parents. They moved to Florida when they didn't want to deal with snow anymore."

"Did you grow up here?"

"Only place I've ever lived," he says. He zips the bag, then reaches for the towel on the floor of the shower. "They never updated it, so it needed a lot of work."

"Why'd you leave?" I can't imagine it: the gift of spending your entire life in a place like this, just to go and rent it out.

Henry looks at me, eyes flickering between my own like he's deciding what to say next. But he doesn't have to respond, in the end—a scream tears through the house, shrill and undulating and distinctly Mei. Henry jerks around, but I'm already scooping up my water glass and grocery list and darting past him.

"Mei?" I call, halfway into the hallway. Henry's right behind me. "Are you okay?"

"Help me!" she shrieks, and a brutal thought flashes across my mind: There's a murderer in my house. There's a murderer in my house on the first full day that I have a guest. My entire life is about to be dead in the water, literally and figuratively.

But when Henry and I hit the landing, I can see Mei in the living room—alone. She's standing on the couch, phone clutched to her chest, hopping up and down.

"Get it!" she says, turning to us with her eyes wide. "Get it, get it, get it!"

I rush toward her, and stop short when I see what she's pointing at. An enormous wolf spider, brown and furry and damn near the size of my palm, perched on the edge of my vintage Turkish rug. One leg twitching into the tufted fringe. I let out an inhuman scream and dart around Henry, back in the direction I came. When I grab on to his arm to hide behind him, he looks down at my fingers—then back up at me. I let go immediately.

"Sorry," I say, flexing out my hand. I think of that first day in his office, the way his forearm tensed when I reached for him. All the ways I touched him in the basement—his chest under my palm, his lips under my fingers.

"Kill it!" Mei wails, and I blink away from Henry. He swallows. "Don't leave me here with it, Lou!"

"What do you want me to do?" I say, as Henry takes a step toward her. "Come *in there* with it?"

"I don't know!" She's still hopping up and down. The spider starts to move, skittering onto the hardwood floor. I yelp and take several steps backward. Mei hollers, "Henry, kill it!"

Henry turns toward me, eyes connecting with mine for half a breath before he plucks the glass and grocery list out of my fingers. For one terrible flash of a moment, I think he's going to make me catch the spider with my bare hands. But then he lifts the glass to his lips and knocks it back, downing what water was left, and flips it upside down to trap the spider in the middle of the living room floor. When he slides the grocery list underneath, lifting the caged spider into the air, Mei repeats, "*KILL IT.*"

"If I did that," he says, making for the back door, "Joss would have my head." He uses his hip to nudge open the squeaky screen. "They're good for the garden. And gentle, as long as you don't bother them."

"As long as you don't bother them," Mei repeats. "What bothers a spider? *Breathing* near it?"

But I'm watching Henry: as he takes the steps into the garden, as he looks both ways and then makes for one of our biggest pines, surrounded by bark. A bough of Russian sage obscures his body as he squats along the gravel path and lowers the water glass to the ground. When he tips it to release the spider, the midday sun catches the glass and sends light streaking across his face, pinched with focus. The spider scurries away, and Henry rests one elbow on his bent knee to watch it dart off to its new life.

When he glances back toward the house, our eyes meet through the screen. *Thank you*, I mouth. His lips lift at one corner, an almost smile. I rub my fingertip against my thumb. Feel the ghost of his lips on the skin there. *Louisa*.

"Um."

I turn, and Grace is standing on the landing in her robe.

"Is everything okay down here?"

Thirteen

Grace stays four nights, says not a single other word to me, and leaves a five-star review before I've even had time to wash her bedding.

"See?" Mei says when I show it to her. "Even just your presence makes people feel better."

"I don't think it's me," I say, and she waves me off.

But it's the house. It's always been the house—first for me, now for Mei and Grace. And for Rashad, who shows up two days after Grace checks out, in a tracksuit the color of aluminum foil. When he rings the doorbell, he's nearly reflective in the window through the door.

"You must be Louisa," he says, thrusting a lime-green suitcase into the entryway. "When I tell you I'm *overcome* to be here."

"I am," I say, taking the duffel that he holds out to me. "Are you Rashad? How was your journey?"

"Nightmarish." He lowers his sunglasses and takes in the house, dark eyes flicking from room to room. "Have you ever flown after spending the entire night crying? I've never been so dehydrated in my life."

"Let's get you some water." I motion him toward the kitchen. "Then I'll show you to your room and you can get settled in."

"The last thing I need is to settle." He harrumphs into an island stool like a deflating balloon. "I can*not* be alone right now—I swear. I've been holed up in my apartment like a vampire, charging up my depression batteries with the full moon. I can't see my friends because they're all *his* friends, too, but if I spend one more minute alone I will truly join the undead—if I haven't already—do I feel human to you? Is this a healthy ninety-eight point six or what?" He tips his forehead at me over the counter, and I rest the back of my hand lightly against it.

"Confirmed human," I say, and slide a glass of water toward him. "Though I understand not feeling that way, especially right after a big loss. It can be disorienting."

"No shit." Rashad drinks the entire glass in one long gulp. Then he closes his eyes and pinches the bridge of his nose. "It's like I'm relearning who I even am, which is so pathetic."

"It's not pathetic." I refill his glass at the fridge. Distantly, I hear Mei's voice—she's upstairs on a work call. "It means you cared."

"Too much," he says, accepting the second glass of water. He's young: early twenties, maybe. Hair buzzed close to his scalp, dark eyes fringed in gorgeous black lashes. "Way, way, *way* too much."

"Why do you say that?" I lean my hip against the counter, settling in. He's the opposite of Grace: no preamble, right into the heart of it, like he's been waiting for someone to tell all this to.

"Because it wasn't mutual." Rashad waves his hands into the space between us, like it's obvious. "Because he dumped my sorry ass the second shit got hard."

"So, there was a fight?"

Rashad sighs, long-suffering, and shoulders off his silver jacket. Underneath it, he wears a T-shirt printed in yellow-and-pink checkerboard. "Hardly even. It was what I'd call a *conversation*, but he acted like I was accusing him of first-degree homicide. We can't talk through a difference of opinion without it turning into the end? That's how little I'm worth to you? Where's the investment?"

"Hmm." I flip on the espresso machine, and Rashad leans toward me over the counter.

"What? What *hmm*?"

I glance at him, reaching into the cabinet for two mugs. "It sounds to me like you know, somewhere in there, that it's not really about what *you're* worth."

His eyebrows—perfectly groomed—hike up. Flatly, he says, "Do I."

"Your partner turned a difference of opinion into a reason to run, whereas you were ready to talk it through."

He just looks at me. I wait for him to pick up the thread on his own, the espresso machine humming. But then he waves his hand, like, *And?*

"You were ready to do the emotional labor it takes to create intimacy." I slide a mug under the spout and, through the window over the sink, see Henry cross the garden. He's in a button-down and a black peacoat, like he came from work. "Which, um—" I stumble. What's he doing here? I force myself to turn back to Rashad. "Which goes to show you have a deeper understanding of what it takes to really be with someone. And maybe he didn't. Is that really"—the back door pushes open, and I finish—"on you?"

We both turn to Henry. His cheeks are clean-shaven, pinked up from the October wind. He's holding a reusable grocery bag.

"Are you staying here, too?" Rashad waves a hand from Henry to me. "Louisa was just making coffee and telling me I'm incredibly emotionally intelligent, if you want to join us."

"Um, no." Henry glances at me. "I'm sorry, I didn't realize you had someone coming today, I should've checked before—"

"It's okay." I think I lost my right to reasonable boundaries when I threw myself at him in the basement. I gesture at the espresso machine. "Do you want a coffee? I'm no expert, but I'm getting better."

Before Henry can reply, Rashad says, "Is this your man?"

The laugh I let out is strangled and quavering, like I'm thirteen again. I look away from Henry immediately. "No, Henry just owns the house."

Henry clears his throat before repeating, "I just own the house."

"My bad," Rashad says. "You had this sweet domestic look to you—like you were bringing her groceries or something. What's in the bag?"

When I glance at Henry, he swallows. "The upstairs faucet was leaking when I came to fix the shower. I went to the hardware store—but I can come back at a better time."

"My faucet?" Rashad asks, glancing between us.

"No." I slide an espresso mug toward him. "A different bathroom, don't worry."

"He can stay." Rashad sips from the mug and flicks his lashes toward Henry. "I don't mind."

I manage a smile in Henry's direction. My skin feels like it's vibrating. "Do you want a coffee first?"

His gaze tracks to the machine, just over my shoulder, and I think of him plucking my water glass out of my hand. Drinking it in one fluid movement. "Take your time," he says, not exactly an answer, as he starts toward the staircase. "I'll come back down for it in a bit."

"Okay," I say, busying myself with a second espresso and trying to pretend it's taking up all my brain space. "Thanks for fixing the sink."

In the silence Henry leaves behind, I can hear Rashad's brain whirring. "You're a loud thinker," I say, and when I glance over my shoulder at him, he's smirking.

"What?"

Rashad swirls his espresso. "He's very pretty."

I betray myself by doing the prepubescent laugh again.

"Is he single?"

I turn back to Rashad, lifting my own espresso to take a sip. "I'm not sure." There's a clunk from upstairs, and as I lean back into the counter we both glance at the ceiling—a bag of hardware store supplies hitting a tile bathroom floor, maybe. "He doesn't wear a ring."

"I noticed that, too," Rashad says, which makes me realize that it's something I *also* noticed, enough to have brought it up without even thinking. "But some folks don't wear them. Want me to ask when he comes back down? I have no shame. We can blame it on my breakup."

"No," I say quickly. We don't need to scheme together about anything—and certainly not about anything related to Henry. "We're focusing on *you*. Where were we?"

"I don't remember," Rashad says, then shoots me a wink as he stands. "I do think I'm ready for a nap, though. Show me where my room is?"

Though I have three more guests arriving over the weekend, tonight it's just Rashad. So when I show him to his room and hand him the check-in questionnaire, I also ask him to pick what's for breakfast in the morning. I'm in the kitchen thirty minutes later, chopping dried cherries for Mei's foolproof ("not saying you're a fool, Lou, just—well, you know") overnight oats, when my phone rings. I expect it to be Goldie—who's taken to twice-daily proof-of-life check-ins—but it isn't. It's my mother.

You can always send her to voicemail, I hear Goldie say. I pick up on the final ring.

"Mom, hi."

"Lou!" She's outside—wind batters through the line. "It's been too long, honey."

I blink across the kitchen. I resent the bitterness that seeps through me, the jadedness—that right away, I know she wants something. My mother tends to call when she needs money, and hardly ever else.

"It has," I say carefully.

"How's the west? The trees are changing colors, yes? And the cold, I'm sure—you're wearing a coat?"

I turn the paring knife in my hand, watching light from the window glint across its blade. "Not too cold, just yet."

"Well, good, good. It's already chilly here so I'm going to Miami, can you believe it!" She laughs, a trill I'd recognize anywhere. "Your mother! On vacation!"

I know better than to take an interest, but I can't help it. "With who?"

"Oh, Mark, honey! I told you about Mark." Of course. Mark, her supervisor at McNeely's, the hardware store where she's worked for the last four months. "He's taking me on a little trip."

I wonder if she's told Goldie yet. If she's calling me because my sister didn't pick up the phone.

Growing up, we were not a family that vacationed. When I was in eighth grade and living with Goldie, Mom took us to a cabin in Hocking Hills—the first time we'd ever stayed anywhere overnight that qualified as a "trip." She paid for it with holiday tips from work; it was January and freezing, awful Ohio weather.

Goldie was at the start of a new semester and buried under homework. When she declined a hike through the frigid slush so she could study for a political science quiz, Mom told her she was ruining the entire vacation. Then Mom dragged me, cold and wet, through the woods as she complained about my ungrateful sister. The sister who'd taken me in, raised me when Mom wouldn't.

By the time we got back to the cabin, Goldie had figured out a ride back to campus for the two of us. We didn't take a trip together again.

On the other end of the line, finally, my mother gets to the point. "Nate still has a place in Miami," she says. "Doesn't he, honey?"

I turn the knife blade into the pad of my thumb—not quite hard enough to break the skin. "He does."

"He'd let us stay, don't you think? Just for a few nights? I'd have called him myself, but I seem to have lost his phone number! Such a sweet boy. And if he's in town, maybe we can have dinner!"

My fingertip turns white, red splotches blooming under the skin. I think about hanging up—I think about how much better it would have been if I hadn't answered in the first place. I thank every star in the infinite universe that she couldn't find Nate's phone number. And then I make myself tell her the truth.

"I don't think that'll be possible. Nate and I broke up."

There's silence, punctuated only by wind on her end of the line. "Oh, Lou," she says finally.

I hear footsteps on the old wooden stairs—the familiar creak as Henry descends into the kitchen. His shirtsleeves are pushed up, his hair rumpled in a way that makes him look young. He has the grocery bag fisted in one hand. He meets my eyes over the long hallway, and I gesture to the espresso machine with my free hand, raising my eyebrows. Henry shakes his head, just once, and raises a hand—like he's saying goodbye.

In my ear, my mother says, "What did you *do*?"

In the foyer, Henry opens the front door.

In my chest, a quiet impulse whispers, *Please don't go.*

Fourteen

"So, where's the hike?"

I blink at Mei, who's standing in front of me in a nano puff jacket and short, braided pigtails. It's Sunday afternoon, and I have a nearly full house: Rashad, on the third night of his weeklong stay; Nan, a widow who arrived from Colorado Springs in a vintage Cadillac; and Bea and Kim, twenty-two-year-old sorority sisters who graduated in the spring and loathe—*loathe*—the Denver dating scene.

"Hike," I repeat. Mei holds up a thin stack of papers and wiggles them in front of me.

"From the check-in questionnaire? Everyone said yes."

I press my eyes shut and shake my head once, hard, to clear it. "Shit, yeah. Sorry—um, is everyone ready, or should I go up and rally the troops?"

Mei tilts her head. "Are you okay? I've never heard you use the phrase *rally the troops* and it feels decidedly un-Lou of you."

"I'm okay," I say, drawing a deep breath. "It's just—"

"Nate?" Her eyes soften with understanding. I know Mei's

missing Andy; our rooms share a wall, and I still hear her sniffling in the dark after everyone's gone to sleep. Being hung up on Nate would make sense, and I'm not sure I could explain the truth to Mei anyway: my mother, the acidity of her voice as she told me I was letting the best thing in my life walk away. As if I have no chance of amounting to anything at all without him.

I know it's not true. That my mother's the last person I should be taking dating advice from. But she's still my mother—and her disapproval cuts as deeply as it ever has, regardless of how much time's passed since we last spoke.

"Nate," I confirm now. Mei reaches for my hand on the counter, and I let her squeeze it. Yesterday I shut myself in my bedroom for hours, raking through Reddit threads from other people who failed their National Counselor Examination. I've felt alone in my failure—but the internet always reminds me that I'm not. It's right there for me to read through: other recent grads, panicking, begging an invisible void of strangers to reassure them they'll be okay. They'll be okay. I'll be o*kay*—whether my mother believes it or not.

I failed the NCE the way you miss a step on the way down the stairs: with heart-dropping, breath-stealing unexpectedness. It never crossed my mind that I wouldn't pass the exam. I'd always been a good student—never the best, never near the worst—always perfectly decent. It was something I was proud of, even, that I didn't feel the insatiable urge to be best. I grew up watching it eat my sister alive. I'd figured out the secret to a good life, I thought: I was absolutely content being just fine. And then, suddenly, I wasn't even fine.

I wanted to blame it on my lackadaisical attitude—that I assumed things would go all right, as they always had before. I studied. Not so much that I didn't have time for a full life, but enough. Plenty. I'd completed thousands of clinical hours. I was already out there in the world, a therapist. This was a box to check—and then I missed all four of its lines entirely.

But it wasn't about my attitude. It wasn't about the hour I spent doing a sugar scrub in the bath when I could have been watching one more YouTube practice video. It was—as with so much else—about Nate.

I took the exam on a late-April Friday, the morning after Say It Now's last show on the European leg of their tour. Nate had been gone for a month; while I got into bed for an early night before my test, he was still standing on a stage in Stockholm. It was nearly dawn there. The post was up on Say It Now's social channels so briefly you'd have missed it—unless, like me, you were scrolling through your feed before you turned out the lights. Unless you were wide awake, staring straight into the pixels, the moment the photo went live.

It stayed up for all of ninety seconds, which was plenty long to take a screenshot. The photo was of Kenji and Abe backstage before the show, Kenji on Abe's back with his drumsticks thrust triumphantly into the air. There was a whole mess of people moving around them: stage crew with cords draped over their arms, Mateo tuning an electric guitar, Roger on his cell phone in the corner of the frame. And then, just the sliver of the face I knew best: Nate, kissing an unfamiliar woman, his hand raised to her cheek. Leather bracelet I'd made for him slung around his lifted wrist.

It was Estelle, of course. A name I know now, and didn't then. I sent Nate the screenshot and lay in our dark bedroom with my heart like a clenched fist. He didn't reply for nearly fifteen hours, long after I'd finished my exam. I didn't sleep one single minute. I took the exam on autopilot, trusting myself to pass it on muscle memory. I did not.

When Nate called me from the Stockholm airport, I was already halfway back to Estes Park. I put him on speakerphone and stayed silent until his miserable voice filled my entire car: *She surprised me, she came out of nowhere, I don't even know her, she's no one, no one, no one. I love you,* he promised. *I'm a fool.*

He was. But no bigger a fool than me, who believed him. Who let his nonsensical story make sense because I didn't want to face what it would mean for it to be a lie. And then, hardly two weeks later, I'd called him, flat voiced and furious, to say I failed my NCE because I'd spent the entire night prior sleepless and sick over that goddamn photograph. Nate apologized. And then he brought Estelle to a hometown show he knew I'd be at and let it all fall apart right in front of my face.

He's still the only one who knows I failed the test. A secret I trusted him with long after he'd stopped giving me reasons to trust him with anything at all.

Yesterday afternoon, scrolling through Reddit, I resolved myself to end this. To draw a line in the sand for myself to step over, to finally book my exam. But two weeks into October, all the autumn dates at the testing center in Estes Park were already booked up. Between the inn and the lingering specter of my own shame, I was terrified I'd bungled it all over again—but managed to find an exam administrator in Fort Collins offering dates into the winter. I booked the furthest one out: December 16. By then, I'll be looming closer and closer to my March 1 deadline for the rentals; by then, I'll need to start figuring out my next step regardless.

It's not so far, really.

Close enough that no one else will ever have to know that I failed.

"Is Henry here yet?" Rashad's the last one downstairs, a vision in plaid flannel and leather hiking boots. Everyone turns to look at him: Nan, walking poles gripped in both hands; Bea and Kim in their matching Carhartt beanies; Mei, who promptly raises her eyebrows at me.

"Is H—" I stutter, brow scrunching together. "Why would Henry be here?"

"Because I invited him," Rashad says, smiling sweetly. He pulls a granola bar from one pocket and rips it open. "I Googled him—did you know he's a vet? He was easy to find."

"Rashad, *no*," I say before I can stop myself. If I keep bothering Henry with drunken mishaps and broken showers and guests calling his office, he's going to shut down this entire operation and I'll be out on my ass before I can even take the exam in December. Not to mention my criminally unprofessional feelings about that strip of his stomach on the bathroom floor—about his soft mouth and the dark flash of his blue eyes as he said my name in the basement, *Louisa*.

"What?" Rashad says. He scans the other guests' faces like they could back him up. "I love looking at him. I'm here to get over my ex, aren't I?"

"Yes," I say, folding my jacket sleeve. "But Henry isn't part of the Comeback Inn, okay? Please don't bug him."

"I wasn't *bugging* him." Rashad splays one hand over his heart. "He was perfectly happy to join us."

"Perfectly happy," I repeat. I can't think of a combination of words *less* suited to Henry's opinion of the inn. "What did he actually say?"

"He said 'sure.'"

I spin around at the sound of Henry's voice, low and dry as ever. As we stand huddled around the kitchen island he comes down the front hallway, wearing that same utility jacket from when the power went out, the one I slid my hand under in the close dark of the basement. I'm getting used to the sight of him here, in my house. I try not to think about how much I like it, or what that means.

"Hi," I say, much too loudly. "I'm so sorry, you don't have to—"

"Louisa." My mouth snaps shut. "Are you turning me away?" The corners of Henry's lips lift, just long enough for me to clock the smile before it's gone. He holds my gaze, traps me, over the length of the hallway. "Be professional."

Rashad hisses. "Oh, girl, he's got you there." My cheeks burn as Rashad reaches forward to bat Henry on the arm. "Thanks for coming."

Henry smiles at Rashad before looking back at me and repeating, "Sure."

"Who's this?" Bea asks, looking from Henry to me as she slides ChapStick over her lips. "A *man* in our midst?"

"Hello?" Rashad says, gesturing at himself. "He's the landlord, I invited him."

"Your landlord?" Bea asks me, eyebrows rising. "Don't you own this place?"

"No," I say, tugging my sleeves down just for something to do with my hands. I'm so flustered I feel like I have a fever. "I run the Comeback Inn, but Henry owns it, and really we shouldn't be bothering him with what we're—"

"He already said he's not bothered," Nan chimes in. She's in her seventies, wearing a sun hat and a bugproof button-down. When she looks at Henry, he's watching me carefully.

Like we're the only two people in the room, Henry says, "Do you want me to leave, Louisa?"

I feel Mei shift beside me. I feel six pairs of eyes on my face. I feel something humming under my skin.

No, is the truth. I can't believe he's going to make me say it.

You should stay, I told him that night the power went out. Henry's still holding my eyes across the length of the kitchen, his gaze blue and blistering and guarded—waiting on me. I think of his laugh, the shock of it in the dark under the house. His gentle fingers in Custard's fur. The way he held out his hand for Nate's car keys.

I say, "You should stay."

Fifteen

In spite of Rashad's staked claim over Henry, it's Nan who winds up glued to his narrow hip. We split into two cars to get to the trailhead—Bea, Kim, and Mei with me; Henry and Rashad in Nan's Cadillac. When they pile out of its powder-blue doors in the parking lot, Nan hooks one carefully manicured hand through his elbow. Rashad trails behind them like a forgotten puppy.

"She was a Cavalier King Charles," Nan is saying as our groups converge next to the pit toilets. It's in the high fifties, the breeze soft as an exhale. "Lived to sixteen! My late husband said it was good genetics, but between you and me, I think it's the whipped cream I slipped her on weekends." Henry smiles at Nan, a real one, showing a white flash of teeth. "Those little treats keep us young!"

"She was lucky to have you," he says, and Nan squeezes his arm.

She glances at me through pink-framed sunglasses. "You helped Lou put together the Comeback Inn?"

"No, Lou was the brains," Mei supplies before either Henry

or I can correct her. "Henry's just the landlord. And the hiking guide, apparently."

"Oh," Henry says, raising his eyebrows at me. "Am I leading this?"

"No," I say quickly. We haven't taken a single step into the wilderness and this whole excursion is headed swiftly off the rails. "First of all, I'm so glad you all signed up for this." I look around the group, avoiding eye contact with Henry since he did *not* sign up for this. "I find nature to be really helpful for processing grief, especially in the early days when it feels so consuming and it's hard to see a world beyond it." In my peripheral vision, Bea reaches for Kim's hand and gives it a squeeze. "The woods remind us there's still good out there, and entire ecosystems that'll keep living and creating oxygen no matter what happens to us." I draw a breath as Henry shifts his weight. "That the world is much bigger than our grief, even when that grief feels enormous. So." I wave an arm toward the trailhead. The path is gobbled up by aspens, their teardrop leaves October-yellow and shivering in the breeze. In a week they'll be engulfed by deep fall—red and orange as flames—but in the lowered shoulder of a warm autumn they're still glistening gold. "This hike is three miles—there's an alternate route that doubles the distance if anyone's feeling like a longer trek. Since we took two cars, we can always split up when we get there."

"Three seems like plenty," Rashad says, and Kim nods in agreement.

"Great," I say. And then a hot swell of insecurity forces me to add: "And if anyone isn't enjoying this, and wants to leave"—my eyes flicker over Henry, who's watching me with an expression I can't even begin to read—"just say the word."

"We're here, honey," Nan says. "Let's get on with it."

"Right," I say, as Mei snorts. "I'll, um, lead the way, then."

I weave through the group and force myself to straighten my shoulders. Doing this work—stepping into my role as a Heartbreak Hotel Proprietor—feels about seven hundred times more stressful with Henry here to watch. I believe every word I said: nature is the greatest force of calm I've ever known. There's nothing better for my own enormous feelings than to be made to feel small. But saying it all in front of Henry turns it into something that feels like a performance I'm being graded on. *Let's try it for six months*, he told me that first day, back in his office. If he hates what he sees—if there's too much about *getting over your ex*—will he cut it all off early?

"So what's your deal?" I hear Rashad say from behind me. Our boots stamp a discordant beat on the trail, snapping twigs and shuffling gravel.

"Probably the same as yours," Mei replies. "I'm a miserable sack of heartbroken bones."

Rashad laughs. "How long ago?"

"Almost two months. You?"

"About a month. I thought maybe this would get me out of the funk."

"It will," Mei says. "Lou's a miracle worker."

I roll my eyes straight at a nearby pine, knotted and towering and unmoved by me. *No pressure.*

"There's no getting *out* of a great love." That's Nan, her voice rising above the whisper of wind in the aspen leaves. "Only a new kind of life that you find on the other side."

"But how long were you married?" Bea asks, her Southern

twang unmistakable. "I was only with my ex for eight months—there's no way he's sticking with me forever."

"He might," Nan says lightly, and I can't help myself—I shoot her a look. "It's up to you, isn't it? How much license you give him to stick around. I was married for thirty-four years and I hope I never have a day I don't think about my Teddy."

"He died, though, right?" Rashad says. A twig splinters under my hiking boot. "I'd want to remember my ex, too, if he went and died on me instead of breaking my heart."

"He did break my heart," Nan says. "Even if he didn't mean to."

"Pretty sure mine meant to," Rashad says, and I call over one shoulder, "It's not apples to apples, okay?" The group falls quiet, so I stop and turn back. "No one's heartbreak is any more or less valid than anyone else's."

I feel Henry's gaze like a magnet, and our eyes snap together. I hear his voice so clearly, that day in my kitchen when the article came out: *That's what this is about? Come stay here to get over your ex-boyfriend?* But I'm not ashamed of this. None of it's trivial.

"Pain is pain," I say, raising my chin. "Loss is loss. You don't get to give permission to let something hurt you—it just does."

"Too true." Mei nods. "Well said, Lou."

I send her a telepathic *Thank you*, and Henry clears his throat. I brace myself for an admonishment, but when he speaks what comes out is: "I think we missed the turnoff." He points back over one shoulder, where a lichen-dotted boulder butts up against the slope of the mountain. We're walled in on one side, trembling aspens as far as the eye can see on the other. "If you wanted to do the three-mile loop?"

I look around, realizing with white-hot embarrassment that he's right. I was so busy eavesdropping on the conversation behind me that I wasn't paying attention.

"Sorry," I say. "I wasn't—"

"Maybe Henry should lead," Rashad says, then smiles at him. "I'll follow you."

"Louisa?" Henry says, as if Rashad hasn't spoken. He waves a hand back the way we came and steps off the trail to let me pass him—like there's no question I'll be the one to lead us. When I pass Henry, his fingertips brush the middle of my spine. I don't know him well enough to know what his gestures mean, but it strikes me immediately as an apology. Whether for correcting me or for saying what he said that day back in my kitchen, I'm not sure.

Bea and Kim start chattering as we make our way back to the turnoff. Behind them, I can just hear Nan: "Have you lost someone, dear?"

I want to stop walking. I want to tell everyone to shut up so I can hear how Henry responds. But I've already fumbled this hike, so I keep my chin lifted and my eyes forward, training every other ounce of energy I have into my ears. Too much of my energy, apparently—my boot catches a root and I trip right in the middle of the trail, letting out a truly regrettable scream on the way down.

I land with my wrists pointed straight out. Lunatic behavior. They fold up under me when my chest hits the dirt, and I just lie there for a moment with my eyes shut—like if I can't see this situation, maybe it won't be real.

"*Bah!*" Mei cries, a wail loud enough to scare off every bird in a two-mile radius. "Oh my god."

I groan, rolling onto my back and flexing my wrists. Not broken. Four faces appear above me: Mei and Nan, Bea and Kim, their brows furrowed in varying stages of concern.

Rashad's voice comes from behind them. "She did that pretty gracefully, don't you think?"

Henry's booted feet land next to my face. "Anything broken?" He peers down at me, washed out by the cloudless sky.

"Just my ego," I say. I'm pretty sure there's a rock immediately under my ass, which should make for a really lovely bruise. I try to prop myself up but am stopped by Henry's sudden movement directly into my space.

"Your hands are bleeding." He's reaching for me before the sentence is out of his mouth, crouched beside my twisted body in the dirt, both of his hands wrapping around my wrists. He holds them up between us like the evidence of a crime—scraped, bloody, freckled with gravel.

I make a noise that's trying to be "whoops" but lands somewhere around "whew." Henry's palms are warm and rough. His fingertips press into my pulse.

"First aid kit?" Mei prompts, and I blink.

"Backpack." I struggle to tip myself into a seat with both of my hands in Henry's. He releases them and helps me stand, taking a backward step as Mei starts rooting around in my pack. When she yanks out the red first aid pouch and hands it to Henry, his eyes flick up to mine—just barely—before he unzips it and pulls out a sleeve of isopropyl pads. I can still feel Mei adjusting things in my backpack when he holds out one hand for mine.

Everyone is watching us. I say, "You guys can keep going, I'll catch up."

"No, no." Rashad's eyebrows are halfway lifted. "We'll wait."

Henry clears his throat, and I meet his eyes before looking away and placing one of my hands in his. He holds it lightly—not like that night in the basement, when I needed him to stand. More so, this time, like he's afraid to get too close.

"This'll sting," he says, but I still hiss when the alcohol meets my broken skin. My hand jerks in his grip, and he tightens his hold on me just a little—his fingertips flexing. "Hold still."

Hold still. What he said to me when I told him the power was out. Everything that happened afterward. I bite my lip, and Henry's eyes lift from my hands to my mouth. His fingers, gently wiping the pad over the heel of my palm, go still.

Answer Nan's question, I think. I want to know what he told her—if he's lost someone, if that flash of rough-edged pain I saw in my kitchen after the *Denver Post* article is what I thought it was: heartbreak. The longer we hold each other's eyes, the more it feels like he actually might tell me.

But of course he doesn't, and his eyes flick back down, and I jerk just as violently when he brings the alcohol to my second hand.

"He said hold still," Mei tells me. I shoot her a look—she stands just behind Henry's shoulder, grinning. She could have helped me with this. Should have. But it's Henry dressing my palms in gauze, wrapping them in the tacky bandaging I've never used before in my life, finally letting them drop into the space between us.

"Be careful," he says softly. I meet his eyes and don't say what I'm thinking—which is that this *does* feel dangerous. That it has nothing to do with the wilderness.

"I want ice cream," Rashad says the minute we're back in the parking lot. My wrapped hands are throbbing, and there's a sheen of sweat on the back of my neck that's made my hair sticky and unbearable. Even in the crispness of autumn, the sun is unforgiving at elevation—it might as well be summer, for how clammy I feel. "Can we get ice cream?"

"I'd do ice cream," Bea says, nudging Kim. "Eh?"

"Have you ever seen me turn down ice cream?" Kim asks, retying her ponytail. It's late afternoon by now—the sun is high and hot across the unshaded lot.

"I'm lactose intolerant," Nan announces. "But I love a sorbet."

"Polliwog's has sorbet," Mei says, turning to me. "Should we go on the way home?"

"I don't want to keep Henry," I say, gesturing in his direction without actually looking at him. It's unclear to me if the throbbing in my palms is from the scrapes or the ghost of his touch, and I'm afraid to discover what other unhinged feelings I might develop if I spend much longer in his general vicinity. "I'm sure he has things to do, and we're his ride home."

What I don't add is that Polliwog's is Nate's spot: the ice cream shop he grew up visiting with his brothers, the one he was so excited to show me that we hadn't unpacked a single box before he took me there on move-in day for a drippy, double-scoop cone.

"Henry?" Mei asks, turning to him. "This plan appears to depend on you."

I force myself, finally, to look at him. He's next to Nan with his shirtsleeves pushed up, utility jacket long stuffed into his backpack. Behind his dark sunglasses I can't make out his eyes, which is for the best—I can't tell if he's looking at me or not when he says, "I like ice cream."

Rashad lets out a whoop and makes for Nan's car.

"Are you sure?" I ask, gesturing one bandaged hand in Henry's direction. "You don't just feel pressured to say that?"

Henry's quiet for a full beat before saying, "No, Louisa, I don't feel pressured to lie about whether or not I like ice cream." Then he turns to follow Nan to her car.

"Nicely done." Mei hooks her arm through mine to drag me behind Bea and Kim. "You okay?"

"Of course," I say, though even to me, my voice sounds slightly strangled. "Why?"

Her voice is low, nearly a whisper. "You seem a little on edge."

I let out a gust of breath. "I did eat shit in front of everyone."

Mei's lips part, but she hesitates, glancing at me and then ahead, where Bea and Kim are waiting at my parked car.

"Say it," I tell her.

"You're being weird about Henry."

I look at him instinctually, but he's not paying attention to us; at Nan's Cadillac, he's waiting for her to slide in behind the wheel so he can close the door.

"No, I'm not."

"Yes, you are." Mei's eyebrows jut up her forehead. "He seems perfectly happy to be here and you keep acting like you can't get away from him fast enough. Even after he played nurse for you."

"No, I—"

She cuts me off with a dry look. "Let it be, okay? Maybe he's here for a reason."

"We keep roping him into things and he's too nice to say no?"

"I was thinking more like: he needs this, too." I meet Mei's eyes. "Maybe this is helpful for him."

I look back at Henry again, letting Mei's words breathe between us in the dry autumn air.

Have you lost someone, dear?

This time, Henry's looking at me, too.

Polliwog's hasn't changed since Nate was a kid; it's what he loved so much about it. *Enduring charm*, he said. Perched at the edge of a soft-shouldered road and painted periwinkle, the wood-slatted storefront is surrounded by pines and always has a line winding to the parking lot. The air smells like waffle cones from the moment we step out of the car.

"Okay, what's everyone's order?" Rashad points one finger around the group as we join him, Nan, and Henry in line. "Says a lot about a person. I read ice cream preferences like star signs—lay 'em on me."

"Lemon sorbet for me," Nan chirps, adjusting the brim of her sun hat. Henry cranes over her to read the chalkboard at the front of the building, the long line of his throat arced in the sun. I think of Nate, pulling me by the hand across the Polliwog's threshold, laughing—*First-timers have to get the Elk Poop.*

"Such a sophisticated choice," Rashad tells her. "A classy and elegant selection for a classy and elegant lady." Nan beams, and Rashad scans over the rest of us. "Who's next?"

"What's *Elk Poop*?" Bea asks, making a pinched face as she squints at the menu. "They can't be serious."

"It's peanut butter with Whoppers in it," I tell her, the words out before I've realized I'm speaking. "Local rules say first-timers have to get it."

"Yuck," she says, but Kim shrugs.

"I'll get it, if that's the rule. Not looking for any more bad karma."

"Bold and curious," Rashad tells her, nodding his approval. "Your flavor selection tells me there are bright and unexpected joys in your future."

"God willing," Kim groans, and Bea nudges her in the arm.

"What's the horoscope on chocolate brownie?" Henry asks, crossing his arms against the breeze as he turns to Rashad. It ruffles through his hair, sending it loose and wild over his forehead.

Rashad lets out a chirped little *hm!* and rolls one hand dramatically in the space between them. "An expected but delicious choice that tells me you're a steady, reliable, and delectable man."

Henry barks a laugh that surprises me so thoroughly I actually jump. The bright flash of his teeth, the backward tip of his throat, the sound of his startled joy. It shreds across the memory of Nate here, and I feel suddenly unsteady, too warm.

"What's yours, Lou?" Rashad asks as we step forward in line. "And don't say mint chip, girl. I'm warning you now that vile toothpaste flavor was my ex's."

"It's lavender," I say, trying to breathe. "They, um—" I wave toward the menu board. "It's honey lavender here."

Mei puts her arm around me, like she knows I'm wavering. I feel Henry watching us.

"Oh, *yes*," Rashad says, clapping once. "I knew you'd come through. Soapy perfumy lavender queen, making things so fresh and clean. Light and floral and unexpectedly complex." He presses his palms together and bows in my direction. "Perfection."

And purple, I don't say. I want to make myself order something different; I want to rewrite this place and change myself into someone else—not Nate's ex-girlfriend, not someone who knows the Elk Poop rule because he held me to it himself.

But when I get to the counter, it's the same woman who's always worked here. Gray-blond curls, a retro diner hat in turquoise paper, a warm smile that says she recognizes me. It's all so familiar that I can't break character. I feel Nate's fingertips on the back of my neck as I order, the way he used to dance them along my spine.

"Honey lavender," I tell her. *Purple girl*, I hear Nate say.

"Louisa."

I blink, and there's Henry. Holding a waffle cone piled with chocolate ice cream, his sunglasses pushed up into his hair. They've left little indents on the sides of his nose. "Are you all right?"

I look from him to the register, where the woman appears slightly confused and is clearly waiting for me to pay. I shake my head and mumble an apology while digging into my back pocket.

"Here." Henry taps his credit card across the reader, offering the woman a smile. "Have a good one."

I jerk my cup of ice cream off the counter and step out of line, clustering immediately into Henry's personal space in the crowded shop. It's all black-and-white checkerboard and chrome accents in here; over the speakers, an old Johnny Cash song plays.

"Everyone else got a table outside," Henry says. I look up at him. We're close enough that I can smell his soap, citrus, and his chocolate ice cream and something else, too—sweat, the scent of being outdoors in the sun. His eyes move over mine. "What happened there?"

I could lie, easily. I could say I'm dehydrated, or I zoned out, or I could thank him for the ice cream and pretend nothing happened at all. But I think of Henry on the trail, telling me to hold still, and I think of him in my basement, calling me *Louisa*, and I think of him that first day in his office—the softness that changed his face when I talked about the house. I think of how he's lost someone, too. I know he has.

"I was remembering something," I tell him. It doesn't make sense—not really. But Henry's eyes hold mine. "And I just got lost in it for a minute."

He nods, then. Someone passes behind him and he steps even closer to me, close enough that my wrist brushes the buttons on his shirt.

"I understand," he says. He tips his head toward the window. He doesn't reach for me to make me follow him, like Nate would have. He only moves, and I follow him on my own. "Let's get some air."

Sixteen

"I heard a rumor you're the handyman."

Henry, unfolding himself from the back seat of Nan's Cadillac, looks over at Bea. It's nearly four and the sun's just starting to lower over my driveway. I love the smell of late afternoon: the sandy gravel of the sunbaked landscape, the spicy perfume of pine needles.

"Did you," Henry says.

"Rashad said you were at the house fixing sinks the other day?"

Henry glances at me before pulling his backpack out of the car. "I fixed one sink, yes."

"Well, my door sticks." Bea tosses hair off her shoulder and smiles without showing any teeth. I exhale through my nose, long and slow. "Maybe you could take a look?"

Henry's become the undisputed star of this hike, of eating ice cream, maybe of this entire project. In his hiking clothes, cheeks pinked up from the sun, he looks like a cross between the Brawny Man and a sexy librarian. I wasn't the only one who watched him lick chocolate ice cream off the inner curve of his thumb at Polliwog's.

"Maybe we should start a list," I say, gesturing everyone toward the house. "I'll put out a notepad in the kitchen so Henry can come take care of everything at once instead of us bothering him every other day."

"Are we bothering you?" Nan asks.

Henry laughs, low and breathy. "Not at all."

"And for little things," I say, raising my voice a couple octaves, "you can just come to me. I can take a look at your door, Bea."

I shoot her a smile, which she returns half-heartedly. I'm already imagining her review: *Clean room, good hiking, hot handyman who made me forget about my ex.* The last thing I need is Henry shutting this down because he's somehow become the key component of everyone recovering from their broken hearts.

But he only says, "I'm here now." And when he walks toward the house, I don't stop him.

"Lou?"

I turn at the sound of a soft, hesitant voice. I thought everyone had gone upstairs to shower, nap, or—in Henry's case—investigate a sticky door, but Kim is standing at the entrance to the kitchen with her hands stuffed in her pockets. She and Bea arrived together, a matched set in the Denver uniform of expensive athleisure and corded flat-brim baseball caps. Bea was their immediate voice: they were sharing the Pine Room and its matching double beds for a little over a week and she was the one who'd booked it for them, fresh off the demise of an eight-month relationship with her college sweetheart. The term *college sweetheart* brought Nate right there into the house's entryway with us, and I'd pushed him away like an unwelcome specter.

Kim, though, has been quiet. I can tell Bea is her safe place—there's something about their dynamic that reminds me of Mei. The way they turn in to each other, keep their heads bent inward like a silent dialogue is always passing back and forth between them. She hasn't made full eye contact with me since showing up at the house, and even now her gaze flickers from my face to the garden windows and back again.

"You okay?" I say. I tip my water bottle upside down in the drying rack next to the sink and reach for a dish towel.

"Um," she says, and I know that without an immediate *yes*, the answer to that question is *no*.

"Here." I motion to one of the island stools, and she ducks her head as she pulls it out. When I sit on the stool next to her, she picks at a loose thread on her sweatshirt instead of looking at me.

"I've been thinking about what you said. On the hike?" Kim glances up at me as if to confirm this.

"Which part?"

"How it's so consuming." Her voice pitches upward at the end of each thing she says, turning her sentences into questions. "Losing someone. And you can't see the world past it."

"Yeah," I say quietly. I can tell there's more she wants to get out; I've learned that if you let the awkward silence linger, someone will always fill it. And if it's not me, it'll be Kim.

"Bea's so angry," she says. She glances over one shoulder, like she's worried her friend will come down the stairs at any moment.

"We both got dumped on grad weekend and it's like it lit this fire in her and made her even—I don't know"—she waves one hand in the space between us—"*more*. And I'm not like that. I can't— I just, I feel like I'm going to disappear."

Her eyes come to mine, red rimmed and watery. "It's like you said," she whispers. "The world doesn't feel the same. I can't see anything except that he doesn't want me anymore."

"I understand that feeling," I tell her. Kim closes her eyes, drawing a rickety breath. "If anger is working for Bea, that's understandable, too. But if you can't access that part of yourself right now, it doesn't mean anything's wrong with you."

Kim's nose scrunches up, like she's holding back a sob. "She's so much stronger than I am."

"I don't think that's fair," I say, and Kim's eyes break open. "There's strength in feeling your sadness, too—instead of burying it in anger."

She shakes her head. "I wish I could be angry, though. I think it would be easier than this."

"Have you talked to Bea about this? Or anyone?"

"No," Kim whispers. "I don't want to bring her down."

I hesitate. "Bea's your friend. She probably wants to know what's really going on with you."

"I'm kind of sick of myself," she says. "I've been circling this drain for, like, four months."

"Have you considered therapy?"

Kim's eyes come to mine. "Isn't that what this is?"

"Oh." The word punches out of me, sharp and surprised. "Um, no, I meant—I meant, a dedicated therapist that you can work with on a regular basis. To help you understand what's holding you here, and how to take care of yourself through it."

"But that's why we came here," Kim says. "To talk to you and work through it."

"I'm a therapist," I say, feeling the near lie grate on the way out. "But I'm not *your* therapist. It'll be so much more beneficial for you to work with someone one-on-one." When she looks helplessly up at me, I add, "I'd be happy to help you find someone, if you like. Before you go. I know it can be intimidating to get started."

Kim sniffles, nodding once. "Okay," she says softly. "Yeah, that would help. Thank you."

When she starts to stand up, I add, "Hey, Kim."

She looks at me, swiping one sweatshirt sleeve under her nose. "Remember the other thing I said, about how heartbreak isn't apples to apples? The same goes for reacting to it. It's not better to be angry or better to be sad. It's just different. But it's all valid."

She manages a smile, frail and fleeting. "Thanks, Lou."

I watch Kim go, rounding the corner toward the dining room in the direction of the first-floor bathroom. When I stand from the stool, turning toward the front hall, I nearly jump out of my skin.

Henry's in the doorframe, one shoulder leaned against the wallpaper. There's a rag in his hands, smudged with oil, wrapped between a few of his fingers like he's been wringing it out. He got some sun, today; the tops of his cheeks are the faintest bit burned.

"How long have you been standing there?"

"A few minutes."

"Are you spying on me?"

"Yes," he says seriously. I have a flash of his eyes in the woods, dipping to my mouth. "I'm spying on you."

I squint at him and he shakes his head, dropping his gaze to the floor as the shadow of a smile tugs at one corner of his mouth. "I fixed the door."

"Great," I say. "Thank you. And I'm sorry everyone's so, um—" I break off, and he looks back up at me. "Obsessed with you."

I think he'll brush it off, tell me it isn't true. But Henry's nothing if not a surprise, and when he says, "Everyone?" I feel it under my skin like a sunburn. I think of my palm on the smooth skin of his jaw, that night in my kitchen, and make myself turn away.

"I'll leave this out for other repairs," I say, reaching into the kitchen's junk drawer for a notepad. "And wait to text you until there are a few you can come take care of at once." I glance up. "So you don't have to keep stopping by."

Henry holds my eyes, still working the rag between his fingers. Leaned into the doorframe, sleeves hiked up to his elbows, he looks like he lives here. It occurs to me that this is the first time he's looked relaxed in the house.

I understand, he told me at Polliwog's. Without knowing why, I believed him.

"If that's what you want," he says.

We stare at each other. "Isn't that what *you* want?"

Before Henry can respond, the garden door whines open.

"Hey." Joss pokes her head into the kitchen, blond ponytail peeking from beneath a baseball cap. She shoots me a wave, then says, "Henry, I saw your car in the driveway. Can I talk to you for a minute outside?"

He looks at me again, righting his weight in the doorframe before nodding at Joss. The door closes behind her and Henry moves toward me, the rag twisted in his fingers, his eyes flicking over mine.

When he speaks, his voice is so low I nearly miss it. So quiet I could have made it up. "Not necessarily," he says.

He drops the greasy rag onto the kitchen island and steps around me, reaching for the screen door. I've been holding my breath for too long to say anything; when the door grouses open, Henry teeters it back and forth a few times. The familiar pitch of it—high but musical—fills the kitchen as he looks up at me.

"Add this to your list," he says.

I swallow. I feel very, very warm. "I like it like that."

Henry's eyes hold mine, his fingers still bracketed around the doorframe. "You like it squeaky?"

I shrug, pulling the rag he dropped into my hands just for something to do. I twist it between my fingers. "I like it how I'm used to it."

Henry's lips twitch—not quite a smile, but something that wants to be. When he finally steps onto the porch and lets the door fall shut behind him, I let out a shuddering exhale that makes my throat hurt.

Through the window above the sink, I watch Joss lead Henry through the woven arbor toward our grove of yellowing aspens. Just far enough away to be completely out of my earshot before she turns to him, frustration on her face, and starts talking.

Henry's back is to me—I can't see his face, only the increasingly rigid set of his shoulders. He was different today: not the Henry who moved so woodenly through my house, but the one who smiled at Custard in that shady spot in the grass. The one who laughed when Rashad called him *delectable*. But all this way across the garden, through the kitchen window, I watch him start to change again.

When Joss glances up at the house, I look quickly away. Like I've been caught spying; like I've seen something private that I wasn't meant to.

Like there's something going on in this house that I don't understand.

Seventeen

I don't sleep that night. For the first time since the breakup, my bedroom feels the distinct lack of Nate. I turn fitfully until five o'clock, waking up from misty half dreams and reaching for his side of the bed like it's where I'll still find him.

It's cruel, dreaming after a loss. I know this. Your sleeping brain forgets, puts you in dreams where things are as they were. I dream of being twenty, a college junior kissing Nate in some sweaty dive bar where he spent two hours performing on a sad excuse for a stage. Twenty-two, decorating the house for our first Christmas in it together. Twenty-three, ordering honey lavender ice cream while he stands next to me in line, laughing as someone behind us asks disgustedly what *Elk Poop* is.

I make coffee in the half dark, blue morning just starting to spill into the kitchen. *Twenty-six*, I remind myself. Nate's second choice, and all alone now.

"Hey."

I turn, blinking bleary-eyed down the front hallway. I haven't turned any lights on, and Rashad emerges like a hologram from the shadows—pixelated and hazy until he gets close. "I thought I heard you down here."

"Sorry," I whisper. "I didn't mean to wake you up."

"Oh, babe." He swats a hand as he lowers onto a barstool. "I don't sleep anyway."

"Still?" I pull down another mug and start making him a latte.

"It's better," he tells me. He's wearing a giant fuzzy hoodie. "But nighttime is the hardest."

"Yeah," I say, pouring milk into the metal pitcher. "I feel that."

"Yeah?" He stifles a yawn behind one hand. "You want to talk about it?"

The kitchen fills with hissing as I steam the milk, saving me from responding. But when I slide Rashad's mug over the counter, he raises his eyebrows pointedly.

"I don't know," I say honestly. "Not really."

He takes a sip of the coffee and then stands, tipping his head toward the living room. "Come on. It's just you and me awake right now anyway."

We sink into the couch, side by side. Outside, a breeze rustles the aspens and they send dancing shadows through the windows that reflect in the mirror over the fireplace.

"You've got a broken heart, too, huh?" He doesn't ask it like a question, not really. He says it like something he already knows.

I wave a hand, vaguely, around the living room. "We all do, in this house."

"Sure," Rashad says. "But we've got you to listen to our drivel. Who's listening to you?"

I smile at him. "I'm all right, Rashad."

He snorts, taking a sip from his mug. "Oscar-worthy work, here, but you're puttering around this house at five a.m. like a widow in mourning."

I groan, leaning my head back on the couch. I close my eyes and leave them shut. "Can we talk about you instead? You said the sleep is getting better?"

"It *is*," he says. "But I leave soon. A week here isn't going to solve my whole situation, right? I've got to keep doing the work."

"That's right," I tell him. "But I'm glad this is helping, at least. And you can always stay longer, you know that."

"It's helping," Rashad says. "But I've got to get back to my job one of these days." There's a moment of silence, and then his hand lands on my knee and jostles it. "I'm waiting, Miss Lou. What's the work *you're* doing?"

My eyes break open and I cast a sidelong glance at him, not moving my head. "Persistent."

He shrugs. "I do get what I want."

I sigh, long and slow. "I went through a breakup, too, recently. A couple months ago. It was for the best, and I've been feeling okay about it, but now . . ." I trail off, stare up at the ceiling. *But now*. Why does it feel so hard, so suddenly?

"But now that beautiful chocolate brownie man is in the picture, making you all confused."

I jerk my head around, and Rashad smirks. "You're not so subtle, okay? We get it: you two have your panties all twisted up for each other."

"That's *not* the situation," I say, sitting up straight.

He mirrors me, putting his mug down on the coffee table. "Isn't it? You don't have to feel guilty, babe." Rashad turns to face me. "There's no requisite mourning period. You can move the *fuck* on."

I blink at him, my throat suddenly tight. I didn't realize how desperately I needed someone to give me permission to let go of this—of Nate, of who I was with him, of the idea I had for so long of what my life would be.

In the dark living room, the world feels hazy and half-real. Like Rashad and I aren't in Estes Park, Colorado, but in a shared dream—a place where we could do anything, say anything. Where we could be honest.

"What if I'm not ready?" I ask.

Rashad tilts his head to one side. "How do you know you're not?"

My sister shows up on a cloudy morning in a terry cloth onesie. She started wearing them when she was pregnant with Quinn and never stopped: spaghetti-strap overalls in soft fabrics that she hoisted on over bralettes in summer, skintight long sleeves in fall. *It's all fun and games until you have to go to the bathroom*, she told me the first time I saw her in one. But they're so clearly her comfort outfit—her go-to for any travel day or homebound weekend—that now, when I picture her, she's always wearing one. The coziness outweighs the peeing issue, apparently.

When I open my front door Quinn has his hand buried in one of the slouchy overall pockets, digging for a snack.

"LOU-LOU!" he screeches at the sight of me, flinging his fingers from the pocket and sending a Werther's Original flying across my driveway. He bolts up the steps and Goldie goes to collect it.

"We went on the airplane!" he shouts as he throws his arms around me. When I pick him up and spin him around, he giggles—the most perfect sound ever uttered on god's green earth. Behind him, Goldie sifts through the browning aspen leaves on my driveway to pick up the candy.

"Did you see clouds?" I ask, peppering his face with kisses. "The moon? An alien?"

"*No*," he chides, grabbing my face in both hands to hold me still. We look at each other, eye to eye. "There was a man in the window seat and Mom said I couldn't bother him."

"Ah," I say, reaching out an arm to fold Goldie into our hug as she arrives at the top of the stairs. "Men are the worst."

"I'm a man!" Quinn protests, his face flanked by our shoulders.

"You're a boy," I say, plopping him down on the landing. "And one day, you'll be the best of men."

"Yeah, the best," Quinn says as he shuffles past me into the house. Goldie puts the Werther's Original in my palm.

"Why are you giving Quinn grandpa candy?"

"They're his favorite," she tells me on a sigh. "'Your children come through you, not from you,' or whatever the saying is."

"Well, you can keep this." I drop it back into her pocket and look up at her. "Hi."

"Hi," she says. Her hands land on my shoulders, grounding me. Goldie and I are the exact same height: five feet, three and a half inches. But she has Mom's blond hair, wispy waves that frame her face like a halo, and her pale blue eyes. I carry the darkness of a man I never met: dishwater hair, not quite brown, and hazel irises that change in the light. "You look tired."

"So do you."

"I just flew across the country with a five-year-old. What's your excuse?"

I wave a hand through the front door. "I run my own business now, remember?"

Goldie lets out a sigh, long and withering. It speaks sentences all on its own: *Yes, I remember this batshit idea of yours. Yes, I remember this inadvisable scheme. Yes, I remember that I'm leaving my pride and joy in a house full of strangers.*

"I want complete details on everyone staying here before I leave Quinn tomorrow," she says. She'll head to Denver in the afternoon for her conference, leaving Quinn and me with a week of our own. "*Especially* any men."

"No men at the moment," I tell her, though Henry's face pops, unbidden, into my mind. Rashad left yesterday, with a lung-flattening hug and a promise to call me at five thirty in the morning when neither of us can sleep. "Just a group of incredibly delightful—if sad—women."

She levels me with her gaze and sidesteps me into the house. "We'll see. Quinn? Where'd you go?"

"I found Mei!" he shouts from the living room. "Remember Mei, Mom?"

"Of course," Goldie says. Mei is Goldie's favorite: the person she wishes I was. When we join them in the living room, Quinn's perched next to Mei on the couch, her work laptop open on the coffee table in front of them. Last I checked, Kim and Bea were upstairs doing a puzzle with Nan.

"Hey, you," Mei says, standing to give Goldie a hug. "Love the overalls."

"Oh," Goldie says, accepting the hug and then waving her off. "They're ancient. But thank you." She pulls away and drops her hands onto Mei's shoulders, just like she did with me. "I was so sorry to hear about Andy."

I resist the rigidity that nags at the base of my spine, threatening to freeze me up. Our whole lives, it's been like this: the warmth Goldie's capable of with others and never with me. Mei's sadness makes sense to her; mine is a problem to solve.

"Who's Andy?" Quinn asks before Mei can respond. She squeezes Goldie's elbow in thanks and then sits back down next to him, tipping her head into the couch cushion.

"Andy was my partner," she says. "But we broke up."

"What's 'partner'?" Quinn asks, leaning closer to her. He's so unbelievably delicious: shiny blond hair, Goldie's blue eyes magnified by little-kid glasses, tiny fingers that curl around Mei's forearm like he can't help but get closer to her.

Mei glances at Goldie before saying, "Do you know what a girlfriend is? Or a boyfriend?"

"Yeah," Quinn says, giggling again like the word itself is a scandal between them.

"It's like that," Mei tells him. "Except Andy is non-binary, which means they aren't a boy or a girl. So we call them my partner, instead of my boyfriend or girlfriend."

"Oh," Quinn says, nodding. He looks up at his mom, then at me, and I think there's a clarifying question coming. But he just says, "Are you sad, Mei?"

She hesitates, and when she lets out a laugh it's halfway to a sob. "My god," she says, pulling him in for a hug. "You're too much. I'm sad, but I'll be okay."

He looks at me over Mei's shoulder. "Do you live with Lou-Lou now?"

"For a little, yeah." They pull apart, and Quinn hikes his feet up onto the couch. His socks have green dinosaurs on them. "Did Lou tell you about the other people who are living with her, too?"

"Mom said *strangers*," Quinn says, leaning closer to her like it's a secret. When he darts a glance at Goldie, she raises her eyebrows.

"They aren't strangers," I say, giving Goldie a look of my own. "Quinn, remember when we went to visit Grandma in Ohio and we stayed at the hotel?"

"With the pool," Quinn confirms. He was three and just learning to swim; his duck-patterned water wings were a bright spot in that interminable weekend.

"It's like that," I tell him. "My house is like a hotel, but small. And there are a few people staying here with Mei and me."

"Will I meet them?" he asks.

"Of course."

"How long will you stay?" Goldie asks Mei, finally taking a seat in one of the armchairs by the fireplace. She's presenting at the conference this week—some kind of immigration law summit—but right now she just looks like my sister: tired, familiar, an unidentifiable stain on the knee of her overalls.

"I don't know," Mei says, glancing over at me. "It's been almost two months. And work said I could have two, but it's been so nice being here—I'm not sure I'll be ready to go back to Denver anytime soon."

"Then you shouldn't," I say. When I drop onto the couch next to Mei, Quinn clamors over her lap to sandwich himself in between us. "Ask for more time. You know they'll give it to you."

"Yeah," she says, tapping her head against mine. We've been

having this conversation for weeks already—and the truth is I'm not ready for Mei to leave. I'm not sure I can do all this without her. "It's just, like, I have to get back to my life eventually, right? How long do I wait before ripping off the Band-Aid?"

"A little longer," I say. "And maybe a little longer after that."

"You'll stay while I'm here?" Quinn asks, and Mei gasps like she's offended.

"*Duh*. You're not getting rid of me."

"Did you break your lease?" Goldie asks. She has her hands folded over her stomach, leaned back in the armchair. "Or are you paying rent in Denver on top of the room rate here?"

Mei glances at me. She isn't paying anything to stay here, of course. But Mei knows our dynamic well enough to know what Goldie's really asking: *Is Louisa making enough money to sustain herself here? Is she safe?*

"I didn't break my lease," Mei says. "So there's that to get back to, too."

"*Ev*entually," I insist, putting my hand on her knee. Quinn places his on top of mine and echoes, "Eventually."

"I'm worried about Mark."

I blink across the kitchen at my sister, surprised she's talked to our mother recently enough to know about Mark. It's only five o'clock on the day she arrived. Quinn's watching TV in the living room. Goldie's peeling baby potatoes over the sink, and she doesn't look up at me when she adds, "What do you know about him?"

"Basically nothing." It's been a week since my phone call with our mother, and I haven't heard from her since. I don't know if she and Mark went to Miami. I don't know if they're even together anymore. "When did you talk to her?"

"Yesterday," Goldie says. There are a few silent beats. "She texted me because she didn't want to *burden* you after your breakup." The way she says it makes it clear that she doesn't think my situation warrants this degree of consideration. "She needed help with their tickets back from Florida."

I stop chopping the carrot in front of me, swallowing the sting of her tone. "Did you pay for the tickets?"

"No," Goldie says, not looking up from her potatoes. "I have a son to provide for. I don't pay for Mom's recklessness anymore."

It's pointed, a dig. I send Mom money often enough to have a line item for it in my budget. It's usually something more practical: she needs groceries to bridge to her next paycheck, or help with her heating bill during an especially frigid February. Goldie always says no—as far as I know, these tickets are the first thing Mom's asked her for in years.

"Then how will she get home?" I ask, hearing the fear in my own voice. "She didn't even ask me—"

"Because I told her not to," Goldie says, finally putting down the vegetable peeler and looking at me. "It's got to stop, Lou. She's an adult."

Of course she's an adult. But she's also our mom. The one who lifted up that blanket in the darkness all those years, tucked my body in against hers. "So she'll be stuck in Florida?"

"No, she put it on a credit card, just like I told her to."

I swallow. Mom's credit score is so bad she can barely lease an apartment. I would never tell her to put something on a credit card. "Why didn't Mark buy the tickets?"

"Apparently he only bought his own." Goldie turns back to the potatoes. "Hence my concern."

I look across the island, down the hall toward the front door. It's shadowy and familiar: the woven runner I bought at a flea market with Mei, the gold-framed photo of Quinn as a baby, the turtle-shaped Tiffany lamp on the side table. *Mom's not here*, I remind myself. *I'm safe*. But it does nothing to loosen the clench of my chest, the whisper that rushes through me: *My fault, my fault, my fault.*

If I told Goldie I felt this way, she'd roll her eyes. She has no patience for my bleeding heart, my inability to let Mom go. So I just tell her, "She wanted to stay at Nate's place in Miami."

"What?" Goldie looks up, peeler poised in one hand. "You didn't tell me that."

"I didn't want to get into it." What I mean is: I'm never able to get into it with *you*. "And she basically acted like my life is over without him, so."

Silence falls. When I hazard a glance up at Goldie, she's looking out the window over the sink. The sun is lowering over the garden, where everything is hunching up for November: the petals dropping from the flowers, the green stalks browning as they cower into themselves.

I want Goldie to say: *That's awful, Lou*. I want her to say: *She shouldn't treat you like that.*

I want her to tell me that I won't ever end up like our mother, dependent on men who discard her like damaged goods—again, and again, and again.

Goldie's eyes flick to mine. She picks up the peeler.

"It isn't," she says. I turn back to my carrots. "You know that it isn't."

Eighteen

"What did *you* enjoy about those things, dear?" Nan is leaning close to Kim on the couch, watching her intently. "The things you love don't cease to exist because you can't do them with him anymore. You can still do them."

"I'm not going to go indoor rock climbing by myself," Kim says, teary-eyed.

Nan throws her hands up. "Why on earth not?"

"I agree," Bea says. She's cross-legged in the armchair next to Mei's, mug of coffee in her lap. "I think you *should* go climbing by yourself, Kim. Like a total *fuck-you*. You don't need Peter to take you to the gym—you have just as much of a right to be there without him."

"What if he's there, though?"

"Then he sees you living your best life," Mei says. Next to her, on a dining chair we've pulled in from the kitchen, Joss nods. We're arranged in a haphazard sort of circle: Mei and Bea in armchairs by the fireplace, Joss on the dining chair, Kim and

Nan tucked in next to me on the couch. "And you get seeing him again for the first time over with. Win-win, right?"

Kim groans, dropping her head back into the couch cushions. "I guess so."

It's Monday afternoon, just after lunch. Nan, Bea, and Kim have forged such a special bond that I'm a little sad to have another booking coming in tomorrow. With Mei and Joss in the mix, it's basically all of my favorite people in one room. Bea and Kim head back to Denver tomorrow, but Nan's decided to stay for a while. *What reason do I have to leave?* she asked me. I'm hesitant to let the dynamic shift, especially since this group has been so open to my programming: hikes, breakfast together every morning, group sessions that usually result in one or all of us weeping into our coffee mugs.

Quinn charmed the pants off of everyone at breakfast, and Goldie's satisfied with the absence of danger at the house (I refrained from telling her I have a new guest—female!—coming tomorrow). She leaves for Denver in an hour, and is upstairs putting Quinn down for a nap before she goes.

"Just because Peter introduced you to climbing doesn't mean he *owns* it," Bea says now. I think of Polliwog's, of Elk Poop ice cream, of Henry. *I understand.* "Even if he thinks he does, that pompous ass."

"Well said," Nan agrees. "Hobbies are for everyone. If being in that gym brings you joy, you need to get back there as soon as you can."

"Plus, endorphins," Mei says. "Exercise is irritatingly effective at making you feel better."

"It's true," Bea says. "And since I can never get you to go to Pilates with me . . ."

Kim rolls her eyes. *"Joss,"* she says, pointedly changing the subject. "Let's discuss your trauma, please."

Joss laughs, chin tipping back. She's cross-legged in the chair with a mug of coffee in both hands—she came in for a warm drink before starting on fall cleanup in the yard, and we convinced her to stay.

"Or something else," I say quickly. "Anything at all."

She nods her head back and forth, like she's deciding what to say. "I've been processing a loss for a bit—a heartbreak." She glances at me, and I give her a sad smile. She's never told me, but then again, I haven't asked. "The garden helps."

"Doesn't it?" Nan asks, and Joss nods.

"I guess what I've been struggling with most," she says, "is everyone else's reactions to it. And managing those, when I'm still trying to manage my *own* pain."

"Why does anyone else get an opinion?" Bea says, indignant. "It's *your* breakup."

"It's a little different, when you get old," Joss says, nudging Bea's knee with her own.

Mei says, "You're not *old*," and Joss waves her off before continuing.

"It's a whole family affair." Joss's eyes flit to mine, and she takes a sip of her coffee. "Everyone has feelings, and you sort of have to navigate them."

I tilt my head, wishing we'd talked about this before. Thinking of my mom's reaction to my breakup. In all the years I've known her, Joss has never mentioned a partner.

"I think it's like on airplanes," I say, shifting in my armchair. "You have to put your own oxygen mask on first—even if other people are struggling around you."

Bea lifts one arm in the air, snapping, and Joss breathes a laugh.

"Take care of yourself first," I add. "Everyone else can wait until you've patched your own pain."

"*Agree*," Mei says, and Joss smiles at me. She's opening her mouth to say something else when the back door pushes open, whining merrily, and suddenly Henry is standing in my house. His eyes flicker across the living room, lighting on one face after another, before landing on me. I think of us after the hike, his low voice telling me, *Not necessarily*, and swallow.

"Sorry to interrupt." He looks startled, a little embarrassed to have walked into a house full of people. He's in dark jeans and a flannel shirt with the sleeves pushed up past his elbows.

I shake my head. "Is everything okay?"

"Yes," Henry says. He glances at Joss, and I follow his gaze. "I just—Joss asked me to stop by for something in the garden. I didn't realize you'd be—" His eyes move back to mine. *Doing therapy? Talking about our feelings?* "Busy."

"Not busy," Joss says, standing. She doesn't look at Henry as she steps around him, placing her mug on the kitchen counter. "Let's talk outside." She waves at me, then smiles across the group. "Thank you."

"Oxygen mask!" Bea calls, and Henry shoots me a bemused look before following Joss outside. I watch them through the window, Joss leading Henry toward the back of the garden until they're partially obstructed by a fringe of pine boughs. I'm not close enough to read his body language, to see if his shoulders tense up as they talk.

"Lou, you okay?"

I jump, turning to find Mei watching me from across the room. "What's going on out there?"

"Nothing," I say quickly. Bea, Kim, and Nan have all turned to look at me. "Sorry, I just zoned out for a second."

"It's all right," Mei says, eyeing me and then squinting out the window. A squirrel skitters down the porch railing, its mouth stuffed with bark. "What are they doing out there?"

"What's who doing out where?" Goldie's voice precedes her down the staircase, and Kim scoots over to make room for her on the couch. When she drops onto the cushion, Mei says, "Ask Lou."

Fantastic. The last person I want to explain Henry to is Goldie, who's eternally suspicious of men. I make the mistake of glancing out the window again—where Henry and Joss are still just within sight—and she cranes forward on the couch to look for herself.

"Who's that?" she asks. She's changed into her conference attire: black slacks, block heels, a herringbone blazer. With her hair in a sleek bun and her freckles hidden beneath a smooth layer of foundation, she looks like the Goldie that the rest of the world gets: Immigration lawyer Goldie. Professionally helpful Goldie.

"Joss," I say. "The groundskeeper."

"And who else?" She looks at me. "I thought there weren't any men staying here."

"There aren't," I say, resigning myself to it. "That's my landlord."

"Henry," Bea adds, slow smile twisting her lips. "He's *soooo*—"

"What's he doing here?" Goldie asks, her eyes narrowing.

I wish I knew, I think. But Goldie latches on to mysteries with the tenacity of an Olympic marathoner, so I just say, "Talking with the groundskeeper."

Bea's standing up to catch a glimpse of Henry in the garden, but Kim yanks her back. Goldie levels me with her gaze but, blessedly, drops it.

"We were talking about Joss's and Kim's ex-beaus," Nan says, looking at Goldie. "Do you have anything you'd like to bring to the group, dear?"

Goldie's eyebrows hike up. "Oh, I'm not here for therapy."

"It's not therapy," I say. Goldie's clinically allergic to discussing her feelings. "We're just talking."

"Where's Quinn's dad?" Bea asks, pulling one knee up to her chest and wrapping her arms around it. "Or is that too personal?"

Goldie stares at her, then drags her eyes to me. "It's pretty personal."

"Ignore her," Kim says.

I say, "Goldie conceived Quinn with a sperm donor."

"*Shit*." Bea lifts her palm toward Goldie for a high five. "Respect. Who needs men?"

Goldie breathes a laugh, touching her palm to Bea's. "Couldn't agree more."

"I love men," Kim sighs. "It's basically my whole problem." She looks at Goldie. "Is it hard, raising him on your own?"

Goldie shrugs. I know it's hard. Know, too, that she'll never admit that to a roomful of strangers. "I basically raised Lou," she says, waving one hand in my direction. "So I've done it on my own before."

I feel my cheeks flush, but Goldie saves me from having to respond. "Can we talk for a minute before I go?"

"Sure," I say, standing. I cast a glance across the group. "You all feel free to keep going—I'll be back."

"I think it's time for me to rest these old bones," Nan says, making to stand.

Mei gets up to help her, and Bea follows. "A nap sounds *great*," she says.

When I lead Goldie into the kitchen, all four women head for the stairs; their voices fade as they disappear.

"Look," Goldie says, leaning one hip into the kitchen island. "I want to talk to you about this rental plan of yours."

I groan, reaching for a crumpled dish towel on the counter and starting to fold it. "Do you have to?"

"Yes." She crosses her arms. "Tell me about the financials. Is it working?"

I hang the towel over the faucet and glance out the window, where Joss and Henry are still talking near the aspens. The window's open to let in the breeze, but they're too far away for me to hear them. "What do you mean by *working*?"

"Are you making enough money to pay your rent?"

"That's not how it's set up. I'm staying here for free and giving most of the income to the landlord."

"That man outside?" Goldie slides in right beside me, following my gaze out the window. I promptly turn around and lean my hip into the counter.

"Yes."

"So how are you making money to cover your other expenses? Groceries? Student loans?"

I feel warmth start to build in my belly. It's shame, I know it is: Goldie always brings this out in me. She was born with a plan and never strayed from it even a centimeter—the fact that I haven't followed the one she had for me makes me feel like a failure.

"I'm using my savings right now." The money that Henry didn't accept, back in his office in August. "I don't have to start paying back my loans yet. And I'm using some of the rental income to cover smaller things like groceries."

"Savings," Goldie picks out. She follows me away from the window, comes to face me at the island. "How long will that last?"

"Long enough."

"Lou, don't be difficult."

"*You* don't be difficult." I sound petulant, but she brings this out of me, too. Without Goldie around, I get to be an adult. But when she's here, she makes me feel young again—and stupid. "I'm handling this, okay?"

"Are you?" She doesn't pull her gaze from mine, doesn't blink. "What happens when that money runs out? You come to me?"

"No," I say, the warmth that began in my stomach rising up into my rib cage, my neck. I can feel my skin going splotchy. "Don't worry, Goldie, I'm not going to ask you for a handout."

"That's not what I'm—"

"I'm not like Mom."

Her mouth snaps shut, and the words hang between us. She looks offended that I'd accuse her of equating me to our mother. But that's what she was doing, whether she knew it or not. It's what we're always doing, how the two of us move through the world. Molded by her.

"I know you're not," she says stiffly. "I only want you to be okay."

"I am okay."

A muscle tenses in the corner of her jaw. "I'm just worried," she says slowly, "that you're doing this hotel . . . *thing* to postpone your career. That it's one more excuse not to get started."

My cheeks are hot now. If this goes on much longer, I'll start crying. Goldie doesn't know that I wanted to get started months ago; she doesn't know that I failed the test. She doesn't know what Nate did to me—not the depth of it, not the things that I tolerated, the weakness that makes me like our mom.

"The Comeback Inn isn't an excuse," I bite out. She doesn't deserve an explanation, but I give it to her anyway. "It's something I really care about."

"But what about a *job*?" Goldie presses. "What about something that'll *pay* you? Do you care about that, or just playing housekeeper in this—"

"Louisa's quite good at this."

We both spin around. Henry's standing on the other side of the screen door to the garden, one hand on the doorknob. He looks at me, jaw pressed into a tense line, before pushing it open and stepping into the kitchen. "I've seen it."

Goldie opens her mouth, looking from Henry to me and back again. I still feel like I'm on the verge of tears, my cheeks hot and clammy. The fact that Henry must have been listening from outside, must have heard all the ways my own sister thinks I'm a failure, makes me want to cover my face like a child.

"I don't get the sense that she's playing at anything," Henry says. The door shuts squeakily behind him and he looks at it, then back at me, before adding, "It seems to me she's helping these people."

I look down at my feet, heart frantic beneath my ribs. I didn't know Henry thought I was good at anything. After all the ways I've made a mess of myself in front of him, I don't know why he's defending me at all. Goldie recovers before I do.

"I'm sorry, who are you?"

"Henry Rhodes." When he extends his hand toward her, she takes it. "I'm Louisa's landlord."

"Marigold Walsh," Goldie says crisply. "Her sister. And we were having a conversation, so if you don't mind—"

"Goldie," I say quietly. Both she and Henry look at me. "I think we should finish this another time." *Or maybe never.*

Goldie looks at her watch. "Fine," she says, in a way that indicates it's clearly not fine. "I need to get going anyway. I'm going to get my things."

She leaves the kitchen in a clatter of heeled footsteps. Henry doesn't move.

"Sorry," I say straight down at my feet.

"What for?"

I look up at him, my face still on fire. He's watching me carefully, that concerned line between his eyebrows, the sunburn gone from his cheeks. They're clean-shaven: smooth and familiar in the kitchen light.

"That was, um—" I swallow, shaking my head a little. "She just worries about me."

"That's what families do," he says. It makes me wonder, straightaway, what his family is like. "But she doesn't have a reason to worry about whether you're doing well at this. You are."

It's maybe the kindest thing anyone's ever said to me. It's, somehow, the exact thing that I need to hear.

I mean to say, *Thank you*. But when Henry's gaze meets mine, when I open my mouth, what comes out is: "I was going to take my nephew to the park in a bit. Do you want to come?"

Nineteen

Quinn's wearing a beanie shaped like a fox face, orange ears pointed skyward. He runs ahead of us down the sidewalk, kicking up leaves, oblivious to the tension that expands and contracts like a held breath between the two adults behind him.

"Goldie lives in New York," I tell Henry, just to say something. He agreed to come to the park without hesitating, but now that we're halfway there and still haven't spoken, I'm worried that inviting him was the wrong choice. We ran into Bill and Martina walking Custard on our way out the door, and seeing Henry with him again reminded me of the dynamic from back in August: Henry, silent with me. Henry, open and lit up and loosened with everyone else. "I only get to see Quinn a couple times a year."

"He loves you," Henry says. He'd watched Quinn bound down the stairs and into my arms when Goldie left, completely unfazed by her going. I'm not too big to admit that it gave me a silly sort of satisfaction after what she'd said to me.

"It's super mutual," I say, and a smile tugs at the edge of his mouth. "He's my favorite person."

"Is she doing it alone?" Henry asks. "Or does he have another parent?"

"Just Goldie." Our footsteps fall in tandem, our shadows stretching long across the sidewalk. "She had him with a donor. She, um—" I catch myself before saying *doesn't trust men*. "She's always known exactly what she wants, and never hesitated to get it."

Henry nods, watching Quinn hop two-footed over a crack in the pavement. "Looks like she's doing a good job."

"I mean, yeah. She's a perfect mom." She came into motherhood like she was made for it: stern but warm, fun but boundaried. Something she'd never seen modeled, she picked up straightaway. There's never been a problem Quinn has presented to her that she hasn't been able to solve. Goldie can be callous, but I'd trust her with life—mine, and anyone else's. "Goldie's good at everything."

"Hm."

I look over at Henry. "What?"

He shrugs, glancing at me. The way the autumn light catches his eyes is criminal. "She's good at *everything*? That can't be true."

"Well, you just met her," I say on a laugh. "Give it some time, and you'll see."

"Can she cook?"

"Better than anyone I know."

"Run?"

"She does the New York City Half every year."

"Draw?"

I tilt my head back and forth. "Decently."

"Give her sister the credit she deserves?"

I catch his eyes, narrowing mine. "Ha-ha."

Henry shrugs again. "I mean it. Giving people we care about space to be themselves, instead of the people we want them to be, is a skill, too."

"That's true," I say slowly.

"And you're good at it." The breeze blows hair over his forehead, and he reaches up one hand to push it back. The threads of silver at his temples glint in the lowering sunlight. "I didn't mean to listen, the other day, when I finished fixing that door. But I heard what you said to Kim."

"About being sad?"

"About grieving how you need to." Henry digs his hands further into his pockets, shoulders coming up to his ears. I picture him in the doorframe that day: his fingers working the rag, his low voice as he stepped around me toward the garden door. "You told her that the way she is is okay. I think she needed to hear it."

It's so validating that my initial urge is to push back on it, thrust away the discomfort of being seen so clearly. But instead, I make myself say, "Thank you, Henry."

He turns to look at me, holds my eyes. *I understand.* "You're welcome."

"Lou-Lou, *look*!" Quinn points ahead of us, where Elk Run Park's brand-new jungle gym rises from the mulch in all its polycarbonate glory. It's surrounded by pine trees and the ring of distant mountains.

"I told you," I say. Henry and I stop next to him, and Quinn absently clenches a hand into the bottom hem of my jacket. "What should we do first?"

Quinn takes it all in, his lips parted. There are a few other families at the park—twins in matching sweaters on the swings, a group of teenagers clustered around the slide. October wind blows, crisp and cold, but Quinn is unfazed.

"Monkey bars?" He looks up at me with a combination of glee and mischief in his eyes.

"Good choice," Henry says, as I drop a hand onto Quinn's fox-capped head.

"You know your mom's rule about monkey bars." They're a big, whopping *no*, right alongside trampolines and contact sports. "But she's not here, huh?"

Quinn lets out a thrilled yelp and runs into the mulch pit.

"I should help him," I say to Henry. "Be right back."

He nods, hands in his jacket pockets. I can feel him watch me go, and when I lift Quinn up to reach the bars, Henry takes a seat on one of the benches at the edge of the park.

"I like your friend," Quinn grunts, breathless as he hoists himself from bar to bar. I keep my hands around his rib cage—I can betray my sister a *little*, but not all the way. "Does he live with you in the big house?"

"No," I say, glancing at Henry again. With one arm hooked over the back of the bench, coat falling open to show a flash of red flannel underneath, he looks like an autumn dream—like an ad for hayrides and spiced cider and pumpkin carving on a back porch at dusk. "He owns the big house."

"He lets you live there without him?"

"Yeah," I say. "It's called a landlord, when you own a house and other people pay you to live there."

"Landlord," Quinn repeats, testing it out. He grunts again, little fingers reaching for the final bar. *"Land. Lord."*

"You done?" He hangs vertical from the bar, strip of his tummy exposed to the cold. I lift him up and he melts into me before dropping to the ground. "Or want to go again?"

"Go again. But I'm gonna get a drink." He points to the water fountain near the entrance of the park, then starts running. "I'll come back!"

I slip my hands into my coat pockets, hunching against the wind. Quinn crosses the mulch, arms swinging, and when he takes the ledge up onto the pavement his sneaker catches the wooden barrier. I watch him fall in slow motion: his arms flinging forward, his shoe popping off, the horrible thud as he hits the ground. In the silence before he starts crying, I gasp, "*Shit.*"

I'm running before the word's left my mouth, but Henry's bench is only a few paces away from Quinn, and he gets to him first.

Quinn's in Henry's lap before I'm off the playground: Henry's knees pressed to the pavement, Quinn's fox hat tucked under his chin, the lost sneaker already scooped into one hand.

"You're safe," Henry says—that low, soothing voice. The first thing I noticed about him, back in his office in August. "Did that hurt you?" Quinn pauses mid-sob to look up at Henry, his eyes tracking over his face like he's unsure whether he remembers him. "Or just scare you?"

I stop beside them, kneeling. Quinn's watery eyes come to mine. "Scare me," he squeaks, looking back up at Henry, who nods. My heart thrashes between my ribs.

"That was a big fall," Henry says. All of him has softened—the cut of his shoulders, the tension he holds in his jaw. That line between his brows, gone now. "It did look scary."

"Hey, buddy," I say shakily. When I hold my arms out, Henry pours Quinn's trembling body into them. "You okay?"

"I'm okay," Quinn says wetly. "Just scared."

"Yeah," I say, meeting Henry's eyes over his shoulder. *Thank you*, I mouth.

Henry says, "He's all right," and slides Quinn's sneaker back onto his socked foot. When he places his hand on the back of Quinn's head, it strikes me that he's done this before. He looks more comfortable in this moment—knelt in the dirt with a sobbing Quinn—than I can remember seeing him since that day with Custard on the lawn.

"Do you have nieces and nephews?" I ask, holding Quinn close as his breathing slows.

Henry's hand drops into his lap. "No," he says. And before I can ask anything else, he helps me to my feet and adds, "Should we get him home?"

Henry stands in the door to my bedroom, watching me pull the covers up to Quinn's chin. There are guest rooms free, but he prefers to sleep with me—the most adorable kind of slumber party. My bedroom is at the back of the house, its windows overlooking the garden, oddly shaped and all the more charming for it. The bed angled into a corner, lamp arcing up behind it; two reading chairs in front of the biggest window; an antique lowboy dresser extending along the far wall, scattered with framed photographs and perfume bottles. Quinn's baby-sized suitcase sits at the foot of the bed.

I've cleaned his scraped palms and covered them in the requested kisses. Aside from being shaken up, he's perfectly fine—a relief for several reasons, not the least of which is that now I don't have to call Goldie.

"He all right?" Henry asks quietly as I close the door behind us. It's nearly five o'clock, well past Quinn's usual naptime, but after the drama of the park, he didn't protest a second nap. My guests are in their rooms, the usual late-afternoon lull where the house is quiet: everyone resting as the sun goes down, or getting ready for dinner.

"Yeah," I say. We lean into opposite sides of the stained wood doorframe, facing each other. The long hallway is dimly lit by milk glass sconces; under our feet, a woven runner muffles the hardwood floor. Henry's collar is half upturned from taking his coat off. "Thanks for your help back there."

Henry shrugs. "I'm glad he's okay."

I take him in: soft flannel, dark jeans, arms crossed over his chest. Hair rumpled from the wind. Eyes gone nearly navy in the shadowy hallway.

"Can I ask you something?"

Henry's voice is soft. "Of course."

"What's your family like?"

Henry inhales, arms tightening around each other like he's protecting himself. "Normal," he tells me, not an answer at all. "I'm an only child. My parents were teachers. They inherited this house from my dad's parents, who built it in the fifties."

I tip my head to one side, studying him. The way he's tucked in on himself.

"What?" he says.

"I'm not going to hurt you."

The line appears between his eyebrows. This time, I don't stop myself from reaching into the space between us—drawing one fingertip over his skin to smooth it out. Henry holds his breath until my hand drops back to my side.

"You look scared," I say softly. "To talk to me about this."

He doesn't deny it. He doesn't say anything at all. He only swallows—steadying—and lets out a breath that parts his lips, shows me the pink of his tongue.

"I won't make you," I say. When I tip back against the wall he leans toward me, making up the distance. "We can talk about something else—like the garden." His eyebrows lift, and I say, "What's going on? I've seen you arguing with Joss twice now."

"We aren't arguing," Henry says. I notice the present tense: that whatever they're fighting about, it isn't resolved. He shifts his weight, bringing us another hair's breadth closer. "Just discussing."

I tilt my head. "Discussing quite animatedly."

"I have a lot of opinions," Henry says, "about plants."

I narrow my eyes, feel my mouth betraying me into a smile. "Really."

"Really," he echoes.

"I wouldn't expect that from you."

"No?" He doesn't blink, doesn't move his gaze from mine. "What would you expect from me?"

I press my lips together. I never know, is the truth. Henry has surprised me in every single way.

"I expect that you make your bed every morning with hospital corners."

He lets out a short breath, halfway to laughter. "Correct."

"I expect that you hated group projects in school."

A real laugh, this time. His eyes close, his teeth flashing, and

I want to make him laugh again and again and again. "Correct," he says.

"I expect," I say, slowly, testing my resolve, "that you still think the Comeback Inn is silly."

Henry tips closer to me. "Incorrect."

I pull my lower lip between my teeth. "I expect you're annoyed by how often you've had to come over here since I started this."

Henry's eyes dip to my mouth. "Incorrect."

"I expect," I say, slowly, "that if I asked you to stay for dinner tonight, you would say yes."

Henry's lips twitch, like he's fighting a smile. He uncrosses his arms. "Correct."

Twenty

"Let me." Henry reaches past me, arching onto his tiptoes. When he lowers a pot from the high cabinet and hands it to me, I force myself to look away from the exposed strip of his stomach.

"Is all this stuff where you left it?" Mei asks from the island. She's putting in her earrings. "Back when you lived here?"

"Not quite," Henry says, leaning his hip into the counter. "I didn't keep my heaviest pots on the top shelf, but"—he raises his hands—"it's Louisa's kitchen now."

Mei barks out a laugh. "Yeah, she's not exactly Michelin-chef material, if you hadn't picked up on that yet."

"Weren't you leaving?" I ask, shooting her a frozen smile.

"I was." She smiles sweetly. "I'll see you tomorrow; give Quinn a hug for me when he wakes up."

Mei's spending the night with some work friends in Denver—a girls' night designed to get her over Andy that she's been dreading ever since it was proposed. *Go*, I'd told her. *Forget about them for one night.* And her miserable, whispered reply: *I'm not ready to forget about them.*

But now I watch her go, in a maroon corduroy dress and platform boots that I could never in one hundred lifetimes pull off. Kim and Bea are having dinner in town, and Nan's been upstairs with a set of paperback romance novels all evening. It's just Henry and me in my quiet kitchen, the setting sun casting us multicolored through the stained glass.

When I open the pantry for a box of Quinn's favorite mac and cheese, I ask, "Where *should* I keep my pots?"

"It's your kitchen," he repeats. But when I hike my eyebrows at him, he points to the cabinet next to the sink, where a pair of low drawers house my cutting boards. "I kept them here."

When I sidestep him to fill the pot with water from the sink, Henry doesn't move: his body is warm and solid, brushing against mine. I glance up at him and quickly away, whisking the pot to the stovetop.

"How long did you live here, on your own? Like, not as your parents' house?"

"Five years," he says. I twist the burner and look back at him as the gas hisses on. He's watching me carefully, a glass of my best red wine ($17) in one hand, and doesn't offer anything more. I wish I didn't have to drag it out of him, all the details I'm ravenous to know—if he was here alone, and why he left when he did, and whether he likes what I've done with the house. Whether he still pictures his life here, when he steps inside.

"Why'd you leave?"

He takes a sip of wine, and I watch the movement of his throat as he swallows. "It was time to move on."

I roll my eyes, and he takes a step closer to me. "Why are you rolling your eyes at me?"

"Because you're impossible."

His eyebrows twitch. "How so?"

"You want to stay for dinner," I say, "which I assume means you want to talk to me." I wait for him to nod his acknowledgment. "But you refuse to answer any of my questions directly."

Henry points to the cabinet. "I told you where I kept my pots."

I roll my eyes again, and he breathes a low laugh. "Fine. You answer one question for me, and I'll answer one for you."

I bite my lip. He tracks the movement with his eyes. There's so much I don't want Henry to know, so many avenues for this deal to go sideways: the status of my counseling license, the shameful way Nate left me, the precarious mess of my mother—always teetering in the background.

But Henry's eyes are dark and liquid in the sunset through the kitchen windows. His fingers are curled just so around the edge of the counter. His mouth is wet and red with wine. I think of him remodeling this kitchen for me—without knowing it—and find, terrifyingly and all at once, that I'd give nearly anything to learn just one concrete thing about him. The family he doesn't want to talk about, the life that took him away from this house. *How do you know*, Rashad asked me that blue-dark morning, *that you aren't ready?*

"Deal," I say softly.

Henry tips his head to the pot, which has started to boil. As I dump in enough macaroni for all three of us, he says, "How did you wind up with Nate?"

I make an involuntary noise, a cross between a squeal and a

laugh. "Wow." I shoot Henry a look over one shoulder, then reach for a spoon to stir the noodles. "Straight to the point."

"Well, if I only get one question."

I turn to him. "I thought we were just going back and forth until one of us refuses to answer."

Henry studies me, the ghost of a smile on his lips. "If that's how you want to play."

"It is."

He nods, then waves a hand at me, giving me the floor.

"We met in college," I say straight into the pasta pot. The last thing I want to think about is Nate, but if this is the *one* thing Henry most wants to know about me—well. "We were just kids."

"Not by the end."

"No," I say, meeting his eyes. I wonder, not for the first time, how much older Henry is than Nate and me.

"And you just hit it off, or . . . ?"

"One question at a time, sir."

"I don't think you finished answering my first one."

"I did," I say, smiling sweetly. "We wound up together after meeting in college."

Henry makes a sound in his throat, a frustrated sort of growl that I feel in my stomach.

"How old are you?" I say into the pot, steam rising to heat my cheeks.

"Thirty-four." He takes a sip of wine and adds, "But I have it on good authority that I have a baby face."

"*No,*" I groan, holding up the pot lid and hiding behind it. *I like your baby face.* I peek at him over the top of it. "You remember that?"

He smiles, but it isn't smug. It's delighted. He's unreasonably, unforgivably handsome. "Do you?"

"Yes," I admit, my cheeks burning. "But I was hoping you didn't."

Henry runs a hand along his jaw. I remember what it felt like: Soft. Hard line of bone. "I've been shaving since, haven't I?"

It lands like an ice cube at the back of my throat—an irrepressible jolt. I whirl toward the pasta pot, fighting to swallow my smile.

From behind me, Henry says, "Do you think I'm old?"

When I look back at him, glass of wine poised halfway to his mouth, I nearly laugh: he's so beautiful, framed in the window, lit orange by the lowering sun. "Is that your question?"

"Yes," he says, smiling.

"No." I reach for my own glass of wine, taking a drink that warms me all the way down. "I don't think you're old, Henry. Besides, maybe I'm thirty-four, too."

"You aren't thirty-four," he says, and I raise my eyebrows. "I have your birthday from the original rental agreement."

I study him. "And you just . . . remembered it?"

He shrugs, completely unembarrassed. "Maybe."

I laugh, and it goes high-pitched before I can help it. "Okay."

"Why'd you stay in Colorado after school if your family's so far away?"

My family. I know he means Goldie and Quinn, not my mother, who's still in Ohio. It's a loaded question, one with so many facets I could spend the rest of the night answering it. I let out a slow breath of air, turning from the stove to face Henry.

"That one's got a *really* long answer," I tell him.

Henry shifts his weight against the counter. Doesn't look away from me. "I have time."

By eight o'clock we've had bowls of mac and cheese with Quinn, watched two episodes of a show about an animated dog, and poured third glasses of wine. When I come back downstairs from putting Quinn to bed, Henry's still on the couch. For a moment I stand in the hallway taking him in: his silver-threaded hair in the lamplight, one hand curved around his wineglass, the dark lines of his legs stretched out over the rug. He looks exactly right in this room: like all my decorating, all these years, was to make him make sense here.

Something aches, painful and good, in the pit of my stomach. Nate's energy was a lit fuse in this house, crackling and then gone. Henry, here, is different: quiet and enormous. Henry, here, makes this house feel more like mine.

"Are you stalling because you know it's my turn?" He looks at me over the curve of his arm, stretched along the back of the couch. I imagine the night coursing ahead of us—the momentum of it, how inevitable Henry seems, the way I feel the hitch of his lips like an ab cramp. Wringing me out.

"Yes," I say on a smile, and he breathes a laugh.

"I'll be nice."

I answered his question about Colorado as carefully as I could: I stayed for Nate, in some ways. For grad school. For a life I'd built away from a complicated relationship with my family. And for this house—for the home it had become to me. Henry fell quiet at that. And at my question, *What are you thinking right now?* he'd said simply, *That I'm glad it was you who moved in.*

I wanted to ask him why. I wanted to hear him say it. But then Quinn was up from his nap, and now it's Henry's turn.

"What did your sister mean?" he asks as I sit down beside him. I leave a foot of space between us on the couch, the size of Quinn's body. This was easier when he was here between us, setting the guardrail. "In the kitchen, about postponing your career?"

I level Henry with my gaze. He says, "What?"

"You said you were going to be *nice*."

"You can forfeit." His fingertips on the couch are centimeters away from my shoulder. "End the game."

But there's more I want to know—all of it, everything about him—and when I bring my eyes back to Henry's, I know that he can tell. That there's hunger in both of us.

"I'm no quitter," I say, and when he laughs the movement of it brings his fingers to the back of my neck. My skin blooms with goose bumps, sending a chill through my spine that goes hot as it reaches my core. "Though that's exactly what Goldie thinks I am, and why she said what she said today."

He's quiet, waiting for me to explain. His fingertips move so gently above the collar of my shirt that I could be imagining it. I can't tell him about the test—can't tell him about my failure, or the half-truths I've told to make the Comeback Inn what it is. But I don't lie. I say, "She wanted me to start working as a therapist the moment I graduated, and because I didn't, I'm a failure in her book. Goldie had a plan for me, and this wasn't it."

"But you're doing that work here," he says. I wish it were true: that I was licensed, that I could legitimize the inn the way he thinks I can. "That's not good enough for her?"

"Uh-uh," I say, holding up my hand. "My turn to ask a question."

Henry lets out a frustrated breath through his nose. "Fine."

"At Polliwog's that day," I say, riding a wild surge of courage. "When I—got lost."

Henry holds my eyes, steady and careful, like he knows what's coming.

"You said you understood." Henry's fingers on my neck go still, but don't move away. I focus on the warmth, the solid pressure of his skin on mine. "How?"

Henry licks his lower lip. Pulls it into his mouth. When he presses his lips together and looks across the room, I think I've done it: forced his forfeit, pushed us to the end of the line. But then Henry puts his wineglass on the coffee table and turns back to look at me, his eyes dark, and says, "Can I show you something?"

Twenty-One

I feel like I've spent weeks watching Henry move through this house: guarded, careful, each footstep chosen with weighted consideration. I've watched him check things with me—a flick of his eyes over mine before he opens a cabinet or steps through a door—asking permission. I've watched him hesitate to take up space here. Watched him so thoughtfully make sure this house feels like mine.

But when Henry leads me up the stairs, he does it like a man in his own home. Someone who knows where to walk so the fourth step doesn't creak, who navigates the narrow landing without flicking on the hallway light.

"Is anyone staying in that bedroom?" He points down the hall to the Lupine Room. It's the smallest of the guest rooms, and the only one facing the street. When I shake my head, Henry leads me toward it.

He twists the doorknob on a steadying breath. Like he's bracing, though this is Henry—who I've only ever seen solid and sure. When I place a hand on his back, warm ridge of muscle under soft flannel, he jumps.

"Sorry," I whisper, dropping my hand. "Sorry, I didn't—"

His eyes track over mine, back and forth. In the dark of the Lupine Room, we could be anywhere: a movie theater, the middle of the woods, outer space.

I say, "Are you okay?" and Henry only swallows. He reaches to twist on the bedside lamp, which casts the room in a low, warm glow. There's a twin-size bed against the wall, white iron frame and sage-green duvet dotted in embroidered daisies. Three scatter rugs layered in the middle of the room. A small desk below the front window, stack of books in its corner.

And Henry, who's taking it in like a painting. Like the longer he looks, the more there is to see. When he pushes the bedroom door softly closed behind us, heat rises to my neck.

"It's here," Henry says, lowering to a squat on the floor. I don't know what *it* is; if *here* is the bedroom or the house or the insulated cocoon that seems to be unfurling around us, warm and soft and dark. "Just—" He breaks off when I crouch beside him on the hardwood. With one look at me, he reaches for the baseboard next to the door and gently pries at the edge of the wallpaper. It was here when Nate and I moved in: cream with a pale green pine needle motif, so delicate that if you let your eyes unfocus it loses all its shape. I watch Henry peel it back, gently, one centimeter at a time. "Sorry," he says, though I'm unsure whether he's apologizing to me or the house. "There."

He drops his hands to his legs, fingers hanging into the space between his thighs. I look at the wall, at his guarded face, back at the wall. He's exposed a sticky-note-sized window into the world beneath the pine wallpaper. In the dim light, it takes me a moment to clock the pattern for what it is: a child's sky, perfect blue, dotted with fluffy clouds and a plump bird and the colorful edge of a hot-air balloon.

"She died when she was three," Henry says. In the silence after his words, a high whine. The alarm of myself: *Oh my god, oh my god, oh my god.* When Henry looks up at me, his eyes are dark and anguished. Here it is, finally—his heartbreak. "Six years ago."

"Henry—"

"We picked this room because of the window." His voice rises an octave, and I understand that he isn't ready for—or doesn't want—my sympathy. "Because Bill and Martina across the street got Custard when she was just a baby—even then, he had paws the size of Molly's face." *Molly.* "She was desperate for a dog. She'd sit on the desk just waiting to see Custard in the yard. My ex-wife was allergic, or we'd have gotten her one; every sick kid should have a dog." He takes a breath. "Custard's nine, and Molly would've been, too, and I see it all the time, but if that dog dies, Louisa, I can't—"

Henry breaks off and it all blends: *Molly, ex-wife, every sick kid.* Custard, here then and now. I have so many questions, but more than anything there's Henry: inches away from me on the floor of his dead daughter's bedroom. The rise and fall of his chest. The way he looks at me now—like he's handed me a grenade, and we're both waiting to see if I'll pull the pin.

"Henry," I say, and he blinks. So slowly he could be falling asleep, turning back time, erasing all this. His eyelashes send shadows over his cheeks. "I hate that you went through that. I'm so sorry."

It's not enough. Nothing could be; I know that. I want to undo it for him, unlearn everything I know about acceptance, about grief, about the requisite pain—I want to take it away. I want to crawl inside of him and press my hands to the hurt.

But Henry says, "Thank you." And when his eyes open, he's the same Henry. Steady and—the shade I've always seen but never been able to name—sad. "Congenital heart disease. We tried everything. I mean—everything. There was nothing else." He shakes his head, making to stand and drawing me with him. His fingers frame my elbow. "My family—you asked. I just." Henry's always so measured with his words, but now they come out stuttered. Unrehearsed, broken. "I was lonely, growing up. It was just me and our animals, my parents working. I wanted a big family. Kids." He swallows, his voice wavering. I picture him with Custard, that day: the way his whole body changed around that sweet, gentle animal. "And I lost all of it."

I reach for him before I've realized I'm doing it—one palm pressed to the flat plane of his chest, my fingers spread over his heart. One of his hands is still lifted—forgotten, maybe, on my elbow. But when he looks down at my fingers on his chest, he releases my arm and spreads his hand over my own. "And now I have this house," he says, straight down at our fingers, "that I can't bring myself to live in or get rid of." His heartbeat bruises under my fingertips. He looks up at me in the soft dark. "Thank you for taking care of it for me."

"Henry," I whisper. I feel like I haven't drawn a breath since he started talking. Like I'm lightheaded and static, like the lines between our bodies are blurring away. "Of course. Of *course*."

He pulls me out of the room and into his chest in the same breath—one moment we're in the dark of Molly's memories and the next we're in the hallway, door knocking shut behind us, Henry's hand next to my head on the wallpaper. He boxes me in, the warm wall of his body, our hands still pressed to his chest.

"Louisa," Henry says. I have the distant thought that someone could see us, that a door could open. I find myself shamefully unable to care. "You said I seemed scared. I am scared." His eyes—that dangerous, trapping blue—are so close to mine that I feel like I'm breathing him, like Henry's all there is. "You scare me."

"No," I say. My free hand rises to his face, his smooth jawline. "Why?"

He shakes his head like he can't explain it, like this is too much. "You must know how long I've wanted this," he says, instead of answering. "Since my office, in August. All those printouts you brought." His eyes hold mine. His hand over my knuckles presses down, grasps me to his chest. When he wets his lower lip, I feel it like the lick of a flame on skin. "The way your nose crinkles when you're trying not to cry. How you yelled at me in the kitchen after the *Denver Post* article. When the power went out. And before." The palm he's braced against the wall slides down, and he releases my hand to frame my hips with both of his own. His voice goes impossibly soft. "Before we met. From the first time I saw you, the day you moved in, and I was so glad that it was you, here." His fingertips flex, ten points of heat pulling me closer. "You didn't remember me, but I couldn't forget you. Not in all this time."

It's too much. It's not nearly enough—I drag his mouth to mine and his lips part, warm warm warm and ravenous, searching, his fingers kneading the base of my spine like this close isn't close enough. Our breath comes fast and ragged, my hands unbuttoning his flannel, the heat of his chest under my palms, all of it melting until I've gone tingly, let go, unrooted.

Henry's hands side lower and lower until they're cupping my ass, and when he presses me into him I feel the hardness beneath his jeans, meeting the seam between my legs in a way that sends heat all the way up to my lungs. When I move against him Henry groans, the sound wrenching from his throat. It makes me think of dropping the espresso machine on his knee, of every moment he's been in this house with me. Of how much more I want.

I slide my hands up his chest, his neck, his jaw. Push the pad of my thumb into his lower lip until he breaks from me, breathing unevenly, his tongue on my fingertip.

"Stay," I whisper. My eyes flick down the hallway—not to my own room, where Quinn sleeps, but to the empty guest suite near the stairs. "Here." Henry swallows, his gaze casting from my eyes to my mouth and back again. He's unbelievable in the half dark: shirt undone, hair mussed, mouth red and swollen. I find that I'm not above begging. "Please."

His thumbs brush my waist—soft. Agonizing. When I tug his hips into mine, his eyes flutter half-shut and he swallows again, pressing his fingertips into my skin to still me. He holds me like that: his eyes hooded, the heave of his breath against my chest. Like he's deciding, like maybe he's going to say no.

But he doesn't, and when he hikes me up onto his hips it's with a new kind of determination. His mouth on mine is certain and sweltering; from the seat of his forearms I arch my back so our chests press together, winding my legs around his waist and letting him carry me the few steps to the Aspen Room. We tumble through the door with a bang loud enough to wake the whole house; I hush Henry on a breath of laughter as he nudges the door behind us, drops me to my feet, latches the lock into place.

"We'll be quiet," he promises, lips lighting on mine, "we'll be good," as I pull him toward the bed in the dark. His mouth finds the pulse in my neck as he tips me backward, as his body moves over mine—his lips sucking at the sensitive skin until I let out a noise I've never heard myself make before.

"*Shhh*," Henry murmurs, soft in the hollow below my ear. His breath is warm, fanning across my chest. He hooks one of my legs around his waist and uses the other hand to frame the top of my head, dipping his mouth to mine as our hips meet in an exquisite, unbearable way that makes me keen. My spine arches and I hear Henry's breath hitch. His voice is strangled and low when he says, "Hold still, Louisa."

"No," I breathe. I ruck my hands under his shirt, exposing the warm expanse of his back. "I don't want to hold still."

Henry laughs, his lips pulling into a smile that I feel against my neck. He runs his hand along my thigh where it's wrapped around him, digging his fingertips into my jeans as he rocks his hips into mine.

"*Henry*," I gasp, scrabbling at his shoulders, his neck, the sides of his face. He lifts his gaze to mine and then kisses me, our lips still touching when he says, "Not tonight. Not with all these people—"

I use my leg to press him into me and his words dissolve into a low groan.

"Henry," I whisper. His warm hands on my waist, that night in the basement; his fingertips on my pulse when I fell in the woods; his mouth, wet and searching, his tongue dipping into the hollow of my collarbone. I want to know every inch of him, all at once. "We'll be so quiet. So good."

"I don't want to be quiet," Henry says. His shirt is hanging on for dear life, tugged nearly to his wrists. Dark shadows wrap around the dips of his biceps, his elbows, the soft undersides of his forearms. "And I don't want—" I drag his face to mine, and he swallows the words. Molds his fingertips into the ridges along my spine and groans, soft and low, when I scrape his bottom lip with my teeth. "To be good," he murmurs, finally.

Henry rolls himself onto one elbow, his breath coming fast and hard as he looks down at me. "I want more than that."

"More?" I whisper, tracing his lips with my fingers in the dark.

"More," he echoes. Heat has pooled, molten, in my belly. His eyes are clear as the autumn sky, blue even in the lightless bedroom. "All of you."

"Yes," I say, and he dips his chin to press his lips to mine. Once, chaste.

"I don't want the first time to be like this." The words land like whispered breath, raising goose bumps. *The first time.* "Stolen."

He's right; I know he is. But I don't want this to end—I'm desperate for it not to end.

"But you'll stay?" I ask, running my hand along his jaw, down his neck, into the dark hair across his chest.

Henry pulls me toward him, sliding us in unison up the mattress to find the pillows, the edge of the blanket. He pushes hair from my face, runs the pad of one thumb along my eyebrow.

"I'll stay," he says.

But it's two o'clock when I wake up, and Henry's gone. My mouth feels swollen and sore. I'm in my bra and underwear, my jeans and sweater in a hopeless pile on the floor next to the bed. Henry's clothes were beside them, when we fell asleep. Now they're alone.

I get dressed and steal into the hallway as quietly as I can—surely Bea and Kim are back by now, and Nan will be long asleep. The door to the Lupine Room is open a few, dark inches, and my heart surges painfully against my rib cage as I walk toward it—imagining Henry alone, in the dark, in his daughter's bedroom. But it's empty: the lights off, an imprint on the bedspread like someone was sitting there, not so long ago. I turn back around and stare down the length of the hallway. It feels bottomless, the thought of him leaving in the middle of the night.

I check on Quinn—fast asleep, mouth fallen open in the glow of his night-light—before creeping downstairs to find my phone. I left it on the coffee table, and it's still there. I see it as soon as I hit the landing, right where I left it last night before going upstairs. But I don't move toward it. I stand frozen in the foyer, staring at the hunched outline of Henry on the couch.

He's leaned forward, elbows braced on his knees, light from the moon in the garden turning his skin silver-blue. He never put his shirt back on. Every muscle in his back is bunched up, straining, like he's trying not to come out of his body. I watch his breath rise and fall.

"Henry," I whisper, scared to startle him. He lifts his head, turning to look at me over one shoulder, and I move toward him in the darkness. When I put my palm on his back he flinches, and as I lower onto the couch beside him he looks back down at his hands, clenched together between his knees.

"I'm sorry," he says, so soft they're barely words at all.

I smooth my hand over his skin—he's hot, nearly feverish. "What happened?"

Henry only shakes his head. I can tell he's trying to steady his breathing, trying to calm himself down. "It's all right," I say. I run my hand along his spine, slow, at the steady pace I want his inhales. Just like Goldie did for me, in dark midnights just like this one, when we were kids and I was too scared to sleep. "Just breathe."

He nods, and my hand moves, and the clock ticks on the mantel. Henry keeps his head ducked; I can't see his face as he syncs his breath to my fingertips, as his muscles loosen under my palm. Eventually he lets go of his own hands and curls one arm around my leg, bracketing my knee with his fingers.

"I'm sorry," he says again. I run my hand up the back of his neck, into his hair, and he finally looks up at me. The line between his eyebrows is deep and worried. I smooth it with my thumb, taking his face in both of my hands as he turns to me on the couch. I shake my head, brushing my thumbs over his cheekbones.

"Are you all right?"

Henry exhales, blinking so slowly I think he might leave his eyes shut. But he opens them, and they're anguished in the thin, silvery light from the moon.

"I wanted to stay," he whispers. "It's hard for me to stay in this house." He draws a shuddering breath, turning to look at the stairs. "You make me wish that weren't true."

"It's okay." I want to hide him against me; I want to take all of this away. I want my safe place to be safe for him, too. I think of that square of wallpaper upstairs—of how much Henry has given me, and how much more I'm terrified to find that I still want. "I understand."

"I'm sorry." Henry pulls me against him, his bare skin warm as he hooks his chin over my shoulder. Spreads all ten of his fingers over my back. "You have no idea how much—"

"Henry." I pull away, needing him to see me as I say this. "You don't need to be sorry for this."

He swallows, nods, looks back at the staircase. "I didn't want to just leave, but I couldn't stay up there. I didn't want to wake you."

"You could have," I say. His shoulders are rising again, tensing toward his ears. I reach forward and steady them with my hands. "This is okay."

Henry's eyes skate over mine, back and forth. "That night the power went out," he says, his voice soft, "you said you thought I hated you. That was never true, Louisa, it's this house. It's so hard for me to be here—I can't figure out—"

He breaks off and I feel it like the rip of a Band-Aid, the sharp sting of how he's looking at me: like he's desperate to fix something so understandably broken.

"You don't have to figure it out tonight," I tell him. He looks so young, and so scared. "You can go home, and rest, and everything will be okay."

"I'm sorry," he says again. "I want to be better at this."

"Please stop apologizing." It's the wrong thing to do, maybe, but the thing I'm aching to do: I tip forward and frame his jaw, push my lips to his, hold him steady until his mouth opens under mine and his arms wrap around my rib cage.

"This doesn't change anything for me," I whisper, smoothing my thumb one last time between his eyebrows. "I wanted tonight so badly. I still want it so badly."

"Louisa," Henry murmurs, and it sounds like goodbye. I feel the house holding us close. "I've been inside out, with wanting you."

Twenty-Two

I wake up to the doorbell. My face is hot, tingling like I'm on the verge of breaking a sweat. I blink up at the ceiling and register that I'm in the living room, flat-backed on the couch, streak of morning sun searing across my cheek. I swallow, and it dislodges the memory of what happened last night: Henry in his daughter's bedroom, Henry's warm body under my hands, Henry kissing me on the front porch and walking to his car under the silver moon.

I couldn't share a bed with Quinn, after that. Couldn't fall asleep with his little-kid breaths puffing into the space beside me, his small hands reaching for mine. Couldn't fall asleep at all, really. My nervous system spent all night in overdrive—I felt like I'd run a marathon, like I was perched at the ledge of myself, poised to fall. My mind wouldn't quiet. Henry's daughter, Henry's ex-wife, Henry's house full of pain and memories that I've spent years walking past without knowing. *Henry, Henry, Henry.* The lines of his body, so different from Nate's. *I've been inside out, with wanting you.*

The doorbell rings again, and I push myself up on the couch. The clock on the side table says that it's 8:04. Another ring, and I yank my nest of throw blankets aside to hustle to the front door. I'm thinking it's Mei, having forgotten her key. Nan, back from a morning walk holding coffee for both of us and unable to open the door.

But it's an unfamiliar woman, wearing a full face of makeup and a BabyBjörn with a shih tzu inside.

"Uh," I say, and her eyebrows rise. I squint against the sun. "Hi. Good morning."

"I'm Shani?" She poses it like a question. "I'm supposed to be checking in?"

I pull a hand through the mess of my hair and try to regain my composure. I'm wearing an ancient pair of sweatpants and an enormous T-shirt, no bra. I summon a smile. "Hi, I'm so sorry—check-in is at four on weekdays."

"Four," Shani repeats, glancing at her watch. The dog tracks the movement before looking up at me. "There's no way I can get in earlier?"

"I need to prep your room," I tell her. *And take a shower. And feed Quinn. And calm the fuck down.* "But we could do, like, noon? There are some nice coffee shops in town, if you want to grab breakfast?"

"Um—"

"We also, uh—" I force myself to sound more authoritative. "We don't take pets here. I'm so sorry. It's in the rental listing."

Shani blinks at me. Her makeup is immaculate, but I've been around enough sad people lately to clock the red at the corners of her eyes, the evidence of a night spent crying. "You don't—" She breaks off again, looking down at the dog. It looks up at her.

When Shani's lip starts to tremble, my resolve evaporates in a puff of smoke.

"You know what, it's fine." I reach out and rub the dog's head, then draw a deep breath. "If you can make noon work, I can make the dog work—as long as she's potty-trained?"

"Oh, of course he is," Shani says. Her eyes come to mine, shining with tears, and she takes a backward step down the front stairs. "Thank you. I'm sorry. I didn't—I'll come back at noon."

"No need to apologize." I smile again. "We'll see you soon."

"Lou?" Quinn calls from behind me, and I shoot Shani one last wave before shutting the door.

"Hey, bud," I say, a little too loudly. If Goldie knew I was making out with Henry in my underwear instead of cuddling her son all night, she'd assassinate me. "How'd you sleep?"

Quinn's standing halfway down the stairs, holding the railing in one hand and his favorite stuffed octopus in the other. His pajama set—pale yellow printed with gumdrops—has ridden up to expose the round swell of his belly.

"Okay," he says, and when I hold out my arms he comes the rest of the way down the stairs so I can pick him up. He's so soft, everything about him, and when I press a kiss to the top of his head I think of Molly—even smaller than Quinn, and sicker, and gone. Of the slope of Henry's shoulders in the moonlight, the ripple of muscles pulled rigid and frantic along his spine. My eyes burn. "Where'd you go?"

"I was right here," I say thickly. "I couldn't sleep and I came down to the couch so I wouldn't bother you."

"Oh." He's extra delicious when he's sleepy, and when his warm head drops onto my shoulder I feel his entire body melt into mine. "Can we have waffles?"

"Of course," I say, swallowing back the tears. I turn on the TV for Quinn, and kiss him until he wriggles away from me, and head into the kitchen to unwrap a pack of Eggos.

We're eating them on the couch when Bea and Kim come downstairs. It's nearly nine thirty and I've got overnight oatmeal warming in the oven, a farewell breakfast before they head back to Denver.

"Morning," I say, rising from the couch. Quinn waves at them before turning back to his show.

"Hey," Bea says, smiling. "We loved the Italian place last night. Thanks for the rec."

"Of course." I flip on Henry's espresso machine and pull two bowls out of the cabinet. I wonder if he's awake yet. If he ever fell asleep. "What did you order?"

"Shrimp scampi," Kim says, pulling out a seat at the island. "And calamari."

"And penne with vodka sauce," Bea adds. "I fucking love vodka s— Oops." She glances at Quinn, slapping a hand over her mouth. "Sorry."

I wave her off. "He's not listening." The truth is Aunt Lou-Lou is Quinn's one-way ticket to uninterrupted screen time, and he's much more interested in taking advantage of it than in anything Bea has to say.

"*And*," Kim says, drawing out the syllable, "I booked a spot at my climbing gym for tomorrow. By myself." She straightens her shoulders as she says it, sitting up taller.

"Good for you!" I reach across the island and squeeze her arm. "I'm so glad you're doing that."

"Yeah, fuck Peter," Bea says, lowering to a whisper on the *fuck*. In a lot of ways, their dynamic is the same as when they arrived: Bea the angry one, all vengeance and roiling rage; Kim the soft one, folded into her sadness. But now they understand each other, and will—I hope—be better support systems for one another when they leave the house.

Kim rolls her eyes and pushes Bea in the arm. When they dig into the oatmeal, I turn away to start their coffees.

"Before we go," Bea says from behind me, "we wanted to ask you something."

The grinder whirs to life, and I wait until it's finished to look back at them—hoping to all that is holy they aren't about to ask what those noises were in the Aspen Room last night. "Shoot."

Bea glances at Kim, like she's nervous. Like this is a secret. A tiny smile tugs at her lips when she looks back up at me. "Are you Nate Payne's ex-girlfriend?"

The question falls through me like cold water. I should have known that this would happen—of course it would. There was a time when Nate's social feeds were full of me. College, the years after. The shadowy outline of my face backstage at a show, our clasped hands in the garden, my name right there for anyone to see. I should have known this curiosity would follow me.

I clear my throat. It feels jarring, to step back there after last night—my body shuddering backward in time. But it's the truth. "I am."

Kim's mouth drops open. Bea nudges her in the shoulder. "I *told* you."

"We recognized your name," Kim says, spoonful of oatmeal forgotten halfway to her mouth. "But we weren't sure— I mean. But, wow. It's really you."

"Purple Girl," Bea says. It feels exactly like Nate meant it when he wrote the song: like pressing on a bruise. It's disorienting, to think of him now. To hear the echo of his laugh overlaid with the memory of Henry's measured breathing on my couch, the rise and fall of his ribs under my hand.

"Is that why you started this place?" Kim waves around. "The Comeback Inn?"

I swallow so hard it makes a clicking noise. "In a way, yes." They don't need to know that this has been my home for four years, that I can't afford it without Nate, that I started this place so I wouldn't be homeless. I volley up a bid to change the subject. "Did you find it helpful? Any feedback for me?"

Bea and Kim look at each other again. They want to keep talking about Nate, I can feel it. But, blessedly, they let it go.

"It was great," Kim says finally. "Seriously. We're going to recommend it to friends. And, like, maybe come back? Next time we need to get out of Denver for a while."

"Anytime," I tell them, drawing a slow breath to calm my nervous system. It's just Bea and Kim—these girls who've filled my house with snuggled hugs and ragged rage and such understandable, familiar sadness. There's no danger here. "Truly."

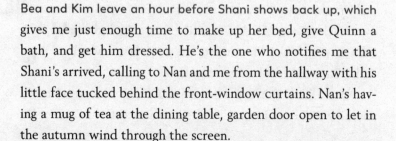

Bea and Kim leave an hour before Shani shows back up, which gives me just enough time to make up her bed, give Quinn a bath, and get him dressed. He's the one who notifies me that Shani's arrived, calling to Nan and me from the hallway with his little face tucked behind the front-window curtains. Nan's having a mug of tea at the dining table, garden door open to let in the autumn wind through the screen.

"That lady's back with her dog!" Quinn shouts, and I put down the bowl I was drying at the sink.

"There's a dog staying here?" Nan asks, peering up at me from above a print copy of *The Denver Post*.

"Yes," I say apologetically. "Kind of by accident. Are you okay with that? I should have asked." It occurs to me that I have more guests arriving while Shani's here and should probably reach out to them, too.

Nan puts down the paper and claps her hands, shoulders hunching up. "Of course!" She stands, shepherding me toward the front door. "The only thing this place has been missing is a dog."

But when I open the front door, the three of us don't get to welcome Shani's dog with open arms. Quinn doesn't get to rub his scruffy little head. Nan doesn't get to coo over his smushed-up, ugly-cute face.

Instead, Shani lets out a hair-raising scream from halfway up the driveway. "Oh my *god*," she cries, scooping the shih tzu off the gravel. "Oh my god, oh my god."

"What?" I call, yanking Quinn up into my arms and hurrying toward her. "What happened?"

"A spider just—he just—" Shani's lifting the dog's face to her own, inspecting every inch of him. "He just tried to eat a spider and then he spit it out and it was *huge*, I mean—" She breaks off, eyes tracking over the driveway like she could find it again. "Oh no. Oh, god, look." She thrusts the dog's face toward my own, and Quinn and I look at him together.

I don't know this dog. His face could look like pretty much anything. But even I can tell that something's off: one side of his mouth is already puffing up like a marshmallow, soft and round and wrong.

"Oh my god," Shani says again, looking around wildly—like there just might be a veterinarian lying around somewhere. "What if he stops breathing?"

"Stops *breathing*?" Quinn repeats, his voice crackling up several pitches.

"Okay," I say, mustering the voice that I use for crisis. For panic attacks. For fresh, uncontrollable grief. "It's going to be okay. I'm going to call a vet."

I hardly have time to think about it before I dial the number. Before it rings once, twice. Before Henry's low, smooth voice meets me on the other end of the line.

"Louisa."

"Henry." I look from Shani to Nan and back again. "I think that spider you saved just attacked someone's dog."

Twenty-Three

"He'll see you right away." Rita stands behind the reception desk and hurries toward us, beelining for the same examination room where I presented Henry with my pitch back in August. We're a sight, I'm sure: Shani, hysterical, cradling her shih tzu (named, I now know, Alfalfa); Quinn, asking questions a mile a minute from the perch of my arms; and Nan, still in her robe, trying to keep everyone calm. As we pass through the lobby, every single person looks up.

The exam room is small: two chairs facing the table. Shani takes one immediately, setting Alfalfa in her lap and watching his face, which seems to swell in size even as she's looking at him. Nan sits next to her, putting one hand on her shoulder and rubbing it in slow circles. Which leaves Quinn and me to stand. I wonder, briefly, if we should even be in here—but then the door opens, and Henry walks through it, and every thought drops directly out of my head.

"I hear someone's been eating questionable snacks," Henry says, motioning for Shani to bring Alfalfa closer. His voice is light, reassuring, warm. Nothing like the shredded whispers against my mouth in the hallway last night: *You scare me. You must know how long I've wanted this.* My hairline prickles with sweat as Shani sets her dog on the exam table.

"I'm Henry Rhodes," Henry says, then nods at the vet tech who followed him into the room—young, closer to my age than Henry's, with a golden retriever smile and thickly muscled arms. "And this is Jorge." Henry's in his white coat, a button-down shirt, his hair carefully combed. The circles under his eyes are faint; you wouldn't know, from looking at him, that he was up all night. I wonder how often this has happened. How much time Henry's spent hiding this part of himself. "He's going to be helping me with Alfalfa."

"It happened so fast," Shani says, her voice high and wavering. "By the time I realized Alfie was going for a spider, he was already spitting it out and shaking his head, and now this."

"That spider didn't want to be eaten, huh?" Henry talks directly to the dog, kind and calm, hands moving from his swollen mouth to his ears to his spine. Like nothing's wrong, like Alfie's face isn't approaching the shape of a basketball. He ducks to look Alfie straight in the eyes, and when his face lights with a smile I feel it in the back of my throat. "We're going to get this sorted out." Henry looks up at Shani, then me. His eyes soften, just a little, as they hold mine. "I'm glad you called."

"Me, too," Shani says tearily.

"Jorge and I are going to take Alfie into the back, if that's okay with you." When Shani nods, Henry scoops the little dog into his arms. *I was lonely*, he'd said. *It was just me and our animals.* This isn't the place for the feelings rising in me like carbonation, for the overwhelming urge to reach for him across the exam table. "We'll get him a Benadryl injection and a steroid to speed it up, plus something for the pain." He lifts Alfie to meet his eyes. "Okay, buddy?" Henry smiles at Shani. "We'll be back soon."

He and Jorge leave the room as quickly as they came, leaving my heart strangling up my windpipe. Shani drops into her chair and sobs.

"Oh, my dear," Nan says. "He's going to be just fine."

"I just can't deal with this on top of everything," she says, hiding her face with both hands. "My ex-girlfriend fought me so hard on keeping Alfie, and it was so stressful, and now I nearly kill him?"

"You didn't nearly kill him," I say, putting Quinn down and taking his hand. I walk over to Shani and Nan, leaning against the exam table so I can face them. "It was an accident completely beyond your control. And he's going to be just fine, okay?"

Shani nods wordlessly, her ribs shuddering with silent sobs. Quinn tugs at my sweatshirt. "Lou-Lou, I need to go to the bathroom."

"Okay." I squeeze his hand, looking at Nan. "We'll be right back."

She nods, one hand still on Shani's shoulder. Quinn and I navigate our way through the lobby to the bathroom, where I boost him up onto the toilet and lift him to wash his hands. The walls are covered in client photos: dogs and cats and an enormous rabbit and even a lizard. I imagine Henry listening to a lizard's heartbeat—his huge hands, its tiny body—and feel it like a stomachache.

"Is Alfie gonna die?" Quinn asks, carefully sudsing up his hands as I hold him up to the pedestal sink.

"No," I say, meeting my own eyes in the mirror. I lower Quinn to the ground and reach for a paper towel. "He's going to be just fine."

Quinn watches me dry his hands. When I toss the towel into the trash, I take them in my own, crouched in front of him. "Are you okay?"

Quinn nods. He has Goldie's eyes—the palest, softest blue. It's like staring at my sister. "Just scared," he says, and I think of Henry in the park. Of Henry last night, how afraid he looked. I pull Quinn into a hug and he wraps his arms around my ribs.

"I know," I say, kissing the top of his head. "That was scary, but everything's going to be okay."

"'Cause Henry's gonna save him," Quinn says, muffled against my shirt.

I draw a deep breath, let it out. "That's right."

It takes thirty minutes for them to bring Alfie back to us. Shani lets out a sob of relief when Jorge carries him into the room, de-puffed and much more normal looking. There's a felt daisy tied to his collar, and I think of that very first day I met Henry, back in August: the giant Bernese mountain dog who greeted me here, the pink lily on its collar.

"He's all right," Jorge says, smiling, as he hands him off to Shani. They brought us another chair from the waiting room, and Quinn's hunched up in my lap playing games on my phone. "Feeling much better now."

"Pretty scary allergic reaction," Henry says, following Jorge inside and closing the door behind them. "But that's all it was." He pulls over a rolling stool and adjusts his slacks to sit down. I imagine crawling onto his lap and have to close my eyes to make the picture go away. "His swelling's gone down really nicely, airway's clear. I'm not concerned about another flare-up, but if he starts to swell again, or you notice any reddening of his skin or difficulty breathing, definitely call us." Henry glances at me, then back at Shani. "You're staying at the Comeback Inn?"

Shani nods, running a hand over Alfie's head. He looks pretty zonked, eyes half-closed, tongue poking between his lips. The daisy makes for starkly cheerful contrast.

"Okay, I'm going to send you home with some Gabapentin in case you notice any signs of residual pain, like drooling or restlessness. And if you're seeing that swelling or redness again, you can always start by giving him a Benadryl at home. Half a pill in some peanut butter usually goes down fine for these guys." Henry folds his hands between his legs, fingers lacing together. "Any questions for me?"

Shani shakes her head, pressing a kiss to Alfie's head. She looks up at Henry through red-rimmed eyes. "No. Thank you so much."

"Of course." He smiles and stands. "Jorge will walk you up to the front and they'll give you those medications at checkout." All of us stand, Jorge opening the door and guiding Shani through.

"Louisa," Henry says from behind us. I turn, Quinn on my hip. "Can I talk to you for a moment?"

I glance down at Quinn, who's completely absorbed in my phone, and back at Henry. "Um." *Yes*, my body says. *Yes*, from the tug in my belly, the heat in my throat. "Nan?"

She stops in the doorway, looking back at us. "Would you mind taking Quinn for just one minute? I'll be right out."

"Of course." She smiles, and when I put him down I slide my hand over the phone screen so he'll look up at me.

"Is it okay if you go to the lobby with Nan while I talk to Henry really quick?"

Quinn looks up at Nan, who reaches for his hand. He takes it before looking back at me, his other hand still clenched around my phone. "Okay," he says, and I smooth my fingers over his hair. Quinn looks up at Henry. "Are you gonna come over again?"

Henry looks at me, then back at Quinn. "Would you like me to?"

"Yeah," Quinn says. "Me and Lou-Lou are doing tattoos this weekend if you want one."

I bite my lip, and Henry tracks the movement before saying, "Tattoos?"

"Temporary," I say. I picked out three packs weeks before Quinn and Goldie arrived: dinosaurs, the solar system, animals. "It's kind of our tradition, the day he leaves."

"My mom hates them," Quinn says, so matter-of-factly that Henry laughs. Even here, in this sterile room, the sound of it does something to me—an ache in my stomach I can't breathe out.

"Well, in that case." He smiles at Quinn before looking at me. "If your aunt is okay with it."

"I'm okay with it," I say, holding Henry's gaze.

"Come on, Quinn," Nan says. She leads him through the doorway, glancing back at me with a conspiratorial look. "Let's let Lou talk to Henry."

The door falls shut behind them, and I tip backward to lean against it. For a moment, neither of us moves. Henry's standing in front of an environmental allergens poster, hands loose at his sides. The air in here feels absolutely still, like it's waiting for us.

"Hi," I say.

His voice is soft. "Hi."

I brush at my neck. "The flowers are a nice touch. On the collars."

Henry's eyes flick to the door behind me, like he's trying to remember anything that happened before it was just the two of us in this room. "Oh," he says. "Yeah—they, um. They make them for me at the senior center. People like them."

A self-conscious flush rises to his cheeks. I want to touch him there. Instead I ask, "How are you feeling?"

Henry swallows. I watch his throat move and imagine it under my mouth. "Better." He takes a step toward me, then draws a breath. "Embarrassed."

"No," I say. The truth is I knew I wanted Henry—it's become an indisputable fact in my body, the way everything inside of me turns toward him like the point on a compass. But last night— his loosening muscles under my palm, his breath steadying in rhythm with the movement of my fingers—it deepened everything. It opened him up to me in a way I can't get out from under my skin. "Please don't be."

He takes another step toward me. "Thank you. And I'm sorry."

"If you apologize to me one more time, I *swear*."

His lips twitch. I want to touch his mouth. "You swear what?"

"I'll tell everyone who works for you that you identify as a delectable chocolate brownie of a man."

Henry laughs, a soft sound. He's still embarrassed; I can see it in the set of his shoulders, the creases at the corners of his eyes. "Louisa, last night—"

He steps closer. Stops a foot away, near enough that either one of us could reach out.

"I put a lot on you." He swallows again, his eyes flickering from me to the wall next to me—like he can't quite hold himself steady. "I told you this really heavy thing, and you were just trying to comfort me, and I worry that I made you feel obligated to—" He breaks off, eyes tracking over mine. "To do more."

Henry looms over me, all dark brows and thick lashes and eyes creased in concern. He's so, so beautiful. I want to reach forward and touch every single part of him.

"Obligated," I repeat.

He nods, both hands sliding into the pockets of his white coat.

"Sort of like how you felt obligated to stay when the power came back on, that night." I lean forward off the wall, inching into his space. I hear his breath catch, nearly soundless. "Or how you felt obligated to come hiking with us." I tip my chin upward, making our eyes as level as I can get them. "Obligated to lie and say you like ice cream."

Henry's lips press together, fighting a smile. "I take your point," he says quietly.

"Good." I brush one hand over the buttons of his coat, curling my fingers into his lapel. His lungs expand, rising to meet them. "Thank you for telling me about Molly."

One of Henry's hands pulls out of his pocket to hold my waist.

"You didn't *make* me feel anything," I tell him, angling my chin upward. "Except—"

"Except?" he urges softly.

"Except," I repeat, and then I pull him into me. His mouth opens under mine, wet heat and soft lips and the bite of his fingertips at my hip to hold me steady. Henry's other hand comes to my throat, his thumb tracking the line of my jaw and tipping it upward to deepen the kiss. He presses me against the door, one leg sliding between my own. I take his bottom lip between my teeth and he groans.

My head tips back, thunking against the door, and I wince.

"Ow," Henry breathes. He lifts a hand to cradle my skull, putting his fingers between me and the door. His eyes track back and forth over mine. "Louisa."

"Henry." I have my hands under his coat, wrapped around his ribs over the thin fabric of his dress shirt.

"I know it hasn't been that long." His thumb is hooked under my sweatshirt, brushing the sensitive skin above my hip bone. "Since Nate."

I press my eyes shut. Nate is the last thing I want to think about right now—especially after that conversation with Bea and Kim this morning. When I open them again, Henry hasn't looked away—he's still watching me, patient and close. "Are you sure this is okay?"

It's more than okay, I could tell him. *I want every part of you that you're willing to give me.*

"Are you?" I say instead. "You mentioned an ex-wife last night."

Henry's eyes move over mine. "Years ago," he says. "It ended right after Molly. She's long gone."

I want to know more—I want to know everything—but I don't press him. "Things with Nate were over for a long time before they ended." I reach up and draw a thumb between Henry's eyebrows, smoothing the line that's formed there. "Please don't think about him."

"I don't think about him," Henry says, dipping his chin. He pushes his lips to mine, soft and sweet and lasting. "I can hardly think about anything, anymore, that isn't you."

Twenty-Four

Mei opens the front door before we've even gotten out of the car—Shani and Alfie, Nan, me carrying a sleeping Quinn.

"There you are!" she calls. She's in sweats and a cropped T-shirt, wet hair brushing her shoulders. "I've been texting—I came home and everyone was just gone."

"It's been quite the afternoon," Nan says, patting Mei's arm as she passes her in the doorframe. "I think our young friend Quinn has the right idea—I'm headed up for a nap."

"I'm sorry," I say, hefting Quinn up the front steps. His head lolls against my shoulder. "Shani's dog got bit by a spider and we had to take him to see Henry, and Quinn's been on my phone the whole time." I gesture back at Shani, who's carrying Alfie. "This is Shani, who's checking in today and already got way more than she bargained for. Shani, Mei—my best friend."

"Hey," Mei says, reaching out to pet Alfie's head. "So sorry you went through that."

"Thanks," Shani says. She still looks a little shaky. "I'm just so glad Louisa was here—she knew exactly what to do."

"Yeah." Mei smiles at me. "She usually does."

"Let me put Quinn down," I say as all three of us cross the threshold. "And then I'll show you to your room, Shani, okay?"

She nods, and I get Quinn tucked into my bed. He melts willingly into the mattress, rolling onto one side, burrowing his head into the pillows. Then I show Shani up the stairs and into the Spruce Room. It takes all of my willpower not to stare at the door of the Lupine Room as we pass. Molly's room—stamped with the memory of Henry tugging me through the door, his body framing mine, his hands on the bare skin of my back.

"Sounds like I missed a big day," Mei says as I come down the stairs. She's filling a glass of water from the fridge and I widen my eyes at her, shaking my head. She doesn't know the half of it.

"Nuts," I say. "I'm so glad her dog's okay—can you imagine? 'Heartbreak Retreat Kills Beloved Dog.'"

"I mean, it wouldn't have been your fault," Mei says. "But yes."

I drag a hand through my hair. "How are *you*? How was your night?"

"It was good." Mei smiles softly. She tips her head toward the back door. "Want to chat on the porch?"

I follow her outside, dropping onto the couch on the back deck. The sun's still high in the sky; it bakes honey-yellow over the garden. I'll tell Mei about Henry, I'll have to—the secret is already fizzing in me, frenzied, desperate to be free.

"We went to RiNo and bopped around and it was honestly, just—" Mei looks at me, letting out a breath and dropping her shoulders. "Nice. To have fun, and forget about things, and be back home and not have it feel terrible."

I nudge her knee with mine. "I'm so glad. I told you it would be good."

"Yes, yes." She waves her hand. "You're always right. But, look, it did really get me thinking."

I raise my eyebrows, and she says, "I should probably think about going back. You know, for good."

"Really?" I try not to let my voice betray my disappointment. Just a couple days ago, she told Goldie she wasn't ready to leave. I want Mei to feel better—of course I do. But I don't want to lose her, either.

"Yeah," she says on an inhale. "It's been so good to be here and spend all day with you and just, like, disconnect from the life I had with Andy. But it's still *my* life, too. Last night reminded me Denver wasn't just Andy—there's a lot of other things I love there. I can't keep hiding."

"You haven't been hiding," I say. "You've been healing."

Mei tilts her head back and forth. "If I'm honest with myself, I think it's been both." She reaches for my hand, sensing without me having to say anything that this news is hard. "I'm so glad I could be here for this, Lou. You're making something really special here." She squeezes my fingers. "And I'm only ever an hour away if you need me."

"I know," I say quietly. I squeeze her hand back. "I'm going to miss you, but I'm really glad you're feeling ready for this."

Mei tips forward and bumps her forehead against mine. When she leans back again, she says, "Thank you."

"When will you go?"

"The weekend, maybe." My heart drops. "So I can get back to work in the office on Monday."

"Okay," I say, forcing a smile. I know she can see how fake it is, and she pulls me into a hug.

"You got this, Lou," Mei says over my shoulder. And then, something that's never been true: "You don't need me."

Mei leaves on Sunday morning, with lots of hugs for me and even more for Quinn. Watching her go feels like being halfway up a rock wall and unclipping my carabiner. I'm not done here, and now I'm left to make the rest of the climb without my support system. Quinn and I stand in the doorway and watch her car roll down the driveway. It's been parked out front since I started the Comeback Inn, and the street feels empty without it.

"Don't be sad, Lou-Lou," Quinn says. He wraps an arm around my leg, hugging it sideways. "We're doing tattoos today, remember?"

"Yeah," I say, ruffling a hand through his hair. I ended up not telling Mei about Henry—it didn't feel important, after our conversation on the back porch. But he'll be here in under an hour. "How could I forget?"

It's quiet in the house; I don't have anyone else checking in for another couple of days, and Shani's mostly kept to herself since Alfie's accident. Nan spends a lot of time reading in her room, or going on walks downtown. So as Quinn and I set up for tattoos in the kitchen, we play his favorite Disney music and pretty much feel like we have the house to ourselves.

Henry rings the doorbell when he arrives, and Quinn goes

running. I have bowls of water and clean towels set out on the counter. I reach to straighten the stack of tattoo sheets, feeling a great wave rise in me: tingling, enormous, threatening to swallow me whole. *Henry, Henry, Henry.*

"Hey, Quinn." His voice carries down the hallway, and when I look up he's crouched in front of my nephew with his elbows propped on his knees. Henry's in jeans and a dark gray T-shirt. His eyes find mine, and it tugs deep in my belly. "Do you have any tattoos yet?"

"No, we waited for you!" Quinn says, reaching out to rest his hands on Henry's shoulders. Kids are amazing—the way they accept intimacy. It's a testament to Goldie's parenting, I know, that the world feels so safe to her son. "How many are you gonna get?"

Henry stands, putting a hand on Quinn's head as they turn toward me. "How many are *you* going to get?"

"*Twenty!*" he cries, then giggles hysterically.

"I don't know about that," I say. Henry lifts Quinn into one of the island stools like he's done it a hundred times before—like Molly used to sit here, maybe, while he made dinner. Then he comes around to me, his hand rising to the small of my back.

"Hi," he says. I want to kiss him, but I know it would open up an entire can of worms with my sister if Quinn saw me do it. So I only say, "Hi," as Henry's thumb brushes the base of my spine.

"Me first!" Quinn says, leaning over the counter to inspect the tattoo sheets. He spreads them out in a fan, considering carefully, before selecting a rocket ship and holding it up to me.

"That one?" I ask, and he nods. "Do you want to pick one for Henry and me, too?"

He ducks back over the counter, finally choosing a pterodactyl for me and what looks like a Komodo dragon for Henry.

"Like the lizard in your bathroom," Quinn says as he hands Henry the sheet. Henry looks between us, eyebrows quirked together.

"At your office," I explain. "We saw all the photos of your clients in the bathroom—there was a lizard."

"*Oh*," Henry says, lifting up Quinn's tattoo selections to examine them. "That's Mr. Stink, the skink." Quinn shrieks with delight and Henry grins at him, setting the tattoos back on the counter. "Good choices."

"Now me." Quinn thrusts his arm over the counter, and I peel the backing off the rocket ship to apply it to his bicep. Henry asks him about home while I wet the tattoo with a towel: where he lives (New York City), if he likes school (yes), if he has any pets of his own (not yet but Mom says when I'm 'ponsible enough). It's unstitching something in my heart, listening to them.

I imagine Henry with his daughter, here in this house. Younger and lighter. The way he must have been with her, the way I know him to be: gentle and sturdy and kind. I pull away and Henry takes Quinn's wrist to examine the tattoo through the paper. They crane toward each other over the island, their heads ducked close, Henry talking about space and stars and the vastness of the universe. *So much to explore*, he tells Quinn. *Maybe by someone like you.*

I lean in to blow on the tattoo, and feel Henry turn to look at me. All three of our faces are inches apart, like children telling secrets at a slumber party. He nudges my hip with his. I feel a sadness I can't quite name: holding a grief that isn't mine, that

I didn't know about, that happened in my happiest place. I peel the paper off Quinn's tattoo.

"Me next?" Henry asks, when Quinn flexes his arm in the space between us.

"Yeah," Quinn says, his eyes flicking to me. "Can I do it?"

"Of course," I say, a little too thickly, and pass him the Komodo dragon. Henry looks at me, his eyebrows twitching together. That line there and then gone, the one I already know so well: *I'm worried*.

I shake my head and curl my hand around his thigh below the counter. My feelings about this aren't his to hold, the way it pushes on my ribs to imagine him living through this. We're here, now—I make myself focus in on it.

Henry extends his forearm over the counter so Quinn can reach it. The underside of his arm is smooth, ropy veins racing up to his elbow. The watch at his wrist has a worn leather band and a thin face full of fine Roman numerals.

"How you want it?" Quinn asks, holding the lizard horizontally and then vertically and then at a haphazard angle.

"Whichever way you think looks best," Henry says. He leans more of his weight into the counter and, below the granite where Quinn can't see, I brush my thumb in a slow rhythm against his thigh. Henry doesn't look at me, but I watch the tips of his ears go pink.

"I think like this," Quinn says, placing the tattoo vertically down the length of Henry's forearm.

"Perfect," Henry says, slightly strangled, and Quinn grins.

By the time his nap rolls around, Quinn's arms are covered in no fewer than seven tattoos. Goldie won't like it, but he's beside himself with glee: a T. rex reaching for the rocket ship, a puppy chasing a shooting star. I have a pterodactyl above my elbow and a mouse on my wrist; Henry made it out with only the one.

Quinn gives Henry a double high five and then complains the entire way up the stairs. He doesn't want to sleep, he isn't tired, he wants to hang out with Henry. *Me, too,* I think. But Goldie will be here in a couple of hours, and she'll never let me hear the end of it if I give her a cranky kid.

When I come back down the stairs, Henry's looking out the window over the sink. Joss has been in the garden since this morning, planting a new tree at the back of the yard. I come up behind him, resting my palm over the ridge of his spine, and he turns to look down at me.

"Pretty tree," I say, and Henry says, "Mmm."

His eyes cast over mine and then he dips his chin, kisses me so lightly that my eyelids are still fluttering shut when he pulls away.

"You all right?" Henry asks, his arm looping around my waist.

I nod and lean into him. "You don't have to stay, if it's hard." His eyes flick back and forth over mine, forget-me-not blue in the light from the window. "I can come to you, next time. We can go anywhere else."

"I want to stay," he tells me. Simple, with no hesitation. "It's hardest at night."

I think of Rashad, his sleeplessness. How the dark of nighttime is so ripe for self-loathing and sorrow.

"Okay," I say, and rise onto my toes to kiss him. "I want you to stay, too."

Henry tips me against the counter, framing my waist, and deepens the kiss.

"Not here," I say, before I'm too far gone to stop him. "Shani could come down—or Nan."

"Mm," Henry murmurs against my neck, hot exhale like he's resigning himself. Finally he looks up at me and tips his head toward the counter, still strewn with tattoo sheets. "Can I pick one for you, then?"

"Sure," I say, quietly, and watch Henry sift through the designs. I press my fingertips to my mouth, to the eager tingling of my lips. He bends over, focused, his light eyes flitting back and forth until he finally settles: a cluster of constellations, delicate stars connected by dashed lines.

"Cute," I say, and he smiles.

"Where do you want it?"

I bite my bottom lip, and Henry reaches out to release it from my teeth. We stand like that, the pad of his thumb pressed to my mouth, until that single point of contact feels inhumanly warm—until I feel like I might evaporate if I can't have more of him.

"Come with me." I take Henry's hand and his fingers thread through mine, hard knots of his knuckles under my fingertips. When I lead him into the first-floor bathroom and close the door, his eyes go dark.

"Okay," he says, so quietly I hardly hear it. "Where do you want it?"

I'm leaned against the counter, Henry facing me. It's a small space—white and black subway tiles, gold mirror, warmly glowing torchère lights. With no room for us to move around each other, he feels more inevitable than ever. It makes me feel numb, my brain hazing out.

I reach for the button of my jeans and undo it, sliding the

zipper down until I can pull aside the fabric and show him my hip bone, the sensitive strip of skin just inward from my pelvis. Henry tracks my movements without blinking. He has the tattoo in one hand and a damp towel in the other. When I rest my hands behind me on the counter, leaning backward to give him access, he swallows.

His eyes flick up to mine and then he lowers to his knees in front of me. He nudges my legs apart. When I brush the hair back from his forehead, he says, "Hold still."

I bite my lip, barely breathing as Henry presses the tattoo to my hip. He's gentle: dabbing the towel over the contact paper, carefully wetting the edges until it sticks to my skin on its own. He drops the towel on the floor behind him and wraps his fingers around my ankle, sliding his hand all the way up my leg before reaching for one edge of the paper and peeling it back. My skin burns—under the fabric of my jeans, where his fingers were; around the edges of the tattoo, where they are now; at the tops of my cheeks, when his eyes come up to mine.

"Beautiful," Henry says, pulling the last edge of the paper away. The constellation spreads from my hip bone to my belly button. I watch him drop the paper and then lean in, hands coming to bracket my thighs, as he blows cool air over the tattoo. His lips are centimeters from my skin. His breath tickles. If it weren't for his hands on my legs, I'd float away entirely.

I close my eyes, and his mouth lands on my stomach. My sharp intake of breath makes him look up, his eyes dark and liquid, and when he says, "Is this okay?" it takes every single one of my faculties to muster a breathless, "Yes." Henry kisses my hip bone, my belly button, the swell of my stomach, the laced edge of my underwear. When his fingers find the waistband of my jeans, I tilt my hips so he can pull them down to my feet. He slides them over my heels and across the room, running his hands up the bare length of my legs, wrapping his fingers around my waist and lifting me so I'm sitting on the edge of the counter.

I tilt backward into the mirror and hiss at the cold. I'm wearing a tank top—easiest for tattoo access—and the glass is freezing between my shoulder blades. Henry pulls his T-shirt over his head in one fluid movement and reaches around me to wrap it over my shoulders. I press my palms to his chest, smooth them up to his collarbone and his jaw. When I pull him in to kiss me it's quick and wet and then he's gone, stamping his mouth to the corner of my lips, to my pulse point, to the top of my shoulder.

He kisses the tattoo and then his lips land between my legs, tongue pressing to the heat of me. I gasp, bucking forward, and thrust a hand into his hair. He kisses the fold of my hip, the inside of my thigh. When he rolls his cheek onto my leg, looking up at me from his knees, I tighten my hand in his hair.

"Can I take these off?" he whispers, one finger hooked through the waistband of my underwear. I nod—I have no words now. Not as he pulls my underwear over my knees, not as he tosses them behind him, not as he presses the flat of his tongue against me.

My head tilts back into the mirror. Henry's hands are warm and rough—wrapped around my thighs, then my ass. Tilting me into him, kneading my skin. With my knees hooked over his bare shoulders he's the only thing keeping me steady. I could slip away; I could disappear; I could drown in this.

When he takes me over the edge my mouth drops open, eyes pressed shut, a broken gasp that's much too loud for the guests upstairs. Henry presses one last kiss between my legs. Then my thigh, my hip bone, the bottom edge of my ribs. He stands, finally. Wraps his arms around my back—I'm sacked out, slumped into the mirror. He wipes the back of one wrist over his lips and then kisses me, careful and slow and torturous.

"Henry," I breathe, and I feel him smile against my mouth.

"Louisa," he says, kissing the corner of my lips, the crest of my cheekbone.

"Let me," I whisper. I drag my hands from his chest to his stomach, over the soft trail of dark hair I noticed that day with Henry spread flat on his back in my shower. My fingertips dip below the waistband of his jeans and he tenses, arms stiffening where they're pressed into the counter on either side of me.

I undo the button and push them down, Henry leaning backward to give me space. When I touch him through the thin fabric of his boxers he flexes into my hand, his forehead dropping to my shoulder. A gust of breath rushes over my chest.

"You don't have to," he says, and I wrap my fingers around him.

"I want to."

And I do. When I slide a hand into Henry's boxers, he's warm and wanting. He groans as my fingers close around him—a soft noise that I could spend the rest of my life listening to. He leans his weight into me as I start to move, like he's weak. Like this takes everything from him. I could get drunk off of it—Henry, vulnerable in my hands, his head on my shoulder and his eyes pressed shut and his breath hot in the space between us. I could stay here forever. I want to.

But then the doorbell rings.

Twenty-Five

"Fuck."

Henry jerks upward, bleary-eyed and flushed. He blinks before stepping backward, my hands sliding out of his boxers.

"She's early," I say, scooting off the counter. When my feet hit the ground I'm immediately in Henry's space, all but pressed against his bare chest. In the stark rush of my adrenaline I see him more clearly than I could before—there's a pink scar running the length of his sternum. "Goldie." I look up at Henry, and he swallows. "I'm so sorry."

"It's okay." Henry drags a hand through his hair, finger-combing it back into some semblance of order. "Let me just—get dressed."

I shuffle around him to find my underwear, yanking it on so quickly it gets completely twisted, and reach for my discarded jeans as the doorbell rings again. She's going to wake Quinn. She's going to make Nan and Shani come downstairs. I imagine all three of them seeing Henry and me emerge from the bathroom together and say, "Could you go out the back door?" before I've even thought it through.

Henry stills, hands on the button of his jeans. Then he looks away from me, finishes buttoning them, and says, "Sure."

I know I've fucked up right away, but there just isn't time. I'm feeling so many things at once—panic, shame, guilt, desire—that I'm nauseous. "It's just, Goldie's so nosy, and she's going to lay into me, I just—" I pull the door open, casting one look back at him. "Thank you."

"Of course," he says again, softly. I want to kiss him again. I want to take his clothes off, really—I want to put my palm against the heat of his flushed face and slide his pants back down and finish what we started. But the doorbell rings again, and I squeak out an unforgivably awkward, "Okay, bye," and make for the hallway. Just before I open the front door, I hear the back one whine shut behind Henry.

My sister stands on the front porch in a blazer, black leather tote bag hiked over one shoulder.

"You didn't have to ring three times," I say. "Quinn's asleep."

Goldie narrows her eyes. "Why are you so red?"

I lift the back of one hand to my face, feel the heat of my skin. "I was, um. Cleaning."

She studies me for another beat before saying, "Okay," and stepping past me into the house.

"How was the conference?"

"Fine," she says, dropping her bag to the floor. "How did Quinn do?"

"Perfect angel," I say. "He tripped at the park and has a few little scrapes on his palms, but I've been disinfecting them and he doesn't even—"

"Why didn't you tell me?"

I blink at her. My brain is still whirring at warp speed: *Henry,*

Henry's mouth, Henry in my hands. Goldie at the door. The doorbell. "Because he was fine? I didn't want to worry you. I handled it."

She lets out a short punch of an exhale. "I'd have liked a heads-up. He's my kid." She starts toward the kitchen. "Can I have some water?"

"Yes—" I follow her, catching up. "I know he's your kid."

"What's all this?" she asks, pointing to the mess of tattoo supplies on the counter before reaching into the cabinet for a glass.

"Temporary tattoos," I say, trying to think of Quinn's rocket ship instead of the constellation on my stomach.

Goldie groans, leaning against the counter next to the fridge and taking a long sip of water. "How many did you give him?"

I press my lips together. "A handful."

"Great," she mutters. No *Thank you for watching my son.* No *How was your weekend?* I feel myself stiffen.

"When's your flight?"

Goldie glances at her watch. "Four hours. So I should probably get him up and start heading to the airport."

"Great." I start gathering the tattoo supplies. I love my sister, but right now I just want her gone.

"We didn't get to finish our conversation about the Comeback Inn."

"Guess you'll have to call me when you get home to finish chewing me out."

She lets out an exasperated sigh, like I'm a child getting on her last nerve. "I'm not trying to chew you out, Lou. I'm trying to look out for you."

"Are you?" I turn, stack of tattoo papers in one hand. "Because it feels like I have a good thing going here, and you don't care because it's not what you imagined for me."

"Is this what *you* imagined for you?" Goldie counters, taking a step closer to me. "Not getting your license? Not practicing with the degree you spent years working toward?"

Shame bubbles in me, hot and painful. She knows exactly where to press so it hurts the most. "I'm going to practice, eventually. But I'm doing this right now."

"When, though?" Goldie's voice rises an octave.

"December." I didn't mean to tell her—I didn't mean to tell anyone at all. But all I want is to shut her up. "I booked the exam. But right now I'm taking care of this house and the people in it—including your kid, by the way."

Goldie doesn't stop to tell me she's glad I booked it. She doesn't compliment me for taking the step she's been badgering me about for months. She just doubles down, twists the knife. "You do this, Lou. You take care of other people to avoid taking care of yourself. But you need to get *your* life in order."

Silence falls between us. I feel tears burning behind my eyes, but I never cry in front of Goldie if I can help it. Nothing's enough for her, especially not me. "Are you done?" I ask softly.

"Yeah." She throws her hands up. "Great talk, Lou. I'm done."

I turn toward the sink—look out over the garden at Joss's new tree—so I don't have to watch her walk away from me.

"Is everything okay?" Shani comes downstairs a few minutes after Quinn and Goldie leave, Alfie in her arms. "I thought I heard, um . . . yelling."

"I'm so sorry." I'm wiping down the kitchen counter, and pause to look at her as she comes toward me and takes a seat at the island. "My sister came to pick up Quinn and we tend to be . . . loud."

She nods. "I get that. I have three sisters."

I imagine three Goldies in my life and want to scream. "Do you get along?"

Shani smiles, tilts her head back and forth. "Sometimes."

I breathe a laugh. "Yeah." When I reach to pet Alfie's head, he licks my palm. "How's he doing?"

"Seems fine," Shani says, rubbing his chest. "I wanted to thank you, again, for helping us. And letting him stay. I swear I'll write you the most glowing review."

"Well, that's not why I did it," I tell her, sliding one of Alfie's velvety ears between my fingers. "But thank you."

We fall silent for a moment, and then Shani says, "I saw the programs card in my room—with hiking and group discussions and everything? I'm sorry I haven't filled it out yet."

"That's okay," I say, turning to hang my wet towel over the faucet. "This space is for you; you don't have to do anything here unless you want to."

"I do want to. I just—I wasn't sure if all that stuff was on offer if it's just me and Nan here?"

"It's always on offer," I say, smiling. "Even if you're the only one here, you can hike or talk with me. But we have a group checking in soon, so you'll have a bit of overlap then if you're more comfortable with more people around."

Shani nods, glancing toward the living room. I get the distinct impression that she's gathering the courage to say something, and wait until she finds the words.

"I wasn't trying to eavesdrop," she says finally. "I swear. But I heard your sister say that, um . . ." She looks back at me. "You're not licensed?"

Jesus *Christ*, Goldie. Below the counter, I press my fingernails into my palm. "That's true," I say, as evenly as I can. "I've completed my counseling degree but haven't taken my licensing exam yet."

I wait for Shani to react to this. I know how I phrased the Comeback Inn page: my therapy degree, my years of counseling. It's all, technically, true—I have nothing to hide. So why do I feel like a filthy liar?

"Makes sense," Shani says. She rubs Alfie's head. "Why's she so mad about it?"

I exhale—Shani's not bothered. No one else needs to be, either.

"That," I say slowly, "is such a good question."

But still, Goldie's words echo: *You do this, Lou. You take care of other people to avoid taking care of yourself.*

I think of Mei, of my mom, of Henry.

You do this.

Twenty-Six

Willa shows up later that week—Halloween—with five friends in tow. All of them are wearing black tiaras. She made the booking two weeks ago, with a note to confirm that all six of them could fit into my three available rooms. With the extra cot I ordered for the Lupine Room, the answer was yes. But I didn't expect this: music blasting from their rental car, black tutus, black wigs.

"It's an un-bachelorette," Willa says when she greets me at the door. "Jamie broke off the engagement a month before we were supposed to go to Nashville." She yanks a woman forward from the back of the pack, bracing both hands on her shoulders. "This is Lucy, our un-bride." Lucy manages a smile and gives me a helpless shrug. "And I'm maid of dishonor."

"Wow," I say. I'm trying to place the feeling at seeing these six women on my doorstep, gathered around Lucy in her heartbreak. I'm flattered they chose the Comeback Inn. I'm moved they still went on a trip together. "Welcome."

The house has a completely different feeling with the un-bachelorette crew upstairs: louder, more laughter, a significant boost in serotonin. Nan borrows one of their wigs and wears it proudly for the entire afternoon. Shani, on the last night of her stay, plays cards with them in the living room while Alfie snores on her lap.

And Henry doesn't text me back. Not in response to the I'm sorry about that timing. Rain check? I sent right after Goldie left. Not in response to the picture I sent this afternoon of Alfie sitting on my coffee table with a black tutu wrapped around him. And not in response to the Please talk to me I sent an hour ago, growing desperate, aching to see his name pop up on my phone. It's nearly nine o'clock, the sun long lowered. I haven't heard from him since Sunday.

"What's going on over there, Lou?" Nan asks, catching my eyes across the living room. Willa and Lucy are snuggled on the couch, their other friends clustered on the floor around the coffee table. One of them is shuffling a deck of cards, another one refilling wineglasses.

"I'm good," I say, pulling on a smile. I'm not good—I'm balancing on the knife's edge of myself. Nan frowns at me, but the other women are talking so loudly she gets swept up in the tide of their conversation.

"Right," Willa's saying, "but the only thing *worse* than canceling a wedding is being married to someone who doesn't actually deserve you."

"Well said," Nan agrees, glancing back at me.

I clear my throat. "You're right, Willa. Lucy, you dodged a bullet—even if it feels, right now, like you took it straight to the heart."

Lucy gives me a watery smile, and one of her friends thrusts a wineglass into her hand. I think of Nate at twenty-three, fresh off his second album, asking me what kind of rings I like. The question had come out of nowhere, out of the darkness, past midnight with his body settled over mine. Sweaty, spent. I hadn't even thought about marriage before then. My mother never married; Goldie would never marry; it had never mattered to me what Nate's title was. He was just my Nate.

But something changed, after that conversation. A new expectation had been introduced into our relationship—that, eventually, there would be a leveling up. And so even as we grew apart, as all the things that made us good for each other fell away, I stayed. I stayed, Nate Payne's *purple girl*, until I was blue in the face from holding my breath.

Henry has felt like an inhale. And sitting in his—my—living room, not knowing if I've ruined things between us, feels like choking.

I see movement in the garden, and my heart lurches into my throat. But it's only Joss, her face hidden by a baseball cap, her hands wrapped around a hose. I leave my guests laughing around the card game and step outside for some fresh air.

"Hey, Lou," Joss calls. "Sorry it's so late. I had a crazy day but I need to give the new tree some water."

"Thank you," I say, tucking my hands into my jacket pockets. I lower onto the porch steps and hunch my shoulders against the cold. "I like it, by the way."

It's some kind of baby pine, very Dr. Seuss, lopsided and furry-looking.

Joss stops to look at it in the garden's fairy lights, leaning on her rake. "Thanks," she says. "Henry hates it."

My chest tenses at his name, and I draw a deep breath that

hurts my ribs. I wonder if that's what they've been fighting about. Why Henry would give a shit about what tree Joss chose for the yard. "Why?"

She turns on the hose. "Not his style, I guess." After a moment, still watering, she adds, "Something happen? I saw him leave in a hurry over the weekend."

Fuck. I press the heels of my hands to my eyes, wishing Mei were here. I should have called her instead of coming outside. "Oh, no," I say. My voice sounds unconvincing, even to me. "He was just fixing something upstairs."

Joss nods. "You okay?"

I push on my knees, standing from the step. "Yeah. Sorry, I just remembered I need to make a phone call."

Joss shoots me an unsure smile and a wave. I'm dialing Mei before I'm even inside, passing the group in the living room and making for the stairs. She picks up just as I'm getting to my bedroom.

"Hey, Lou. You okay?"

Am I so terrible at hiding my emotions? I haven't even spoken yet. But, I mean: "No."

I hear a door close over the line. "What happened?"

"Henry went down on me in my bathroom and then Goldie showed up and I kind of kicked him out and now I'm pretty sure he hates me."

Mei is silent for five full seconds. "Wait, *what?*" Then she asks a string of questions in such rapid succession I have no time to answer any of them: "Hot landlord Henry? In your *bathroom?* While Quinn was there? Did Goldie know? Why would you kick him out?"

"Because I panicked," I say, flapping my hands around the

bedroom even though she can't see me. "I didn't want Goldie to know and make it a whole other thing about how I'm distracted from my career or not taking my life seriously or whatever else."

"Oh my god," Mei says. "Okay, damn. Okay. Why do you think he hates you?"

"It's been *four days*, Mei, and he still isn't texting me back."

"Does he usually . . . text you back?" I can hear Mei playing catch-up, and feel guilty for not telling her about this sooner.

"No," I say, "I don't know, we haven't really texted before."

"So maybe he's busy?"

"For four whole days? Maybe I'm just stupid and I hurt his feelings and he'll kick me out of—"

"Lou?" There's a rapid knock at my door, followed by Willa's voice. "Can you come back? We need you?"

"Fuck," I whisper into the phone. "I'm neglecting my house duties, I've got to go. Sorry, Mei."

"Okay, well, call me back. Jesus." She sounds exasperated, like she can't catch her breath. "Clearly you have a lot to fill me in on."

"I know, I'm sorry." I stand from the bed, my face burning. "I'm sorry, I'm sorry. Bye."

I draw a sharp breath and yank the door open, plastering on a smile. "Willa, hi. What's up?"

She grins, reaching one hand up against the doorframe and leaning into it dramatically. "We want to go out. And we want you to come with us."

There's one bar open past ten in Estes Park: Ophelia's Saloon. I've been exactly once, years ago with Nate when the guys from

Say It Now stayed over for a weekend and needed a little more *go* than our quiet mountain home could provide. It's dark inside, all wood panels and mounted animal heads—the kind of décor only a cretin carnivore could love. It's Halloween, and it's packed.

Lucy's entourage makes short work of getting her to the front of the line and ordering a round of absurdly blue shots that make me think of Henry's irises. I've barely knocked mine back when I decide to text him again.

> I'm at Ophelia's with some guests.
> Will you please come?

"Okay, Lou, what do you want next?" Willa's eyebrows are hiked at me over the head of one of her other friends, a short woman with box braids named Dahlia. Willa has incredible energy—she commands every single room she enters. Somehow, she's managed to get the bartender's undivided attention in this packed space.

"Oh, I'm good," I say. I can already feel the liquor, whatever it was, burning in the pit of my stomach.

"You sure?" Willa shouts. She and her friends are all wearing their black tutus; I'm decidedly unfestive in my usual jeans and a black V-neck T-shirt. The music is earsplitting, a heinous mash of country and EDM that vibrates up through the soles of my boots. "We're doing cosmos."

They make *cosmos* here? I glance down at my phone, which remains silent. I hate myself for fucking this up so fast.

"Okay, yeah," I tell Willa. It's a holiday, after all. "I'll do a cosmo."

I'm at the bottom of it, slurping the last dregs of pink from my glass, when I decide to text Henry again.

Please, I send. I'm sorry.

Lucy's little sister, Eloise, knocks her hip into mine. We're dancing in a circle in the middle of the sweaty room; it's mostly old men in motorcycle jackets in here, sipping whiskey and standing perfectly still. I text Henry again, correcting myself.

Sorry.

"Who's that?" Eloise shouts over the music. "No men!"

"He's my landlord!" I tell her. "Not a *man* man."

She shrugs, appeased, and angles the straw of her drink into her mouth, missing once before she gets it.

"*Fuck Jamie!*" Willa screams in the split-second lull between songs. All six of us other girls—Nan and Shani stayed home—shout it back to her. Somewhere between the first and second cosmos, the call-and-response has become something of a bit.

Lucy lifts her drink in the air. "And *fuck* the wedding industrial complex!"

Everyone repeats it back to her with varying degrees of accuracy. The next song starts and their voices drown out; my phone buzzes in my hand and I nearly scream.

Henry's text is three words: Are you drinking?

I look at the empty cosmo glass in my hand. I was planning to stop now, but he doesn't need to know that.

Will you come here if I am?

The three dots appear on-screen. Disappear, reappear.

Yes, he says.

I bite my lip. Next to me, Willa wraps Lucy in a hug and sways both of them back and forth.

Then yes.

If it's possible, Henry looks even more out of place in Ophelia's than he did that very first day at the house. No leather jacket; certainly no costume. He shows up in jeans and his leather boots, a thin wool sweater, his hair combed back. I'm stupidly relieved to see that he shaved. The un-bachelorette party is still squirming on the dance floor, but I've carved out a Lou-sized notch of breathing room on a barstool; when Henry steps through the door and starts scanning, I raise my arm in the air.

His eyes land on me, and a weird thing happens to his body—like a static shock, or a misstep where you manage to catch yourself before you fall. A twisted mix of fear and relief. It scares me, how well I can already read him. How much time I've already spent learning what his movements mean—the tug of his lip between his teeth, the rise of his shoulders, the scrunch of his brow.

Henry cuts through the crowd without hesitating. When he's near enough I reach for him, bring his face close to mine so I can speak right into his ear. "I'm sorry."

He pulls back, casts his eyes over mine. I say it again, dropping my hands from where they've landed on his chest—just in case he doesn't want this, just in case I'm already overstepping. But Henry picks them up, wraps them back around him, moves into my space so his hips part my legs and my back presses to the bar.

He dips his head so his lips are at my ear and says, simply, "Thank you."

"I could have stayed in that bathroom with you forever." I spread my fingers across his rib cage, hold him to me. "I should have. I'm sorry."

"Forever?" he says, pulling back far enough to meet my eyes. Behind him, the room is a blur of colored lights.

"I mean." I breathe a laugh that shudders on the way out, shaky with relief. "You know what I mean."

Henry pushes hair out of my face. "I was thinking a bed would be good, next time."

I bite my lip, swallowing a smile. When I stand, it brings me flush against his body. "Dance with me."

I make to pull him into the fray and he stops me, all five fingertips flexing into my waist. "I'm sorry, too," he says. His eyes flick back and forth over mine, like he wants to be sure I'm paying attention. "I was trying to sort out my feelings, but I shouldn't have—" He stops, swallows. "I should have texted you back."

I blink, a bitten-off smile making my lips twitch. "You should have," I agree. His thumb has found its way under my shirt. "I was losing my mind, not hearing from you."

"I'm sorry," he says again. He dips his forehead so it lands on mine, closes his eyes. "It's been a while since I've done this."

"*This?*" I ask, tipping back so he has to look at me. His eyes flutter open, and he draws a deep breath. *Been with someone*, I think he's going to say. He looks embarrassed.

"Talked about how I'm feeling." Henry swallows, his eyes flickering away from me before coming back again. "Or processed something with someone else, instead of just . . . here."

He lifts two fingers to his temple. "It's not an excuse. I'll get better."

I smooth my thumb between his eyebrows, run my hand into his hair, and settle my fingers around the back of his neck. He leans into my palm and I want to work him open, know every feeling he's ever had.

"How are you feeling now?" I ask.

Henry smiles, shy, and tugs my hips against his. "Relieved." His gaze dips to my mouth before rising back to meet mine. "You?"

I kiss him once before saying, "Like I want to dance."

Henry laughs, glancing around. Lucy and Co. are too many cosmos deep to care that I've brought a man into our midst, or even to remember that I'm here at all.

"This music's awful," Henry says.

He's right—it's still an impossible cacophony of house music and bluegrass, twangy strings and booming bass. But when I pull him away from the bar he comes with me, and in the tangle of the dance floor he winds both arms around my waist—a Henry-shaped bubble in the chaos.

"Did you drive here?" he asks me, nearly a shout over the music.

"No!" I have one hand wound around his neck, one pressed flush to his chest. "We took the only rideshare in Estes Park."

Henry nods, glancing over the crowd like he's trying to figure out who *we* is.

"Wait," I say, standing still so I can get him in focus. "Is that why you came? You thought I'd try to drive myself home?"

"I came," Henry says, dragging me back into a sway, "because I have this new ailment where I feel sick if I haven't seen you in a few days." I mash my lips together to keep from smiling, and Henry ducks close to my ear again. "But maybe I wanted to drive you home myself."

"You'll have to take all of us," I tell him, leaning back and gesturing around the bar.

Henry tips his head to the right, where a man in leathers is sipping a Coors. "Even the guy in the Harley jacket?"

"No, just the jilted bride and her five drunk friends. We'll squeeze."

Henry shakes his head, a smile tugging at his lips, and dips his chin to kiss me. "Fine," he says. "One condition."

I wind my arms around his neck, pressing our bodies together in the dark. "I'm listening."

Henry's fingers spread wide and warm over the small of my back. "I always go to Florida, the first half of November. Help my parents for a while."

First *half*? I feel my mouth going pouty. It's the cosmos—it's the *damn* cosmos—but I can't help it when I blurt, "But I just got you back."

Henry's eyes find mine in the dark. They glint, crinkling up in a way that's so pleased I'm almost glad I said it. He dips his mouth to my ear. "Spend Thanksgiving with me, when I get back." The words are soft—nervous—at their edges. When I pull back to look at him, he's watching me carefully. There's something so vulnerable in the tense line of his mouth that I tip forward without thinking to soften his lips with my own.

"Is that a yes?" His words, right against my mouth, are so quiet I nearly miss them. He meets my eyes, and his face splits into a smile when I nod.

"It's a yes." A *yes* that pings inside me like a shiver, rattling. *Yes.*

Henry tugs me closer into the warm wall of his body. "Good," he says, and starts to move us in time to the music. The shiver only grows when he brushes his lips against my ear and whispers, "I promise I'll make it worth the wait."

Twenty-Seven

Thanksgiving is a cold, sunny Thursday that I wake up to alone. For the first time since September, my house is empty: Lucy, Willa, and the rest of their friends are gone; Nan flew home yesterday. She'll be back after visiting her family in Pennsylvania, and everyone else I care about is scattered like dandelion filaments across the country: Mei's at home in California; Goldie and Quinn are in New York; my mother, I assume, is with Mark in Ohio. Usually I spend Thanksgiving with Nate's family in Denver, but this year—well.

When Henry dropped us back at the house after dancing at Ophelia's, he crowded me into the doorframe as everyone else tumbled upstairs. His hands were cold from the October chill, raising goose bumps on my neck when he lifted them to my face.

"Thank you," I'd told him, and he answered by kissing me long and slow before walking back to his car. I haven't seen him since then—just a string of texts, back and forth, photos of the

Florida coast, and one I wish you were here with me sent past midnight that wrung through me like a muscle spasm.

Now I'm parked in front of his condo: one in a row of identical units overlooking Lake Estes. My phone buzzes as I stare up at his door—Goldie, the first time I've heard from her since she left nearly a month ago. It's a photo of Quinn in a construction-paper hat shaped like a turkey, grinning so hard his eyes are pressed shut. Beneath it: *Happy Thanksgiving*. I send a heart emoji and nothing else; I'm still mad at her. Goldie's the last person I want to think about right now.

Henry's door is nondescript, a carbon copy of the ones on either side of it. I hear his footsteps before I see him, each one thudding in my chest like a heartbeat. He opens the door in a deep green wool sweater and dark jeans. Socked feet. Clean-shaven. When he smiles, it's small and shy and it makes me want to launch myself at him.

But I only say, "Hi," and he says, "Hi."

I hold out the pie I spent all morning making: Nan's recipe, apples with cinnamon and homemade piecrust she prepared for me in advance. "Pie."

Henry takes it. "Thank you."

"Least I could do," I say as he ushers me through the doorframe. "Considering where we left things."

Holding the pie with both hands, Henry watches me unzip my boots. His condo is clean and plain: gray walls, neutral furniture, a few framed paintings that look like they belong in a hotel room. It's nothing like the house, and it squeezes my heart to imagine him here alone, all these years, just down the street from me. Coming home from work to this emptiness.

"Where did we leave things?" Henry says.

I take the pie from his hands and set it on the entryway table behind me. When I step into Henry's space, an inch away but not touching him, he inhales. "You don't remember?"

"Remind me," he says, and I rise onto my tiptoes to press my lips to his. The feeling I've been longing for since that night at Ophelia's—warm and soft and Henry.

He wraps both arms around my waist, pulling me into him. I'm heat and hunger—forget the pie, forget Thanksgiving in its entirety—he makes me feel unmoored, insane, inside out. I knew he couldn't stay over after Ophelia's, that it wouldn't have been right to invite him in as the un-bachelorette crew's laughter echoed through the house. Knew, too, that he may not have wanted to stay after what happened the first time. I knew these things, but they did nothing to douse the heat of my wanting— especially knowing it would be so long before I'd see him again.

Henry leans me against the wall, now, his knee nudging mine apart and sliding up between my legs. I tip backward, finding his eyes.

"Don't start something you aren't planning to finish," I whisper.

His lips twitch. "Who says I'm not planning to finish?"

But then he releases me, a sudden *whoosh* of cold, and steps backward. His hand slides the length of my arm before lacing our fingers together. He nods his head down the hall. "Come in."

I bite my lip, and his eyes darken. He reaches out to unhook my lip from my teeth.

"Hungry?" he asks softly.

"Starving."

"Good." He leads me further into the house, and I follow. "Let's eat."

Henry's small, tidy kitchen smells like rosemary. When he pulls a turkey breast from the oven with paw-print-patterned oven mitts, I take a sip from my wineglass. It's disorienting, to watch him here—this man who restored my historic home with brass faucets and stained glass and printed wallpaper, the only point of light in his own gray, standard-issue house. I know without checking that none of the doors in this condo creak like music, like a song I'd learn by heart.

"Can we talk about what happened last month?" Henry says, his back to me. He slides the mitts off and reaches for a thermometer. Straightaway, I think of him in the first-floor bathroom. His cheek pressed to my thigh, his chin tilted up to look at me, his knees on the woven bath mat.

I cross my legs on the stool at his island, squeezing. "Which part?"

Henry sets the thermometer aside and turns to me, hands braced against the counter on either side of his hips. Music plays, softly, from speakers in the ceiling. "Louisa."

I could get drunk from it, the way he says my name. "Yes?"

"The part where your sister showed up and you shooed me out the back door like a delinquent teenager."

I take another sip of wine. "Ah. That part."

"That part," Henry says. He crosses his long legs at the ankles and glances down at his feet; when he looks back up, there's a pink flush across his cheekbones. "Are you ashamed of me?"

Oh, god. Am I ashamed of *Henry*? Henry, who reached for

that roll of paper towels the day I cried in his office, who's every animal's favorite person. Whose expressions bear his feelings so clearly—like his face is the book that taught me to read.

"No," I say, as quickly as I can get the word out. I don't tell him what pops, unbidden, to the roof of my mouth: I'm ashamed of *me*. "Of course not."

"Then, what? You clearly didn't want her to see me again."

"I was trying to protect—" I break off. Protect him? Protect myself? I wave a hand between us. "This." This vulnerable thing that's flickered between us since the start, that crystalized so sharply in the dark of my living room back in October at two o'clock in the morning. "Goldie's so judgmental, I was worried she'd—I don't know." I take a breath and let it out, my shoulders slumping. I know I owe him an explanation, but I so, so keenly don't want to talk about her. I want to stay Henry's version of me: the woman who's cared for his house all these years, the woman who steps up. Not Goldie's version: the woman who hasn't amounted to anything yet. "It would have been complicated."

Henry studies me. His arms are crossed over his chest, sweater tugged up above the bones of his wrists. I want to walk over and untwist the pretzel of his body. "I'm okay with complicated."

I swirl the wine in my glass, instead, watching it move. "Fine," I say, drawing another breath. When I look back up at Henry, he hasn't shifted a centimeter: legs crossed at the ankles, eyes unwavering on mine. "Goldie and I had a hard childhood. It wasn't—" I look away from him, out the kitchen windows, where the last licks of daylight sink over the lake. "It wasn't all bad. But our mom was—is—tough." I inhale slowly and then tell him what I hardly tell anyone; not because I need to, but because he showed me something, that night on the couch. "She was diagnosed with borderline personality disorder when I was in elementary school, and there was almost always an awful boyfriend in the picture. It all just—" I glance at Henry and quickly away. His eyes are too endless, too soft. "It made Goldie really scared all the time. She needs to control everything, even me. And she's really distrustful of men." I take a long sip of wine, steeling myself to look at him and add, "I didn't want her to mess this up."

Henry shifts off the counter, stepping around the island. He swivels my stool so that I'm facing him, his hips bracketed by my knees, and tips my chin up so I have to meet his eyes.

"Thank you for telling me that," he says quietly. He presses his lips to mine. "And I'm sorry."

"You don't have to be sorry." I lean my forehead into his sternum, breathe in the heady smell of his citrusy soap, of the spices he's been cooking with, of his skin. "It's just like I said: complicated."

Henry's hand smooths over my hair, warm and grounding. I bookend his ribs with my palms. "How was your trip?"

"It was fine," he says on an exhale. "A little too long."

I nudge my chin into his chest so I can look up at him. "Why do you go this time of year? Why not for the holidays?"

Henry studies me, his hand moving over my hair before coming to rest at the base of my skull. I can see him deciding how much to tell me, weighing how far to let me in—and I'm relieved when he says, "It's tough, doing the holidays with them."

I brush my thumbs over his ribs. This moment feels tenuous—like this close, honest version of Henry is a firefly I've managed to catch open-palmed. "Tough how?"

He swallows. "It's a nostalgic time of year. Sometimes they get—" He breaks off, eyes moving over mine like he could find the words there. "Sometimes it's too much."

"About Molly," I say quietly, so he doesn't have to. When he nods, his eyes flutter shut—like that hurt, even just hearing it.

"I love them," he says. That word in his mouth hits me low and warm. "I want to be with them, and I want to help them, and it's good for me to be there. But it's better for all of us if I come back home before things get heavy."

I nod, and his hands move to frame my face. "I understand."

Henry's leaning to kiss me when, over the speakers, I hear the opening notes of a song I'd be able to place anywhere. The guitar chords pluck right between my ribs.

"*No*," I groan, wriggling out of his grip. All at once, I'm absolutely overstimulated. "Can you change the song?"

Henry blinks, confused. "I—yeah. Yes."

But he's slow to find his phone, rifling through a bowl on his coffee table, and Nate's already singing: "*She reads with her lip between her teeth; asleep, her breath falls slow and sweet; she always wakes up reaching for me.*" It's the acoustic version, of course. Nate last year, instead of at twenty: his voice a little huskier, rougher on the vowels. "*Purple, like the lake before a storm, like the mountains in the morning—*"

The music cuts, stuttering into the Beatles' "Hey Jude." I blink, hard, to clear my head. That song sounds like my old life, one that has no place in this kitchen with Henry and his parents and Molly. Henry's still looking at his phone and I can picture the album art, there in his palm: Nate's dorm room at CU, a pair of girls' sneakers lined up next to the bed, mine. *Say It Now*, below the photo. *Purple Girl (Acoustic)*.

Henry's voice is low. "I didn't realize that would be on this playlist."

"It's fine," I say. Like that article about Nate and Estelle in *People*, this kind of thing will find me. "It's everywhere."

Henry's quiet. When he walks back over to the island, he doesn't touch me. "Does it upset you? To hear it."

"Not really." I swirl my wine again just to have something to do with my hands. I look up at him and there's something guarded in his eyes—this reminder of my past, of a person who loved me once, doesn't mean something only to me. Nate's the reason Henry and I know one another at all. "I'd just rather not think about him, you know?"

"Mmm." Henry reaches over the counter, stilling my hand. I stare at our fingers, there on the granite: his knuckles curved over mine like shelter. He waits for me to look up at him to ask, "It's about you, isn't it?"

I feel heat building under the bones in my chest, grief or panic or fear. I don't want Nate to take this moment from me. "Yes," I say, turning back to watch Henry's thumb trace a line over my wrist. "But it's old. It was a lifetime ago."

"You've never seemed purple, to me." I look up at him, surprised. He keeps tracing my skin, watching his thumb move. "It's a sad song. He makes you sound sad."

"I was, a little."

Henry nods, winding his fingers between my own. When our eyes meet, he says, "Me, too."

"But I'm not so much," I tell him, "anymore."

Henry's extraordinary eyes move over mine, searching. I stand, putting my hands on his face and bringing his lips down to mine. Against my mouth, between one kiss and the next, he says, "Me, too."

Henry turns on his fireplace after dinner, gas flame clicking on to fill the living room with warm light. He carries our wineglasses to the coffee table and I pick up the apple pie, rummaging through his drawers until I find two forks. When I sink into the couch next to him, I hold one out.

"I do have plates," he says, his arm following the line of my shoulders along the back of the couch.

"This is how we always did it," I say, spearing my fork into one edge of the pie. "Growing up."

"Your mom, too?" He follows my lead, digging in.

"Yeah, she loves the holidays. We'd always go to one of her friends' houses but she'd make sure there was a pie just for the three of us—me and Goldie and her."

Henry chews thoughtfully. "This is delicious."

"It was mostly Nan," I assure him. "She made the dough for me."

"Well," he says, "the filling is the best part."

"Oh, yeah?" I ask, smiling, and he says, "Without question."

Henry has crumbs at the corner of his mouth, cinnamon on his lips. The pie is good—but I'm tired of waiting. I take the fork from his hand and drop it into the dish with my own, sliding it onto the coffee table and climbing into his lap. His hands steady my waist as I settle onto him, as I dip my head and kiss the corner of his lips. Run my tongue over the crumbs there, the sugar.

"Done with the pie?" he asks quietly. In the firelight, his eyes are liquid and warm. I think of that first night in the Aspen Room, Henry's breathless voice in the dark. *I want more than that. All of you.*

"Done," I confirm, and then I roll my hips against his. Air punches out of him, his eyes fluttering shut. His fingertips dig into my jeans.

"Louisa," he says, his voice low and rough.

I press my mouth to his ear, kiss the corner of his jaw. His hands slide up my back, warm beneath my cardigan. When I take his head into my hands he gives me the weight of him, leans into my fingers, opens his mouth under my own. In the warm, breathless space between our lips, I whisper, "Are you still scared of me?"

"Terrified," he says, and then he kisses my throat, sucks at the arch of my neck, grazes his teeth along my skin so that I shiver.

My voice is barely a sound at all. "Do you want to take me upstairs?"

"I want," Henry says, pressing his lips to mine, "to take my time with you."

His words move through me like warm water, a slick rush. When I push my hands under his sweater he lifts his arms and lets me pull it over his head. It drops to the floor behind the couch, leaves his hair mussed and wild. The white T-shirt he has on underneath is thin and tight, pulled taut over the lines of his chest.

"You first," I say against his mouth, unbuttoning his jeans. But he traps my hands in his, pulling them behind my back so my spine arches, pushing my chest into his.

"No." Henry starts to unbutton my sweater, one slow step at a time. "You first." He pushes the fabric over my shoulders so it pools at my wrists, taking me in—pale yellow bra, floral lace, nearly translucent. He swallows, frames my ribs with his warm hands. Looks up at me. "Always you first."

"Why?"

His thumbs stroke the bottom edge of my bra, raising goose bumps. His voice sounds scraped. "Because you're so gorgeous like this." His hands slide upward, palming my breasts. "Because I want to watch you. Because I'm selfish."

My eyes fall shut, throat tipping back, as Henry unhooks the clasp of my bra and pulls it away. He slides me onto the couch beside him, tipping me backward and starting on my jeans, my underwear. When I'm completely naked underneath him he kicks off his own jeans and settles on top of me—warm weight, his heartbeat thudding against mine—and frames my face with one hand.

"You're beautiful," he says, and I bite my lip. He ducks his head and pulls it between his own teeth, a low growl vibrating from his throat. "I can't think when you do that."

I reach down between us, finding him hard and straining against the fabric of his boxers. "Henry," I say, breathless. "Let me."

But as I slide a hand under his waistband and wrap it around him, his own fingers brush the ridge of my hip bone, the crease of my hip, finally parting me. My breath catches, chin tipping backward, and he kisses my exposed throat—hot and wet and graceless.

"Is this okay?" he whispers, his fingertips circling torturously. I nod, focusing all I have on keeping my own rhythm—but then

Henry's fingers are inside of me, and his tongue is slick against the pulse in my throat, and I lose my grip on everything. On Henry, on reality, on the steadiness of my own breathing.

"That's good," Henry says, low and close. "You're so beautiful."

I whimper as he finds something hot and vulnerable inside of me—a place that makes my stomach muscles tense, my breath come short. He traces it again and again, his own need straining against my hip, his breath across my chest as my head tips back and I cry out—loud, broken, defenseless.

Henry presses a kiss to my temple. "Hold still." He stands, disappearing as I drop an arm over my forehead, elbow cocked toward the ceiling. I try to slow my breathing, calm the tremors coursing up from my core to my throat. *Henry, Henry, Henry.* I can't make out what song plays, now, over the speakers. I can't form a coherent thought at all.

I hear rustling, his footsteps. When he lifts my arm from over my eyes, I smile up at him with what I can only imagine looks like a drunken lack of muscle control. "Come here," he murmurs, helping me to my feet.

He's pushed the coffee table aside and layered a pile of throw blankets and pillows on the floor in front of the fire. It's the sweetest thing I've ever seen; when I look up at him, flushed and carefully gauging my reaction, it makes me want to swallow him whole.

"So much for 'a bed, next time,'" I say.

Henry's hand wraps around my hip, his chest pressing into my bare back. I feel him against my tailbone and every muscle in my abdomen aches. As his hand sinks lower, he says, "Do you want to go all the way upstairs?"

I shake my head and turn in his arms, fisting my hands into the bottom hem of his shirt to draw it up and over his head. Henry lowers me to the floor, where the blankets are velvet-soft on my bare skin. He runs a warm palm over my hip, my rib cage, my breast, teasing one nipple between his thumb and finger.

"I know you wanted to take your time," I say, reaching under his waistband. I close my fingers around the length of him and he flexes into my palm. "But I don't know how much longer I can wait."

He groans as I pick up my rhythm, breathless. He's propped on one elbow above me, his hair falling forward to brush my forehead. I squeeze, gently, and his eyes open, tracking back and forth over mine. "Louisa, are you sure?"

"Henry." He holds my gaze. "Are you going to make me beg?"

His lips part. "I don't—"

"Please," I whisper, stroking him one more time, watching his eyes flutter closed and open again. "*Please.*"

He lowers onto me, kissing me open-mouthed, one hand reaching down to wrap my leg around his hip. "Off," I say, nudging at the waistband of his boxers. He pulls away to discard them and, when he comes back, presses the full length of his body against mine.

"Tell me what you want," he murmurs, kissing along the underside of my jaw. "I have condoms. Lube."

"Both," I say, running my fingernails up the length of his back. He's broad and warm and I never, ever, ever want to stop touching him. "Please."

I watch him kneel, reaching for a condom on the coffee table and rolling it on. He's beautiful in the firelight: the long lines of his torso, silver-glinted hair falling into his face. I can barely see the pink ridge of that scar along his sternum, half-hidden by dark hair. Before I get a good look he's back, poised over me with his hand between my legs.

"A little cold," he whispers, spreading me open with lube on his fingers. I wriggle beneath him, and he smiles. "Sorry."

"Don't be sorry." I pull him down on top of me, wrapping my arms around his shoulders. He kisses the arch of my neck and then props himself onto his elbows, one hand framing my face, his fingers curved over the top of my head.

"Okay?" he asks, quiet and close. Every centimeter of my body is incandescent with longing.

"More than," I whisper, and Henry moves into me, and I'm done for.

He's heavy-lidded, after—soft lines of his body on the blankets next to me, dark lashes casting shadows from the fire. He rests one big hand on my stomach. Rooting me down, keeping me close.

"How do you feel?" Henry murmurs, his eyes barely open.

I swallow. I feel hot and spent and tingly. I feel exhausted and high. "Dehydrated."

Henry smiles, propping himself up to look at me in earnest. He taps my forehead with two fingers. "How do you feel here?"

"Happy," I say softly. Consumingly so.

Henry dips his chin, kisses me gently. "Yeah."

He gets up to bring me a glass of water, and when he lowers back to the floor beside me that scar catches in the light. I run my hand over his chest, where his skin is hot and damp with sweat. "What happened here?"

Henry rolls onto his back and I move with him, bracing one arm on the ground and drawing my fingers over the scar. It's soft and smooth—healed.

He looks down at my fingers, watching them trace his skin. "It's a tattoo."

"Really?" I get closer to it—the uneven, pink lines, the pucker marks like there were staples in his skin. "It looks so real."

"Yeah," he says on an exhale. I look up at him and he places his hand over mine, hiding the tattoo from both of us. "Molly had this big surgery when she was two." He says it straight up at the ceiling. "They opened up her whole chest. She was so small."

I prop myself up taller, rising on my elbow to get a better look at him. There's a blanket draped over us and it slides with me, pooling at my waist.

"The scar really freaked her out, after," Henry says. "She'd cry seeing it in the mirror, or feeling it under her clothes." He tilts his chin, angling his head on the floor to meet my eyes. "I got the tattoo so I'd have a matching one. So she could see that it wasn't so scary, and as she grew up, she wouldn't feel different because of it." He licks his lower lip, lets out a breath. That line, anguished and familiar, cuts between his eyebrows. "But she died a few months after I got it, so I'll never know if it helped her."

I move his hand away from the tattoo and press my mouth to it. He inhales under my lips, sharp and surprised. *I lost all of it.*

"Having you helped her," I say, looking back up at him with my chin propped on his sternum. How couldn't it have? Henry's softness, his patience. I could choke on the feeling rising in my throat, hot and painful as tears. "It's really beautiful, Henry."

He swallows, his eyes flickering from me to the ceiling.

"You know what's sad," he says, drawing an unsteady breath,

"is six years later, my fingers still twitch every time I step into a crosswalk. Reaching for her hand."

His words land like a burn, tender to the touch. I rest my cheek over his heart—it's pounding, still. Fast and frantic.

"Can you tell me about her?" I ask quietly. "Something you loved about her."

Henry's silent for a long time, the only sound his heartbeat under my ear. "I loved everything about her," he says finally. He's looking into the fire, and even as his thumb traces the line of my shoulder blade, he doesn't meet my gaze. When he rolls me over, dropping his mouth to mine and parting my lips with his tongue, I see it for what it is—a change of subject, the closing of a door. He can let me in, but not this far.

"Henry," I whisper later, when the lights are all off and he's half-asleep on the pillows beside me. My brain won't quiet—this night has turned it to a riptide of my mother, of "Purple Girl," of Molly. Of Henry most of all.

"Mmm?" His arm is warm around my waist, holding me in place.

"You said I've never seemed purple, to you." I watch his face in the dark. "What color am I?"

Henry's quiet for half a moment. And then, without opening his eyes, he says, "Yellow." He pulls me closer, his hands spread warm and wide over my back, his lips at my ear. "Sunrise."

Twenty-Eight

I wake up to the low buzz of my phone on Henry's nightstand. We came upstairs at some point between midnight and three a.m.—Henry's big hands in the dark, wrapping me in a blanket and leading me to his bedroom. It's as neat and simple as every other part of his house, like he hardly lives here at all.

I squint at my phone screen: *Marigoldie (7)*. Shit. There are two missed calls, too. A voicemail. Henry's still asleep, turned toward me with both hands tucked under his pillow like a child. In the half dark he looks young and safe. I think of his tattoo, of the way he quieted me about Molly, and slide out of his bed as carefully as I can.

The throw blanket from last night is heaped on the floor, and I wrap it around myself before slipping out of his bedroom. Goldie picks up on the second ring, like she's been waiting for me—which, of course she has.

"Finally," she says by way of greeting. Pale morning light casts Henry's condo, and all the evidence of our evening, weak blue. Half-full wineglasses next to the picked-apart pie on the coffee table; pile of pillows and twisted blankets on the living room floor. "Did you listen to my voicemail?"

"No," I say croakily. I head for Henry's balcony—I need space from him, from the night we had, to talk to my sister. "I just woke up."

"Well, Mom's getting evicted." I freeze, one hand on the sliding door. I feel Goldie's words in my body—like punches, bruising and cruel.

I step onto the balcony, sliding the door shut behind me. "Why?"

"Because she hasn't been paying her rent, obviously."

"It's not obvious, Goldie, can you please not condescend to me right now?"

"I'm not—" She breaks off, sighing forcefully into my ear. I lean over the railing, blanket pulled tight around me in the morning chill. Everything is covered in shimmering, crystalline frost. "I'm not trying to fight with you, Lou. I need your help figuring this out."

"So she called you?" I ask, watching fog shift over the lake. The sun hasn't crested the mountains yet and everything feels insulated and half-real.

"Yes, last night, lucky me, on literal Thanksgiving. She said you have *too much going on* right now to deal with this. Because apparently getting dumped is more stressful than parenting a five-year-old."

I close my eyes. *It's not a competition*, I want to scream. *You chose Quinn.*

"What did she say?" I bite out.

"That she needs to back-pay her rent by Monday or she's out on December first."

"Can Mark help her?"

"She doesn't want to ask him, of course. She wants us to deal with it." In the background, music swells—whatever Quinn's watching on TV, I'm sure. He only gets screen time in a crisis. "Can you call her? You're good at these kinds of things. Dealing with her."

I feel the words like a slap, like an echo of what she said to me in my kitchen just a few weeks ago: *You do this, Lou—you take care of other people to avoid taking care of yourself.* Which is it? How am I supposed to focus on myself when she always leaves Mom's crises to me?

My throat burns, bile rising. We've always been this way; I know we have—Goldie the logical one, shutting Mom out because it's not *right*. Me, the arbiter of feelings, letting her back in because she's *family*. It's always me, caring for people. Holding Mei on my couch after her breakup with Andy. Telling Kim her pain is as valid as Bea's anger. Rushing Shani and Alfie to the vet. Falling for Henry—heartbroken in his own, permanent way.

It's all I'm capable of, maybe. Being a fixer. It's what people want from me. I have the sudden, unsteadying thought that maybe it's the reason I'm on this balcony at all—because Henry, too, is a project.

"This week is crazy without childcare," Goldie continues, when I still haven't said anything. "And frankly, I don't have the money to loan her. I have my *own* rent due on the first and Quinn's day care is increasing their prices in Jan—"

"I get it." My voice sounds icy, even to me. "I'll deal with it."

Goldie hesitates. I think, for one hair's breadth of a moment, that she might ask if I'm okay. If I have the capacity to be "good at this kind of thing" right now. But she just says, "Okay, great. Thanks."

"Okay," I say, curling my fingers around the cold railing. I squeeze until my knuckles turn white. "I'm going to go."

"Yeah," Goldie says. "Let me know how it winds up."

I don't give myself time to think about it before dialing my mother's phone number—time to brace, or take a deep breath, or play out the potential catastrophes. When she picks up, she sounds as delighted as ever.

"Lou! Happy Thanksgiving, baby. I didn't think I'd hear from you."

"Well, Goldie called me."

Mom sighs, like this whole thing is a trivial inconvenience. "I told her not to bother you with this," she says. "I know you're going through such a tough time."

Hearing her say it, I realize it isn't true. This time *doesn't* feel tough. This time feels precious: the Comeback Inn, two months living with Mei, my week with Quinn. Henry, and every part of my life that's changed because of him.

But this is how my mother understands the world—one relationship to the next, the desolate wasteland of finding yourself freshly single.

I don't correct her. I just say, "Tell me what's going on."

Her explanation is wandering and illogical, a string of causes and effects that don't quite add up to the basic truth, which is that she owes her landlord six thousand dollars in three days.

"Why haven't you been paying your rent, Mom?"

She laughs, though there's nothing funny about it. "I just lost track of it, Lou, it was a silly mistake. We've been in Florida, and then I've been so worried about you, it's just been slipping my mind."

I bristle at the casual insinuation that this is even a little bit my fault. "How much money do you have right now?"

Mom makes a high, wavering noise, like she's trying to remember. "About seven hundred dollars?"

I press my eyes shut. I have two thousand dollars in my bank account. I could give her *maybe* half of that without fearing for my life. Which gets us to $1,700. A slight $4,300 shy.

"Can you borrow some money from Mark?"

"Oh, honey, no—I don't want to bother him with this. If I need to leave my place, though, he's offered for me to stay with him until—"

"No," I say, cutting her off. Mom moving in with one of her horrible boyfriends has always been the worst-case scenario. If there's one thing Goldie and I agree on, it's that she can't be dependent on a man for the roof over her head. "Is there anyone else who could loan you some money?"

Mom hesitates. She has the grace to sound embarrassed when she says, "Well, maybe my daughters?"

"I don't have that kind of money."

"But with you and Goldie together?"

"And then what?" I ask. On Lake Estes, a kayaker puts in near the parking lot—sending ripples over the still water. "How do you pay your rent next month, once you're caught up?"

"I'll pick up more shifts at the store," she says. "I'll figure it out, if I can just get out of this hole. I promise."

She means it—I know she does. She's meant every promise she's ever made to me, maybe most of all the ones she didn't keep.

"Give me today to figure it out," I say. I count the kayaker's strokes through the water, trying to ground myself. "I'll call you back."

"Oh, thank you, honey. I can always count on you, Lou, my sweet girl."

The door slides open behind me and I jump. Henry fills the doorframe—sleepy eyed, his hair a ruffled mess that so begs to be touched I feel it in my fingertips. He's in a white T-shirt and gray sweatpants that hang low on his hips. I've thought of waking up to Henry, but I never thought of it quite like this; in the exact same breath, I want to run from him and reach for him.

"Come inside," he whispers, holding an arm toward me. "It's freezing."

"I have to go," I say into the phone, stepping toward him. "I'll call you."

Mom's still thanking me as I hang up, over and over, the grateful tone I've heard from her all my life. Every time she messes up. Every time I fix it.

"Are you okay?" Henry closes the sliding door behind me. He looks half-awake and confused, blinking rapidly like he's trying to get me in focus. I'm wrapped in the throw blanket like a mummy—it's pulled tightly enough around me to cut off my circulation. Now that I'm off the phone I can feel the blood rushing back into my body, feel all my limbs again. And Henry's right: it was freezing out there. I start shaking almost immediately.

"Come here," he says, guiding me to the couch. He picks up the extra blankets from the floor and tucks them around me until I'm cocooned like a bug, my teeth chattering and my phone still clenched in my hand. Henry sits next to me and holds his arm out. I tip into him without thinking, pressing my head into his shoulder. He's so, so warm.

"What happened?" he asks, one hand sweeping up and down my arm. It's quick and firm—the way you'd chafe your hands together in the cold, the way you'd rub a newborn puppy to help it breathe. The movement grounds me, reminds me of my body. I take a long breath and hold it.

"It was my mom," I say, trying to still the shaking. I can't quite tell if it's from the cold or the panic. "She's going to get evicted."

Henry's hand doesn't stop moving. Outside, the sun crests the mountains, and his living room fills with yellow light; it all feels quiet and soft and I have the strange thought that I'm home sick from school.

"Why?" he asks. I hear Goldie: *Because she hasn't been paying her rent, obviously.*

But I only say, "I need to send her some money by tomorrow."

Henry's quiet. When he shifts away from me, it's to turn on the couch so we can look at each other. I miss his hand on my arm immediately. "How much?"

I rub a fist between my eyes, working out the beginnings of a headache. "More than I have."

Henry reaches for my fist and uncurls my fingers to thread them through his own. My hands are stinging and pink. "Louisa, has she done this before? Asked you for money?"

Only every year since I left home, I think. "A few times."

"And do you feel like you—" He hesitates, eyes scanning back and forth over mine. "Do you feel like you need to give it to her?"

I can hear the questions he's really asking: *Is this your job? Is this a fair sacrifice for her to ask you to make? How much of yourself will you give to her?*

But Henry doesn't know the depth of it. The weak place inside of me that my mother presses on every time. The boundary I've never been able to build between us.

"Yes," I say, unable to look at him. I want to be alone, suddenly—I want to hide. I don't want him to see this, the way I can't stop with her.

"Okay," Henry says. I pull my hand from his and twist my fingers back into a frigid fist. "How can I help?"

Twenty-Nine

The house is empty when I get home. No Nan at the kitchen table, no guests closing doors or turning on showers or padding down the hallway upstairs. I waited until I was a block from Henry's house—out of his sight line on the off chance he was watching me drive away—to start crying. I drove around the lake with my eyes blurred, traffic lights turning to watercolor. I asked Goldie to match my thousand dollars and didn't tell her where the rest of the money was coming from; when she asked if two grand was enough to fix the problem, I lied and told her yes. Goldie hates sending our mother money, but *eviction* was an emergency enough for her to follow my lead for once.

It eats through me bite by bite. As I unlock my front door, as I breathe in the house—oiled wood, books, home—as I drop my keys in the dish by the stairs. Henry sending me a wire before I could even finish asking. A cut of the Comeback Inn profits; the money that was supposed to be replacing my rent. The bottomless, sickening shame of it.

You don't have to help her, I'd said. And he'd looked at me as though he could see right through to my torn, red interior. Told me, *You know I'm not doing this for her.*

But it kept swirling in me, churning like an unsteady sea. That Goldie was right—*You do this.* That she expects it of me. That my mother does. That I give more than I get, and it lands me back here every time. With Nate, who took advantage of me the minute I stopped paying attention; in a house designed to heal everyone but me; in a new relationship with a man who can give me his money but not his memories.

My mind turns it over, again and again, wearing the image smooth: the two of us on Henry's living room floor, me asking about Molly and Henry covering my body with his to quiet me. I'm awful at being shut out. I need to be needed; the longing hurts in a deep, primal place. Henry even *told* me, that night at Ophelia's—he warned me that he was bad at this and I'm still here, letting myself be devastated by it. I hear Goldie's voice every time I close my eyes: *You do this.*

I pull my favorite throw blanket off the back of the couch and bury myself under it, sinking into the cushions and pressing my face into a throw pillow. I have two days alone in the house before Nan comes back. Another day after that before my next round of guests starts to trickle in.

I started the Comeback Inn to care for people—because the part of me that knows how to nurture others has always felt like the best and truest part. But as I breathe into the cross-stitched pillow cover, as my eyes burn with tears, I wonder if that's all I'll ever get to be, all I'm capable of. If the power I thought I held by being needed is just a weakness; if I've sought out sadness in others so I don't have to confront my own. If Henry's heartbreak is what drew me to him, too.

If I'm only ever a caretaker.

If there's something broken and sick inside of me.

Mei calls later that afternoon, when the sun's started to sink through the kitchen windows and I'm still on the couch, HGTV playing softly from the other side of the living room. I have a string of texts from Goldie—I sent my 1k, and then She texted me that it's taken care of, and then Thank you for handling. There's one from my mother, too: Thank you my sweet girl xx

"How was your Thanksgiving with Hot Henry?" Mei says when I pick up. I gave her the full story after our night at Ophelia's, and I'm so grateful to the Louisa of last month for getting into it so that I don't have to muster the entire tale now.

"I mean," I say, propping myself onto a ramp of throw pillows. "Hot."

Mei exhales on a squeal. "Do tell."

"Well, we—" I hesitate. On TV, a woman in denim overalls whales a sledgehammer through her drywall. "You know."

"Louisa Arlene Walsh. I'm *thrilled*."

"Thanks," I say, then realize how flat it sounds. I try again. "Really."

"What's wrong?" Mei says. I hear a door close, and picture her walking into her childhood bedroom in Pasadena. "Was it bad?"

"No." I pull at a loose thread on the blanket. "It was the best." I swallow and tip my head backward, squeezing my eyes shut. "Like, dangerously good."

"Okay," she says slowly. "So what's the problem?"

He's in pain, I could tell her. *He's been married, he's been a*

father, he's had a whole life I know nothing about. I can already feel myself being pulled under, wanting to heal him.

"Mei, am I just, like—" I sigh, opening my eyes again to look straight up at the ceiling. It's the least colorful part of the house, stark and white, and all at once that makes me devastatingly sad. "Everyone's mom?"

She hesitates. "What?"

"Henry's had this—bad stuff happen to him. In the past. And I'm already just, like, desperate to get to the bottom of it and make him talk about it and help him get past it and I just—" I groan, exasperated with myself. "Goldie said this thing to me, when she was here. That I'm always taking care of other people so I don't have to take care of myself. With the Comeback Inn, and with my mom, and now, I don't know, maybe that's what I'm—"

"Did something happen with your mom?"

"Yeah," I say, my voice going small. "She almost got evicted so we had to send her money today." I don't clarify who I mean by *we*.

"Fuck," Mei says. "I'm sorry, Lou. That's so stressful."

"Yeah, thanks." I yank the loose thread so hard that it pulls open a pinhole in the blanket. Perfect. "It is."

"It sucks you have to parent her. And it's shitty Goldie said that to you, *especially* because you being the way you are makes Goldie's life way easier. Does she get that?" Mei's voice crackles with an angry laugh. "I mean, she gets to have this arm's-length, peaceful distance from your mom because she knows *you'll* handle shit. She gets to create these boundaries as a direct result of *you* being so nurturing and kind—not to mention all you do for Quinn, like taking care of him when she has work shit? Hello? Are we operating on the same plane of existence, here?"

I blink up at the ceiling, clearing tears from my eyes. She's right.

"She tells you not to answer when your mom calls," Mei continues. "She tells you not to send her money. But then there's a crisis and who does she expect to handle it? *You.* Because she knows you will, because you always have, and she's lucky for it."

I squeeze my eyes shut. "I think that's my point," I whisper. "I think maybe I'm a doormat."

"No," Mei says emphatically. "How giving you are is one of the most special things about you."

I know Mei's just trying to make me feel better, but it pushes on the bruise already forming underneath my ribs. What makes me special is that I'm always willing to clean up after everyone else. I'm terrified my only worth is the role I'm so desperate to play for the people around me—and that if I don't figure it out soon, I might disappear entirely.

A knock on the kitchen door breaks me out of this spiral, and I crane over the back of the couch to see Joss framed in the window. I throw a wave in her direction and swipe at my eyes. "Hey," I say to Mei, "can I call you back?"

"Of course," Mei says. "I'm here for you, yeah?"

"Thank you," I say, and drop my phone onto the couch. Joss is pink-cheeked in the cold, her shoulders hunched up around her ears.

"Hi," she says, a little breathless, when I open the door. "Is it okay if I come in for a sec?"

"Of course." I step backward, letting her dart around me before quickly closing the door against the chill. "You okay?"

"It is *freezing* out there." She lifts her hands to her mouth and huffs into them. "I've been trying to get the lights up, but my hands are numb." She always does Christmas lights in the garden immediately after Thanksgiving so we can enjoy them for the entirety of December. There's nothing quite so beautiful as my pine trees dusted in snow, string lights glowing through the white. "Still haven't fixed that squeaky door, huh?"

"I'm used to it." I shrug, gesturing her into a seat at the kitchen island. "I didn't even realize you were out there. I can make you some tea?"

"That would be great." She smiles and rubs her hands together. "I think I'm done for today, but I probably shouldn't drive until I regain feeling in my hands."

"Wise." I put the kettle on and reach into the cabinet next to the sink, rifling around for my tea box. "How was your Thanksgiving?"

"Calm," she says. Unbidden, I think, *Must be nice.* "My parents are in Fort Collins. My brother and his partner always fly in with the kids, but it's an easy commute for me."

"Lucky." I rip the foil on her tea bag, glancing back over one shoulder. "Did you grow up there?"

"Sure did," she says. "Jeremy—my brother—couldn't wait to get out of here, but I've never wanted to leave Colorado."

"Can't imagine why," I say, smiling. Joss props her elbows on the island and I lean against the counter.

"How was it with your family?" I venture. "With what you said, about your breakup—how they took it hard?"

Joss's eyebrows tic, like maybe she's surprised that I remember. "Oh, better," she says. But something in her voice is breezy, and I know even before she does it that she's going to change the subject. "How was your holiday?"

I hesitate for a beat too long—do I tell her I spent it with

Henry, her boss? Also kind of *my* boss? Do I lie? There's no real reason to keep it from her, but her dismissive response about her own holiday makes me feel like I shouldn't get into mine. Plus, after spending the entire day rotting on my couch, I'm not even sure I have the strength. So I only force a smile and say, "Fine."

She tilts her head. "Only fine?"

The teakettle whines, saving me. I bat a hand in Joss's direction as I move toward it and tell her, "My mom's kind of intense. There was a whole drama."

"Ah," she says. "The holidays always bring it out."

"Yeah," I say on a sigh, sliding the mug toward her over the counter.

She accepts it with a smile, steam rising into the space between us. "Do you want to talk about it?"

I tilt my head back and forth, making an exaggerated show of considering. Joss is kind and warm and honest—I know I could share this with her. We've known each other for four years. But the reality is we don't really *know* each other. I didn't know until so recently that Joss had separated from a partner; I hardly know anything about her personal life at all. I don't know if she has a good relationship with her own mother, or what she does when she isn't in the garden. And my mom feels like a lot to get into—with Joss, or with anyone.

"I don't think I have the energy," I tell her, honestly. "But thank you for asking."

"Fair," Joss says. She takes a sip of her tea. "Family's hard."

She doesn't have to tell me twice.

Thirty

I spend the next day and a half at the desk in my bedroom, scrolling through licensing exam study guides and writing notes longhand. Through the bay window, I see Joss come and then go on Saturday. She puts Christmas lights on every tree except the new one—the baby pine that Henry hates. Thinking about him makes my stomach go tight, and I force myself to stop.

The day ticks by, the sun lowering. When I get to section three in my practice exam, Helping Relationships, Goldie's voice whispers through the room—so vivid it's like she's breathing up through my floorboards. *You do this, Lou. You do this.* Helping everyone else.

I press my pencil so firmly into my notepad that the lead snaps. I need to center myself in my own life. Help *myself* for once. When Henry texts me at five to ask if I want to meet for dinner, I tell him that I can't.

It isn't true; I don't even eat dinner that night. But when I think of Henry—his low voice in my ear, *You're so beautiful*—it tugs so hard and so deep inside of me that I know I'm ruined. That being near Henry is a danger, a vast hole opening up, a void I'm desperate to fall into. I want him so violently that I can't see myself clearly. I know that if I meet him—if I touch him, if I catch even the shallowest scrape of the sadness I'm frantic to fix—I'll turn myself inside out trying to be a balm. I'll break every promise I've made to myself in the last twenty-four hours.

I need him, my body screams.

And my brain, in a stern voice that sounds a lot like my sister's, replies: *You need space.*

"Home sweet home," Nan says, stepping through the threshold and opening her arms for a hug. Her perfume, floral and familiar, fills the foyer. "I missed you."

"I missed you, too." I take her suitcase and start up the stairs toward her room. "How was your Thanksgiving?"

"Superb," she says, following me. "I have new twin grandsons and they're just perfection. Cherubic. Too small to cause much trouble."

"Congratulations." I set her suitcase on the foot of her bed. "What does your family think of you staying here?"

"They're always bugging me to take a vacation," Nan says. "This is just one long one."

I smile, twisting my watch around my wrist. "I'm glad it feels that way."

Nan lowers to the edge of the bed, patting the mattress beside her. When I sit, she asks, "How was your Thanksgiving?"

I tilt my head back and forth, trying to decide how honest I should be. "Mixed bag."

"You stayed here?"

I nod, and Nan raises one eyebrow. "Alone?"

In the split second of my hesitation, Nan makes a satisfied little *harrumph*. "You were with Henry, weren't you?"

I splutter, already feeling heat in my cheeks. "How did you know?"

"I may be old," Nan says, tapping her brow, "but my eyes still work. You two are like magnets underwater—drawn to each other, pushing everything else out of the way."

I laugh, my first real one in days. "Okay."

"He's a catch," Nan says, shrugging. "So are you." I nudge my knee against hers and she adds, "Why a 'mixed bag'?"

"Just some family stuff." I offer her a small smile. "I'm sure you know how it is."

"Yes and no," she says, surprising me. I expected her to agree, to brush it off—*Of course I do*, or *Who doesn't?* "I know *my* family's stuff. But I expect yours is different, as are all of our problems."

"Yeah," I say, letting out a breath of a laugh and twisting my fingers together. "You're right."

"So?" She leans toward me, raising both eyebrows this time. "What's going on?"

"Nan," I say, smoothing my palms over my jeans. "We don't have to—you're here for *you*, yeah? How did your first Thanksgiving without Teddy feel?"

"Don't call upon my dead husband to change the subject, Lou. If you're upset, we can talk about it." She waves a hand toward her open door, the house beyond it. "Isn't that the point of this place?"

"Yeah, for *you*," I say. "For the guests."

"Well," Nan counters, "it's us two here right now."

I think of Rashad, back in October—that predawn morning we spent on the couch together. How much I needed him then.

"I had to help my mom with some bills," I tell Nan. "And it was stressful."

Her hand moves to cover mine where it still rests on my leg. Her skin is warm and papery soft. "That does sound stressful. Were you able to be open with Henry about it? Lean on him for support?"

Too much so, I think. If I'm honest, it's another reason I've been avoiding him the last few days: shame.

"Yeah," I say, straight down at my lap. "And it feels kind of embarrassing, because he's had some stuff going on, too, and I can tell he doesn't really want to talk to me about it. So I feel like I'm asking too much, or I *am* too much."

"My dear." Nan squeezes my hand. "There could never be too much Lou in this world."

I look up at her, exhaling on a smile. "Thanks."

"And sometimes we have to show people how to love us, or how to trust us, or how to care for us—by giving them that gift first." She shrugs. "It's not fair. But it's okay to go first. It's bighearted and brave."

What if, I think, *we never meet in the middle?* What if I wind up back where I've always been: giving and giving and giving with such imbalance that the person I love knows all my softest places, all the ways to bend me? What if this ends like Nate? Like my mother?

I don't say any of this. But almost as if I did—as if she heard me loud and clear—Nan adds, "Your openness is your superpower, Lou, not your weakness. Don't let the world convince you otherwise."

Pauline arrives the next afternoon, her knock jaunty and complicated, like the secret code of a child at a tree house door. It snowed overnight and she's in a down parka that reaches her knees. When I open the door Custard's framed across the street behind her, tail wagging as he watches us from his fenced-in front yard, paws hidden in the snow. I think of Henry back in August—the afternoon sun in his eyes, his fingers combing through Custard's fur. The longing feels like a corset, flattening me.

Pauline's in her midforties and frustrated after a string of duds (her words, from the lengthy email she sent me after booking). I have a feeling she and Nan are going to be fast friends. As soon as she sees me, she shouts my name like we've known each other for years.

"Welcome," I say, ushering her over the threshold on a smile. "How was your journey?"

"Easy as pie." Pauline lives in Utah, and drove over the state line for her four-night stay. "Gorgeous weather on 70. View after view after view."

"I do love that drive," I say. "Did you—"

"And look what I found at the gas station in town!" She thrusts a newspaper into my hands and unwinds a scarf from around her neck. As she shakes out her perfectly blown-out hair I look down at the copy of *The Estes Park Trail-Gazette*, marked with today's date.

All of it hits me at the exact same time, disparate pieces of information clustering up at the front of my skull to jockey for my attention:

The headline: ESTES HOME WITH HEARTBREAKING HISTORY BECOMES A HAVEN FOR THE BROKENHEARTED.

The lede: *For the last few months, the Comeback Inn—a bed-and-breakfast in Estes Park's Ponderosa Ranch neighborhood—has welcomed heartbroken out-of-staters and Coloradans alike into its warm embrace. It's a heartwarming turn of events for a home with a painful past.*

The photograph: My house from the sidewalk. A head-on shot of the front porch, the wide wooden door. Unfamiliar flowerpots lining the steps. A family of three clustered at the top: Henry, a small girl on his lap. His arm around a woman.

The woman: Joss.

My gardener, my friend. The person who sat in my kitchen just a couple days ago, drinking my tea.

And, apparently, Henry's ex-wife.

Thirty-One

The photograph is sweet poison. I'm frozen in the entryway, clutching it two-handed. Henry's hair is so dark, no silver at his temples, shorter than I've ever seen it. His smile is broad and open-mouthed, like he's coming down from a laugh. One hand holds Molly against him, fingers splayed over her belly, her legs tucked over his own. She's tiny: smaller than Quinn, in a velvet dress and ruffly socks. I imagine Henry putting them on her and it traps the breath in my throat.

"It's a lovely profile," Pauline says. She bends over to unzip her boots. "Some of your past guests are even quoted! They just rave about you."

But her words meet me like water, beading up and evaporating. I can hardly hear her over the ringing in my ears. Over the wail of details pelting me, relentless, one after another after another.

Henry's fingers bracketed around Joss's shoulder. The angle of her head, tipped toward him. The palm of her hand on his knee. I can feel it in my own hand, like a burn: the memory of touching him. Joss is smiling straight into the camera and it's like she's looking directly at me. *You idiot*, I hear. From Joss or from Goldie or from myself, I'm not sure. *You absolute fool.*

"Is everything all right?" Pauline asks. Distantly, I'm aware of Nan coming down the stairs. "You look a bit pale."

"Everything's fine," I say, in a voice that sounds nothing like my own. It's breathless and wavering. "Let me show you to your room."

Nan takes the paper from my hands without a word, scanning it in the entryway while I bring Pauline's bags up the stairs. While I show her the activities card. While I point out her bathroom, where just a couple months ago Henry was spread flat on his back to fix the shower. While I move on autopilot, the truth spreading through me like a virus. *Henry and Joss. Henry and Joss, here, in your house. Henry and Joss in love, Henry and Joss with a child, Henry and Joss fighting in the garden. Henry and Joss with an entire life you could never understand.*

"The gardener," Nan says, when I come back down the stairs. She points to Joss's face before looking up at mine. "She and Henry were married?"

I nod, and Nan's eyes cloud with understanding. "You didn't know," she says.

"I need to—" I don't know where the sentence is going when I start it. *Crawl into a hole*, maybe. I reach for my phone, my car keys. Think of Joss sitting in my living room this fall, talking about her heartbreak. Of Henry, right there, walking in on it. "If Pauline needs anything, can you help her? I'm sorry. I'll be back."

"Of course," Nan says. Her hand rests on my forearm for just a brief moment, grounding me. "We'll be here."

"Thank you." I toe on my sneakers and pull open the front

door. I trip on my way to the car—my eyes glued to my phone instead of the ground. Snow fills one of my shoes, soaking my sock through to the skin.

I text Mei first: Joss is Henry's ex-wife. Then Henry himself: There's an article about your family in the paper. You could have told me about Joss. When I drop behind the wheel I have no idea where I'm planning to go; I just know I need to be away from the house. Away from the front steps where Joss and Henry sat with their daughter. Away from that patch of wallpaper in the Lupine Room.

Mei calls me at the exact same time Henry's text comes through: Where are you? I send her to voicemail and turn the car on. It's frigid today—the first week of December. My breath condenses like smoke, obscures the house through my windshield.

I put the car in reverse and back out of the driveway, churning up frozen gravel. Where am I? Where *am* I? I start driving toward the lake, directionless, letting the green lights determine my path. I shouldn't be driving, probably—my chest is shaking, breaths coming rickety and forced. The road is slick with patches of ice, everyone taking it slow and careful.

The betrayal feels bottomless. All the times Joss could have told me. All the times Henry should have. I feel like the stupidest woman to ever set foot on earth. I hate both of them for making a fool of me.

I'm at a red light near the turnoff for Rocky Mountain National Park when someone honks at me, pointed and prolonged. It jolts me into the present: I clutch the wheel and look up at the rearview mirror, where Henry's black SUV looms immediately behind my bumper. There's snow clustered at the bottom of his windshield. He points left, saying something that I can't hear. I want to drive away and never show him my face again; I want to crawl through his window and cling to him like a koala bear; I want to throttle him for keeping something like this from me.

The light turns green, and when I don't move, the car behind Henry honks at us both. Henry waves left again, more dramatically this time. I clench the steering wheel and flip on my signal.

I wind through a residential neighborhood, Henry right behind me. I think about driving home, or to his place, or to the highway. I wonder how long he'd follow me, wonder what he could possibly have to say when I finally run out of gas. But after we've looped through the neighborhood twice and I still haven't figured out what I want to do, Henry lays on his horn again. I watch him reach for his phone, his car slowing, and then my phone lights up in the cup holder: *Pull over.*

The neighborhood opens up to undeveloped land, fields of winter-crisp reeds cut by a trickling ravine that winds all the way to Lake Estes. It's frozen today: a floe of ice through the grass. I pull onto the shoulder and put my car in park. The field is ringed in mountains, Longs Peak snowy and commanding in the distance. Before I've even had a chance to take a deep breath, Henry's body fills my window.

"Are you stalking me?" I demand, looking up at him through the glass. It sounds bratty and unhinged, which is exactly how I feel.

"I was driving to the house and I saw your car," Henry says. He tries to open my door, but it's locked. "Can you open this, please?"

For a second I let myself imagine not opening it. Turning the car back on, rolling away from Henry, leaving him standing in the field like the exact kind of idiot he's turned me into. But I make the mistake of meeting his eyes, and it's excruciatingly clear. I can't drive away from Henry—not from the worried line between his brows, not from his infuriatingly beautiful face.

I open the door, and he takes a step backward. I lean against it as soon as it's closed, putting as much space between us as possible, tears rising in my throat like a threat. I swallow.

"Louisa," Henry says. He takes a deep breath and sets his shoulders like he's bracing for me. Already, his cheeks are pink from the cold. It's unbearable, the way he wears every feeling so honestly on his face. "That's not the way I wanted you to find out about Joss and me."

Joss and me. I feel it like a slap.

"You lied," I say. Wind blows across the meadow, rustling the snow-laced grass, and I hunch into myself. I left in a rush; all I'm wearing is a long-sleeve T-shirt. Henry starts to shoulder out of his coat. "When I asked about her. You said she was long gone."

"That wasn't a lie." Henry steps forward to wrap the coat around me, and I shrink away from him. He freezes, eyes tracking over me, before stepping backward and holding the coat in the space between us. On principle, I don't want it—but I'm already shaking, and I also don't want to have this conversation while trembling like a pathetic damsel. I take it, hunching into its borrowed warmth. "My romantic relationship with Joss *is* long gone. It's been more than five years since the divorce. Longer since it was over between us."

"That's not the same, and you know it." The coat smells like Henry. Citrus soap, aftershave, everything good. My body betrays me by wrapping it even further around my shoulders, burrowing into him. "Joss isn't *gone*—she's right here. I thought she was my friend."

"She is your friend," Henry says, and I let out a sharp exhale. It's so patronizing—like I'm a child.

"Friends don't keep things like this from each other."

Henry's wearing a button-down, and I wonder if he came from work. Wind teases through his hair and I watch goose bumps rise on his neck, the dip in his collarbone. I make myself look away as he says, "Our relationship to the house is complicated. She takes care of the garden because it makes her feel close to Molly. I manage the rentals because I can't bear to sell it." He takes a step closer to me, eyes serious and searching on mine. "But our relationship to each other is simple, Louisa. We were partners once. We went through something incomprehensible together. Now we take care of the house. That's it."

"Then what were you fighting about, in the garden?"

He blinks. His nose is turning pink. "Nothing," he says, and I shake my head.

"I can't be with someone who keeps secrets from me." It's out before I've thought it through; before I've even realized that it's true. Nate had an entire life I didn't know about. Now Henry does, too—after I sat, shaking with panicked adrenaline, on his couch. After I told him all of it.

"It wasn't a secret," Henry says, taking a half step closer. "I would have told you, I—"

"When?" I angle my chin upward, don't move my gaze from his. "Why should I believe that?"

"You really think I'm lying?" Henry asks, his voice rising. It's the loudest I've heard him since that day in my kitchen, when the *Denver Post* article came out and I caught the very first glimpse of his jagged, broken heart.

"Maybe!" I cry, throwing my hands up. "I don't know what to believe now, Henry, I—"

"Believe this," he says, and reaches for me. His hands are cold, framing my face. "The past few months with you have torn my life apart." His eyes track over mine—sharp, paralyzing blue in the afternoon light. "There were years when I didn't want anything at all. Not to remember any of it, not to feel anything, not to imagine a future. The rest of my life, without her."

I bite my lip, and Henry's eyes flick to my mouth. He lowers his hands so they're on my neck, thumbs tracing my jaw. "But you—" He breaks off. His eyes search mine, and I wait. Henry draws a shaking breath. "I imagine it, with you. I want—" He stops again, dropping his hands and shrugging helplessly. He takes half a step backward, giving me space. When he speaks again, his voice is so soft I hardly hear it. "I want."

Me, too, I think. I want Henry so badly it leaves me breathless—the defeated slope of his shoulders, and the earnestness of his gaze on mine, and the flush creeping up his neck. I want to touch him there. I want to hear him say my name like he did that night at his house, wrecked and breathless. I've imagined it, too. I've imagined all of it.

But I force myself to speak. "Then why did you keep this from me?"

Henry exhales, looking out over the open space. He licks his lower lip and then rubs his palm over his mouth, covers it with his hand, gathers himself. "Because it's hard," he says finally. "Because there's so much pain in that house, and between Joss and me, and I didn't want to—I wasn't ready to bring that to you."

I feel my eyebrows pull together. Wave a hand half-heartedly into the space between us. "I've shown you my whole mess, Henry. Nate, my mom."

"I know," he says, taking a step toward me. I'm so cold, even in his coat—he must be freezing. "And then you disappeared."

My head snaps up. "What?"

"You think I haven't noticed you distancing yourself from me since Thanksgiving?" His eyes move back and forth over mine. "You happen to be at my house when your mom calls, so, okay, you feel like you have to tell me. You let me into this part of your life, basically by accident, and then you shut me out. What am I supposed to think, Louisa?" His dark eyebrows rise. "That I should make things *more* complicated? Tell you about Joss?"

"That's not—" I shake my head, trying to clear it. Why is this conversation turning onto me? "That's not fair."

"No?" Henry doesn't blink. "Then where have you been the past few days?"

Licking my wounds, I think. *Trying to see past how desperately I care about you.*

"I meant what I said," he continues when I still haven't responded. "You scare me shitless." A car whips past us on the road, and Henry turns to watch it over one shoulder. I stare at his face in profile: flushed in the bitter chill, dark and severe and familiar. He turns back to me. "I knew about you for years, but to actually know you—" His jaw clenches, lets go. "How incredible you are. How you have this way of making every room you walk into feel better, and warmer, and safe. How I want you so badly I can't even sleep." My eyes film over with tears, blurring him as he takes a step closer. This hurts too much; more than I have room for in my body. "Now that I know you, I can't—" Henry's eyes trace back and forth over mine. Then he swallows, his voice going soft. "Please don't cry."

It only tightens the vise on my throat, and when I bite my lip to try to swallow my tears Henry reaches for me. He tucks me in against him, his cheek on my hair, and I let him.

"Sweetheart," he murmurs. It blooms in my chest like a bruise. *I don't want to call you what everyone else calls you.* "Please. I've been so terrified to get attached to anything, terrified I'll lose it, especially you." His lungs rise against my cheek. I can feel his heart beating—even through the coat, even through the cold—quick and hard. "So why would I, after feeling you push away from me, tell you something that I know is complicated? That I know is going to be hard for you to hear?"

I squeeze my eyes shut and force myself to move away from him. He doesn't fight it; his arms drop to his sides, his eyes scanning my face as I wipe my cheeks dry. "That's not how it works," I say. "You can't pick and choose which parts of yourself to give me, Henry, it has to be all of it. I can't have you halfway."

"No," he says, urgent, one hand reaching for mine. "That's not what I mean."

"It is." I cut him off. Detangle my fingers from his and jam them into his coat pocket. I can't be this person: giving all of myself to someone who's holding back. "I can't."

Henry blinks. When he takes a step backward his eyes sweep over me, like he's assessing damage or looking for someone he recognizes. "Can't what?"

I bite my lip to hold back my tears, and it doesn't work.

When they leak onto my cheeks the wind chills them to ice. "Can't do this. You lied."

"Louisa," he says, reaching for me and then dropping his hands. He looks scared, wrecked. It hurts like a bone bruise, like something under the skin. "Please. I didn't."

"Henry, you did."

"Well, what about you?" His arms lift as his voice goes rough, uncontrolled. "I Googled you."

My mind blurs, all the things he could find: "Purple Girl," Nate cheating, every unflattering photograph from Say It Now shows in college. But it doesn't occur to me what Henry's talking about. What he means. What of course, of course, of *course* he means.

"You aren't a therapist," he says, and it hangs in the cold air between us. "I know you aren't licensed here. You lied to me, too."

I blink the tears out of my eyes, trying to see him clearly. How long has he been sitting on this? Why hasn't it mattered until now?

"That's not the same," I say thinly.

"No?" Henry sounds ruined—like something's snapped inside of him. I want to cover my face so I don't have to see him like this, anguished because of something I've done. "Why not?"

"I just wanted you to believe in me," I say. I sniff against the wind, wipe a hand roughly over my eyes. "I just wanted you to trust me, Henry."

"Me, too," he says. "That's exactly what I wanted, too."

I look up at him. The intensity of his gaze, the pain on his face—clear, consuming. I can't think of a single thing to say, a single way to fix this. I have the distinct, saw-toothed thought that I'm hurting him. That if I'd just left Henry alone, we'd both be better off.

"I'm going to go," I say, and reach for my car door.

"Please." His hand lands on my arm, but when I look over my shoulder, he lets go. "Louisa, I don't want you to leave like this." He clears his throat. "I don't want you to leave at all."

It tugs me open, loosening a stitch that unravels everything I've been trying to hold together. I feel my nose scrunch, my body's very last-ditch attempt not to cry. "I'm sorry," I manage—and then I'm in my car, and I'm closing the door, and I'm driving away. When I glance up, just once, Henry's standing on the shoulder in the rearview.

I'm halfway home before I realize I'm still wearing his coat.

Thirty-Two

The first thing I see when I get back to the house is Joss's car. I think about turning right back around and driving clear on to Nebraska, but make myself put the car in park. This is still my house—though for how much longer, I'm not sure.

The door to the garden is propped open. I move toward it like a ghost, half-real. Joss has her back to me, crouched over a bed of ivy in a down jacket; she's trimming it back, piling snow-dusted leaves into a bag. When my sneakers land on the path next to her knee, she looks up at me.

"Hey, Lou."

She looks more beautiful than ever: that Nordic blond hair, the dusting of freckles on the bridge of her nose. I picture her and Henry getting married, having Molly, sitting with her in a hospital room while their lives fall apart. I'm not mad at her—I'm devastated.

"I know about you and Henry," I say. "There was an article in the paper."

Joss is silent. She doesn't even blink. But then she looks

down at the bed, surveying her progress, and stands. She pulls her gloves off and puts them on top of her bag.

"I wish you'd told me."

She lets out a breath that condenses in the space between us. "When could I have, though?"

I feel my head rear back and will myself to keep it together. "Literally anytime? In all the years I've lived here?"

"In all the years you've lived here, Henry was hardly in the picture." She lifts her eyebrows. "It wasn't until this fall, with the rentals, that he started coming around. It was a nonissue."

"But we were friends," I insist. *Weren't we?* "It wasn't a non-issue. He was part of your life."

Joss studies me, speaking slowly. "Henry will always be a part of my past. But it's been a long time since we've been involved with each other in any meaningful way."

It sounds so similar to what Henry told me that I can't help but wonder if they talked about this. "What about this fall?" I press. "When you told us all about your heartbreak, and how losing him even impacted your family?"

"I wasn't talking about Henry," Joss says. She looks surprised, like this hadn't even occurred to her. "I was talking about Molly."

I swallow. Feel her words as heat in my cheeks. *Of course.*

"But you own the house together?" I force out.

Joss shakes her head. "The house is Henry's. It's been in his family forever—I just manage the garden, for Molly." When I don't respond, she keeps talking. "Henry told me he was inviting you to Thanksgiving." This hits like whiplash, the memory of her in my kitchen just a few days ago, asking if I had a nice holiday. She knew, even then. "Not that I need to be informed, and certainly not that I need to give permission. I didn't know, before then, that you were involved." I look up at her, and she tucks her hands into her jacket pockets. "And even if I had, how should I have told you? 'By the way, I was married to your new boyfriend'?"

"Henry's not—"

"It already felt too late," Joss says. "Like by then, it was up to Henry to tell you, when he was ready."

I shake my head. He could tell Joss about *me*, but not the other way around? "I don't know if he would've ever been ready."

"He's a good person, Lou. So are you." Joss gestures to herself. "Don't hold this against him."

I don't know what to say to this. Of course Henry's a good person. It gives me a stomachache, to think about how magnetic he is—about all the ways I want to be close to him.

"What were you fighting about?" I hear myself say. "I saw you in the garden, fighting. Twice."

Joss's eyebrows flicker up. "Oh," she says. When her eyes cast across the garden, landing on the new tree, I turn to look at it, too. She clears her throat. "After Molly died, we talked about planting a pine tree for her. But then we were going through a divorce, and then you and Nate moved in, and it kind of just—" She glances back at me. "Well, we stopped talking about it. But I've seen a lot more of Henry this fall than I have in a long time, with him at the house. And I wanted to finally do it, and he didn't think it was the right time, and it just—" She waves her hand in the air, trailing off.

"It just?" I prompt.

Joss looks at me. "He didn't want to talk about it. He doesn't want to talk about her."

You don't say, I think.

"So I bought a tree anyway, and didn't consult him on it, and then he was mad about that."

"That's stupid," I say, and Joss snorts a laugh.

"I was taking your advice." Her smile softens into a line, her lips tucking in between her teeth. Like she's nervous to tell me this, like she doesn't want me to be angry. "Putting my oxygen mask on. Doing what I needed to, to heal."

I think of what she said, back in my living room this fall. *Everyone has feelings, and you sort of have to navigate them.* Of Henry, his lips at my throat on his own living room floor. That tattoo tracing a line over his chest.

"He won't talk to me about her."

Joss nods. When she looks down at her boots, I nearly apologize—I shouldn't be talking about this with her. But then she says, "I'm glad that he told you about Molly at all. He has a tough time about her."

A cluster of pine needles floats through the air, landing on Joss's sleeve. "I'm sure you do, too," I say, and she looks up at me.

She shrugs, one-shouldered. "Of course." For a moment, we regard each other in silence. I don't know what to do now, what could make this better. I have the sharp, sinking feeling that the answer is nothing. Joss reaches forward and touches my arm—when I look down, I realize I still have Henry's jacket on, and feel like the world's biggest asshole.

"Look, Lou," she says. "I'm not going to tell you not to be mad at him. I know you've been through a lot, and he has, too. But for what it's worth—" She draws a deep breath, her hand falling from my arm. "Henry and I went through the worst possible thing together. We weren't right for each other, in the end, but I'm always going to be glad it was him, in that with me." A cloud moves overhead, sending sunlight straight into her eyes. "He's who you want, when everything goes to shit. He makes mistakes." She shrugs. "But he's who you want."

I'm walking Joss to her truck a few minutes later when Mei's car pulls into the driveway. When she sees me she throws her hands up in the air, like I've completely exasperated her.

"Did you drop your phone into a sinkhole?" she says, stepping out onto the gravel. "I've been trying you for the last hour."

"So you just—" I dig into my pocket for my phone, clocking six missed calls and as many text messages from Mei. And, even more ominously, a handful from Goldie. "Drove here?"

"Yes!" Mei cries, slamming her car door. "I thought you were in crisis."

I glance at Joss, who's piling lawn bags into her flatbed. Mei follows my gaze and seems to realize, for the first time, that we aren't alone out here.

"Hey, Mei," Joss says, casually. She's maybe the most self-possessed person I've ever met.

"Uh," Mei says, glancing at me. "Hi?"

"It's fine," I say, tucking my phone back into my pocket and moving toward her for a hug. "We're mad at Henry, not Joss."

Mei squeezes me. "Okay, noted."

"Take care of yourself," Joss says, looking at me as she pulls open her truck door. "Okay?"

I nod, and lift my hand in a wave. Mei and I watch Joss roll down the street. Then Mei looks at me. "What the fuck?"

"Yeah," I say on an exhale. "What the *fuck*."

"Did you talk to Henry? What did Joss say? Are you okay?"

"Come inside." I hook my arm through hers. "I'm freezing."

"What is this coat?" Mei asks, angling away from me to get a better look at it as we move up the front steps. "I don't hate it, but it's big on you."

"It's Henry's," I mumble. "We were talking outside, and I was cold."

"Hm," Mei says. "A liar and a gentleman."

"Indeed."

"Well?" Nan's voice greets us the moment we open the front door. She's standing next to Pauline in the entryway, both of them holding mugs of tea and looking at me expectantly. "What happened?"

"Nan!" Mei says, stepping toward her for a hug. "You're still here!"

"Leave Lou?" Nan says, smiling at me over Mei's shoulder. "I don't think so. Now come in the living room and tell us what happened with that Henry."

It feels like a soft landing place, here with Mei and Nan and Pauline. The way they usher me to the couch and drop a blanket over me and busy themselves gathering tea and pillows. But I'm talked out—and when my phone rings again, I find myself grateful for the distraction.

It's Goldie, of course. I pick up against my better judgment.

"Hi," I say, and Goldie starts talking a mile a minute, her words rushing into each other.

"Lou, it's Mom. I don't know exactly what happened but her rent didn't get paid and she's out of her place; Mark called me and said she's 'flown off the handle'—his words—he doesn't want her staying with him; this has all unraveled in the last twenty-four hours and I think we need to go out there and sort it. To Ohio. Right away."

I've sat up straighter on the couch with every one of her sentences. Nan, Pauline, and Mei have all stopped what they're doing to look at me.

"But I sent her the money," I say dumbly. Like that hasn't backfired before; like I'm incapable of learning my own stupid lesson. "Enough to cover—"

"Mark said something about being late on her insurance, didn't you say that was drawing this fall? So maybe it went to that, or maybe she blew it all on something else, Lou, I mean—does it matter? This is the situation. This is—"

"It does matter." It's Henry's money. It's Comeback Inn money. I should never, ever, ever have let him get involved in this.

"It doesn't," Goldie says. "She's doing what she always does, Lou—when she has enough money, she spends it on something stupid. We know this. We *know* this."

She's mad at herself—I can hear it in her voice. But she's mad at me, too.

"I called her and she just blew the whole thing off," Goldie says. "It's impossible to get her to talk it through. We need to be there—I mean, Mark's going to kick her out. She'll be on the street."

I notice the *we*. That my sister isn't asking me to handle this; she's suggesting we do it together. But even still, the dread is like a blanket. Going home—to Ohio, to our mother—is the last thing I want to do. But I know, even before I respond, that I'll go. Of course I will.

"Okay," I say. "I'll look at flights."

"Right," Goldie says. "I'm going to try—I mean, I don't think I can get Quinn ready today, it's already four—maybe first thing in the morning? I'll look at tickets and text you? We can stay at that place near the old high school—with the pool Quinn likes?"

"Yeah." My voice is soft, trailing away. I close my eyes. "Sounds good."

The line clicks off. I leave my eyes closed.

"Lou?" It's Mei, hesitant. "What's going on?"

I sniff, opening my eyes and stuffing myself away. All the pain of this morning; Henry's anguished eyes on mine; his hand dropping from my arm. I put myself in fix-it mode. The thing I'm best at.

"My mom's sick," I say. "I need to go to Ohio."

Behind Mei, Nan and Pauline look at each other. "Pauline," I say, standing, "I'm so sorry. I promise it's not always such a mess here—today's just been . . . I mean." I wave a hand in the air and look at Mei. "I'm going to have to close."

"Close?" Nan says, talking a step toward me. "The inn?"

"Yeah. I'm so sorry. I just—I don't know how long I'll be gone. I don't know when I'll be back." I'm processing in real time, saying the words in the exact moment I think them. "There won't be anyone to tend to the house, who knows where everything is. I'm leaving in the morning, I think—"

"I'm coming with you," Mei says. When I open my mouth to protest, she holds up a hand. "When Andy left, you helped me. It's my turn. I'll be your chauffeur, or babysit Quinn so you and Goldie can handle shit, or whatever you need. I'll email work. It'll be fine."

I don't know what to say. The thought of Mei there with me makes it all so much more bearable that I could burst into tears on the spot.

"And I'll manage things here," Nan says. I shoot her a wet-eyed smile, shaking my head.

"Nan, no, I can't ask you to—"

"I know who you *can* ask," Mei says. We regard each other in silence. Like an underscore, her eyebrows lift.

Henry answers on the first ring.

"Thank god," he says, but I can't sink into him. I think of Joss, in the garden: *He's who you want, when everything goes to shit.* Of Henry, in his living room: *You know I'm not doing this for her.*

"Henry," I say. And then I ask for the one thing I've always been so awful at accepting. "I need help."

Thirty-Three

The Columbus airport is gilded for Christmas—all flocked trees and string-light stars and snowflake window clings in the souvenir shops. Quinn points out every decoration as we make our way toward the car rentals. He's holding my hand, like the one grounding force tethering me to this earth.

"So this is Ohio," Mei says, taking in the gray morning through the terminal's tall windows.

"This is Ohio," Goldie confirms. She's been full throttle since we met her at her gate twenty minutes ago; before I could even give Quinn a hug she'd thrust her phone into my hand, open to her notes app riddled with residential treatment facilities in Columbus. This is where Goldie shines: not with feelings, but with logistics. I'd handed it back to her and picked up my nephew.

"Are you ready to see the pool?" I ask him now. We step onto the escalator and he clenches my hand for balance.

"Yeah," Quinn says. "Mom packed my Christmas swim trunks."

"Christmas swim trunks," I say, raising my eyebrows at Goldie. "How appropriate."

"I do what I can," she mumbles, still scrolling through her phone. The plan is for Mei to bring Quinn to the hotel so Goldie and I can meet Mom at Mark's house. She knows we're coming, but doesn't seem to see this for what it is—an intervention, an eviction, the demise of her relationship.

"Mei, did you bring your swimsuit?" Quinn cranes around to look at her over one shoulder, and I pick him up to set him on the solid ground at the end of the escalator.

"Duh," Mei says. "We're gonna play mermaids until you're wrinkled up like a prune."

Quinn giggles, hopping a little. "*Gross!*"

Mei smiles at him and then finds my eyes, reaching forward to squeeze my shoulder. I spent the plane ride studying for the NCE, which I'm retaking in a couple weeks. With Mei asleep in the window seat beside me, there was no one to see me do it—to pull up the practice test on my computer, tick through the multiple-choice questions until my eyes felt twitchy and sharp. It was easier than thinking about what waited for me on the other end of the flight: my mother, my hometown, all of my memories. Easier, too, than thinking about what I was leaving behind: Henry.

He'd agreed to manage things at the house without hesitation. Even after I told him the money was gone; even after I told him I had three more people checking in this week. His low voice was right there, the entire plane ride: *Whatever you need.* I pushed it away. Narrowed the world until it was only my practice test and me.

"When do I see Grandma?" Quinn asks as Goldie clips him

into his car seat. Our rental is a microscopic Kia, its back seat barely big enough for Mei and Quinn. She's holding her suitcase on her lap because there isn't room for it in the trunk.

"Probably tomorrow," Goldie tells him. "Mom and Aunt Lou-Lou need to help her with some grown-up stuff first."

Quinn nods seriously, like he understands the gravity of the situation. When his eyes meet mine, I feel like I could cry. I drive so that Goldie can make her phone calls—checking availability at the facilities she's found. Checking if they take Medicare. Checking if Medicare covers the costs in their entirety.

Columbus spreads flat and familiar before me. I feel sixteen again, driving home from whoever's house I'd spent the night at so I wouldn't be home alone with Mom. Eighteen, leaving for college and feeling it like the deepest breath I'd ever taken. Twenty, with Goldie for Christmas and missing Nate, desperate to get back to the life we'd made together.

And twenty-six, as I am now. Henry here like a stitch in my side, an ache I can't knead out.

Mark lives in a development near the mall where I worked in high school. When I turn left into his neighborhood, we pass the gas station where I used to buy Sour Patch Kids before my shifts. There's leftover snow slushed into brown piles in the gutters.

"I hate this," I say, the first words either Goldie or I have spoken since dropping Mei and Quinn at the hotel.

She looks over at me. We haven't talked about our own shit, about what went down when she visited in October or how tense things have been between us since then. I haven't talked to her about what Mei said to me, about the double standard

Goldie's held me to all these years. But the way she's taken on communication with Mark and inpatient research tells me she feels bad for dropping the Thanksgiving rent situation on me.

"Yeah, well." She looks out the window, leaving it at that.

Mom's car is parked on the street in front of a low brick bungalow. It's the 1990s Maxima she's had since we were kids—faded maroon and rusted around the wheels. I want to sit in the car for a minute, to take a deep breath and remind myself that I'm not in danger and push Henry's face out of my mind for the one millionth time since leaving Colorado. But Goldie's already opening her door and stepping out into the frigid morning.

"Let's go," she says, so I do.

Mom answers the door in jeans and a hoodie, dark eyeliner, her hair dyed a deep red that's faded to bruised purple.

"My babies!" she cries, pulling us in for hugs. Mark isn't here; he asked us to *deal* with Mom while he was at work, like a coward. Mom smells like she always has: the stale cling of cigarettes, not quite masked by her favorite perfume. "I'm so glad you're home."

"We're not *home*," Goldie says, closing the front door behind us. "We're here to clean up your mess."

"Goldie," I say, releasing our mother.

"What?" Goldie's eyes flick to mine before looking back at Mom. "She needs to hear it."

It's unsurprising. Goldie wears her honesty like a medal of honor, like a gift—but in this situation, as in so many situations before, it's not helpful.

"Oh, Marigold," Mom says, swatting a hand at her. "Don't start with me. Let me show you girls what I've been working on."

She doesn't wait for us to reply, just starts across the living room. It's depressingly *male* in here: overstuffed, lumpy armchairs with plastic-handled recliners; a couch with thin, matching throw pillows; empty beer cans lined up like chess pieces on the coffee table.

"I'm decorating," Mom says, leading us down a dim hallway and into a bedroom. There are shopping bags strewn over the floor, the desk, the unmade bed. "Dani at work told me about this great store over at the mall, you remember Dani, she's Yolanda the owner's daughter, sweet kid. Younger than you, Lou." Mom reaches for a throw pillow, intricately beaded and distinctly uncomfortable looking. "Mark, bless him, has no taste. So I'm sprucing up. I ordered some bedding this morning, and there's—"

"Who's paying?" Goldie says.

Mom blinks. She starts reaching for discarded bags, arranging them into a stack. Goldie moves toward her and I put my hand on her arm.

"Mom," I say, gently. "Where are your things? From your house—your clothes?"

She looks up at me, stack of bags suspended between us. "At home, baby. I've just got the one bag." She waves vaguely at the corner of the room, where a black suitcase sits open on the floor. "I'll be back there soon, so I only brought my necessities."

"Okay," I hear myself say. I imagine the rest of her things rounded up by a maid service, hauled to a dumpster or dropped in a Goodwill bin. I imagine Goldie and me back here in a month, when Mom is stable and back on her own somewhere, helping her rebuy everything she left at her old apartment. But that's a problem for later. "Can we help you pack up so we can all leave together?"

Mom stares at me. Since I was a kid, I've pictured these moments as a game of Operation. Thread the needle, remove the organ, avoid her triggers. She's always been one wrong word from exploding. I've always been so much better at steering her than Goldie.

"Leave?" she says, every trace of excitement dropping out of her voice. "Why would I leave?"

"This is Mark's house—" Goldie says, and I hold up my hand to silence her. For once, she does as I ask.

"Goldie and I want to bring you somewhere safe," I say. Mom stares at me. "You can't stay with Mark. He asked us to help you move out."

Silence stutters between us. Mom swallows. "He did?"

I nod. It would be easier to lie, maybe—to trick her somehow, to get her out of here. But she deserves the truth. "You can't stay here anymore, and you can't go back to your apartment because you didn't pay the rent."

Mom blinks rapidly, her cheeks diffusing pink. I glance at Goldie before looking back at her. "We found somewhere you can go, until you find another apartment. Residential treatment."

I wait for her to respond to this, but her eyes only dart back and forth over mine.

"You'll be safe there," I say. My voice only wavers a little. "You'll be able to talk to a therapist, and—"

"I don't want to talk to a therapist." The words shoot out of our mother, loud and sharp.

"Well, you need to," Goldie says. "It's not a negotiation."

"Goldie," I say, cutting my eyes at her. "Stop." I can feel Mom teetering on the precarious edge of her anger, and Goldie's only going to make it worse. I reach for Mom's arm, and she looks up at me.

"I don't need therapy, Lou." Her voice has a shredded quality: she's scared. "This was just a silly mistake with the rent. It isn't about therapy. It isn't about that."

"Okay," I say. My chest is tight and suffocating, but I force my voice to come out smooth. "Then it can just be about a safe place for you to stay until you find a new apartment. We'll go there together, okay?" I glance at my sister, whose arms are crossed. "All three of us. You trust me, right?"

Slowly, my mother nods. She looks at Goldie, then back at me. "Mhm," she says, not quite a word. But it's enough—enough for me to ease the bags out of her hands, for Goldie to zip up her suitcase, for us to pick through the rest of Mark's house for our mother's scattered things.

By the time we settle her into the back seat of the Kia, Mom's eyes are wet with tears. She reminds me of Quinn, back here—small and helpless.

"Mom," I say. My mother looks up at me, and then I do lie to her. "Everything's okay."

After dropping her off at the only treatment option Goldie could find with an immediate opening, we meet Quinn and Mei at the hotel pool. Goldie hauls Quinn out of the water without hesitation—even as he splashes her, even as he protests. She wraps him in a towel and whisks him up to the room for a nap and doesn't say anything to either of us. We haven't spoken since leaving the facility.

The last image I have of our mother—scorched into me like a sunburn—is her red face, mottled with anger and fear. Realizing she has no option but to stay where we've taken her; that another man has let her down; that she needs more help than she knows how to get on her own. I haven't been able to take a full breath since we showed up at Mark's house.

Mei watches me sit down on the pool chair beside her, stretching my legs out in front of me. The whole room feels humid and close, no one here but us, the pool water still swaying with the echo of Quinn's kicking feet. I stare at my shoes and try to remember how to breathe.

"Do you want to talk about it?" Mei asks.

I press my eyes shut. My mother crying, two nurses with their hands on her elbows, everyone in the waiting room watching us pass through. I shake my head.

"Okay," Mei says. Her hand lands on mine, unclenching it from its fist and winding our fingers together. "You're a good daughter and a good person and I love you."

I squeeze her fingers. "I'm an idiot."

"No, Lou. This was the right thing to do, even if it feels like shit."

"Not that," I whisper. I've been here before, breaking my mother's heart. I've felt this specific brand of impossible. But there's another hurt, rattling between my ribs—a new, bottomless sort of loss.

"I thought I had this so figured out," I say, finally opening my eyes. Mei's right there, blurry. "With my stupid heartbreak hotel. I was doing so well about Nate. I thought I was so strong and had it so together and could teach everyone else how to recover because I was so—so *good* at it." I sniff, and Mei squeezes my hand. "But I was never good at it, Mei, I just didn't love him anymore. I thought I had it all figured out, but I just didn't care enough. And now—" My voice squeaks off. I shake my head, looking out over the pool.

Today, with my mom, dislodged all of it: How devastated I am that Henry's held back with me. How embarrassed I am that he's known I've been lying about my license for months. How absolutely miserable I am without him. How entirely wrecked.

Every time I felt scared today—as I shushed my sister, as I parented my mom, as I left her in an unfamiliar place full of strangers—it was Henry I wanted. Henry I wished was there with me: the solid wall of his body, the low rumble of his voice. *I understand*, that day in the fall at Polliwog's. His own loss shaking through him that night on my living room couch.

He's become my safe place, the feeling I yearn for when I'm afraid. And I've gone and pushed him away.

"I had no idea what I was talking about," I tell Mei now. "None at all."

She scoots onto my pool chair, wrapping her arms around me until we're twisted on the rubber slats like a couple of snakes—clunky and uncomfortable and too warm. I tuck my face into her shoulder. She squeezes me even closer. We stay like that, breathing, until I lose track of time.

Thirty-Four

If there's one word I would never use to describe my mother, it's *reserved*. She can be kind, and loving, and magnetic, and fun—but she's never once kept her big feelings to herself. When Goldie and I arrive to visit her the next morning, though, it's exactly how she looks: Like she's buttoned everything in. Like she's swallowing her anger.

"Morning, Mom," Goldie says. She leads me into the room—two beds separated by a thin curtain. Mom's is closest to the window, and the other is unoccupied, though a paperback novel splayed open on the pillow indicates someone's been here recently.

"Good morning," she replies. She's sitting on the edge of her bed in gray sweatpants and a matching crewneck sweater, blue socks. Her hands are folded in her lap, one thumb picking at the back of her knuckle. She's fidgety, unsettled. I wonder how much rage it took to get her here—how long she was furious with us before she accepted this. It's so painful to imagine her here alone all night that I force myself to stop.

"Did you sleep okay?" I ask. I know I didn't; Mei and I stayed up most of the night watching baking show reruns on the hotel room TV. She fell asleep sometime around two—I flitted in and out until finally giving up and going for coffee at six o'clock. Goldie and Quinn had their own room, and she'd kept her distance.

Mom nods, teeth worrying at her lip. When we sit in the chairs across from her, her hand darts out to clasp mine. "I'm so sorry about Nathan," she says. I can feel Goldie turn to look at me, but I hold Mom's eyes. Familiar and sad and the exact same color as my sister's.

I could be angry, I know. That in this moment, with everything she's put us through, this is what she's choosing to apologize for. But I know that she means it. That her heart is broken for me; that this is the way she loves me; that this is easier for her to talk about than the reality of what's happening in this room. I squeeze her hand. "Thanks, Mom. It's okay."

"He was a good boy," she says. "But you'll find someone else."

I nod. Think of Henry, his tattoo under my ear as I lay on his chest. "How are you feeling?"

Mom breathes a laugh, raspy. When she waves a hand around the room, anger flares on her face. "Mark isn't who I thought he was."

I watch Goldie digest this. Her lips pressing together, her chest rising with breath. She's furious; I can see it. This isn't about Mark, and I know—I *know*—she wants Mom to acknowledge that. But I also know that Mom knows it. That it's just too hard to say the rest of this out loud: that she's sick; that she always has been; that it isn't her fault and her healing isn't linear and, all those things being true, it's painful for us to be back here together. I know Goldie knows all of this, too. And I love her so much when she says quietly, "Men are trash."

Mom laughs. Her big one, belly-deep and scratchy. "Truer words never spoken, baby. All these boys who take and take and take and give you nothing in return."

I think of myself, this fall, in my kitchen. Of Goldie: *You do this, Lou. You take care of other people to avoid taking care of yourself.* And of Henry, who's taken every single opportunity I've ever given him to care for me right back. There's power in being the person someone needs—but there's power in accepting what you need, too.

My mother reaches for both of our hands, this time. "I love you," she says. I look at my sister, whose eyes sparkle with tears that she's quick to blink away. "I don't want you worrying about me, now."

When Goldie and I step through the sliding glass doors, the sun's emerged from behind Ohio's characteristic blanket of gray clouds. It makes the sidewalk sparkle: bits of granite dust, or whatever it is.

"That was hard," I say. Mom will be here for at least the next month, talking to a therapist every day. "Thanks for going easy on her."

Goldie slides her hands into the pockets of her wool coat. She looks out over the parking lot like it holds the secrets to the universe. "You taught me how to do that, you know."

"Do what?"

Goldie looks at me. "Say something that's kind and true, instead of just true." She turns away again. "Instead of just saying the thing I want to say."

I nod, taking this in. Before I can even respond, she's talking again—straight out at the rows of parked cars. "I know I'm too hard on you sometimes. That I can be honest *over* being kind, instead of both." She turns to me. "It's only because I love you, and I want you to be okay."

"I know," I say. "But I need you to trust me more. To take care of myself." I swallow, and make myself say the next bit out loud. "You trusting me feels like love. Because you're so smart, and so successful, and when you trust me—it makes me trust me, too. I need that from you."

She blinks, nodding once and then looking down at her boots. "Okay," she says. "Okay, that makes sense."

I sniff, hard, in the cold. "And it's not fair of you to accuse me of taking care of everyone else at the expense of myself, but then leave me to deal with Mom on my own. It's not fair to crucify me for the thing you clearly expect me to do."

Goldie's lips part. "That's not what—I don't mean to—"

I force myself to let her keep spluttering. It's a rare thing, to see my sister at a loss for words.

"I don't *expect* you to take care of Mom," she says finally. She doesn't look sorry, like I wanted her to. She looks pissed. "I just know you *will*, because you always *do*, which is my whole point."

"But I have to take care of her," I say, my voice rising. "Because I know you're not going to, so who does that leave, Goldie?"

Goldie spreads her hands. "I'm here, aren't I? When it's a real problem, I'm here."

"It's always a real problem!"

Goldie takes a step closer to me, leaning into my space. "Mom taking an ill-advised vacation that she can't afford is not a real problem, Lou, it's a *mistake*. And she's going to keep making them if you're always there to fix things for her."

My eyes sting. "So it's my fault she's in this mess."

"Absolutely not," Goldie snarls. "Don't even say that. Mom is a grown woman, responsible for all of her own shit, and you're her *child*, Lou. It makes me livid, watching her expect you to solve things for her." She leans away, but her eyes hold mine, angry and unblinking. "You've got to let that go. It's not your burden."

I swipe at my eyes, sniffing inelegantly into the cold. It's always felt like my burden. Like it belongs to me as much as my hair, my fingernails.

"I would rather die," Goldie says, "than have Quinn ever feel the way Mom's made you feel. Like I expect him to sacrifice *any* part of his own happiness to clean up after me."

"You would never do that to Quinn," I whisper.

"No," Goldie says. Her voice is like flint, sparking. "And Mom should never have done it to you."

I think of all the years I lived with Goldie. All the mornings she drove me to school before class, all the pieces of her childhood that she missed because of me. "Or you," I say. "All that time you raised me, instead of her."

Goldie blinks, the fury breaking from her face. Her eyes flicker away from mine, down to the sidewalk. I say, "Thank you."

"You don't need to thank me."

I take a step closer. "Mom needs to, but she probably won't, and you should get to hear it."

Goldie looks up at me. Swallows. "Then thank you, also. From Mom."

I nod. And then I take a shuddering breath and say, "I failed my NCE."

Goldie's head snaps back, her eyes flaring wide. "What? When?"

"Right after I finished my clinical hours," I tell her, "just like I planned." A couple walks through the double doors, arm in arm, and we step out of the way. I've essentially forgotten where we are, or that anyone could have overheard that entire exchange. But it's too late now. "Nate was in Stockholm with Say It Now. He cheated on me the night before the test, and I saw a picture of it, and it totally got in my head."

Goldie stares at me, unblinking.

"I failed it." My voice thins out, but I force myself to shrug—like this is even a little bit casual, like this isn't the scariest thing I've ever said out loud to my sister. "And I had to wait to retake it. But I'm going to, on the sixteenth. So that's why I've been doing all this stuff, with the house. Because I couldn't do anything else yet."

Goldie glances out at the cars, in through the glass doors, back at me. Like she's looking for something, though I can't imagine what. "Why didn't you just tell me?"

I laugh, an insuppressible gasp. "Tell Goldie Walsh that I *failed*? Goldie Walsh who went to college on a full-ride merit scholarship? Who got a perfect score on her LSAT? Goldie Walsh who—"

"Stop it." She holds up her hand. "I'm your *sister*, Lou, you can tell me anything."

"Can I?"

The question hangs between us, damning. Goldie's nose wrinkles, and I realize that she's about to cry.

"Yeah," she says, shakily. "Of course you fucking can."

"But you would've been so mad at me," I say. "For letting Nate—"

"Fuck Nate," Goldie says. I laugh again, my own eyes blurring with tears. "Truly fuck him for fucking with you like that, especially in a way that impacted your career. I've always hated him."

"I know," I say, wiping my eyes. She swipes at hers, too—surreptitious, but impossible to miss.

"Lou, I'm sorry." She raises her chin, like she's leaning into the apology. "I'm sorry I made you feel like there's anything you can't share with me."

"Thank you," I say. I can count on one hand the number of times Goldie's apologized to me in our lifetime.

"I'm really proud of you," she says. My throat tightens like a vise, and I swat my hand at her. "No, I mean it. I don't say it enough." She waves toward the double doors. "And that, in there? I mean, you've always been so much better at this really hard shit than I am. Mom's lucky to have someone like you—who gets it. I know her diagnosis comes from trauma and I know she's been through it, but it's so hard for me to separate that from how much she's hurt us, and how angry I am, but you—" Goldie breaks off, draws a breath. She's never said any of this to me before—not ever. "You're impressive," she finishes, quieter. "I mean it."

She's completely blurred out in front of me. My voice is thick and strangled when I say, "We're a good team."

She nods. I close the distance between us, finally hugging her against me. She melts into it, letting out a puff of breath over my shoulder. "We are."

"And if there's nothing I can't share with you . . ." I say, leaning back to find her eyes. I swipe at my tears, and Goldie raises her eyebrows. "I do need to get back to Colorado, like, *now*. But I have a good reason."

Thirty-Five

"Excuse me!" Mei tugs me through the terminal, rolling suitcase clicking behind her. "We've gotta go see about a guy!" She shoots me a shit-eating grin over one shoulder. "I love saying that."

"I can tell," I say, but I squeeze her hand.

We landed back in Denver a little past five, dark ridge of mountains just visible as the wheels hit the tarmac. All I heard from Henry while we were in Ohio was a couple confirmations of check-ins and one very respectful I hope everything's going all right. There's so much I want to tell him—that I should never have lied to him, that I don't need to push him, that I'll take whatever he's ready to give me for as long as he's willing to give it to me—that I can't say it over text. It's a conversation we need to have in person. These are things I need to say straight to his disarming blue eyes, to his lip tugged between his teeth, to the concerned line between his eyebrows.

"What do you think he'll do when he sees you?" Mei says. We step through the sliding doors onto the walkway toward long-term parking, and a frigid wind blows my coat open. "I think propose."

I shriek a laugh, and Mei giggles ferociously. We're high on the impulsiveness of this plan—on the speed with which we rebooked our plane tickets, hauled our asses to the airport, drafted a speech for me to win Henry back. And partaking in Mei's excitement is easier than slipping into my fear—because what happens if Henry's *not* thrilled to see me? What if I pushed him too far, and the damage is done?

"I don't know," I say, shaking out my hands. "I don't know, I don't know, I just need to get there and see him and I'll figure it out as I go."

"Totally." Mei nods seriously. "We're gonna read the room. We're gonna gauge his body language. But I'm pretty sure it'll say: *Let me ravish you immediately.*"

I smack her in the arm, exhaling a laugh that condenses in the cold air between us. After the past couple days, it feels good—better than good—to laugh.

Goldie and Quinn stayed in Ohio; she'd already taken the week off work and wanted to spend a few more days with Mom. Usually it's me handling the emotional fallout after the logistics are in order. I'm relieved and grateful and not a little weepy to see Goldie step up and do it instead.

Go get him, she'd said, walking me to my cab outside our Columbus hotel. *We've got things under control here.* When I hugged Quinn, savoring his warmth and his softness and his smell, he'd echoed her: *We got this, Lou-Lou.*

"I'm driving," Mei says now. She plucks my car keys out of my hand and opens the trunk. "I'm way too worked up to sit still for an hour and a half."

When I slide my suitcase into the trunk, she flaps her hands at me. "Hurry! We have places to be!"

"What if he hates me?" I say, slamming the hatch and walking around to the passenger seat. We slide in at the same time, hunching into the stale cold of the car. "What if he never wants to see me again?"

"What if an asteroid the exact size of the Comeback Inn catapults through the atmosphere and blows it up at the precise moment we pull into the driveway?" Mei throws the car into reverse and shoots me a withering look. "Don't be stupid. Let's go see about a guy."

The house is all lit up when we get there, nearly seven o'clock. Someone's hung string lights on the porch, and I can see a Christmas tree glowing from the entryway. Picturing Henry doing all this turns my heart into a bloody pulp. Or maybe it was Nan? But she wouldn't know where the decorations are kept, tucked into cardboard boxes in the far corner of the murder basement. She wouldn't know to string lights on the fiddle leaf in the living room—a tradition I told Henry about when we were wrapped, sweaty and spent, in those blankets on Thanksgiving. I can see it through the narrow window by the staircase, sparse and sparkling, and feel it like a fist clenched around my throat.

"His car's not here," I manage. Mei parks in my usual spot and peers up at the house through the windshield.

"Maybe he ran to the store?" She looks over at me. "So you surprise him when he gets back?"

"Maybe," I say, but my hands are already shaking. "Maybe

this was stupid. *God.* Maybe I should have called first, Mei, I mean, what were we thinking? He could be—"

"Stop." She grabs for my hand, looking at me seriously. Her face is mostly in shadow, lit on one side by the warm glow from the house. "This isn't stupid, it's romantic as hell. We're going to go inside, and figure out where he is, and take it from there. Okay?"

I nod once, sharply. I feel like I'm going to come out of my skin. "Okay."

"Okay," she repeats, and then she reaches across my body and pushes open my door.

I hear voices as soon as we step into the foyer—laughter and warm murmuring and the low notes of holiday jazz over the living room speaker. The smell of the house breathes through me like a lullaby, stilling every live nerve under my skin.

"Hello?" Nan's voice rises, and the others peter out. "Who is it?"

"It's Lou," I say, kicking off my boots. By the time I round the corner toward the living room Nan's made it to the hallway to meet me. There are three other women sitting by the fire—Pauline among them—and I wave distractedly in their direction.

"Lou!" Nan says. She's wearing a cable-knit sweater and fuzzy socks. Her hands land on my arms. "You're back!" Then, as if remembering something awful, she takes a sharp intake of breath and presses a hand to her mouth. She looks at the other women, wide-eyed. "Oh no," she breathes.

"What?" I say. Distantly, I'm aware of Mei walking up behind me. "Where's Henry?"

Nan's gaze comes back up to mine. Her fingers are still covering her lips when she repeats, "Oh no."

"Nan," Mei says, and Nan's eyes dart to her. "What's going on?"

"Henry's gone," Pauline says, from the living room. All three of us turn to look at her.

"*Gone?*" I say.

"Gone," Nan confirms. Her hand, small and warm, lands on the crook of my elbow. "To Ohio, Lou. Just a few hours ago. To find you."

Thirty-Six

The story unfolds in bits and pieces, all four of my guests—Nan and Pauline, new arrivals Daria and Leigh—talking over each other to deliver the details. *Sad puppy*, Pauline says. *He was moping*, Nan adds. And then, from Daria, the simplest description of them all: *Heartbroken*.

"So we sat him down," Nan tells us, sipping from her mug of tea, "and said—look, Henry. There's nothing stopping you from going over there to Ohio and getting her."

"It's a *gesture*," Pauline says, nodding.

"But he was nervous," Nan says. "Thought maybe you needed space from him. But I said: If I know our Lou, what she needs is a hug."

My eyes fill with tears, hot and blurry.

"I said: Our Lou's not the type to want space."

"It's true," Mei says, gathering me into a squishy embrace.

"So we spring into action." Pauline gestures between the four of them. "Leigh's booking a flight, Daria's packing some snacks, Nan's figuring out what hotel you went to."

I shake my head, rubbing at my eyes. What the *hell* did I do to deserve these people? Maybe they never needed me at all. Maybe it wasn't me helping anyone heal, but the space we created together, here—the simple fact of our connectedness, of sharing our pain. Maybe all healing requires is a taking of turns. Leaning on whoever has the strength in each fleeting moment.

"And then Henry leaves," Nan says now. "Just after noon. Nervous wreck. Very charming." She looks at her watch. "His flight was at four o'clock. Should be landed by now."

I pull out my phone, snapping a selfie on the living room couch—huddled in a blanket, hair limp from flying, eyes wet with tears. Smiling in spite of myself. I send it to Henry, and add: Come home? Nan filled me in.

His reply comes through minutes later. A selfie of his own: Henry's dark eyebrows, his unbelievable eyes. His smile, soft and exhausted and relieved. He's standing in front of a giant sign dotted in snowflake decals that says WELCOME TO COLUMBUS!

And just two words: Hold still.

But I don't. Henry takes a six a.m. flight out of Ohio, and I drive straight back to the Denver airport to meet him. There's no way I'm sleeping anyway—and I refuse to wait one minute longer than I need to. I park in the short-term lot this time and hightail it to Arrivals, huddled in my coat. A week into December, and it's decidedly winter.

I wait for Henry at the center of the sprawling terminal. Waves of people come up from the airport trams, one escalator load after another after another. I'm rising onto my tiptoes and lowering back down, rhythmic, like if I can just keep moving, my nerves will stay at bay. But then Henry ascends up the escalator, and his eyes lock on mine, and my heart drops entirely out of my body onto the scuffed tile floor.

I wave to him. *Wave.* Like a preschooler in a dance recital. Like he hasn't already seen me, like that secret smile isn't spreading over his face, like every step he closes between us doesn't nudge me closer to certain death. I've been holding my breath for too long. When he gets to me, I gasp for air and say, "How was Ohio?"

Henry says, "Lonelier than anticipated."

He's a foot away from me, black suitcase parked next to his feet. In his wool coat and marled sweater he looks like a Christmas card, like a goddamn dream, like I made him up.

"I'm sorry," I say, and he takes a half step closer.

"*I'm* sorry."

I shake my head. "I've been so stupid, Henry. I'm sorry I lied about my license. I'm sorry I disappeared after Thanksgiving—I got scared and it was silly of me; I'd told you about my mom and I could feel you holding back about Molly and I got completely in my head about it."

Henry's eyes track back and forth over mine, taking this in. The crowd parts around us, a break in the current, but I know that if I stop talking now, I'll never get the rest of this out.

"I got scared that I was doing what I always do," I say. "Give all of myself, and take care of everyone around me, even if I don't get it back. I'm always disappearing in my relationships because I take care of the other person and I forget—I mean, I *love* taking care of people, and I want to do it, but I have a tendency to just—to let it be unbalanced? And Goldie was giving me such a hard time, and I just—" I break off, sucking in an open-mouthed breath that makes Henry smile. It touches his eyes in the most exquisite way, so they go iridescent under the overhead lights. "I was so wrong, Henry. I want you to share everything with me because I want to share everything with you—but it doesn't have to be now. You can take all the time you need about Molly." I swallow, heat radiating from my face. "You've taken care of me so well, and so often, and in every way I've asked and even ones I haven't. The past couple days with my mom were so tough and they made me think so much about you, and about everything, and how it's okay to care for people if they care for you back. It's good. *You're* good. I want to do this with you. I want"—my eyes flicker over his—"I want to hold your hand at every crosswalk." I draw a long, shaking breath. "If you'll let me."

Henry closes the distance between us, hands framing my face, and murmurs, "I'm going to kiss you now," right against my mouth. I sink into him like an exhale, like something trapped let free. His lips are soft and warm, his arms dropping to wrap around my waist. When he lifts me off my feet I bury my face in his shoulder and breathe him in. *I could stay here*, I think. I could live at the Denver International Airport if it meant being somewhere with Henry.

"I don't want you to disappear," he says, lowering me to the floor. My arms tuck in against his chest. "Not ever, for any reason, and especially not in our relationship. You couldn't. You're the brightest thing—" Henry stops, swallowing. That line appears between his brows, there and gone, like he's working through the words but then, finally, finds them. "That first night, when I couldn't sleep at the house, I thought I'd ruined this before it could even begin. But then you found me, and you didn't try to fix me."

"Fix you?" I push my hands up his chest, bracket his jaw between my fingers.

"Or explain it away." His voice is soft, and the terminal is loud, but my whole body is tuned to him: to every dip of his words, every brush of his fingertips under my coat at the small of my back. "All I've wanted, all this time, is to explain it away. To force some kind of logic into what happened, to train my feelings into some other shape that hurts less." Henry's hands slide upward, framing my ribs, and ease me even closer. "That doesn't end in you in bed without me."

I imagine him, that night: the fevered heat of his skin, the shudder of his breathing under my palm. The way he pulled me into him, after, and pressed me to the hurt.

"You saw me as I am," Henry says simply. "And you told me it was okay, and for the first time, I believed it." I brush my thumb over his cheek and he tilts into the touch, the slightest tip of his chin into my palm. "You have this way of seeing people, Louisa. It feels like cheating, how lucky I am when you turn your gaze on me."

I pull his face to mine, rising to my toes as his fingers spread to steady me. Our mouths meet, and his soft exhale is a whisper in the clamor of the terminal, and I want to tell him that I could spend my whole life learning him. My whole life seeing only him, and it wouldn't be enough.

"I'm sorry I made you feel isolated about Molly," Henry says into the space between our lips. "And I'm sorry I didn't tell you, sooner, about Joss." He dips his chin, pressing his mouth to mine again—like he's reminding himself that he can, like he can't quite help it. "That was wrong. I want to share everything with you, too—I'm just a little out of practice."

"We have time," I tell him. It's a gift. It's the truth. All this time that's spread before us—it aches right at the center of my rib cage, imagining it. The longing for something already held in my hands. "I'll be here when you're ready."

Henry makes a sound that's not quite an exhale, not quite a word. He carries it to my lips and it tastes like relief.

"Joss told me about the tree," I say, quietly, as we pull apart. Henry's fingers splay over my lower back, rooting me to him. "That you thought it wasn't the right time. Why?"

When he lifts one shoulder in half a shrug, it's sad and vulnerable. Softly, he says, "Because the house is yours, now."

"It'll *always* be hers, too." I tuck my fingers around the back of his neck. Smooth my thumb over one clean-shaven cheek. "You don't have to erase any of yourself to have a life with me."

Henry tips forward, forehead coming to rest on mine, and closes his eyes. "I worried," he says quietly, "that if I showed you my past, it would scare you away."

I shake my head, our noses brushing. Lower my palms to his chest and pull away so he has to look me in the eyes. "You can give me anything, Henry. Any part of you. I'll take care of it."

"And you," he says. One hand rises from my waist to my cheek. "You don't know how it killed me not to be with you, these last couple days. To be stuck here, imagining you—" He shakes his head, just barely, his eyes like sunlight on mine. Like the single point that illuminates everything else, that makes me real and visible at all. "Imagining what you were going through, and being so far away. Your mom—?"

"She's okay," I tell him, barely a whisper. His fingertips curl around the base of my skull, tipping my face to his as his eyes cast over me.

"And you?"

I feel weightless, is the truth. With my hip in the crook of Henry's elbow and his gaze on me like this—perceptive, protective—I feel like I could trust the world to carry me. Trust myself, too.

"I'm okay."

He exhales, long and slow, through his nose. "That's the most important."

"Not the *most*," I say, and Henry dips his mouth to mine.

"It's the most important," he murmurs, "to me."

I part my lips and he meets me there without hesitation, the warm slide of his tongue and the pressure of all five of his fingertips holding me steady. I forget we're in the middle of an airport; I forget the day's hardly begun at all—that the sun hasn't risen, that the rest of the world isn't as illuminated as I feel, right in this moment.

"Louisa," Henry says, soft, at the corner of my mouth. The three rumbled syllables of my name, my favorite sound. "It's only ever been the fear of losing you that's made me keep things from you. That it would be too complicated, or too painful, or you wouldn't want to be with someone as brokenhearted as me." He pulls back just the smallest distance, half a breath, so he can meet my eyes. "I'd have done anything to keep you close. Anything not to lose you again."

"You won't." We look at each other, the crowd moving around

us, holiday music playing low and soft from somewhere across the terminal. I have the sudden thought that I want to do every good and bad and human thing with Henry Rhodes.

"And besides," I say. Henry's eyebrows rise. "I'm good with heartbreak, remember?"

Thirty-Seven

Six months later

There's a lot to learn about someone, in the beginning. That Henry drinks tea, not coffee. That the espresso machine was a gift from a client whose puppy he saved from parvo. That he always keeps music on in the house. That he can't hold a conversation while he's cooking, and that there's a spot just behind his ear—soft and secret—that makes his whole body relax when I press my lips to it.

Each Henry I meet is my favorite Henry. Henry sleeping over, for the first time, at the house—his steady breathing in my dark bedroom, the way he tucked my body into his like armor. Henry in snow pants, taking me skiing on my twenty-seventh birthday. Henry in New York, holding my hand at Quinn's preschool graduation. Henry in the quiet at the end of the day—his low voice, his warm hands, our past lives falling away like ghosts.

And now, Henry sitting barefoot on the floor of our new

house. Henry in worn jeans and a T-shirt. Henry passing me a carton of pad thai.

"I picked out the bean sprouts," he says.

I dig in with my chopsticks. "My hero."

"You hear from Nan today?"

"Yeah." The sun's just setting through the living room windows, sinking behind Longs Peak. It's why we picked this place, for its view of the mountains. "She got back last night and said she's already planning her next cruise."

Henry smiles, shaking his head. "Nan Russo: *Around the World in 80 Days*."

Since leaving the Comeback Inn, Nan's been on one trip after another. Her time in Estes Park convinced her that she needed to find herself away from the house she'd spent all those decades in with Teddy, and when the inn closed last month, she went straight to Barbados. We get dispatches from her at least weekly—photos of drippy caramel sunrises, off-center selfies of her familiar smile flanked by beaches or rainforests.

"I hope I'm like her, when I'm seventy-five."

Henry nudges me with his foot. "I hope you're like you, when you're seventy-five."

"Hangry and unemployed?"

Henry puts down his food and reaches for me, sliding me across the floor until I'm right in front of him, my legs wrapping around his waist. "Thoughtful and kind," he says. "Funny and wise." He kisses me, then hovers his lips right above my ear. "And desperately, hopelessly in love with me."

I pull back to find his eyes, winding my legs tighter around his hips. "Desperately, huh?"

"Oh," Henry says softly, tucking a loose strand of hair behind my ear. *"Desperately."*

I smile, framing his face between my hands. The room is full of boxes—his things, neatly organized; and mine, haphazardly thrown together in my hurry to get out of the house before the movers showed up. It took months of discussion to wind up here: conversations between Joss and Henry, Henry and his parents, Henry and me. It was the right choice, but—as is so often the case—not an easy one, to put the house up for rent.

The Comeback Inn had run its course: I passed the NCE in December, and spent the spring interviewing for a full-time counseling job. I wanted to keep the house open through the rest of my bookings, which stretched to the end of February like we'd always planned. I kept living there, afterward: when the rooms were only mine again, when Mei could come up on the weekend and take her pick—no Rashad or Nan or anyone at all ducking through a doorframe into the upstairs hallway. The quiet was jarring, at first. But then it was good.

Part of me wanted to keep running the hotel, in that early part of winter when things with Henry were so new and euphoric. In just six months I'd fallen into it all like an old pair of jeans: the seams of the Comeback Inn fit me right. But when my guests trickled away—when the house became, again, what it had always been to me—I remembered the rest of myself, and I couldn't ignore her.

There's a version of Lou out there, on some other timeline, running a house for the brokenhearted until she's wiry and wrinkled. But this version—the one I am here with Henry and Mei, with Goldie and Quinn and my mother—knows her family is the splinter under her skin. Knows it's her life's work to tend that wound, and to live with it, and to find acceptance in the aching.

It took a few months to figure it out: to talk with my grad school professors, to network with old classmates. It was April when one of them connected me to an acquaintance of an acquaintance—a woman about to retire from her family therapy practice just down the highway in Loveland. I start in August, a year to the day from that awful night with Nate in Denver. When it all came crashing down, and I was broken enough that I had no choice but to put myself together into a better shape than before.

Henry was choosy with the renter. *It's only ever been you*, he told me—and I told him my one condition was he wasn't allowed to fall in love with his tenant again. He laughed at that. My favorite sound of all.

Grace's application came in May. We were eating dinner on the back porch at the house, the evening cool and wet after rain. The sky was pink.

"Louisa," Henry said—in his soft, rumbly way. He held his phone out to me and I felt it like a zipper sliding into place: Grace, my very first guest at the inn, whose shower didn't work and who barely spoke a word to me and who loved this place so much, it turns out, that she wants to move her kids up here.

You never know, is the truth—what people are going through, or what you mean to them.

"Two kids," I told Henry. His eyes crinkled at that. "They're going to love it here."

I'll always carry the house with me. Its cozy, familiar rooms; the soft landing it gave to me and so many others; Custard the dog and his gently wagging tail, still right there across the street. Henry will carry it, too. It's the right choice, to start new together somewhere else. But the house will be there, if we need it—a part of us, without defining who we become next.

I was so scared to lose it, but I know now that home isn't a place; it's a feeling. It's a rootedness that we make for ourselves. The deep knowing that no matter where we go, we belong. And I have that—it was never the house. It was Goldie, and it was Mei, and it was me. It was Henry.

"I have something for you," I say to him now. Henry's face is tipped up to mine, and I drop a soft kiss onto his mouth.

"Mm?" His fingertips grip into my waist before letting me untangle myself from him, get to my feet, cross our echoing house toward the kitchen. There's one box in the center of the kitchen floor, marked with a Sharpie star so I'd know exactly where to find it. I slice the packing tape with a box cutter and pull out the tissue-paper-wrapped rectangle I packed very last.

When I hand it to Henry, he looks up at me with his eyebrows drawn together. I reach out to smudge away the line. "What's this?"

I lower to the floor in front of him. "Just open it."

He's as careful with it as he is with everything else—animals, his words, my heart. He peels back the tissue paper in neat layers and stacks them beside him on the floor. When he gets down to the frame and turns it over, I watch his eyes flick across it—quick and unblinking, taking it in. He cradles it in both hands, quiet.

"Do you like it?" I whisper.

Finally, Henry looks up at me. His eyes are glazed with tears—extraordinary, winter blue underwater.

"Thank you," he says, looking back down at the frame. He runs the pad of one thumb across it. I crawl toward him, wrapping my arm around his shoulders so we can look at it together. A torn square of Molly's wallpaper: perfect, spotless sky; happy clouds; red bird singing into the morning.

Henry swipes a hand over his eyes, and I tuck my feet into his lap. He puts the frame down on the floor, facing us, and hugs my legs into his body.

"She'll be here," I say, resting my cheek against his arm. "With you. No matter where we go."

Because that's the thing, about hearts—broken or aching or otherwise. They don't belong to any one time or place. We carry them with us: bruised and scabbed over, healing and changing, always and inherently our own.

"I love you," Henry tells me. And there's room for that, too. Every broken heart keeps beating, in the end.

So will mine; so will his.

So will yours.

Acknowledgments

At the Comeback Inn, Lou discovers that it can take a village to heal us—and the truth is, most things are made better with a village behind them. This book, for certain.

Thank you to my agent, Katie Shea Boutillier—every story starts with a "What if . . . ?" email to you, and your belief in this one has buoyed me from the start.

To my editor, Mary Baker—it was clear from our first conversation that you saw this book exactly how I did, which is really the greatest gift a writer can ask for. It's been such a privilege to realize the vision together. Thank you for so thoughtfully shaping this novel, and for looking out for Lou and Henry with such warmth along the way. I couldn't feel luckier to work with you.

Thank you to the entire team at Berkley for shepherding this book into the world with immense talent and care: Daniel Brount, Katie Ferraro, Anna Venckus, Christine Legon, Lindsey Tulloch, Lila Selle, and Kalie Barnes-Young.

To my sensitivity reader, Kayla Bettis-Weber, LCSW—thank you for meeting Lou and her mom where they were and helping me both understand them better and write them more honestly on the page. Your insights about therapy, trauma, and BPD have been invaluable to me. And thank you to Kaitlyn Topolewski for connecting us (and for everything else, too).

Early readers are the guardian angels of every book, and I'm so grateful to mine: Kelly Duran, Emily Glickman, Matthew Hubbard, Samantha Markum, Andrea Massaro, and Elyse Pomerantz. Somehow I seem to have rounded up the smartest, kindest people on the planet and convinced them to be my friends. Thank you.

Thank you also to the writers I can always lean on to celebrate and commiserate—Crystal J. Bell, Maggie Boehme, Marisa Kanter, Jenna Miller, Mackenzie Reed, Taylor Roberts, Kelsey Rodkey, Jessie Weaver, more people I'm inevitably forgetting and will remember in horror at two a.m.—I'm so lucky to be alive *right now* to get to do this career with you.

And I must thank Rachel Lynn Solomon for telling me on that patio in Los Angeles that I had to write this one (also for accurately predicting its exact title change—you were right! You always are). Your encouragement has meant more to me over the years than I can truly articulate.

Thank you to my parents, whose life in Estes Park inspired so much of this book—I love every weekend in the mountains with you. To Tucker, the star of my favorite love story. And to our dogs, Puffin and Lilly, who teach me more about love every day.

Finally, of course, to you. Romance readers are my favorite people. Thank you for making space and time for love in your one precious life—especially Lou and Henry's.

The Heartbreak Hotel

Ellen O'Clover

READERS GUIDE

Discussion Questions

1. Henry notices Lou for the first time years before their love story begins. Have you ever formed an important relationship after an initial missed connection?

2. The Comeback Inn is a place to heal from grief in any of its forms. What do Lou and her guests learn about grieving in their time at the inn? How does grief both hold these characters back and help them grow?

3. We meet Lou at a tough moment in her career, when she's struggling with Goldie's perception of her as a failure. How do Lou's and Goldie's understandings of success change by the end of the book? How do you measure success in your own life and career?

4. Lou and Henry are both keeping secrets. Are these secrets understandable? Forgivable? Would you have kept the same secrets in Lou's or Henry's shoes?

5. If you could spend a day with one guest from the Comeback Inn, who would you choose and why?

6. Are you more of a Lou—open about discussing pain and grief—or more of a Henry—reserved about the hard things? Has that changed over time? How has it shaped your experiences?

7. Henry is a veterinarian. What role do animals play in Henry's life and in this book? What role have animals played in your life?

8. Lou and Mei take turns supporting each other—Lou, after Mei's breakup; Mei, when Lou's mom is in trouble. How does platonic love play a role in this love story? How have close friends supported you through tough moments in your own life?

9. Would you ever want to run a bed-and-breakfast? Why or why not?

10. Lou and Goldie have different experiences of, and approaches to, their mother. What creates this rift? How do their relationships change by the end of the book?

11. What do you think it is about Lou that makes Henry want to start really living again after experiencing so much grief? What is it about Henry that makes Lou want to trust again?

DISCUSSION QUESTIONS

12. Lou naturally falls into a caretaker role in many of her relationships. Where is the line between being a supportive friend and being taken advantage of? Have you ever felt like "the mom friend" in your own life? This tends to be a woman's role—why do you think that is?

13. Lou's recipe for processing grief includes open conversation, time outside, and rest. What tools have helped you work through grief in your own life?

14. Lou and Goldie are opposites, but they love each other immensely. Do you have any relationships like this? How do you navigate differences between the close people in your life?

15. Should Lou have closed the Comeback Inn? Do you think it's closed for good?

16. If Lou and Henry got a sequel, what would be next for them?

Photo by Noah Berg

Ellen O'Clover writes stories about love, identity, and belonging for both teens and adults. She grew up in Ohio and studied creative writing at the Johns Hopkins University before moving west to Colorado, where she lives in a little green house under a giant aspen tree with her rocket scientist husband and two perfect bulldogs.

VISIT ELLEN O'CLOVER ONLINE

EllenOClover.com
EllenOClover
EllenOClover

Ready to find
your next great read?

Let us help.

Visit prh.com/nextread

Penguin
Random
House